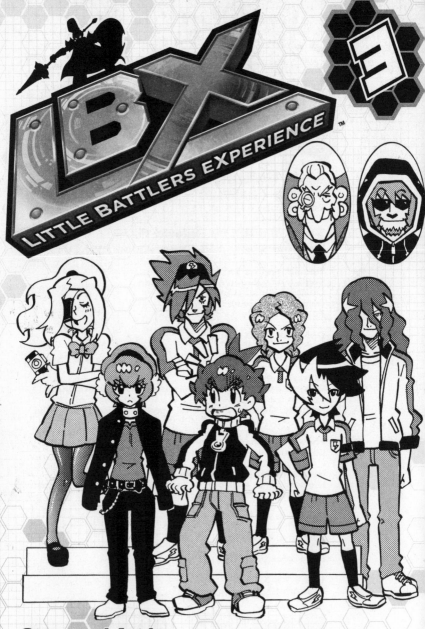

LBX
LITTLE BATTLERS EXPERIENCE™

3

Story and Art by
HIDEAKI FUJII
Original Story and Supervision by LEVEL-5

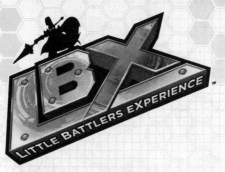

LBX Volume 3
WORLD CHANGER
Perfect Square Edition

Story and Art by Hideaki FUJII
Original Story and Supervision by LEVEL-5

Translation/Tetsuichiro Miyaki
English Adaptation/Aubrey Sitterson
Lettering/Annaliese Christman
Design/Izumi Evers
Editor/Joel Enos

DANBALL SENKI Vol.3
by Hideaki FUJII
© 2011 Hideaki FUJII
© LEVEL-5 Inc.
All rights reserved.
Original Japanese edition published by SHOGAKUKAN.
English translation rights in the United States of
America, Canada, the United Kingdom, Ireland, Australia
and New Zealand arranged with SHOGAKUKAN.

The stories, characters and incidents mentioned in this
publication are entirely fictional.

Printed in the U.S.A.

Published by VIZ Media, LLC
P.O. Box 77010
San Francisco, CA 94107

10 9 8 7 6 5 4 3 2 1
First printing, January 2015

www.perfectsquare.com

www.viz.com

PARENTAL ADVISORY
LBX is rated A and is
suitable for readers of
all ages.
ratings.viz.com

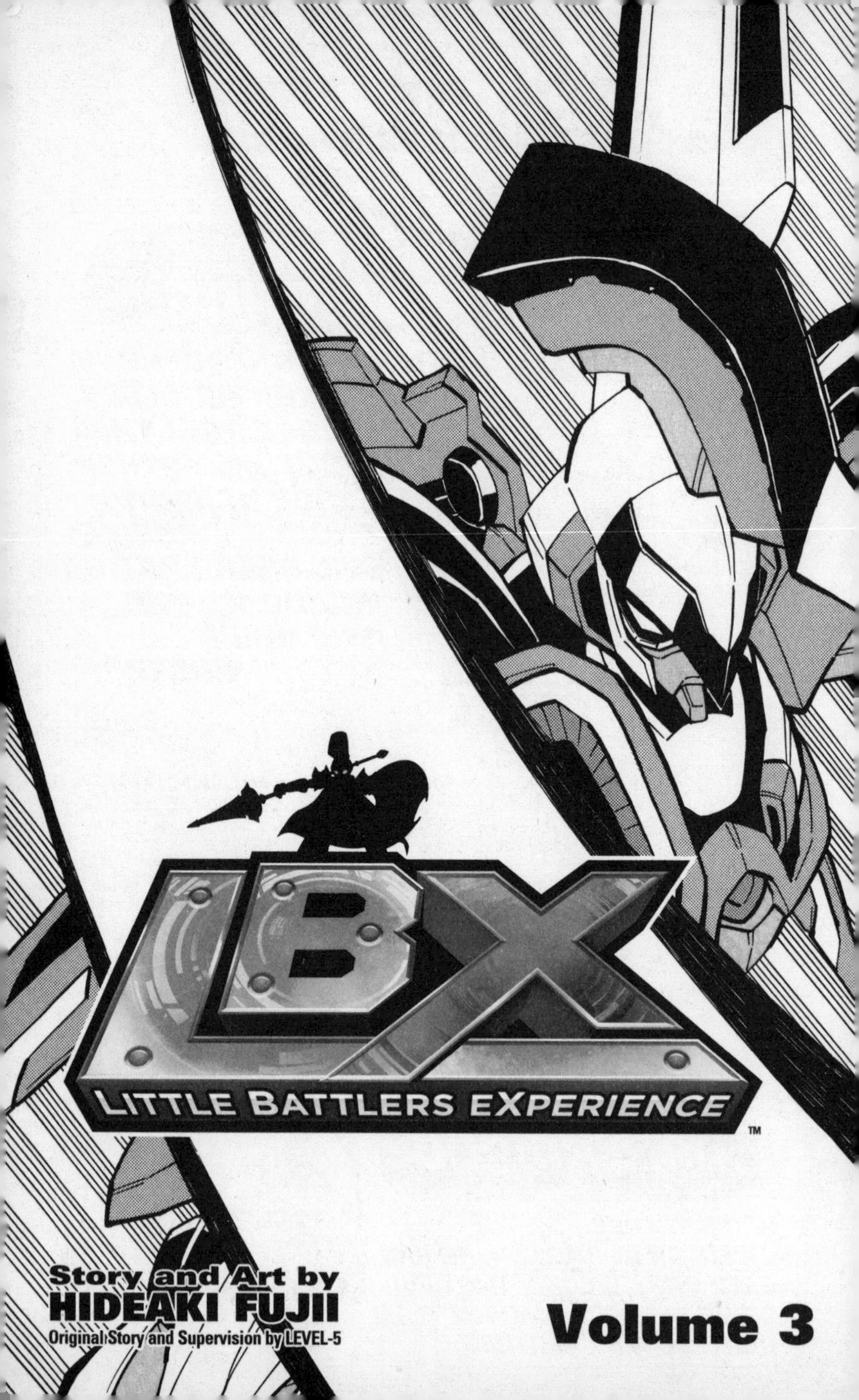

LBX
LITTLE BATTLERS eXPERIENCE™

Story and Art by
HIDEAKI FUJII
Original Story and Supervision by LEVEL-5

Volume 3

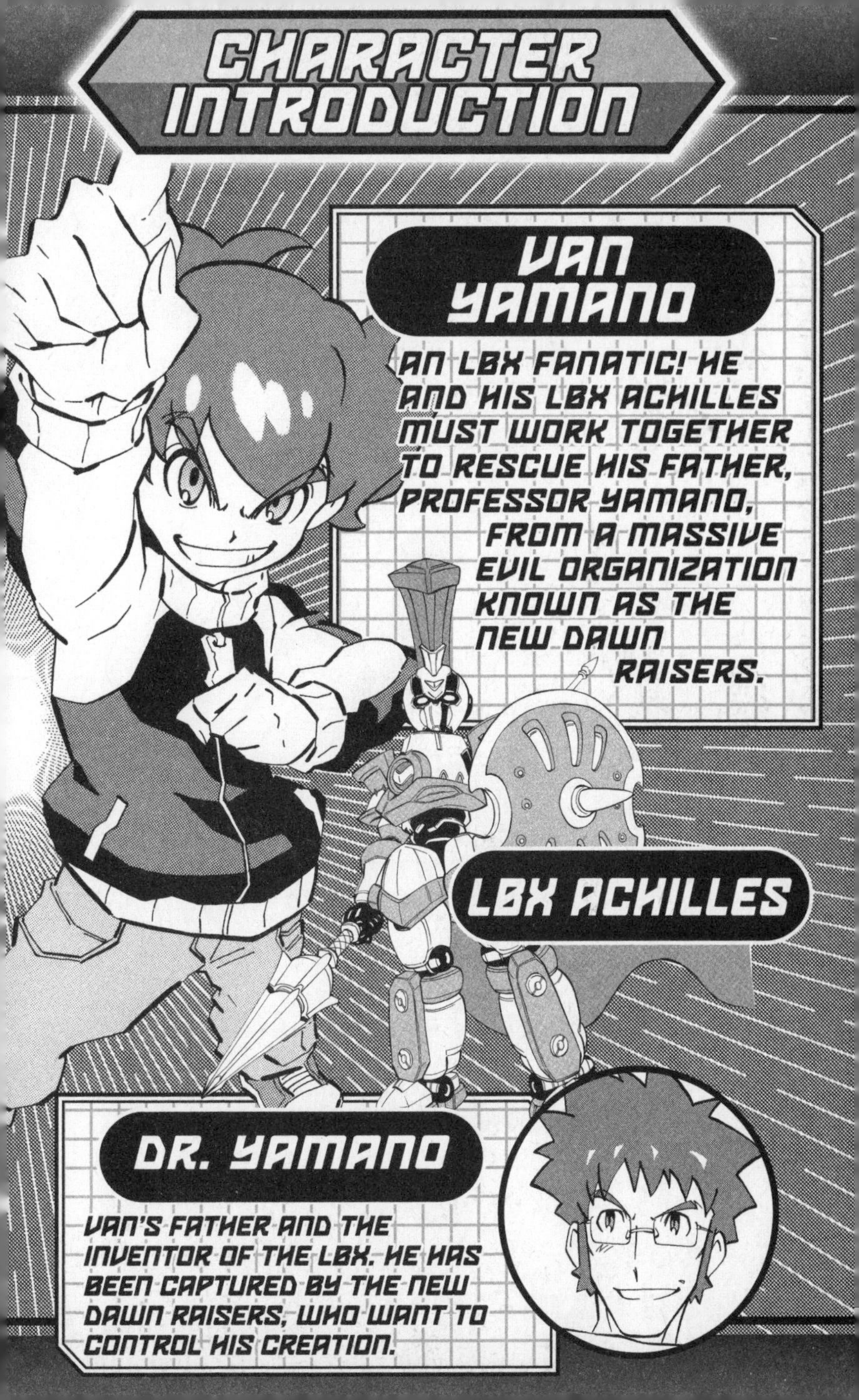
CHARACTER INTRODUCTION
VAN YAMANO
AN LBX FANATIC! HE AND HIS LBX ACHILLES MUST WORK TOGETHER TO RESCUE HIS FATHER, PROFESSOR YAMANO, FROM A MASSIVE EVIL ORGANIZATION KNOWN AS THE NEW DAWN RAISERS.
LBX ACHILLES
DR. YAMANO
VAN'S FATHER AND THE INVENTOR OF THE LBX. HE HAS BEEN CAPTURED BY THE NEW DAWN RAISERS, WHO WANT TO CONTROL HIS CREATION.

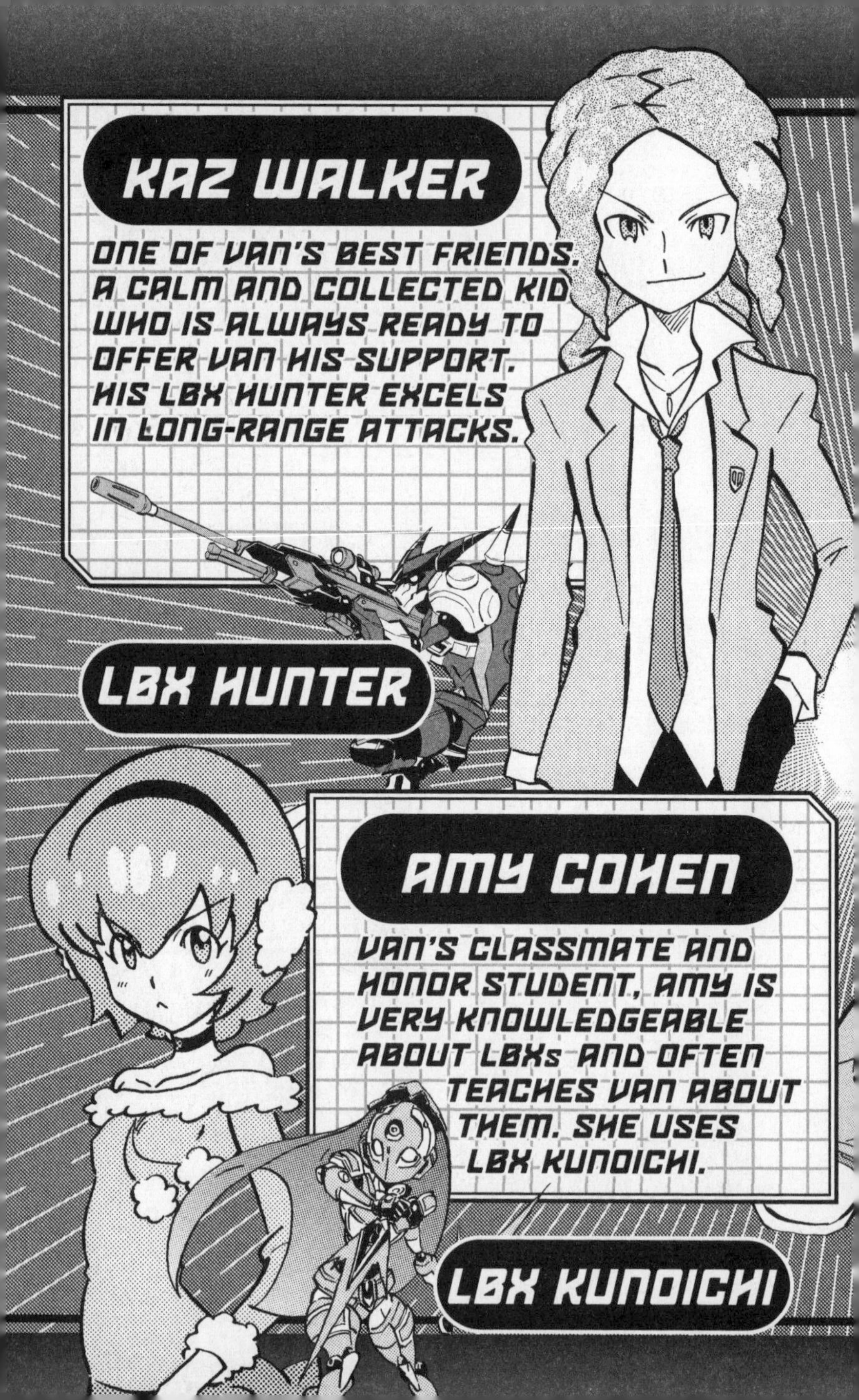
KAZ WALKER
ONE OF VAN'S BEST FRIENDS. A CALM AND COLLECTED KID WHO IS ALWAYS READY TO OFFER VAN HIS SUPPORT. HIS LBX HUNTER EXCELS IN LONG-RANGE ATTACKS.
LBX HUNTER
AMY COHEN
VAN'S CLASSMATE AND HONOR STUDENT, AMY IS VERY KNOWLEDGEABLE ABOUT LBXs AND OFTEN TEACHES VAN ABOUT THEM. SHE USES LBX KUNOICHI.
LBX KUNOICHI

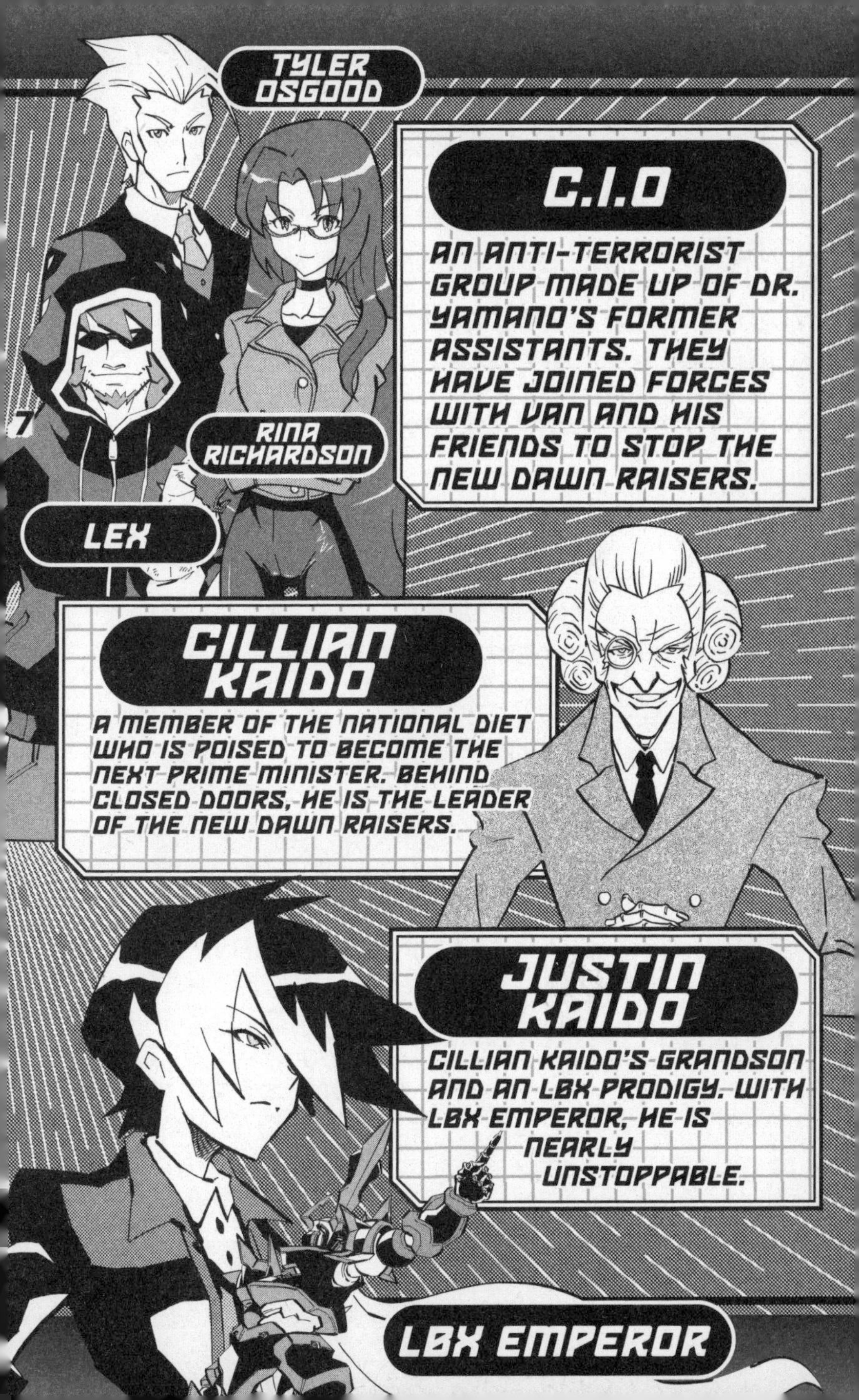
TYLER OSGOOD
C.I.O
AN ANTI-TERRORIST GROUP MADE UP OF DR. YAMANO'S FORMER ASSISTANTS. THEY HAVE JOINED FORCES WITH VAN AND HIS FRIENDS TO STOP THE NEW DAWN RAISERS.
RINA RICHARDSON
LEX
CILLIAN KAIDO
A MEMBER OF THE NATIONAL DIET WHO IS POISED TO BECOME THE NEXT PRIME MINISTER. BEHIND CLOSED DOORS, HE IS THE LEADER OF THE NEW DAWN RAISERS.
JUSTIN KAIDO
CILLIAN KAIDO'S GRANDSON AND AN LBX PRODIGY. WITH LBX EMPEROR, HE IS NEARLY UNSTOPPABLE.
LBX EMPEROR

TABLE OF CONTENTS

NOW... IT'S ALL UP TO... VAN...
!!!
WHAT WAS THAT YOU WERE SAYING ABOUT 10 SECONDS ?!

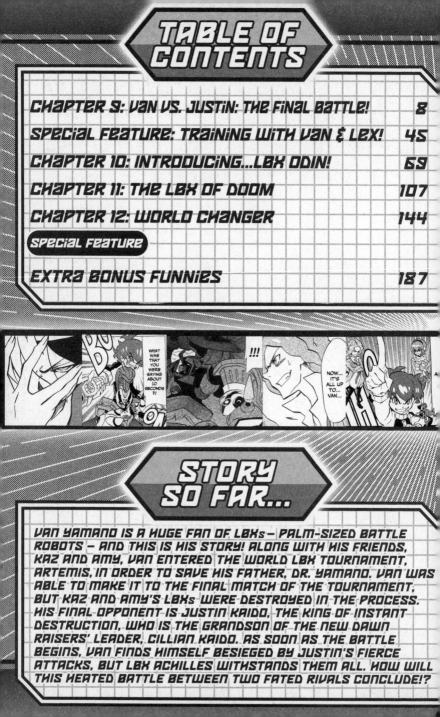

STORY SO FAR...

VAN YAMANO IS A HUGE FAN OF LBXs – PALM-SIZED BATTLE ROBOTS – AND THIS IS HIS STORY! ALONG WITH HIS FRIENDS, KAZ AND AMY, VAN ENTERED THE WORLD LBX TOURNAMENT, ARTEMIS, IN ORDER TO SAVE HIS FATHER, DR. YAMANO. VAN WAS ABLE TO MAKE IT TO THE FINAL MATCH OF THE TOURNAMENT, BUT KAZ AND AMY'S LBXs WERE DESTROYED IN THE PROCESS. HIS FINAL OPPONENT IS JUSTIN KAIDO, THE KING OF INSTANT DESTRUCTION, WHO IS THE GRANDSON OF THE NEW DAWN RAISERS' LEADER, CILLIAN KAIDO. AS SOON AS THE BATTLE BEGINS, VAN FINDS HIMSELF BESIEGED BY JUSTIN'S FIERCE ATTACKS, BUT LBX ACHILLES WITHSTANDS THEM ALL. HOW WILL THIS HEATED BATTLE BETWEEN TWO FATED RIVALS CONCLUDE!?

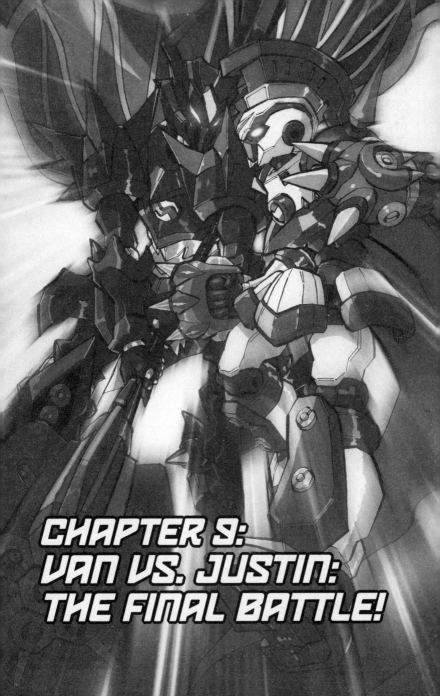

CHAPTER 9: VAN VS. JUSTIN: THE FINAL BATTLE!

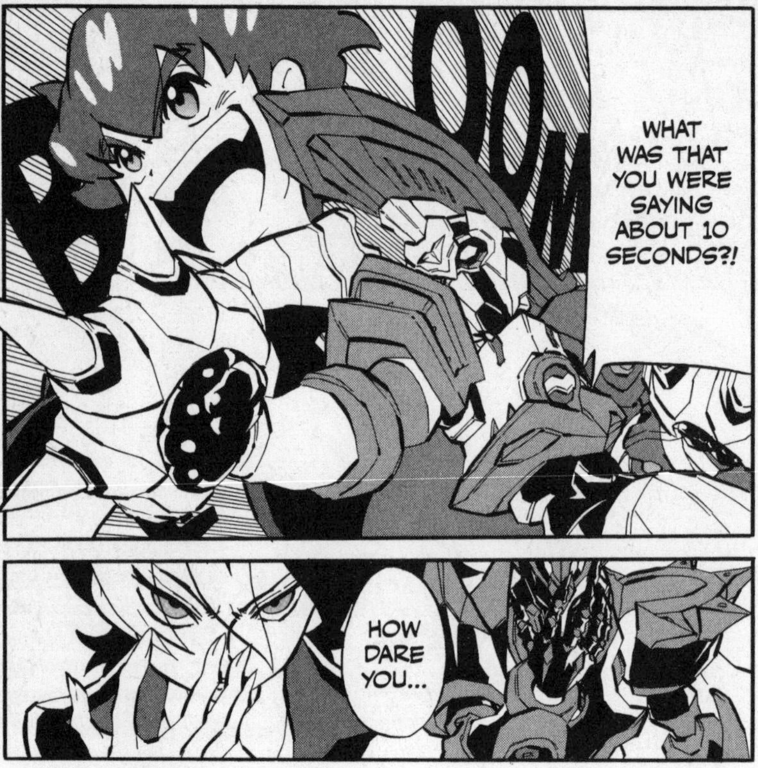
WHAT WAS THAT YOU WERE SAYING ABOUT 10 SECONDS?!
HOW DARE YOU...

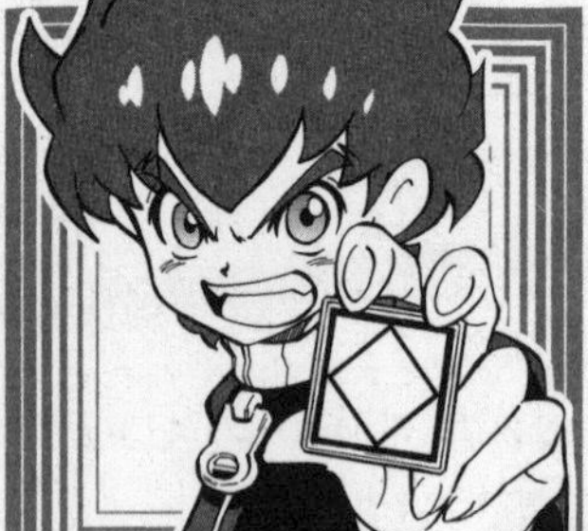

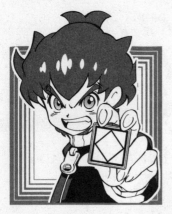

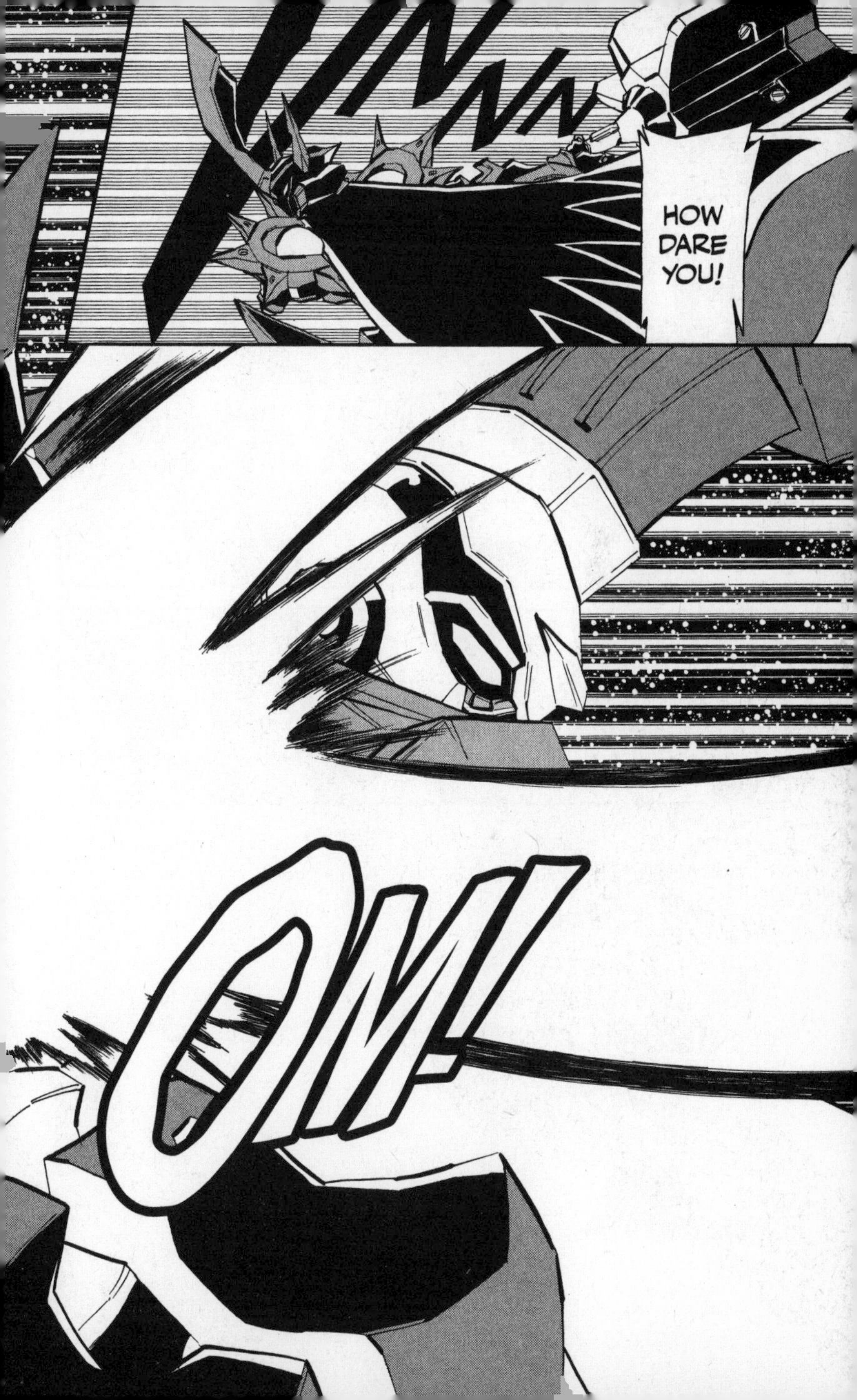
HOW DARE YOU!
OM!

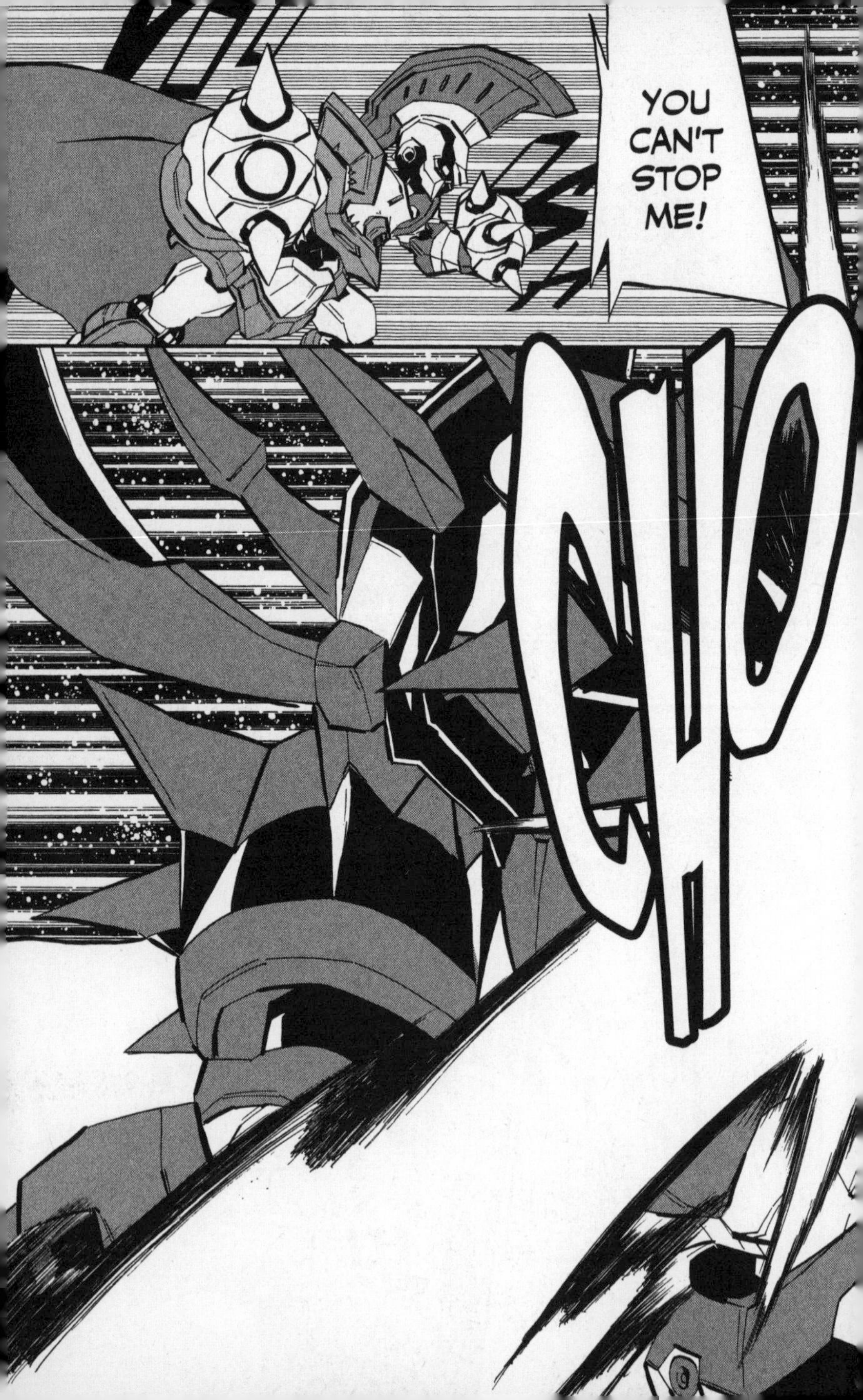
YOU CAN'T STOP ME!

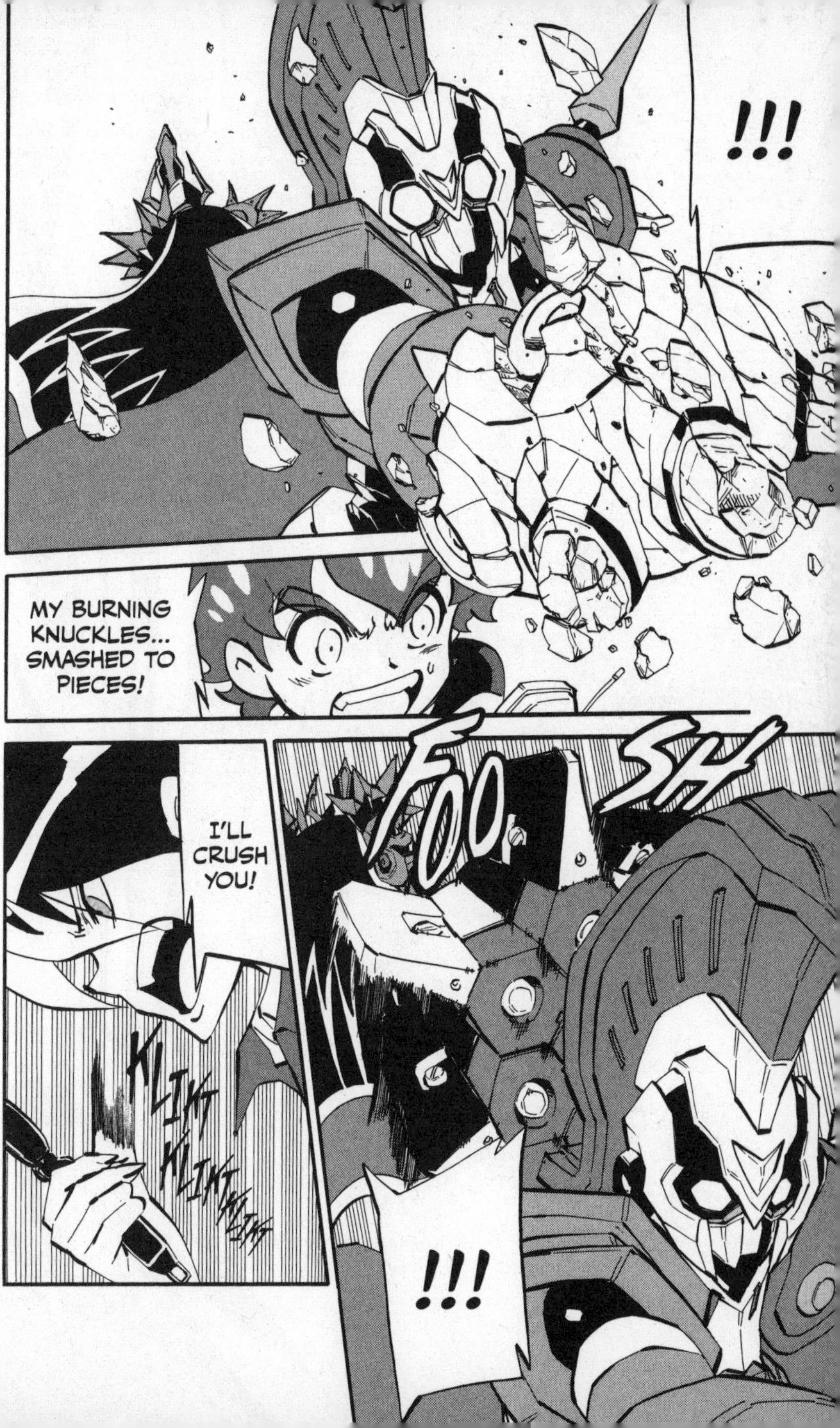
!!!
MY BURNING KNUCKLES... SMASHED TO PIECES!
FOO SH
!!!
I'LL CRUSH YOU!

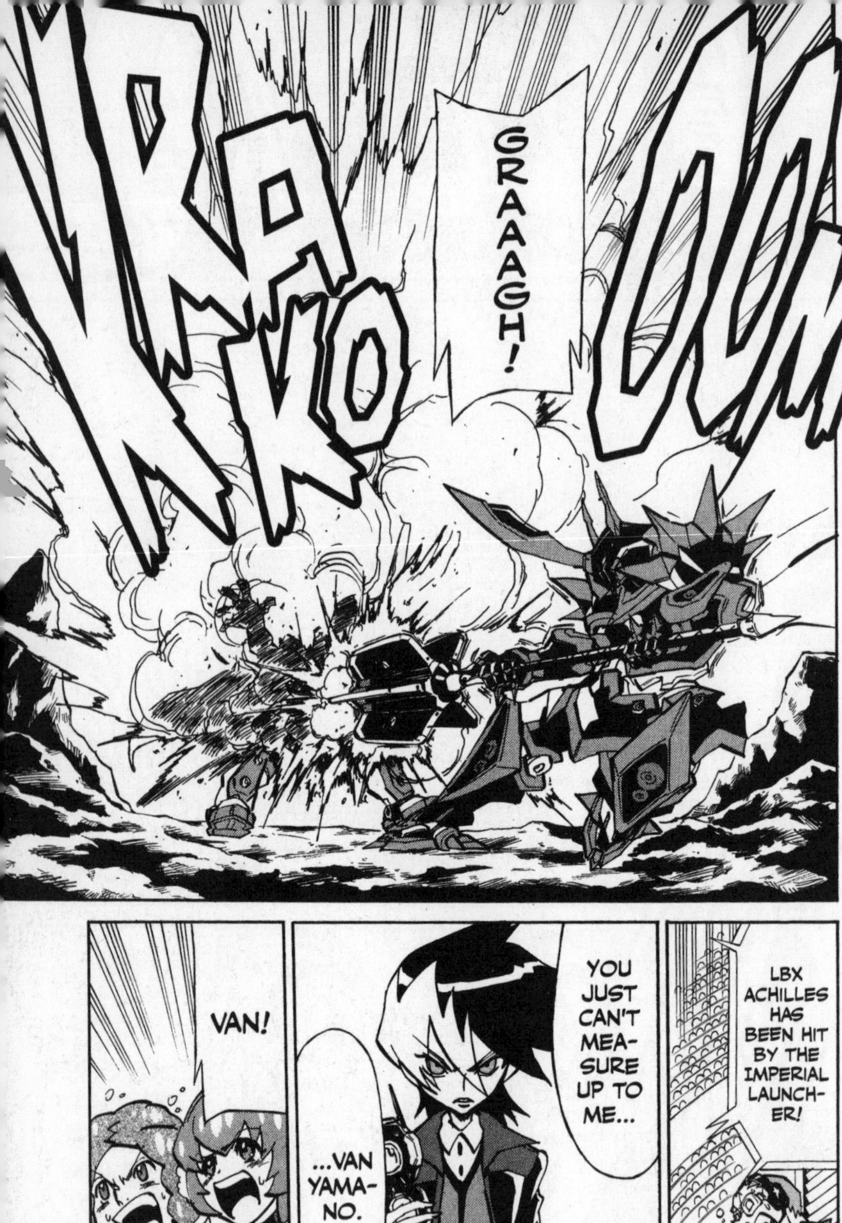
KRA
KO
OOM
GRAAAGH!
LBX ACHILLES HAS BEEN HIT BY THE IMPERIAL LAUNCHER!
YOU JUST CAN'T MEASURE UP TO ME...
...VAN YAMANO.
VAN!

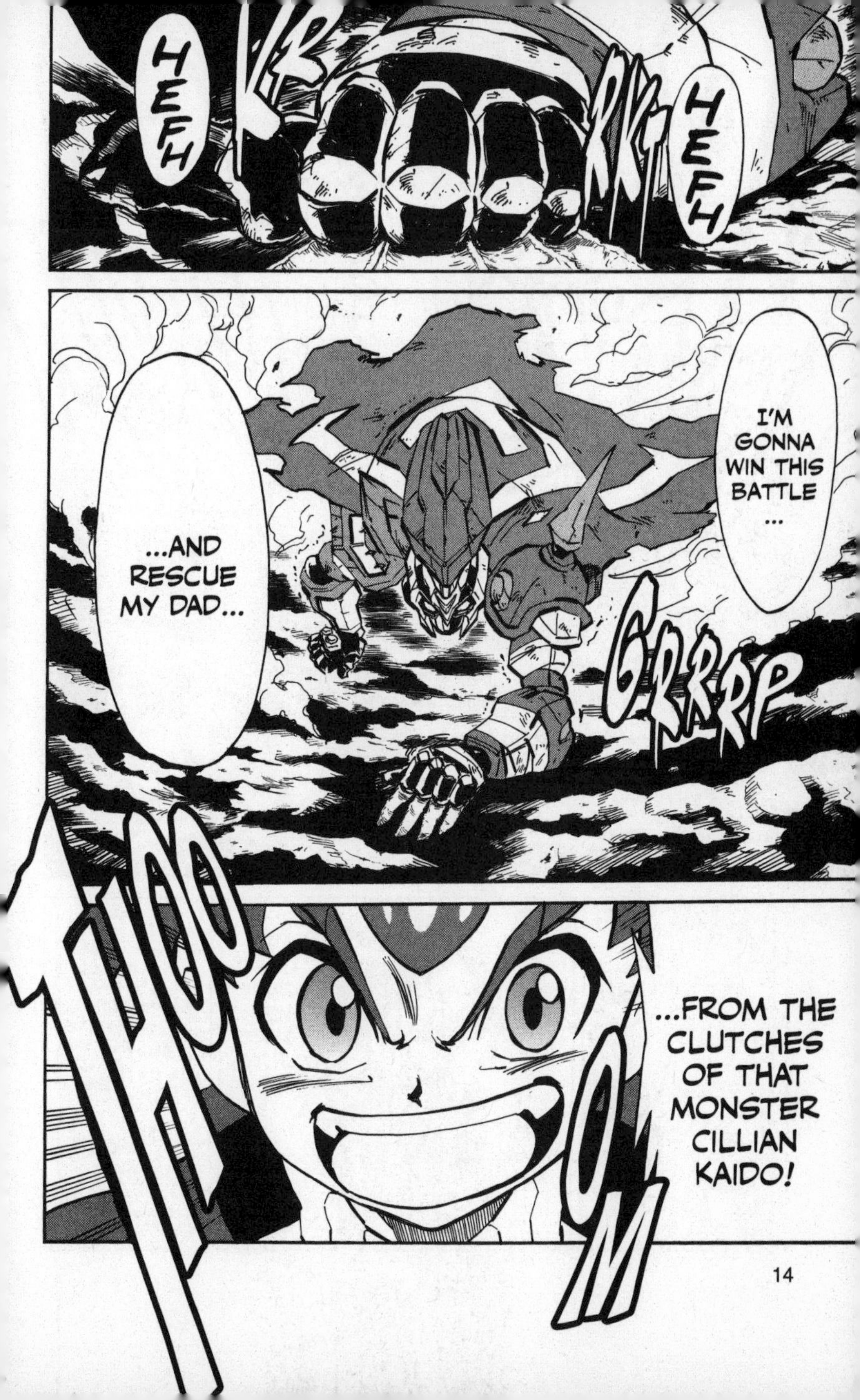
HEFH
HEFH
I'M GONNA WIN THIS BATTLE ...
...AND RESCUE MY DAD...
GRRRP
...FROM THE CLUTCHES OF THAT MONSTER CILLIAN KAIDO!

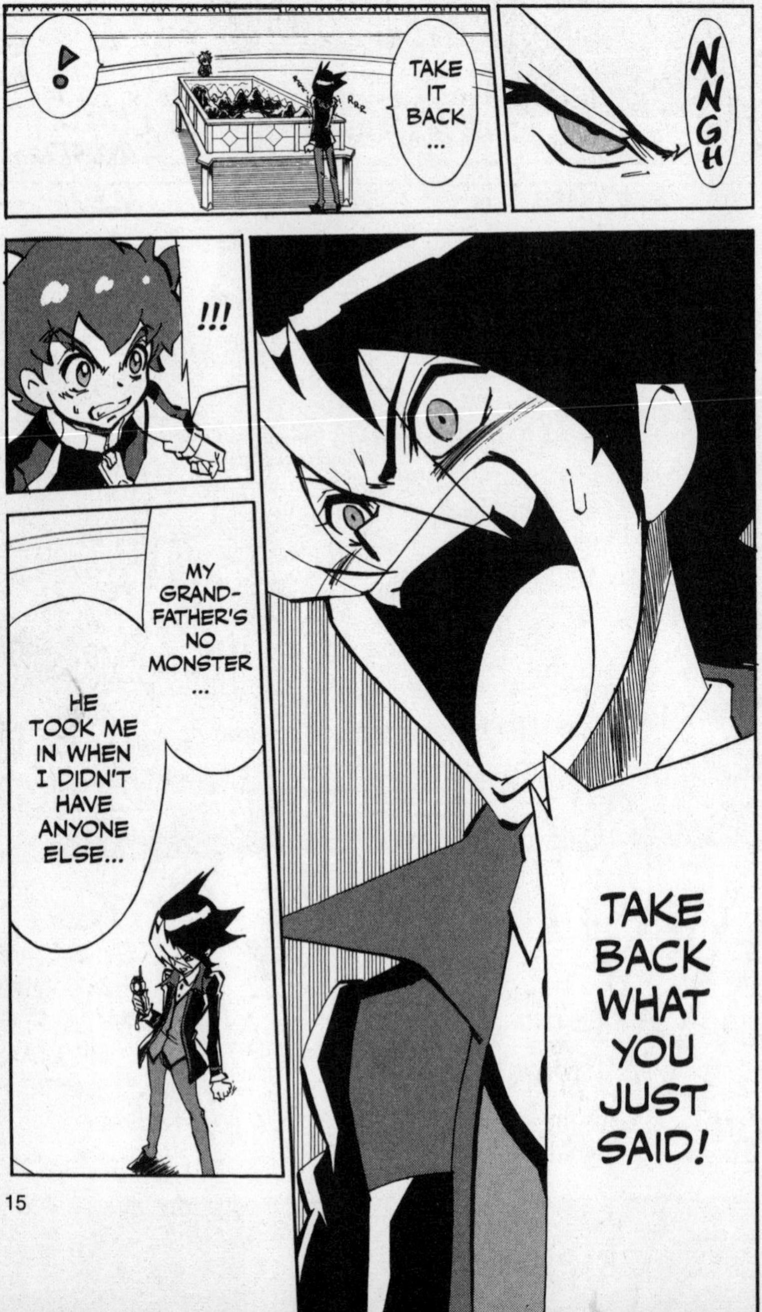
NNGH
TAKE IT BACK ...
RRR... RRR
!
TAKE BACK WHAT YOU JUST SAID!
!!!
MY GRANDFATHER'S NO MONSTER ...
HE TOOK ME IN WHEN I DIDN'T HAVE ANYONE ELSE...

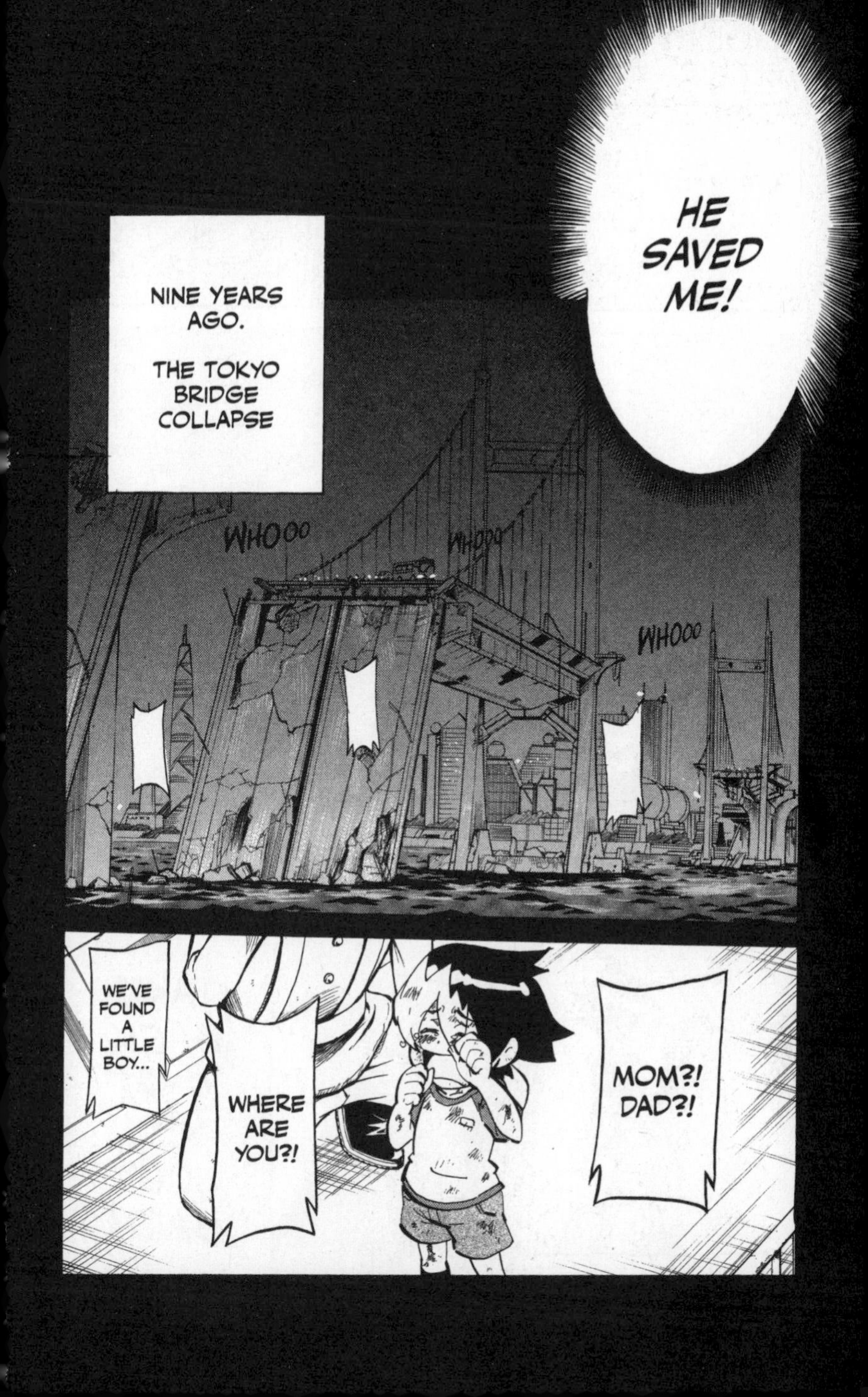
HE SAVED ME!
NINE YEARS AGO.
THE TOKYO BRIDGE COLLAPSE
WHOOO
WHOOO
WHOOO
MOM?! DAD?!
WHERE ARE YOU?!
WE'VE FOUND A LITTLE BOY...

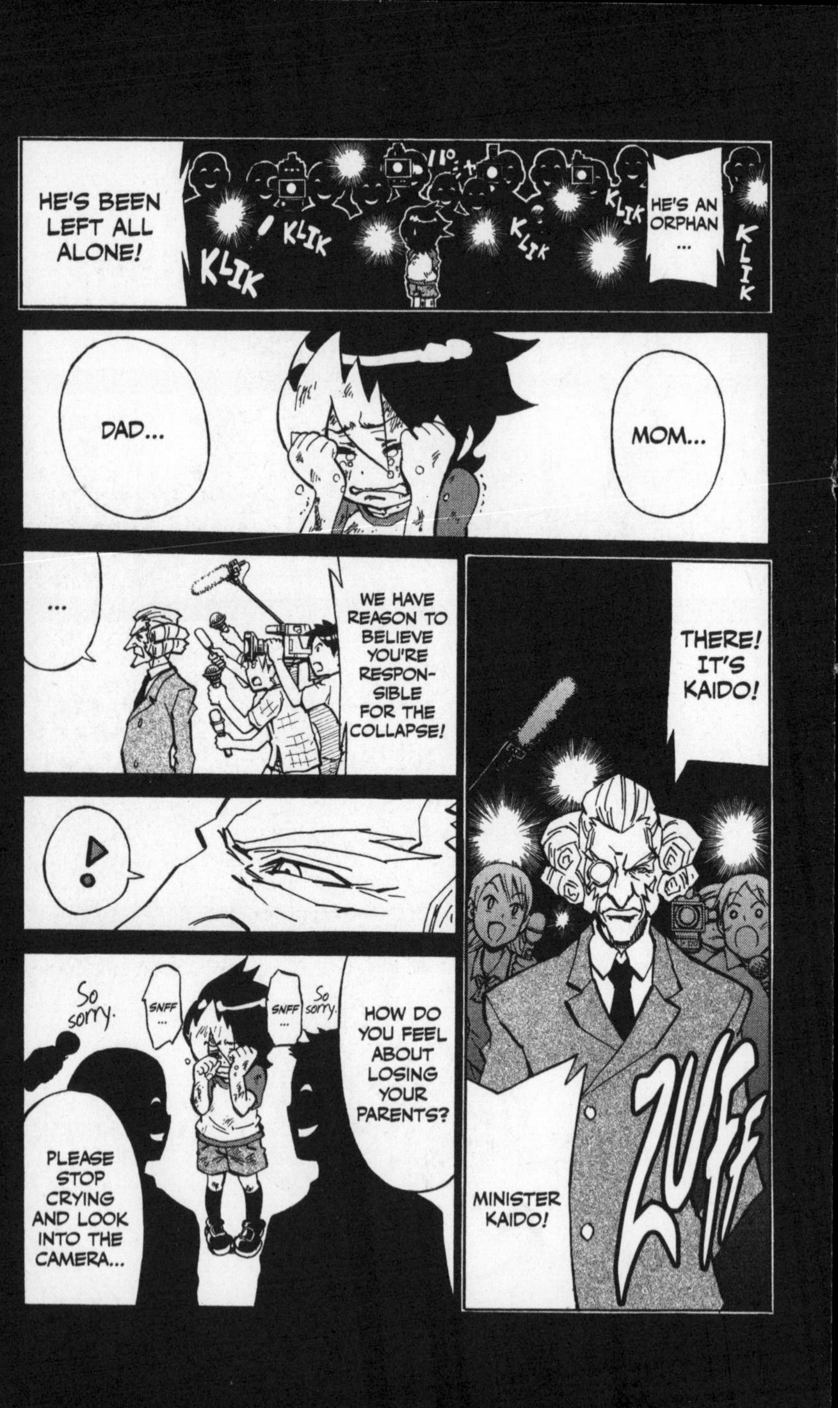
HE'S AN ORPHAN ...
KLIK
KLIK
KLIK
KLIK
KLIK
HE'S BEEN LEFT ALL ALONE!
MOM...
DAD...
THERE! IT'S KAIDO!
ZUFF
MINISTER KAIDO!
WE HAVE REASON TO BELIEVE YOU'RE RESPON-SIBLE FOR THE COLLAPSE!
...
!
HOW DO YOU FEEL ABOUT LOSING YOUR PARENTS?
So sorry.
SNFF ...
SNFF ...
So sorry.
PLEASE STOP CRYING AND LOOK INTO THE CAMERA...

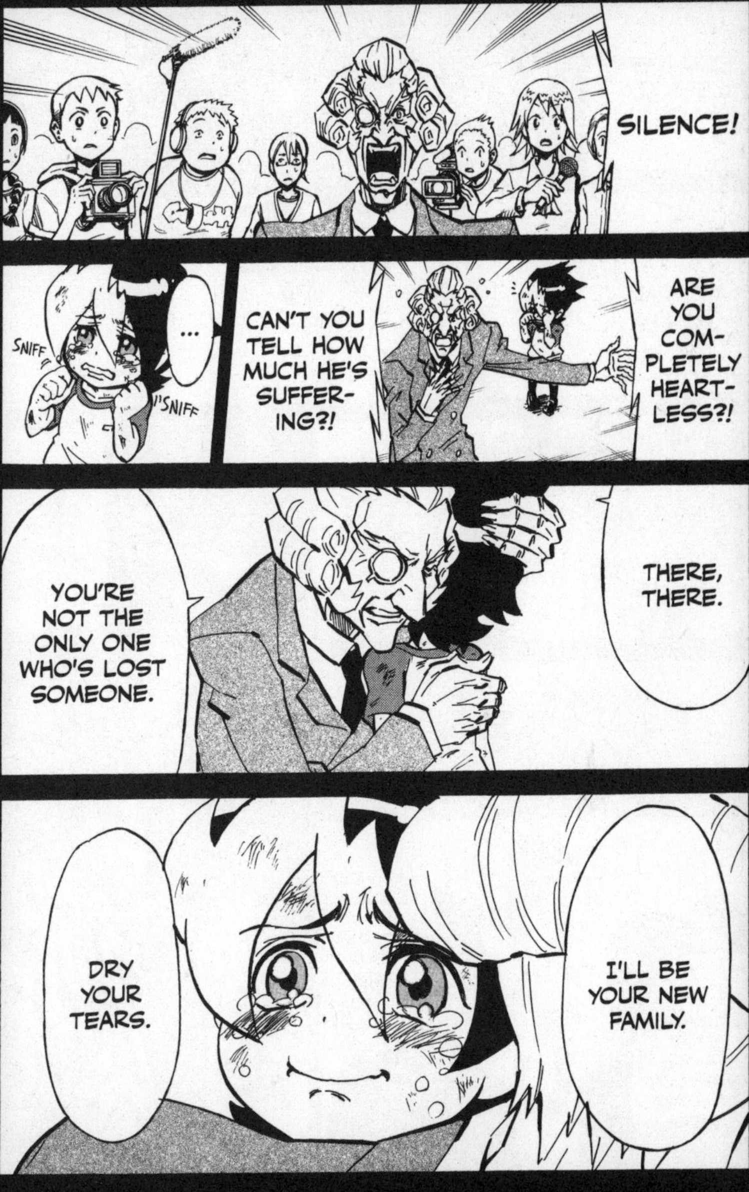
SILENCE!
ARE YOU COM-PLETELY HEART-LESS?!
CAN'T YOU TELL HOW MUCH HE'S SUFFER-ING?!
...
SNIFF
SNIFF
THERE, THERE.
YOU'RE NOT THE ONLY ONE WHO'S LOST SOMEONE.
I'LL BE YOUR NEW FAMILY.
DRY YOUR TEARS.

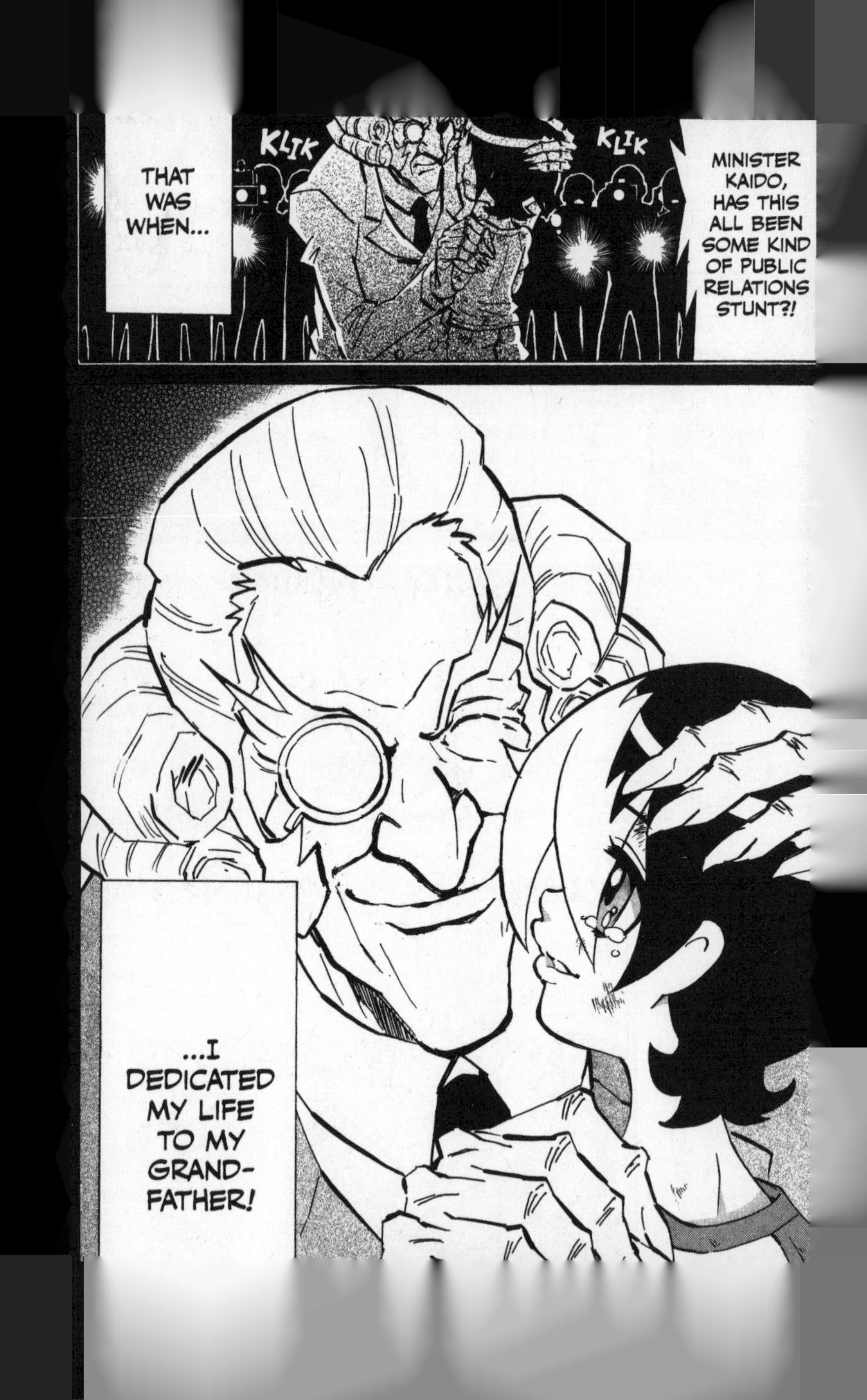
MINISTER KAIDO, HAS THIS ALL BEEN SOME KIND OF PUBLIC RELATIONS STUNT?!
KLIK
KLIK
THAT WAS WHEN...
...I DEDICATED MY LIFE TO MY GRAND-FATHER!

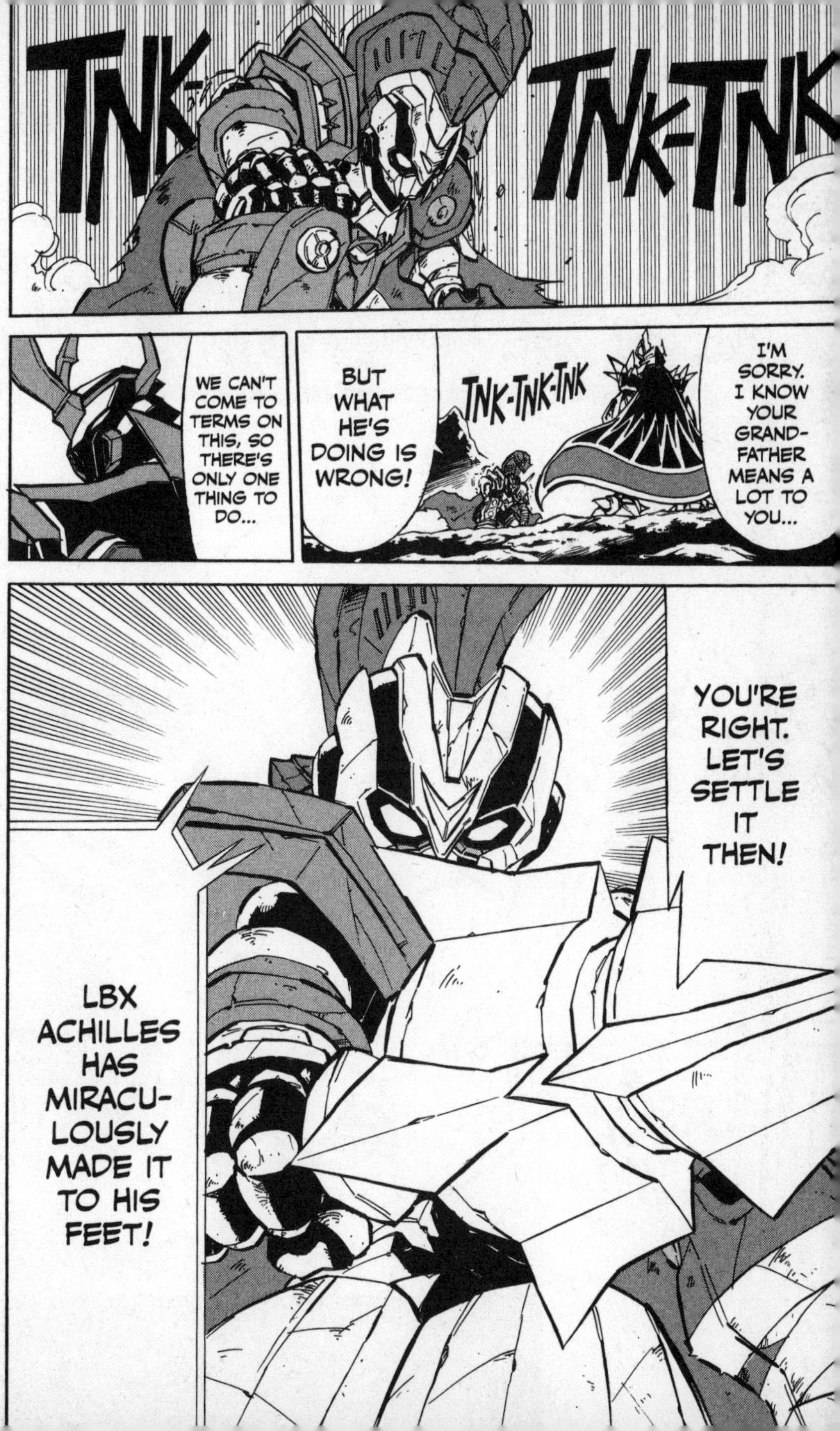
TNK-TNK
TNK-
I'M SORRY. I KNOW YOUR GRANDFATHER MEANS A LOT TO YOU...
TNK-TNK-TNK
BUT WHAT HE'S DOING IS WRONG!
WE CAN'T COME TO TERMS ON THIS, SO THERE'S ONLY ONE THING TO DO...
YOU'RE RIGHT. LET'S SETTLE IT THEN!
LBX ACHILLES HAS MIRACULOUSLY MADE IT TO HIS FEET!

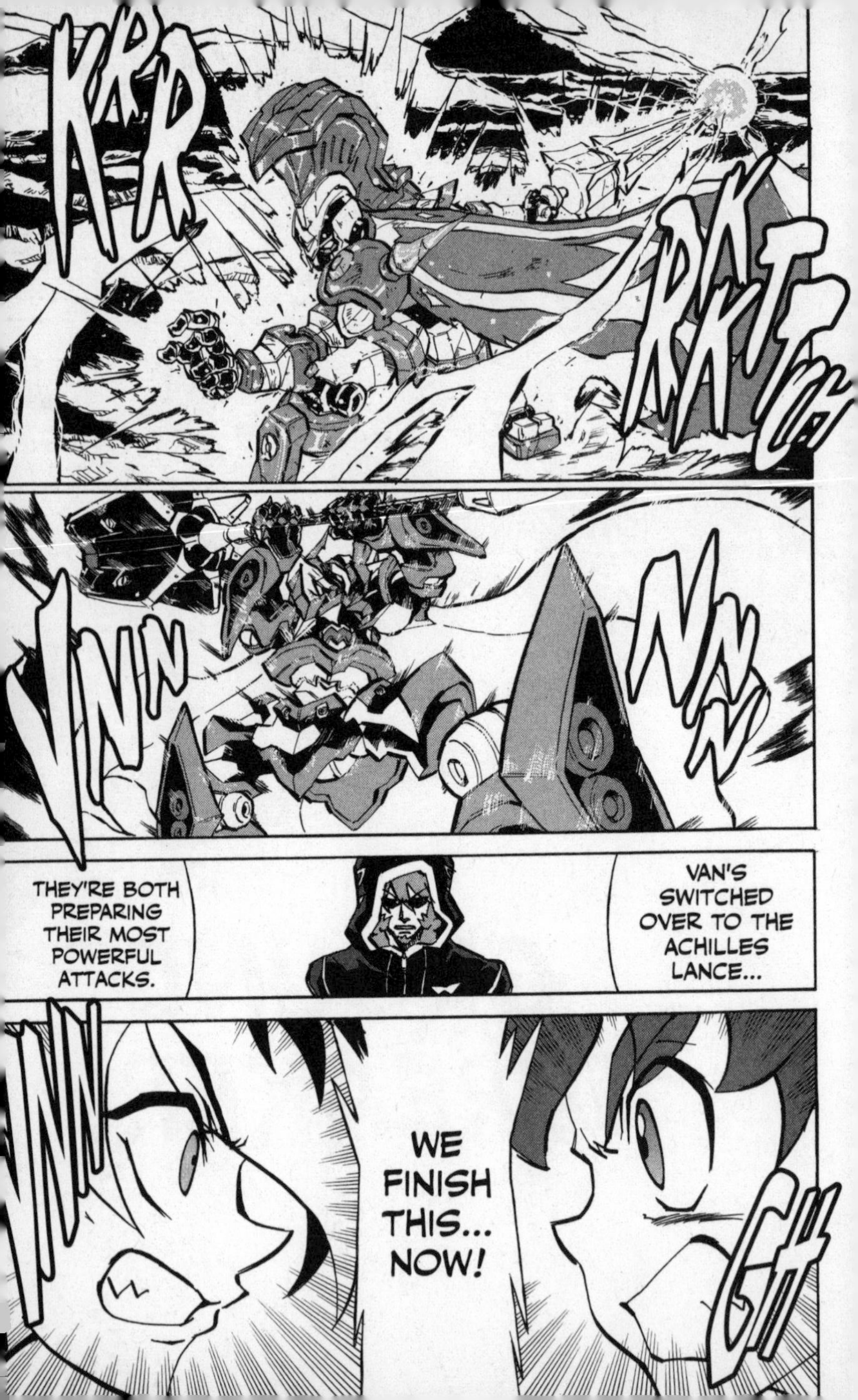
VAN'S SWITCHED OVER TO THE ACHILLES LANCE...
THEY'RE BOTH PREPARING THEIR MOST POWERFUL ATTACKS.
WE FINISH THIS... NOW!

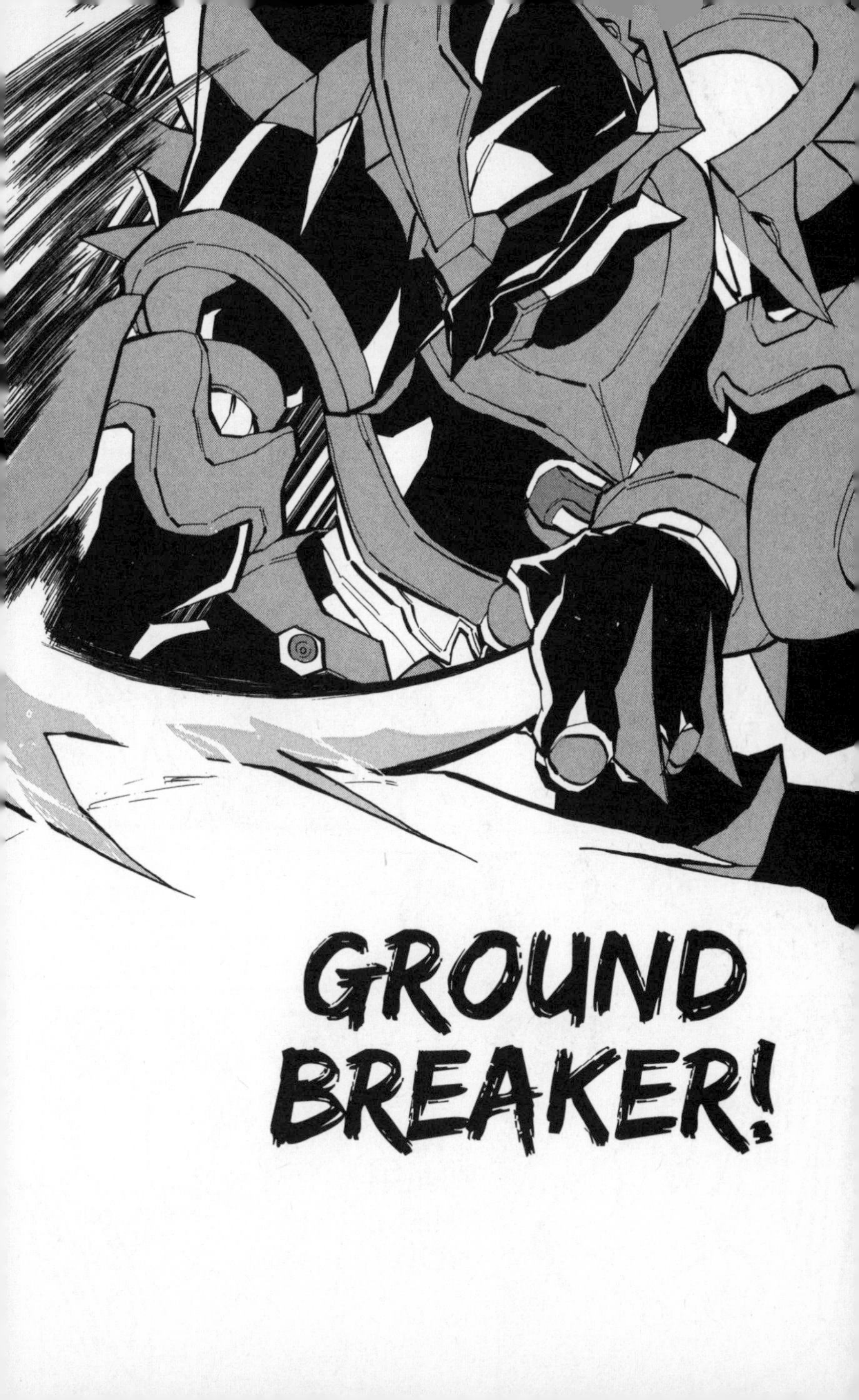
GROUND BREAKER!

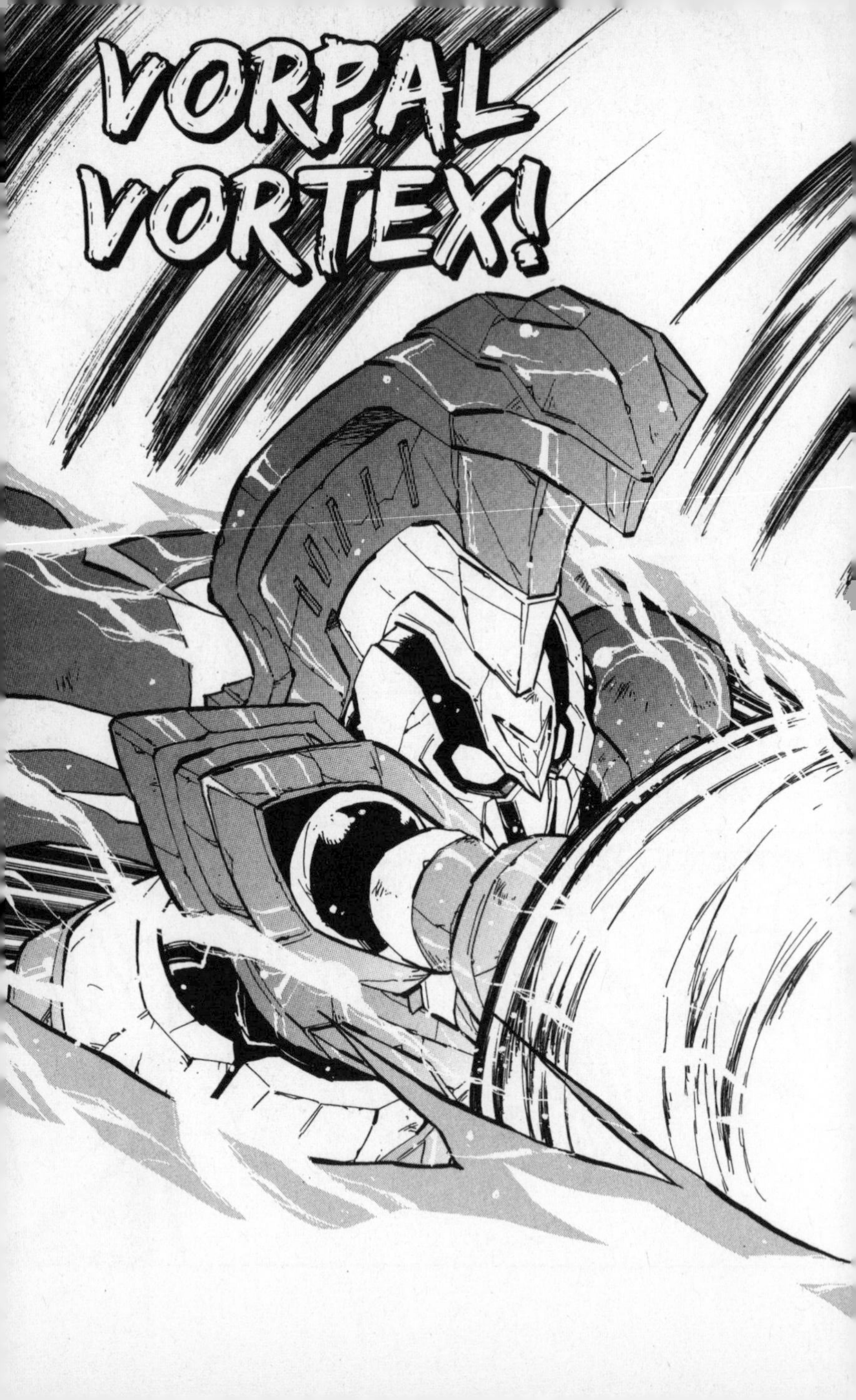
VORPAL VORTEX!

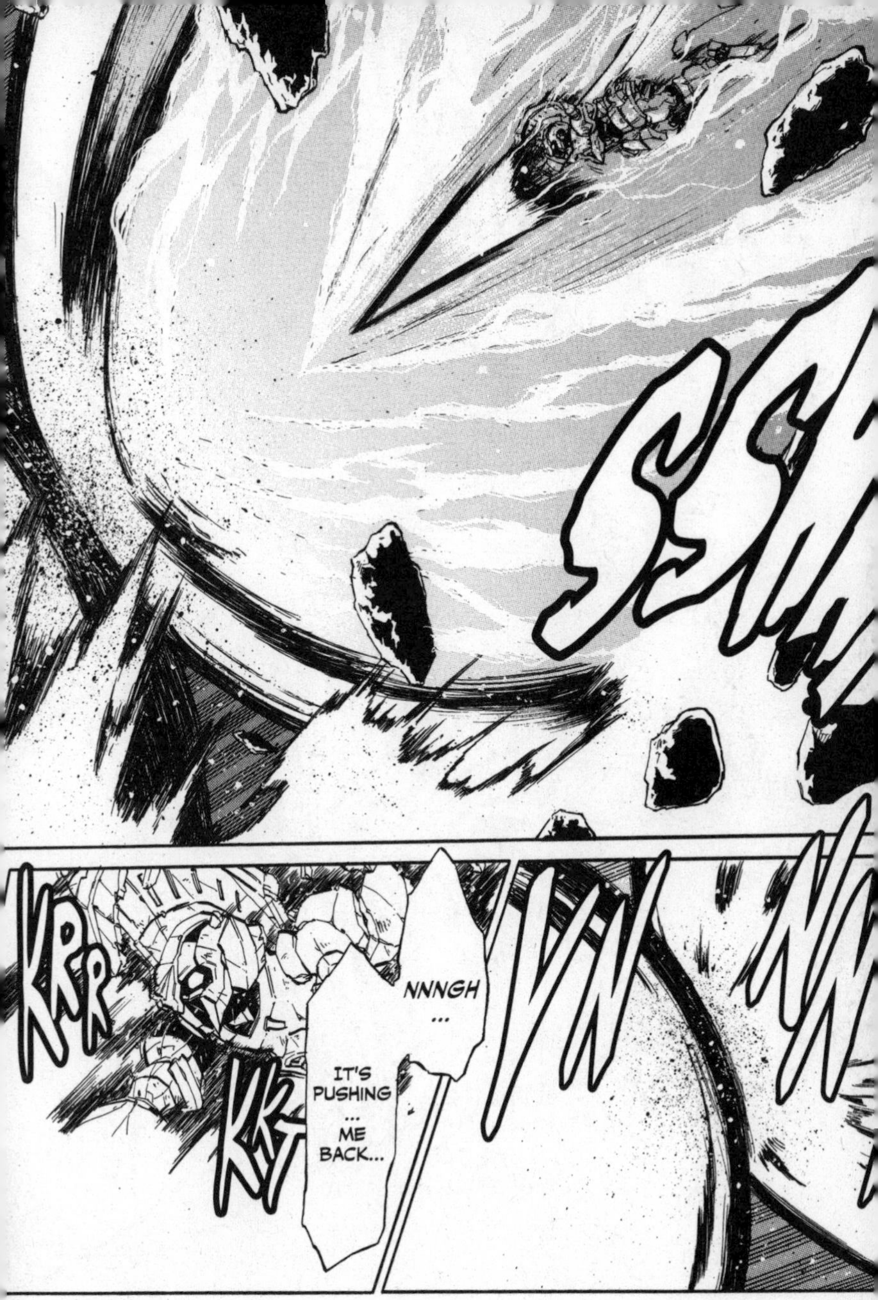
NNNGH ...
IT'S PUSHING ... ME BACK...

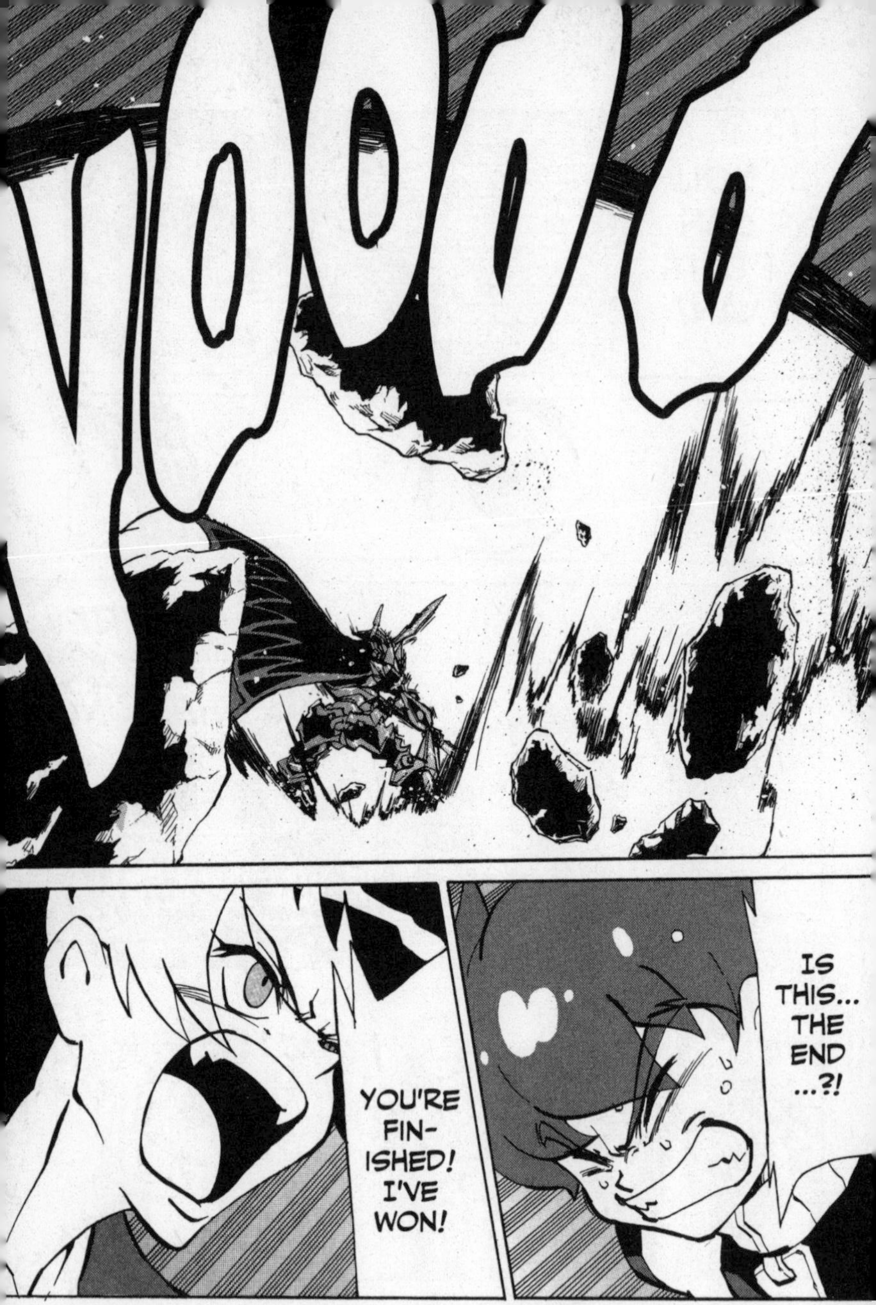
IS THIS... THE END ...?!
YOU'RE FIN-ISHED! I'VE WON!

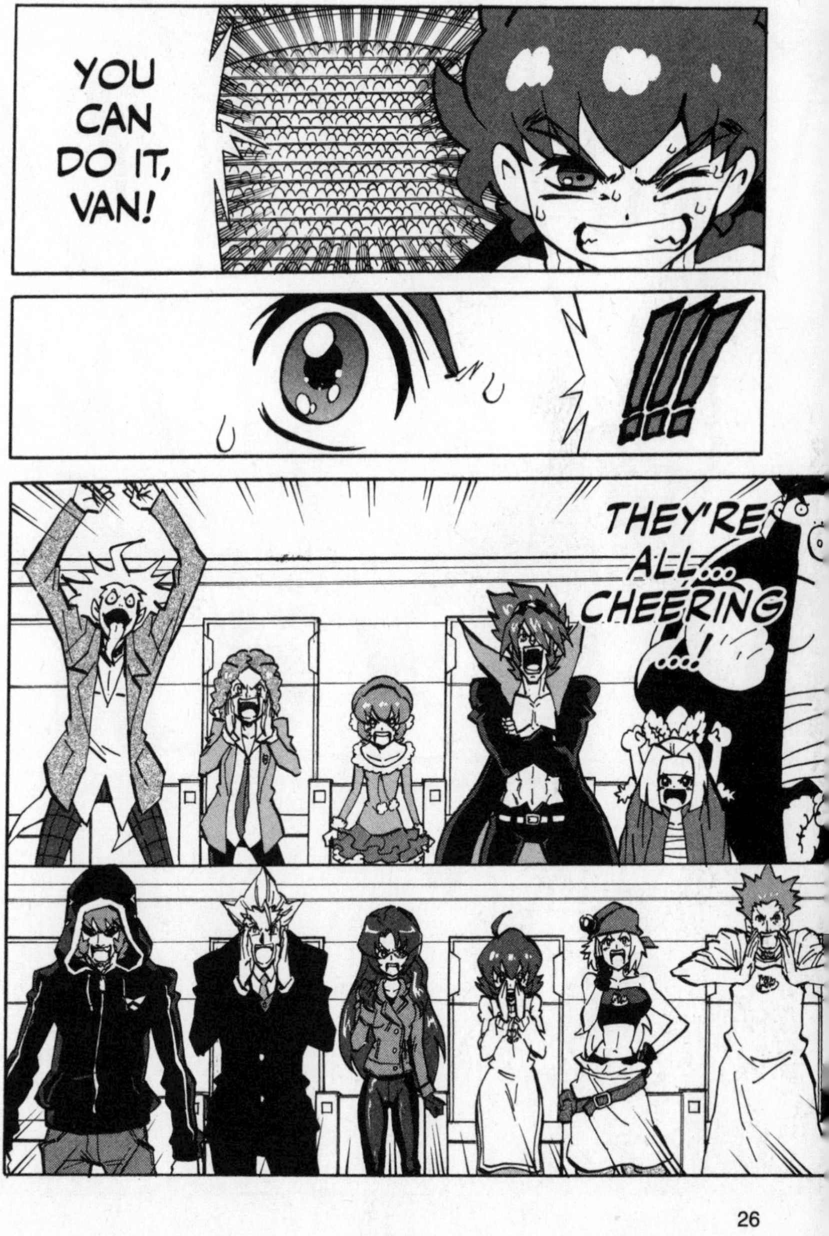
YOU CAN DO IT, VAN!
THEY'RE ALL... CHEERING...!

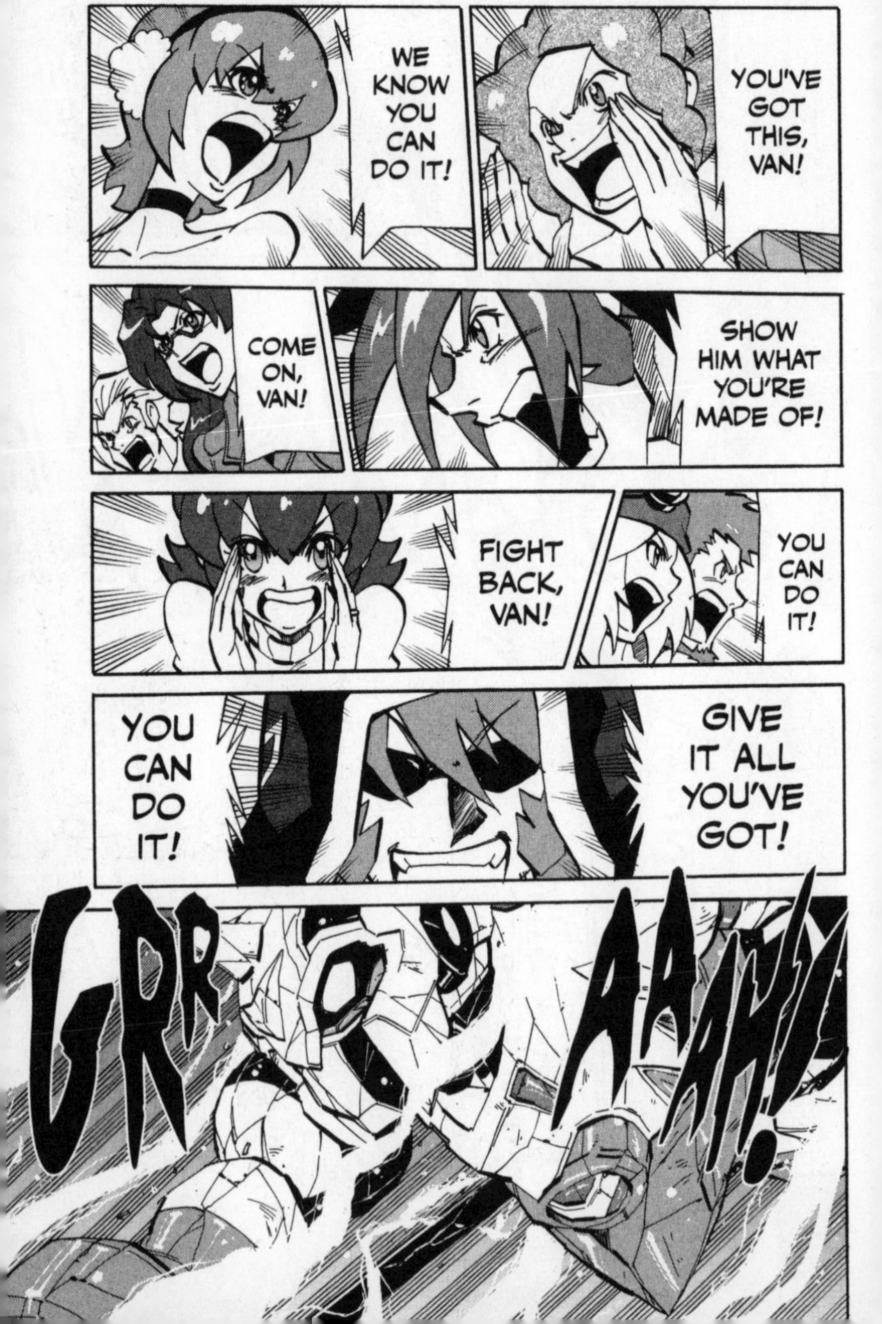
YOU'VE GOT THIS, VAN!
WE KNOW YOU CAN DO IT!
SHOW HIM WHAT YOU'RE MADE OF!
COME ON, VAN!
YOU CAN DO IT!
FIGHT BACK, VAN!
GIVE IT ALL YOU'VE GOT!
YOU CAN DO IT!
GRR AAAH!!

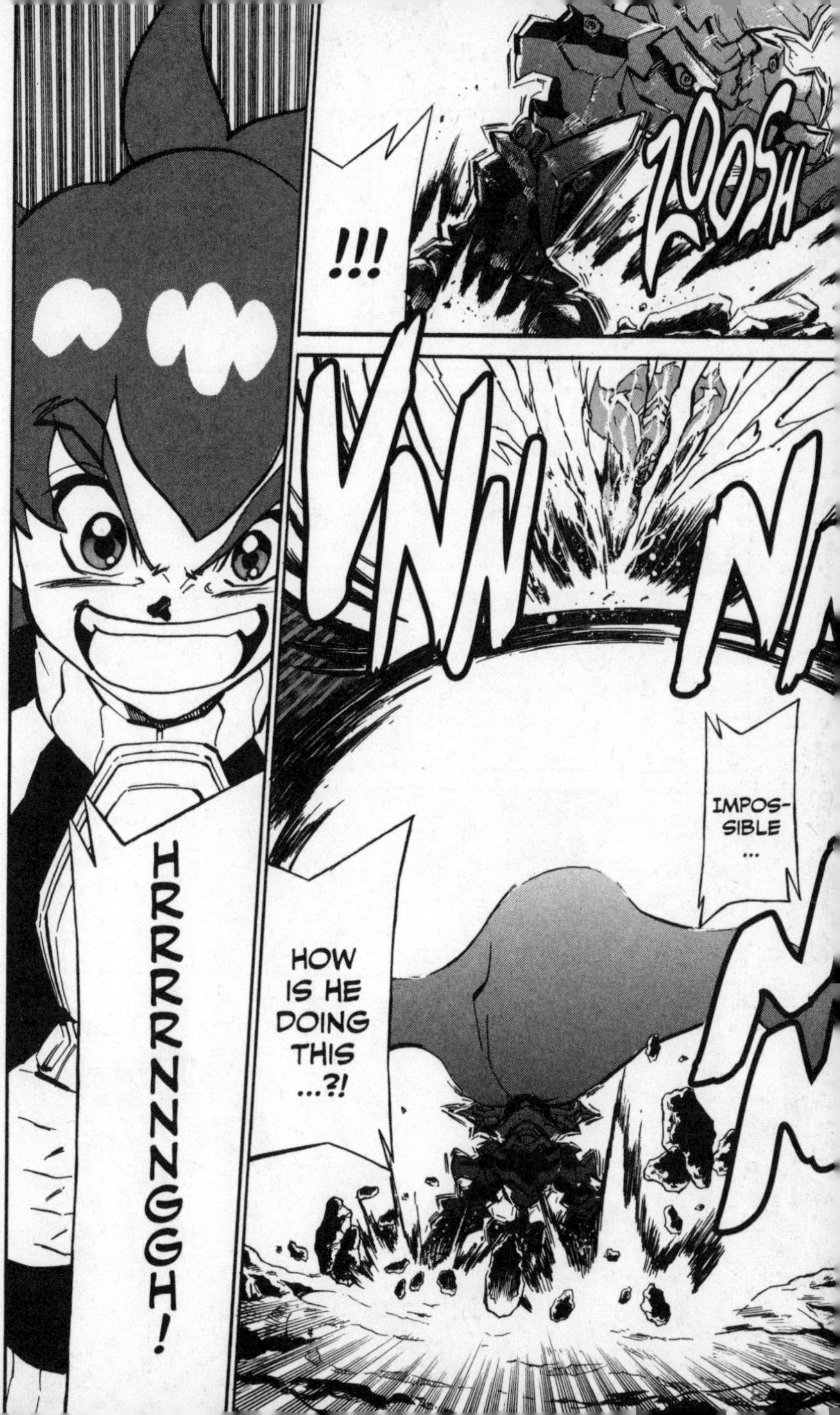
ZOOSH
!!!
IMPOSSIBLE...
HOW IS HE DOING THIS...?!
HRRRRNNNGGH!

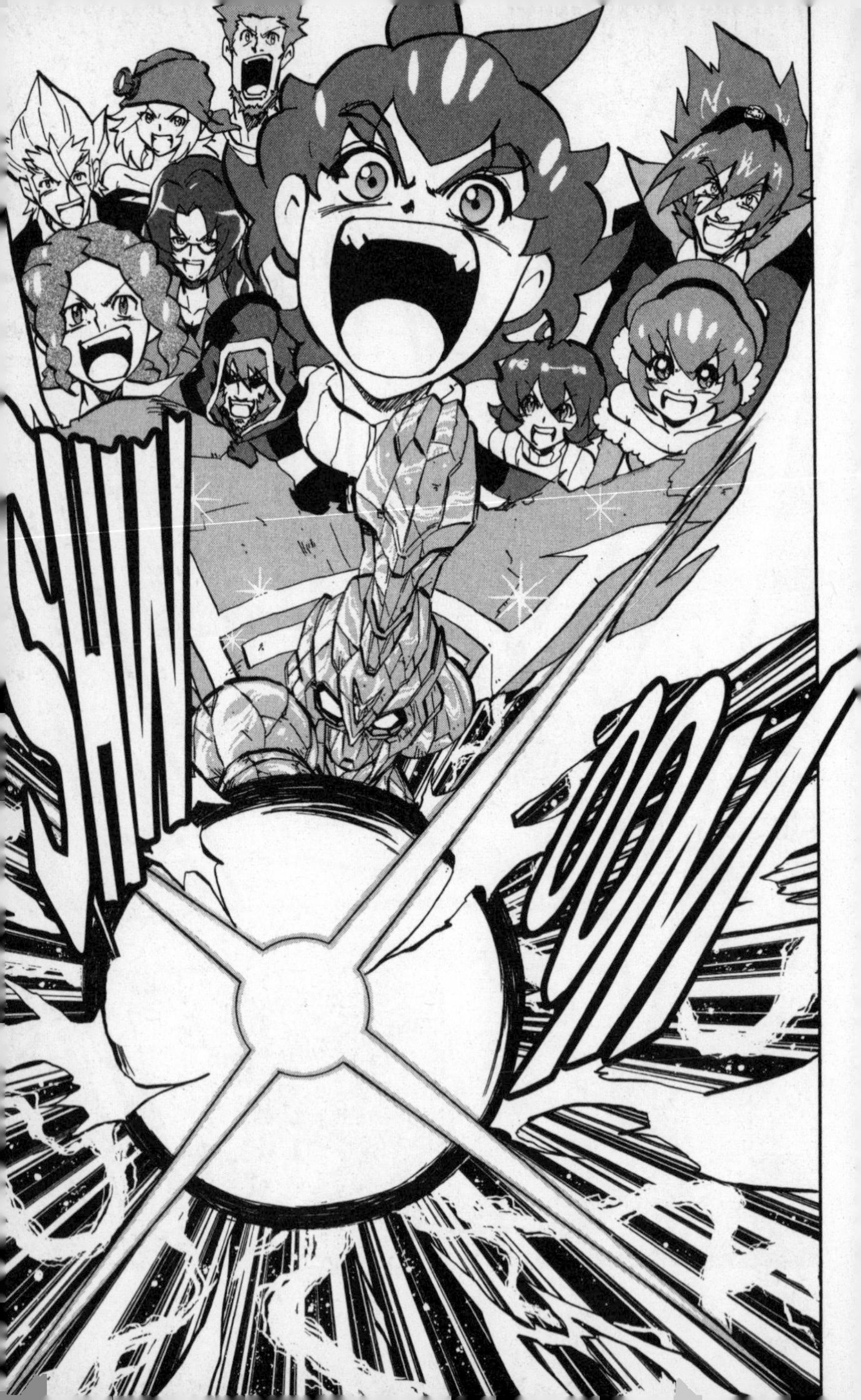

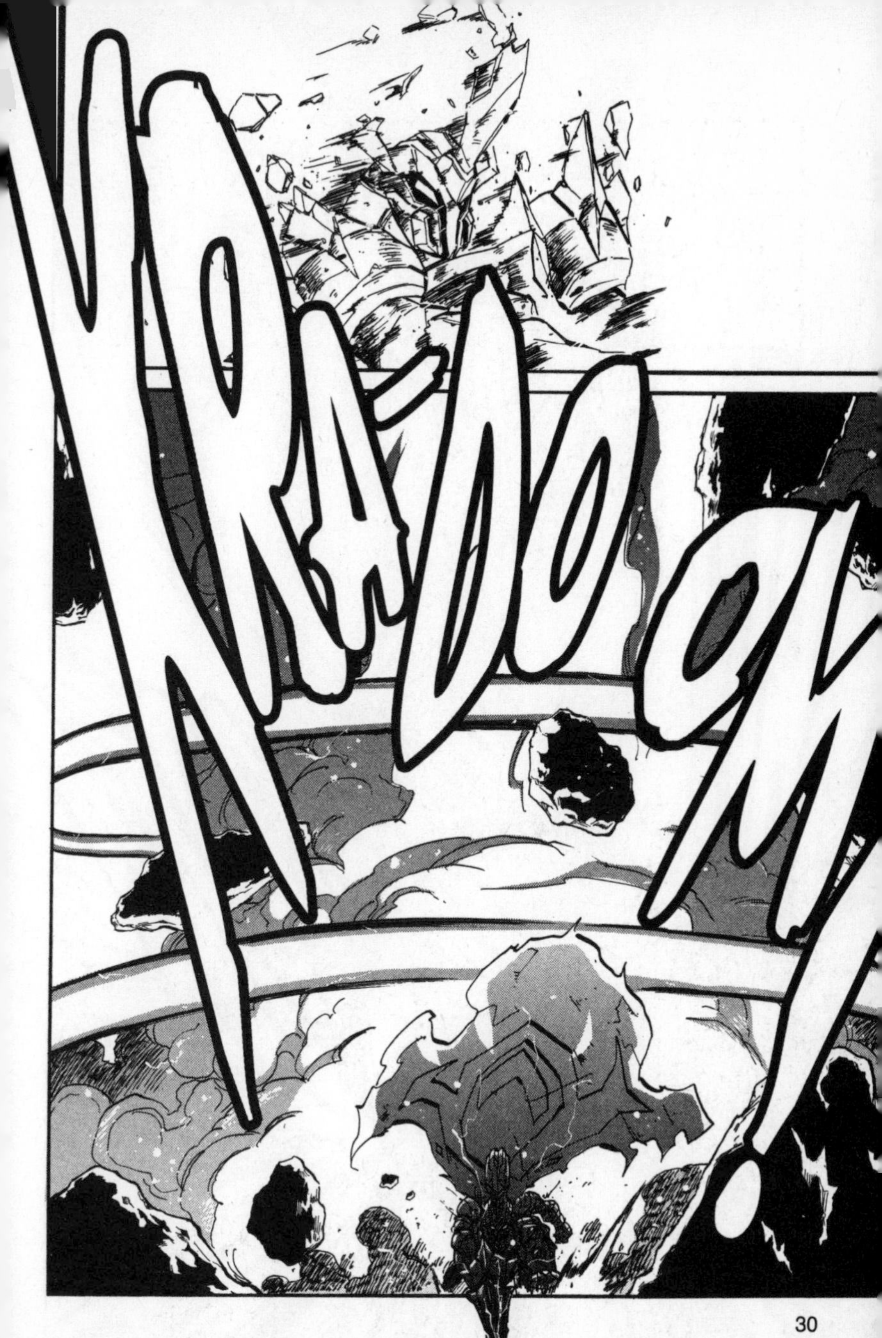
KRADOOM!

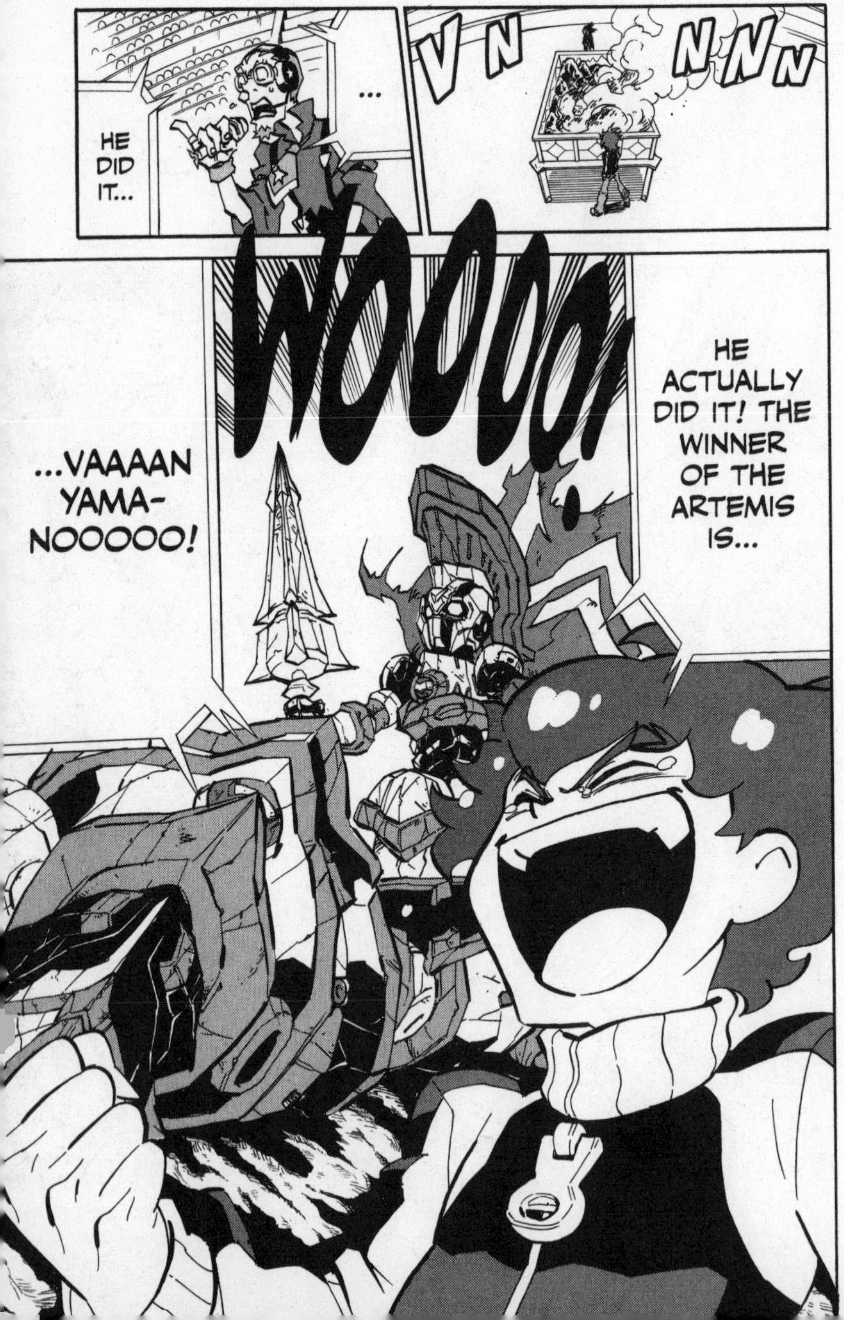
VN NNNN
...
HE DID IT...
WOOOO!
HE ACTUALLY DID IT! THE WINNER OF THE ARTEMIS IS...
...VAAAAN YAMA-NOOOOO!

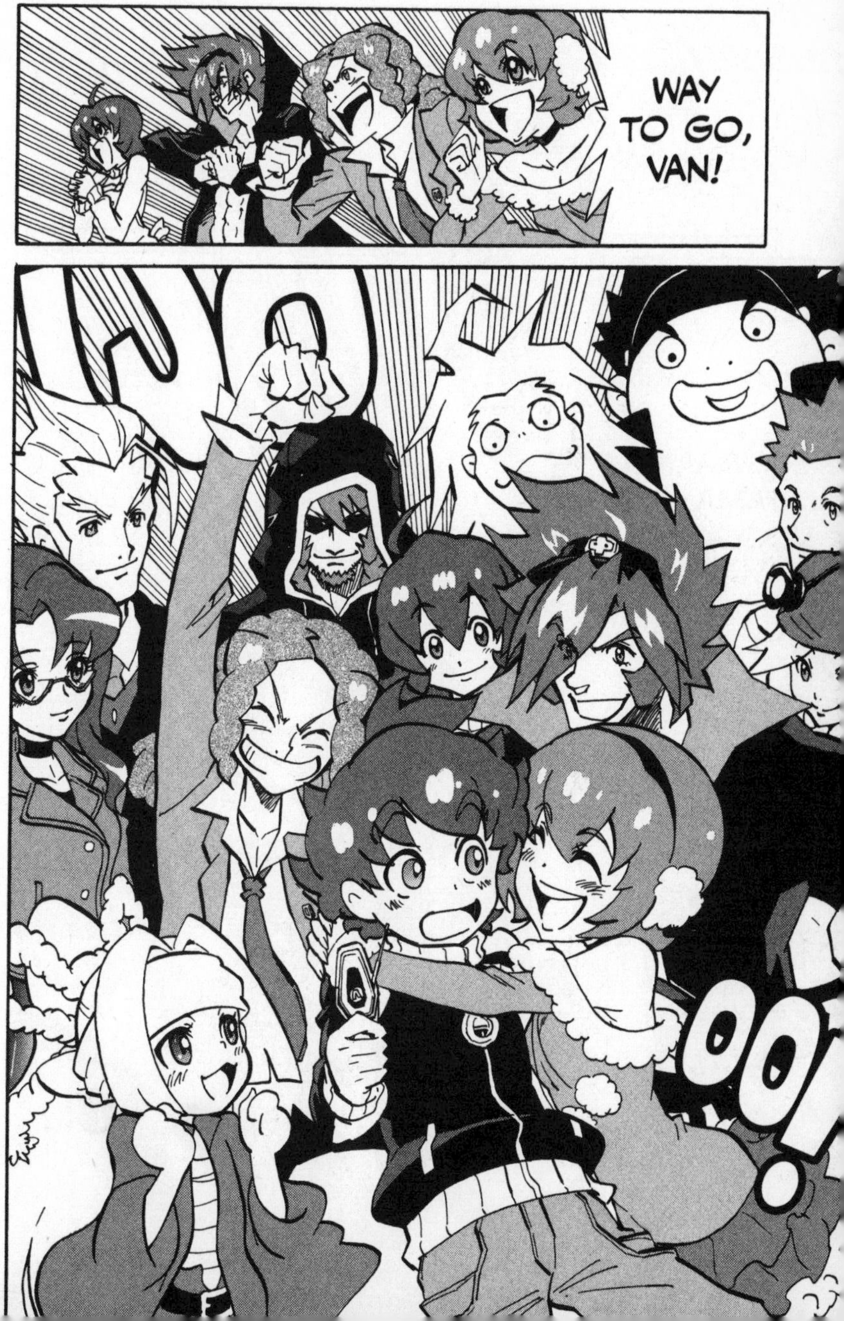
WAY TO GO, VAN!

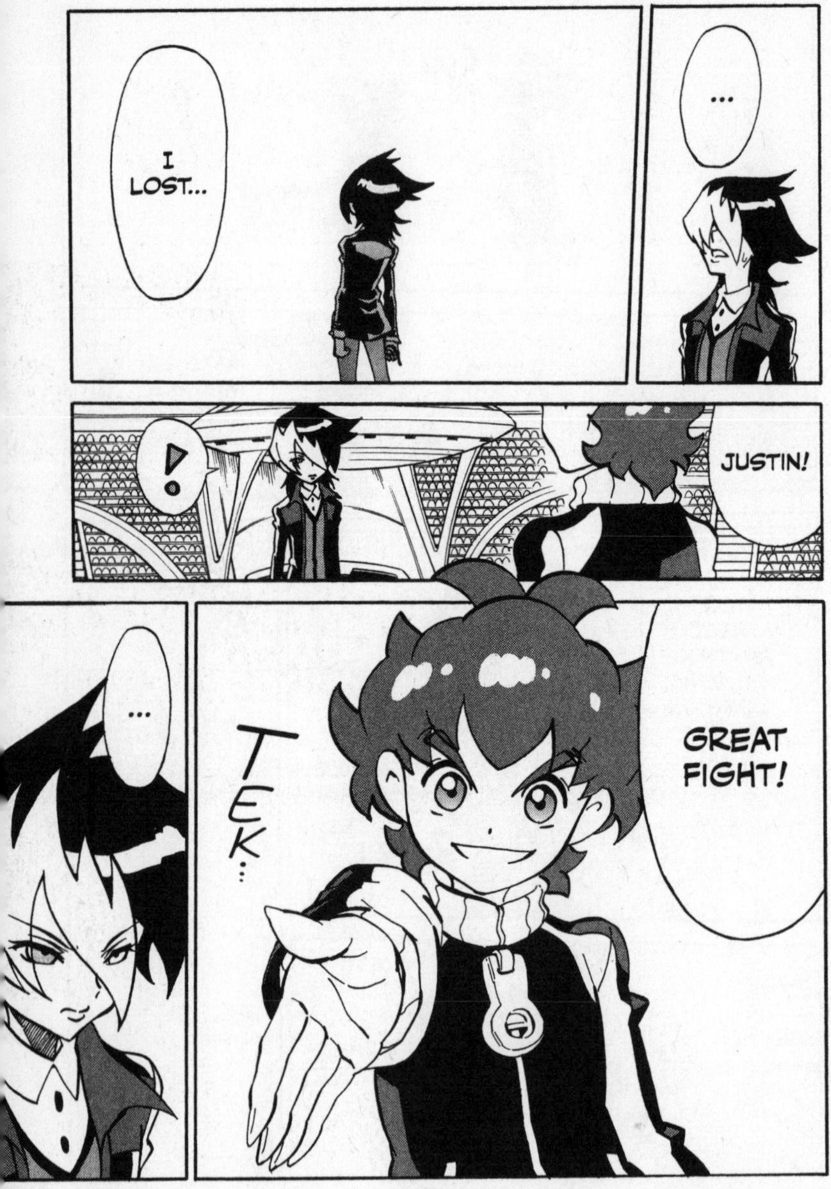
...
I LOST...
JUSTIN!
!
GREAT FIGHT!
TEK...
...

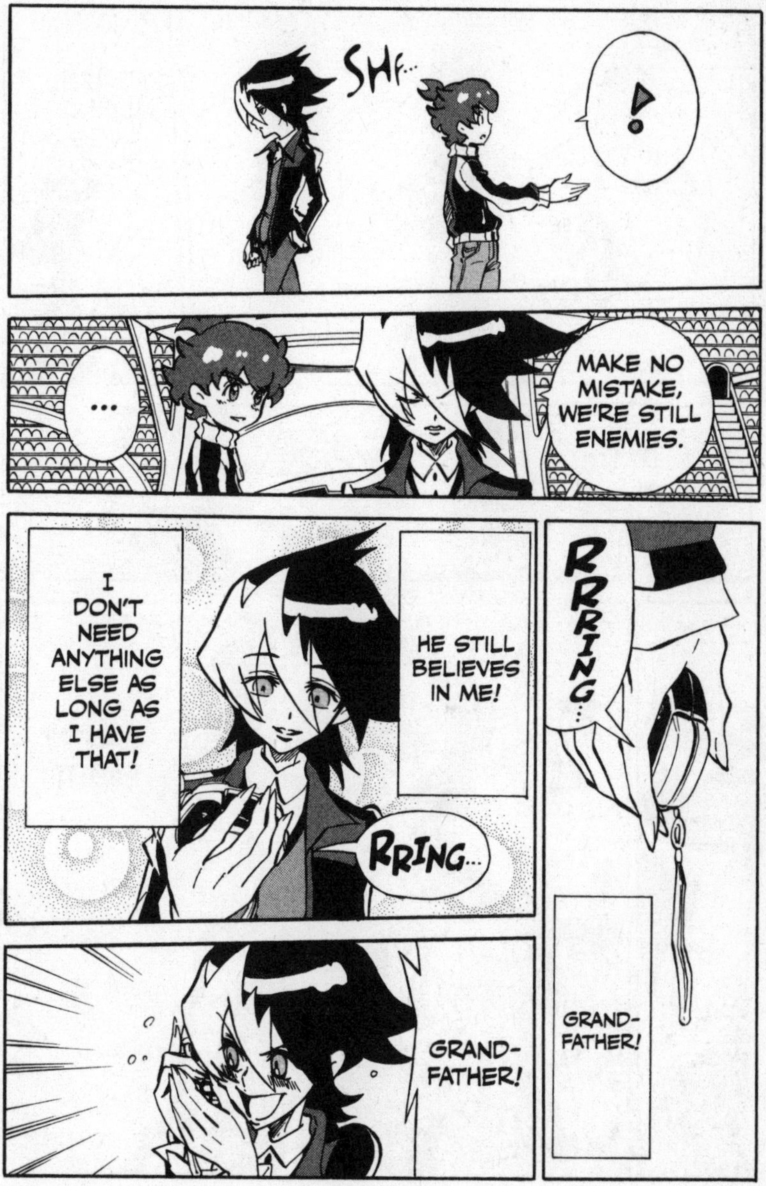
SHF...
!
MAKE NO MISTAKE, WE'RE STILL ENEMIES.
...
RRRING...
GRAND-FATHER!
HE STILL BELIEVES IN ME!
I DON'T NEED ANYTHING ELSE AS LONG AS I HAVE THAT!
RRING...
GRAND-FATHER!

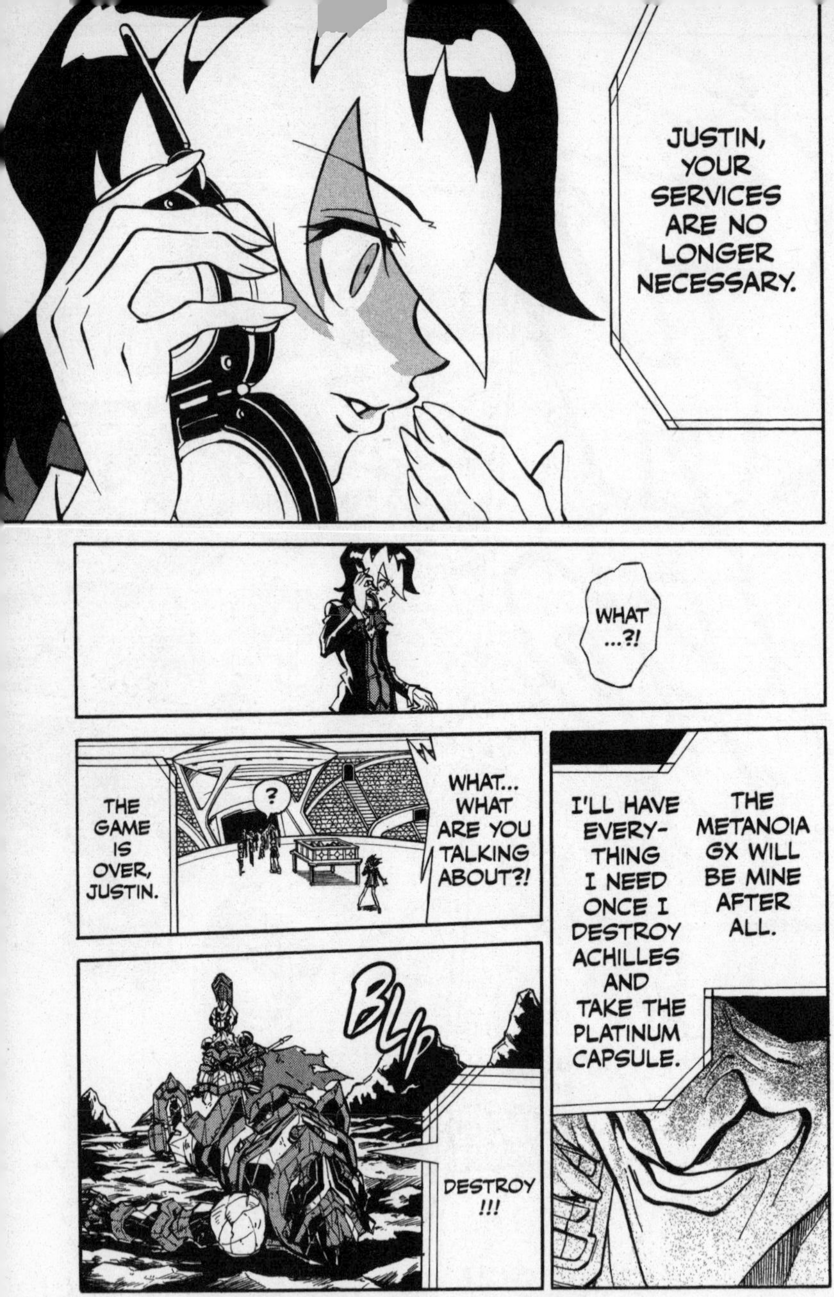
JUSTIN, YOUR SERVICES ARE NO LONGER NECESSARY.
WHAT ...?!
THE METANOIA GX WILL BE MINE AFTER ALL.
I'LL HAVE EVERYTHING I NEED ONCE I DESTROY ACHILLES AND TAKE THE PLATINUM CAPSULE.
WHAT... WHAT ARE YOU TALKING ABOUT?!
?
THE GAME IS OVER, JUSTIN.
BLIP
DESTROY !!!

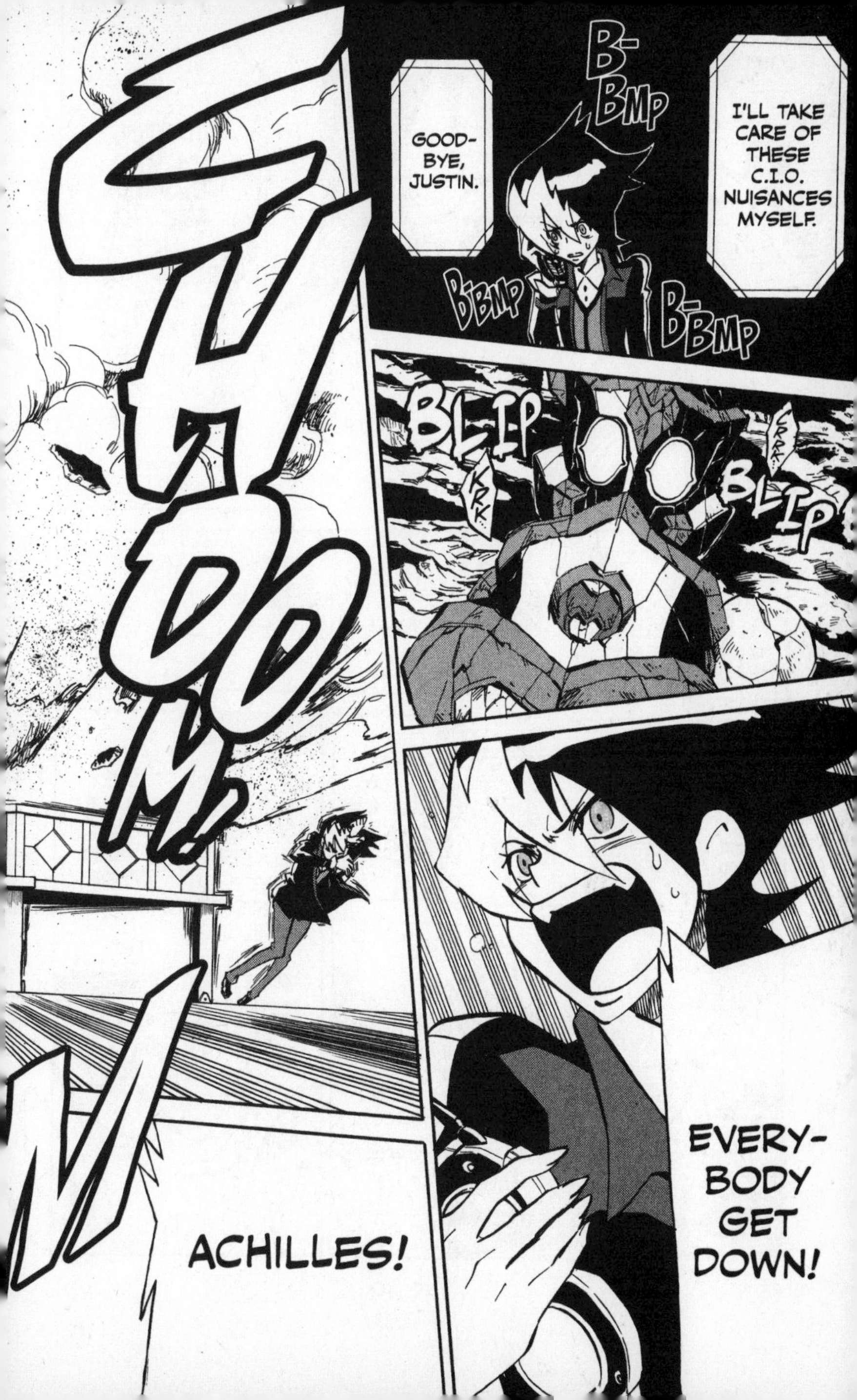
I'LL TAKE CARE OF THESE C.I.O. NUISANCES MYSELF.
B-BMP
GOOD-BYE, JUSTIN.
B-BMP
B-BMP
CRRK
BLIP
BLIP
KRK
EVERY-BODY GET DOWN!
SHDOOM!
ACHILLES!

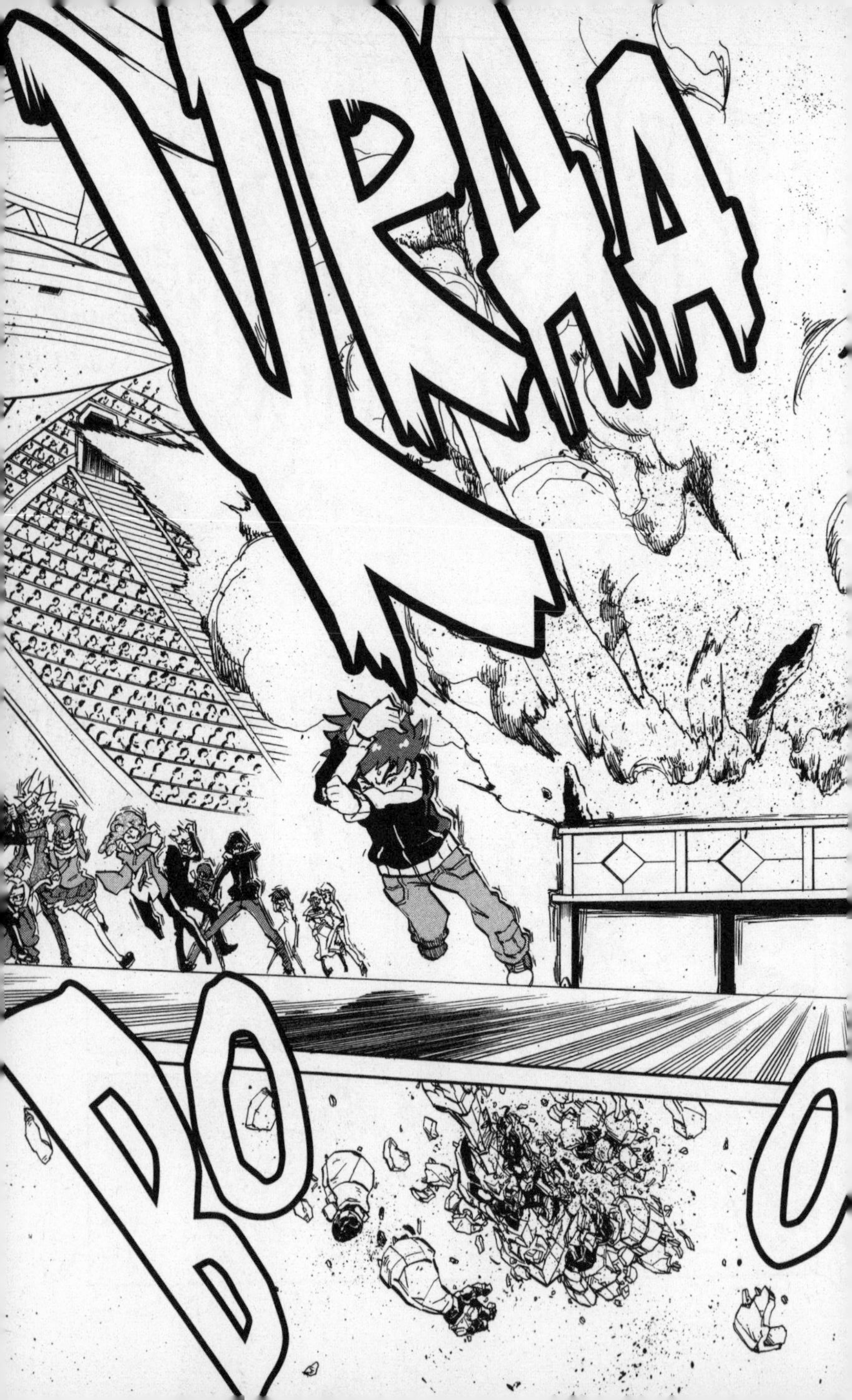

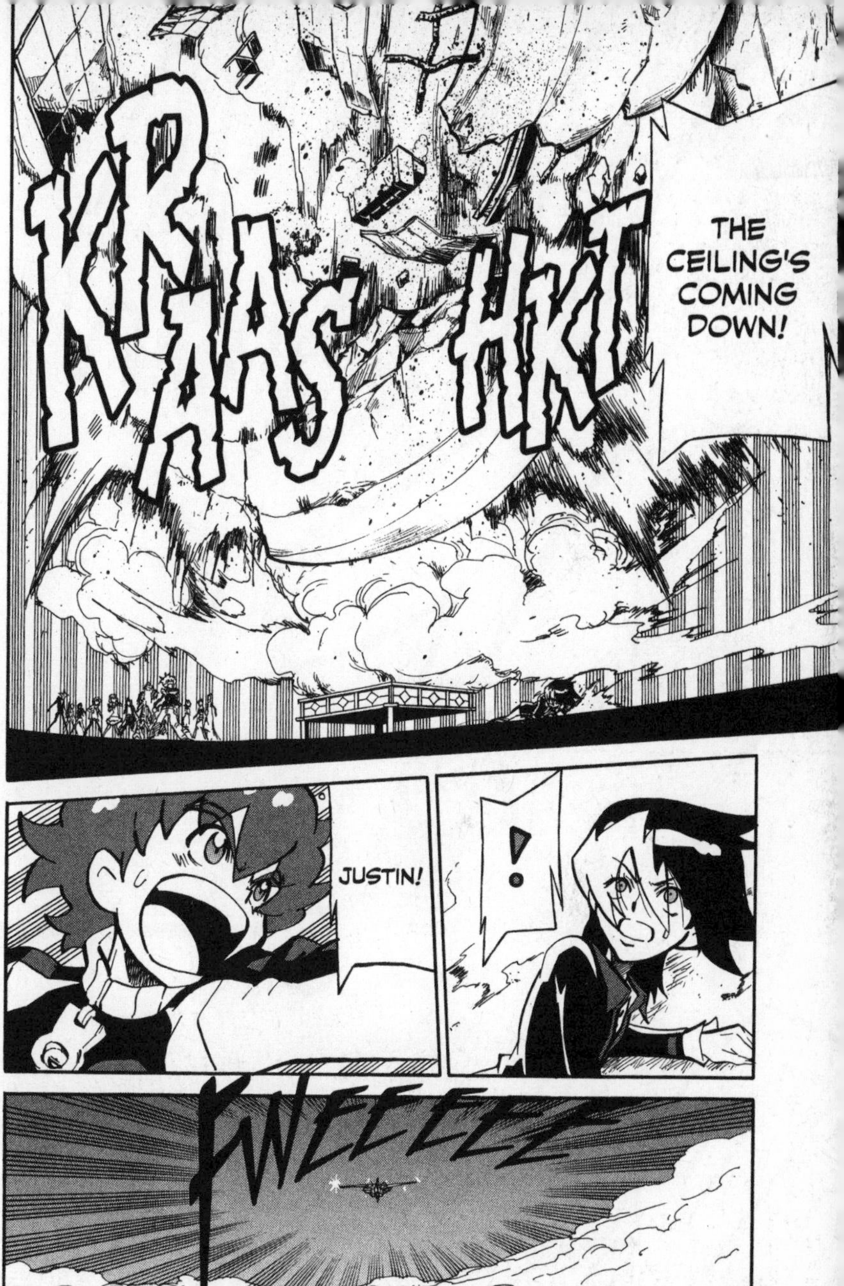
KRAASHKT
THE CEILING'S COMING DOWN!
!
JUSTIN!
FWEEEEE

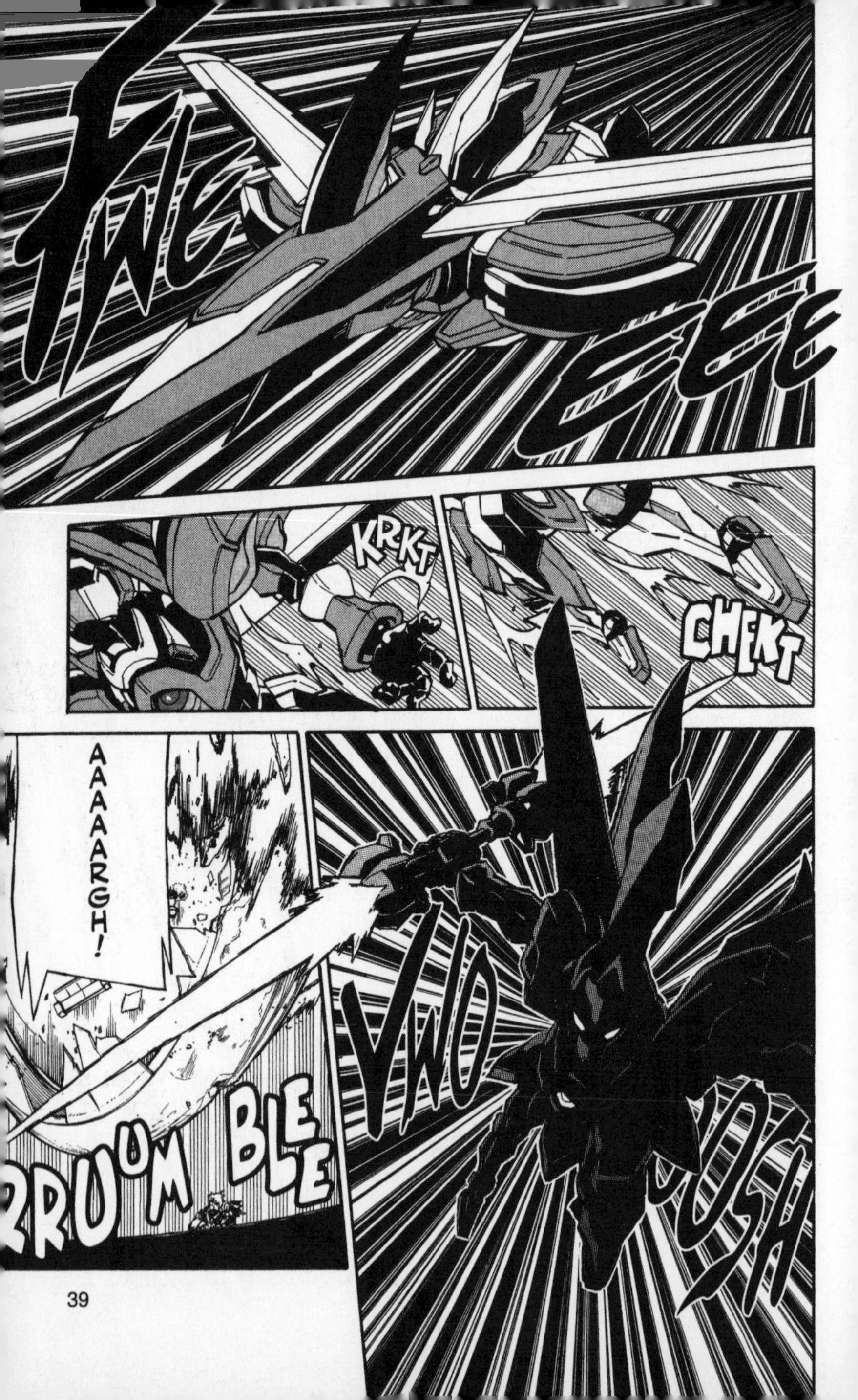
FWEEEE
CHEKT
KRKT
VWOOSH
AAAAAARGH!
RRUUMBLE

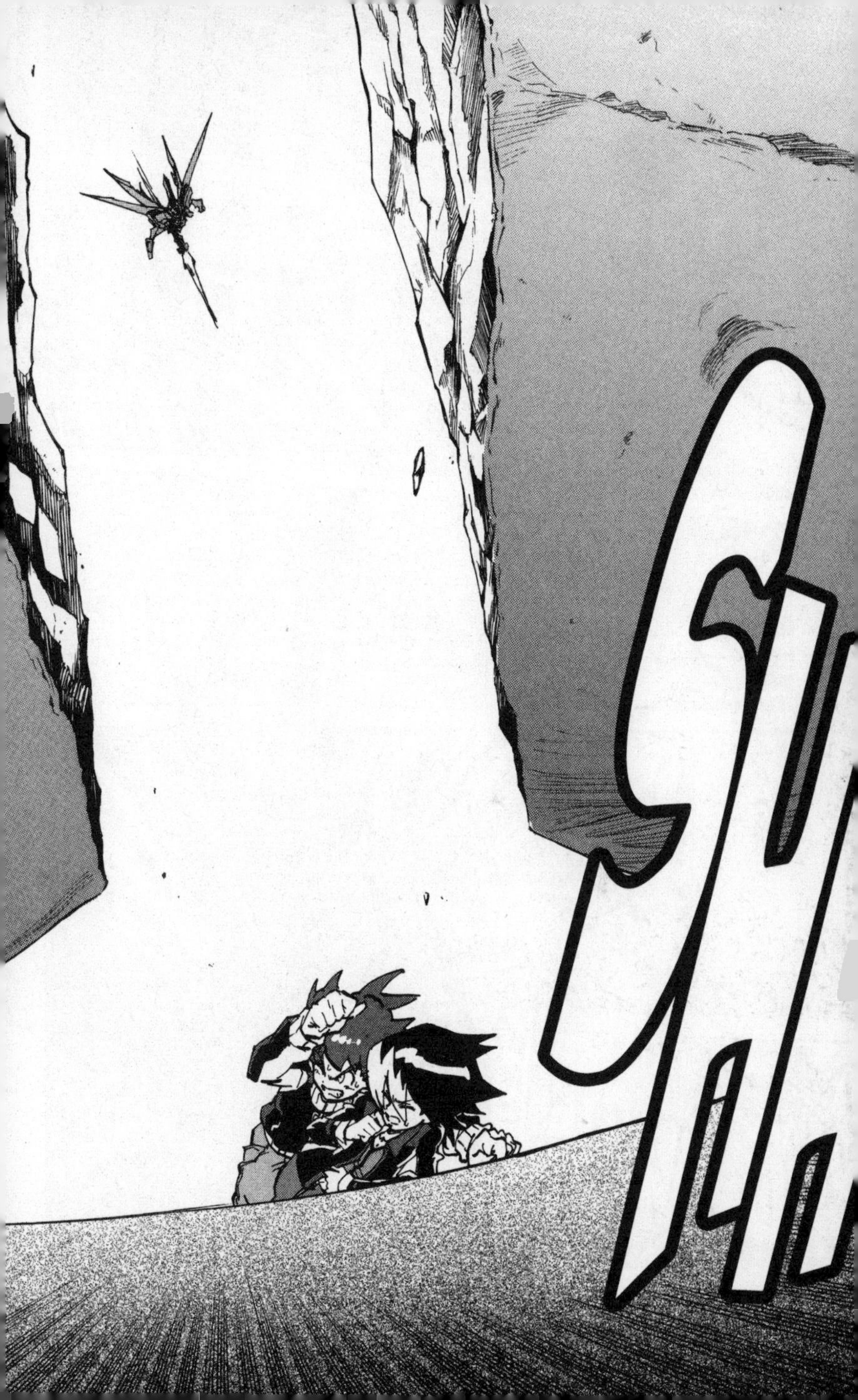

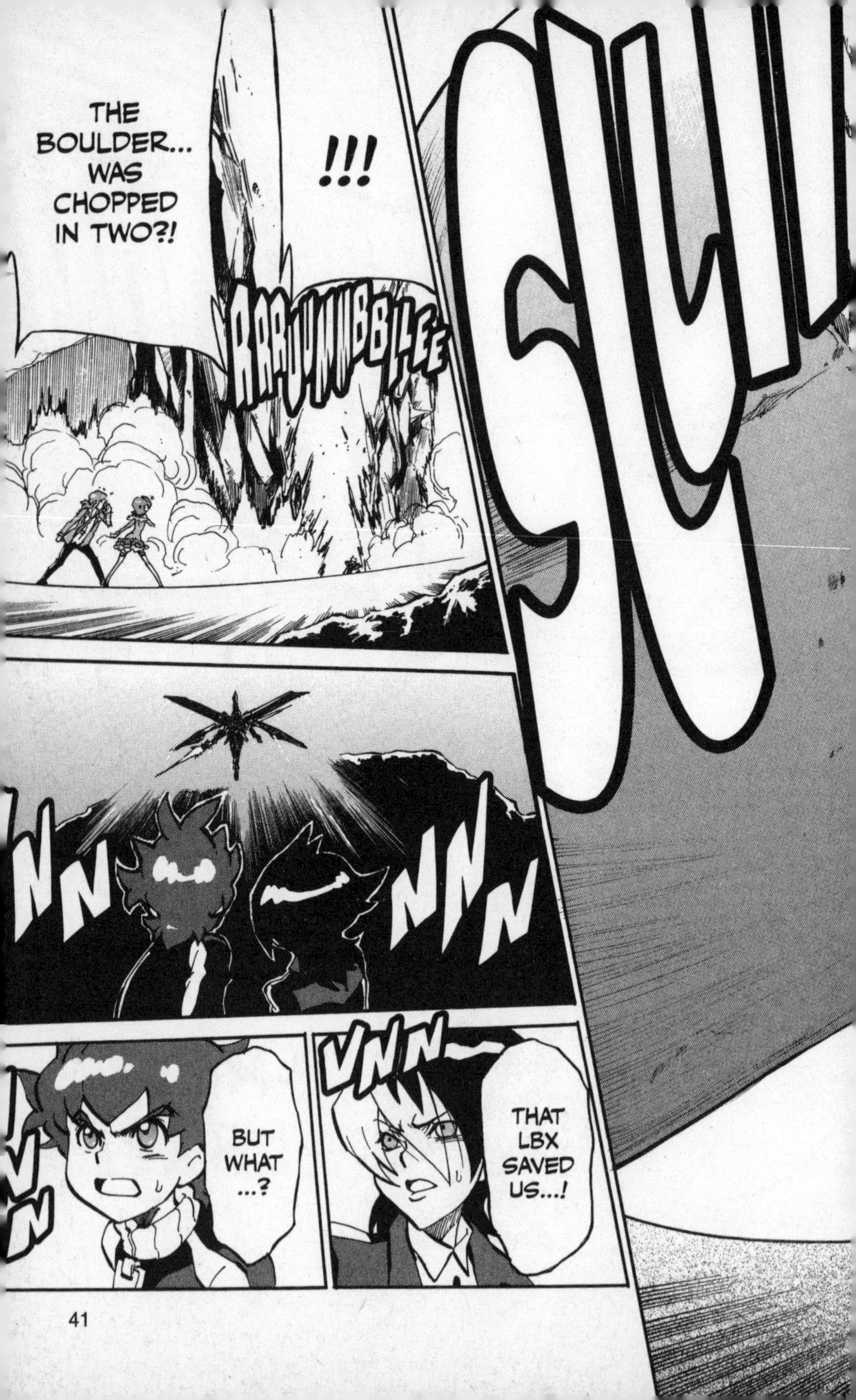
!!!
THE BOULDER... WAS CHOPPED IN TWO?!
RRRUMMBBLLEE
NNNN
NNNN
VNN
THAT LBX SAVED US...!
BUT WHAT ...?
VNNN

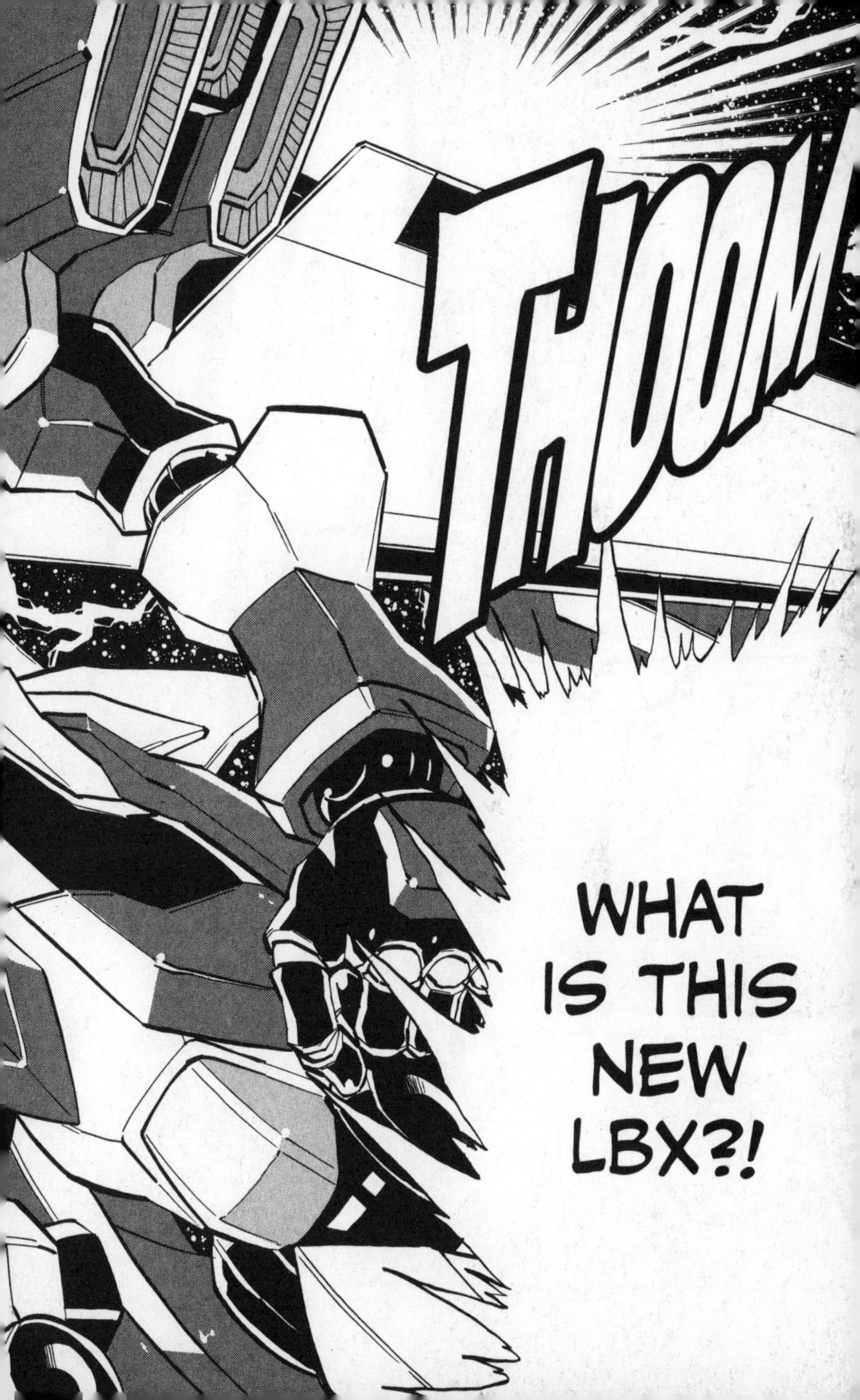
THOOM
WHAT IS THIS NEW LBX?!

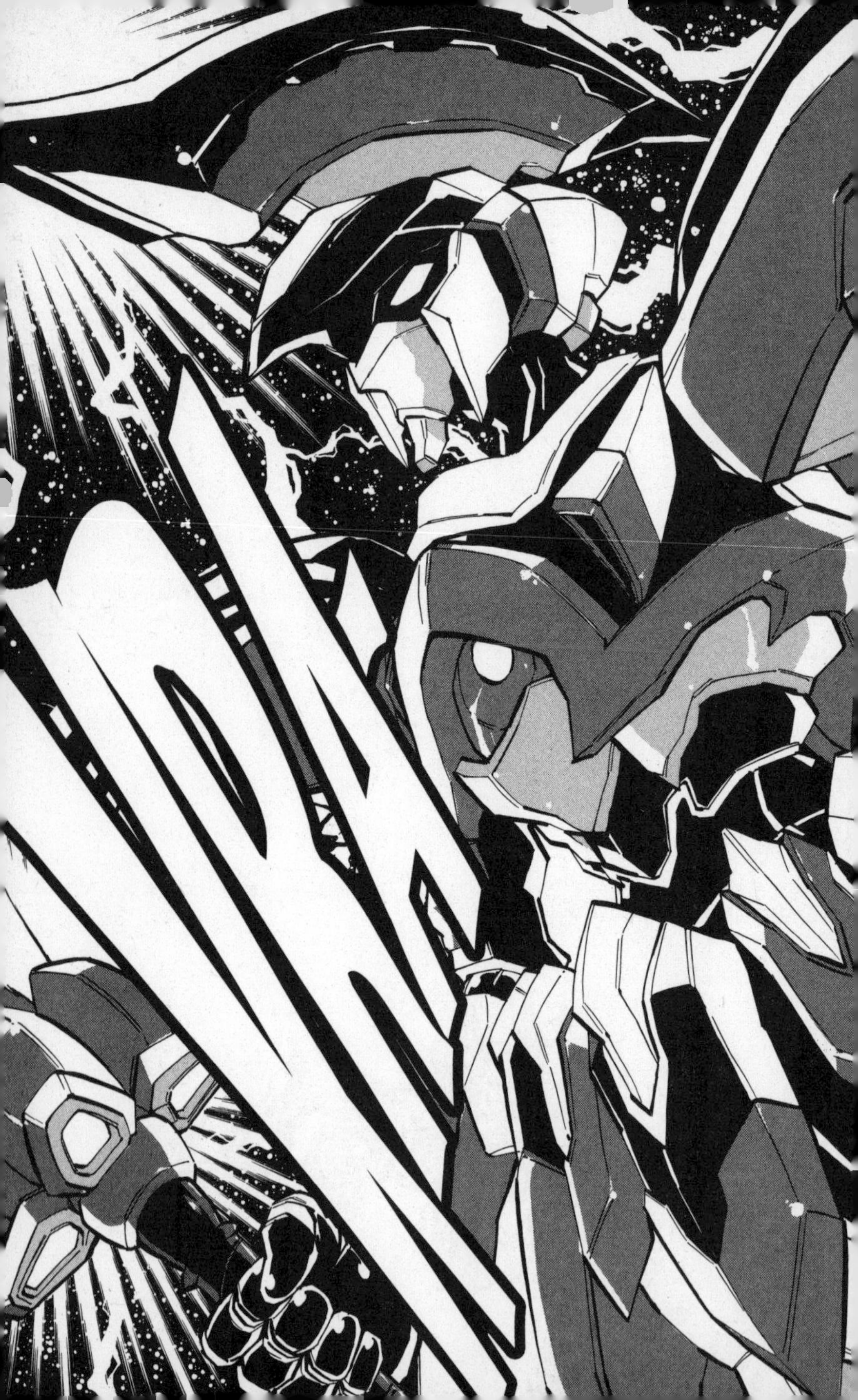

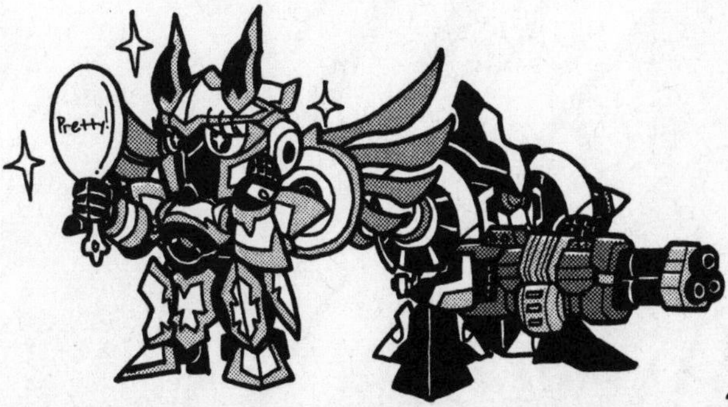
Pretty!

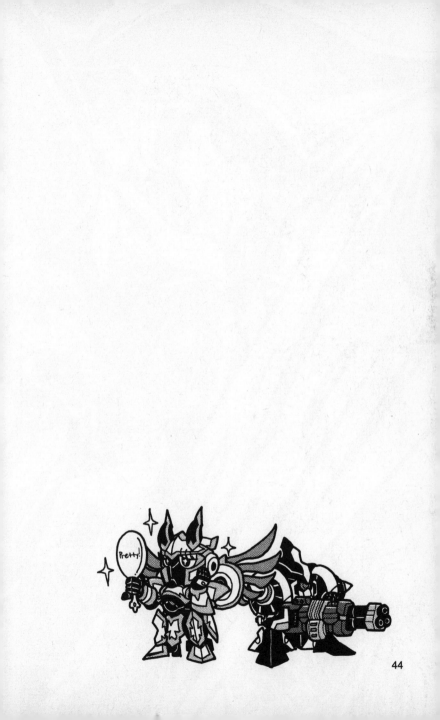

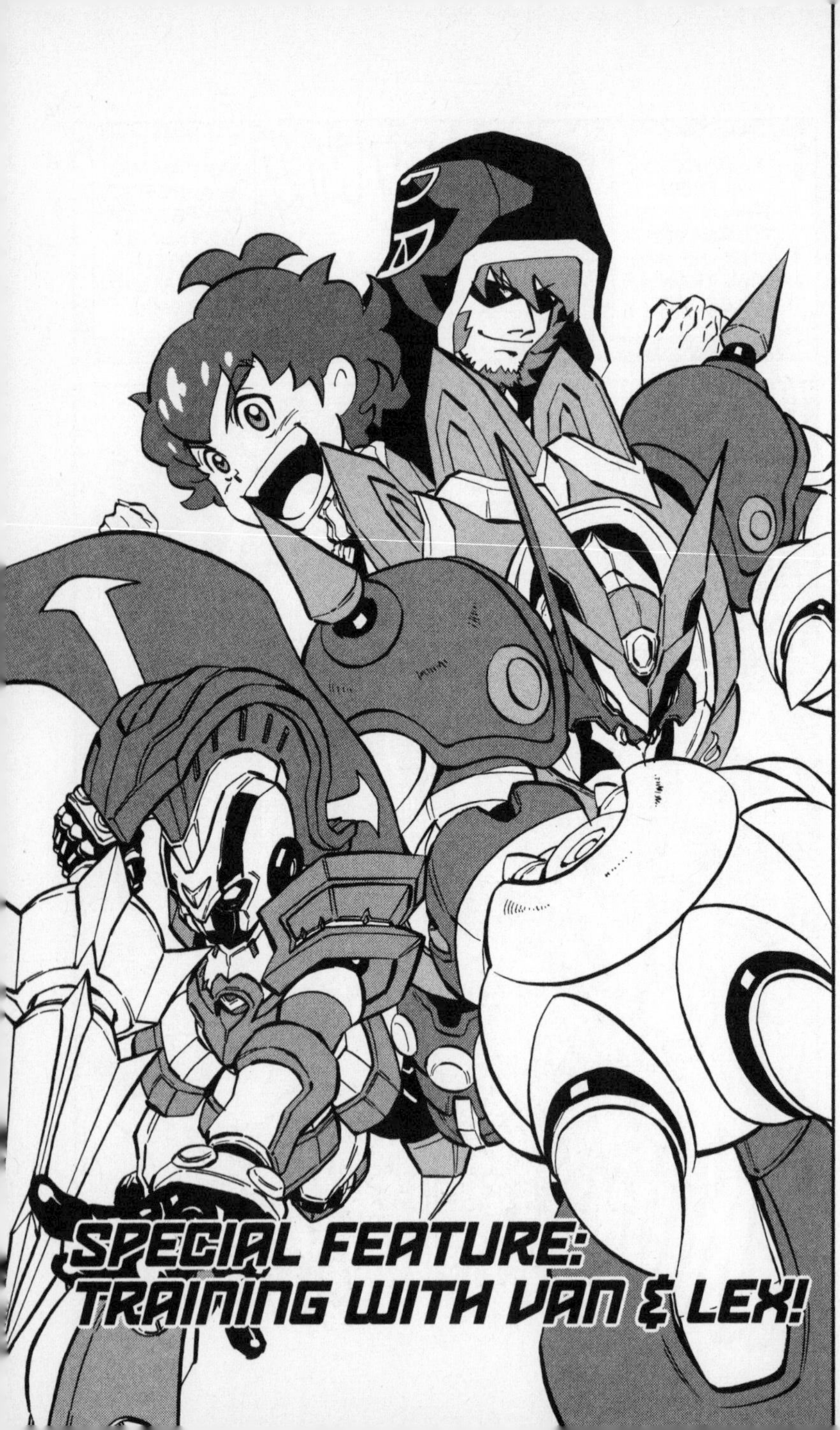
SPECIAL FEATURE:
TRAINING WITH VAN & LEX!

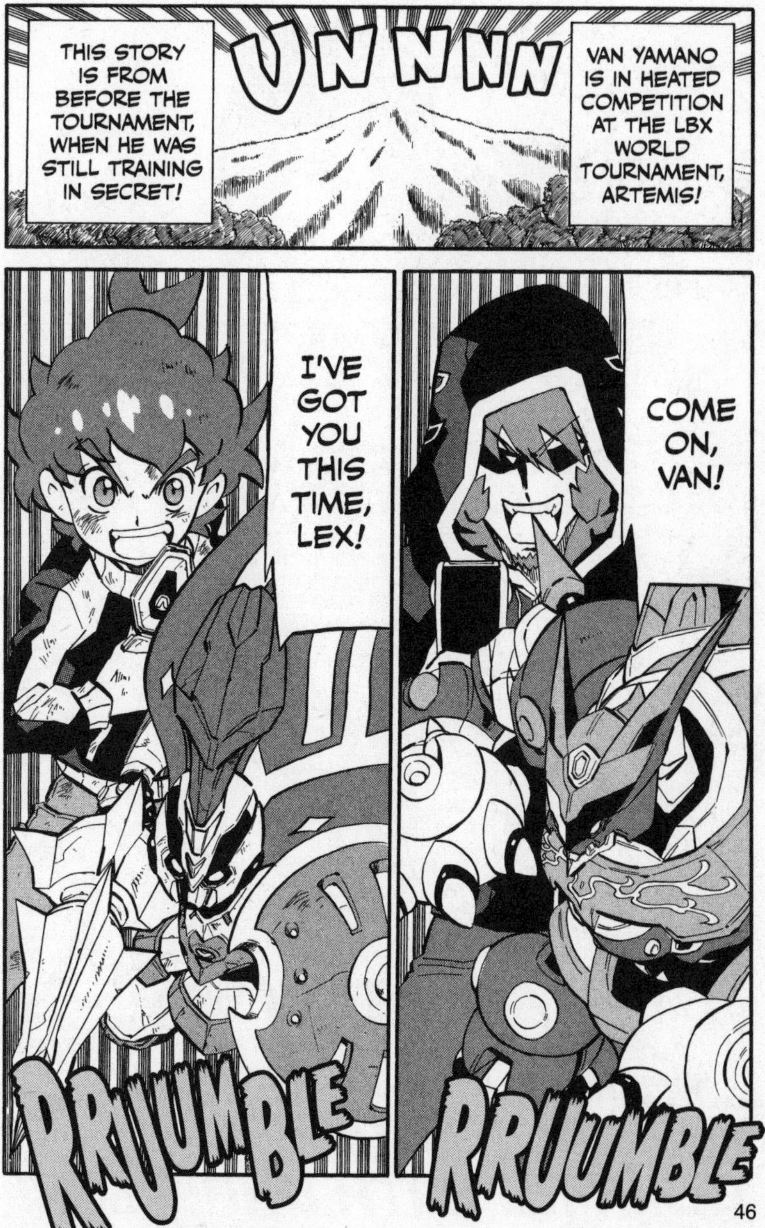
VAN YAMANO IS IN HEATED COMPETITION AT THE LBX WORLD TOURNAMENT, ARTEMIS!
UNNNN
THIS STORY IS FROM BEFORE THE TOURNAMENT, WHEN HE WAS STILL TRAINING IN SECRET!
COME ON, VAN!
RRUUMBLE
I'VE GOT YOU THIS TIME, LEX!
RRUUMBLE

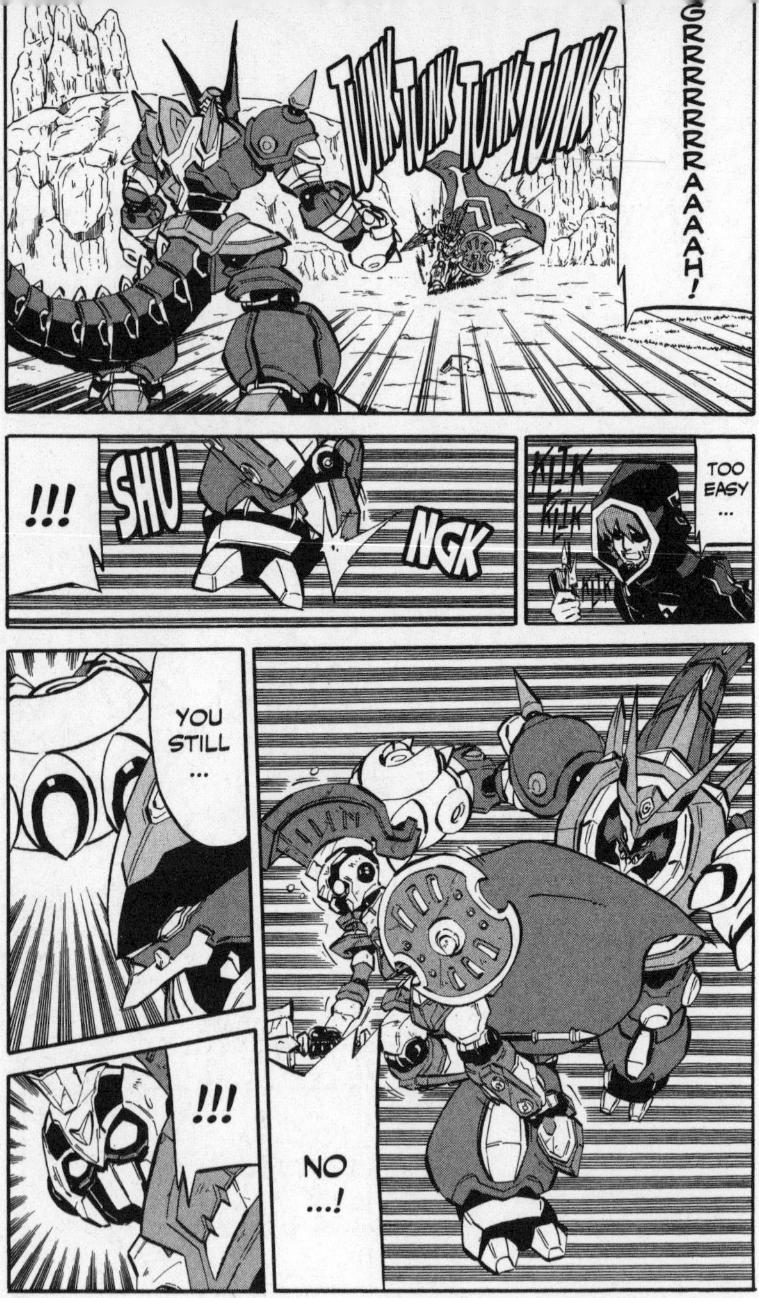
GRRRRRRAAAAH!
TUNK TUNK TUNK TUNK
KLIK KLIK KLIK
TOO EASY ...
SHU NGK
!!!
NO ...!
YOU STILL ...
!!!

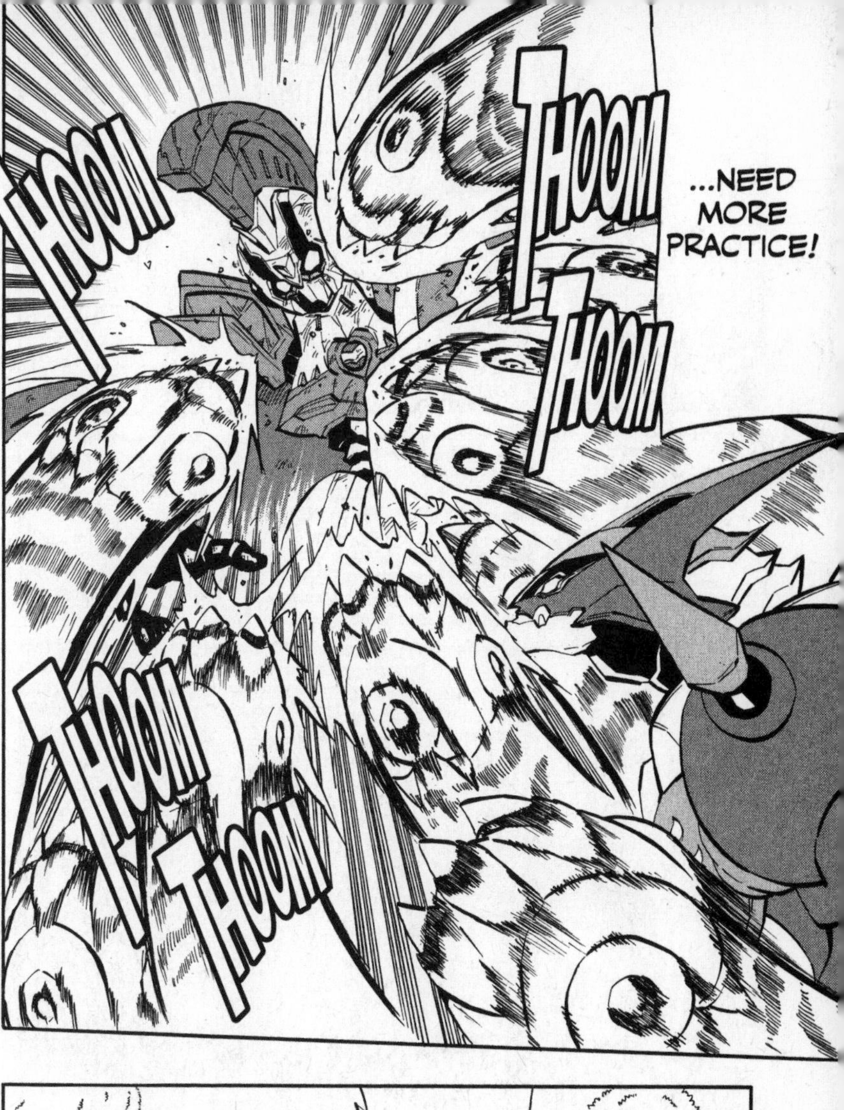
...NEED MORE PRACTICE!
THOOM
THOOM
THOOM
THOOM
THOOM

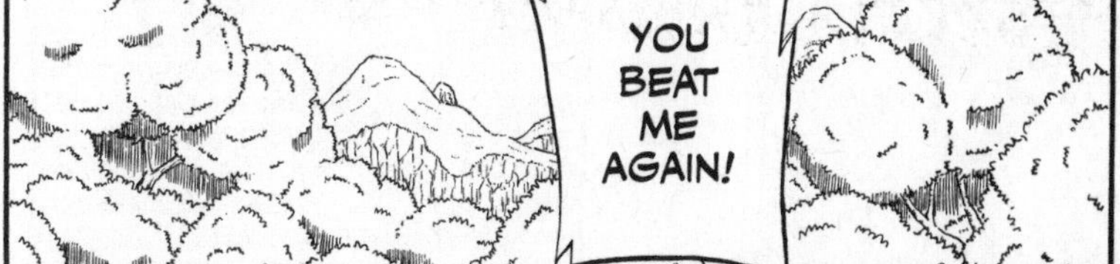
YOU BEAT ME AGAIN!

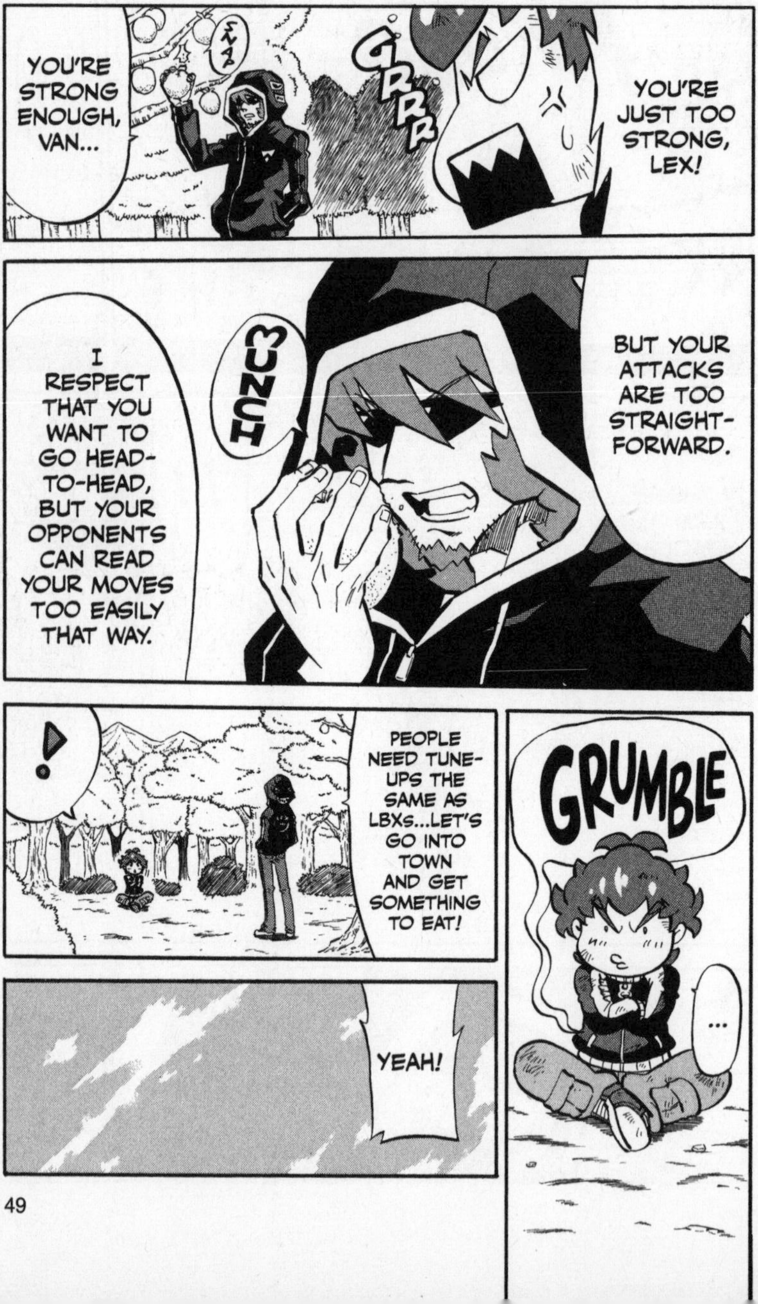
YOU'RE JUST TOO STRONG, LEX!
GRRR
SNAP
YOU'RE STRONG ENOUGH, VAN...
BUT YOUR ATTACKS ARE TOO STRAIGHT-FORWARD.
MUNCH
I RESPECT THAT YOU WANT TO GO HEAD-TO-HEAD, BUT YOUR OPPONENTS CAN READ YOUR MOVES TOO EASILY THAT WAY.
GRUMBLE
...
PEOPLE NEED TUNE-UPS THE SAME AS LBXs...LET'S GO INTO TOWN AND GET SOMETHING TO EAT!
!
YEAH!

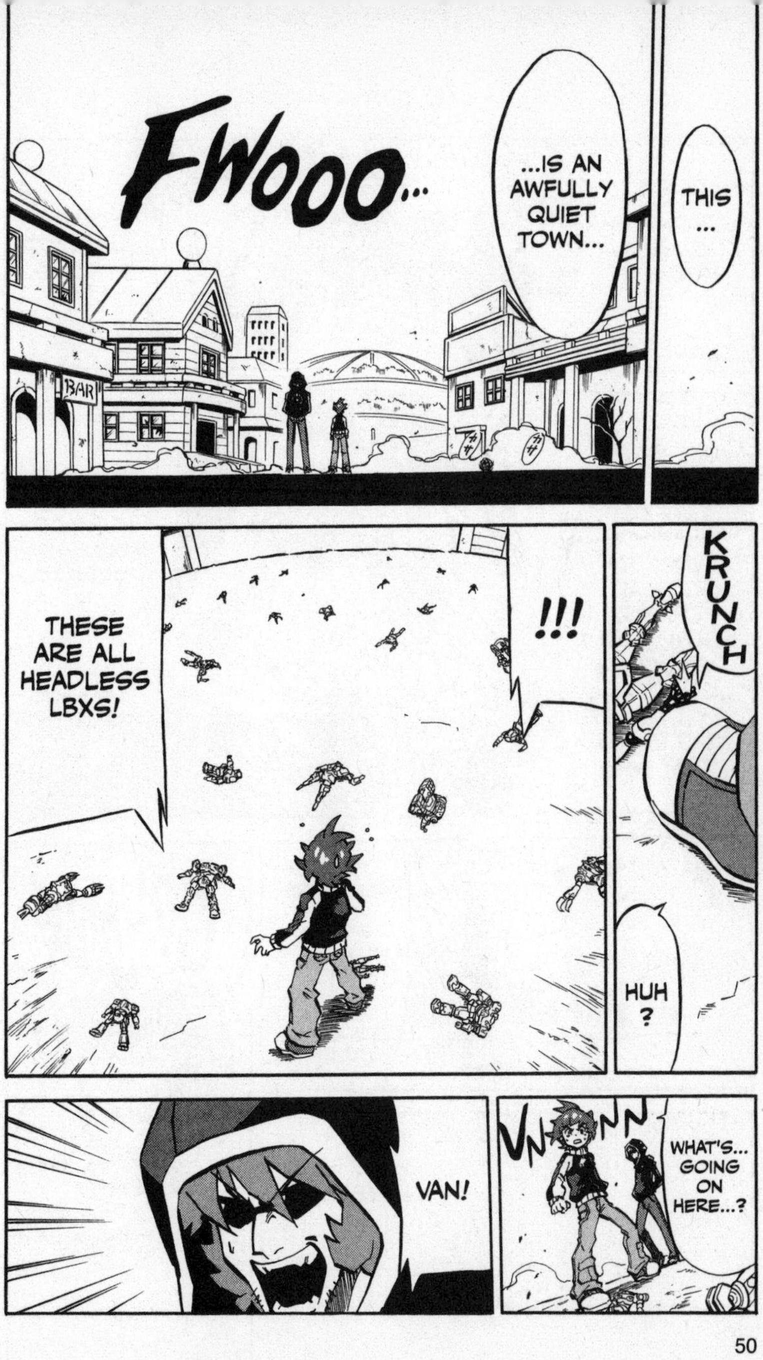
THIS ...
...IS AN AWFULLY QUIET TOWN...
FWOOO...
KRUNCH
HUH ?
!!!
THESE ARE ALL HEADLESS LBXS!
VNNN
WHAT'S... GOING ON HERE...?
VAN!

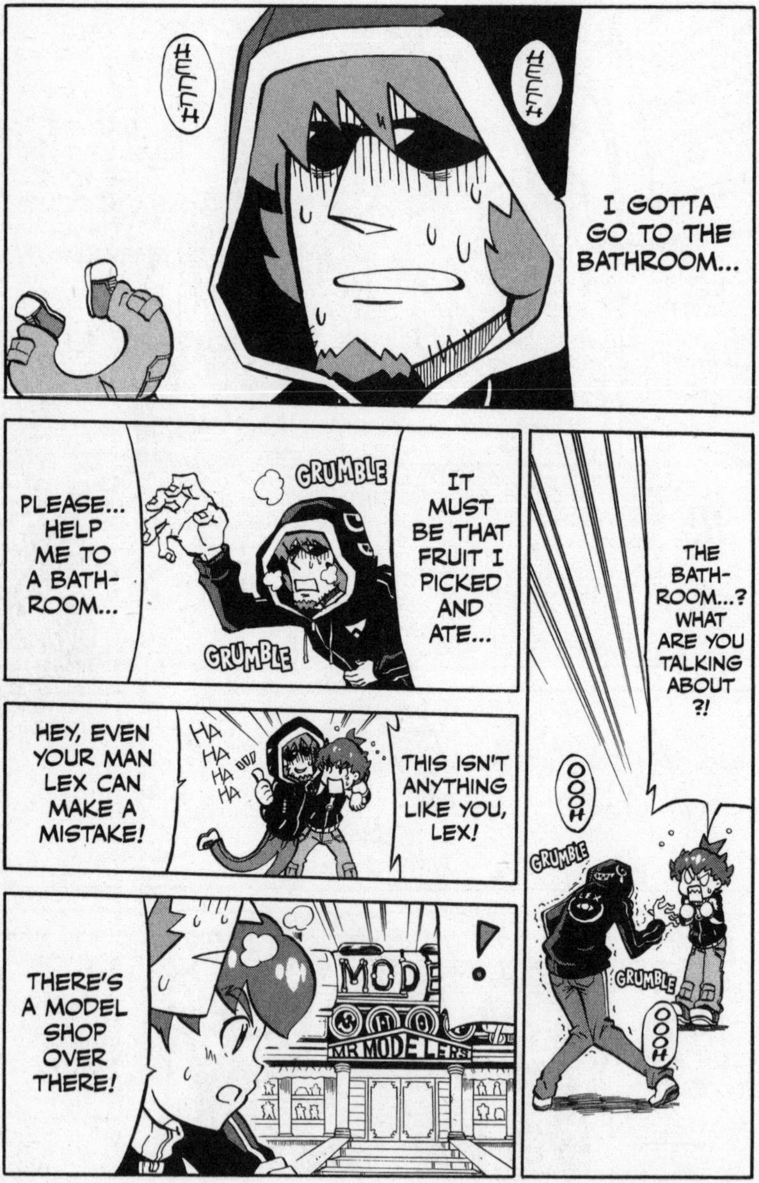
HEECH
HEECH
I GOTTA GO TO THE BATHROOM...
THE BATH-ROOM...? WHAT ARE YOU TALKING ABOUT?!
OOOH
GRUMBLE
GRUMBLE
OOOH
IT MUST BE THAT FRUIT I PICKED AND ATE...
GRUMBLE
PLEASE... HELP ME TO A BATH-ROOM...
GRUMBLE
THIS ISN'T ANYTHING LIKE YOU, LEX!
HA HA HA HA
HEY, EVEN YOUR MAN LEX CAN MAKE A MISTAKE!
!
MOD
MR MODELERS
THERE'S A MODEL SHOP OVER THERE!

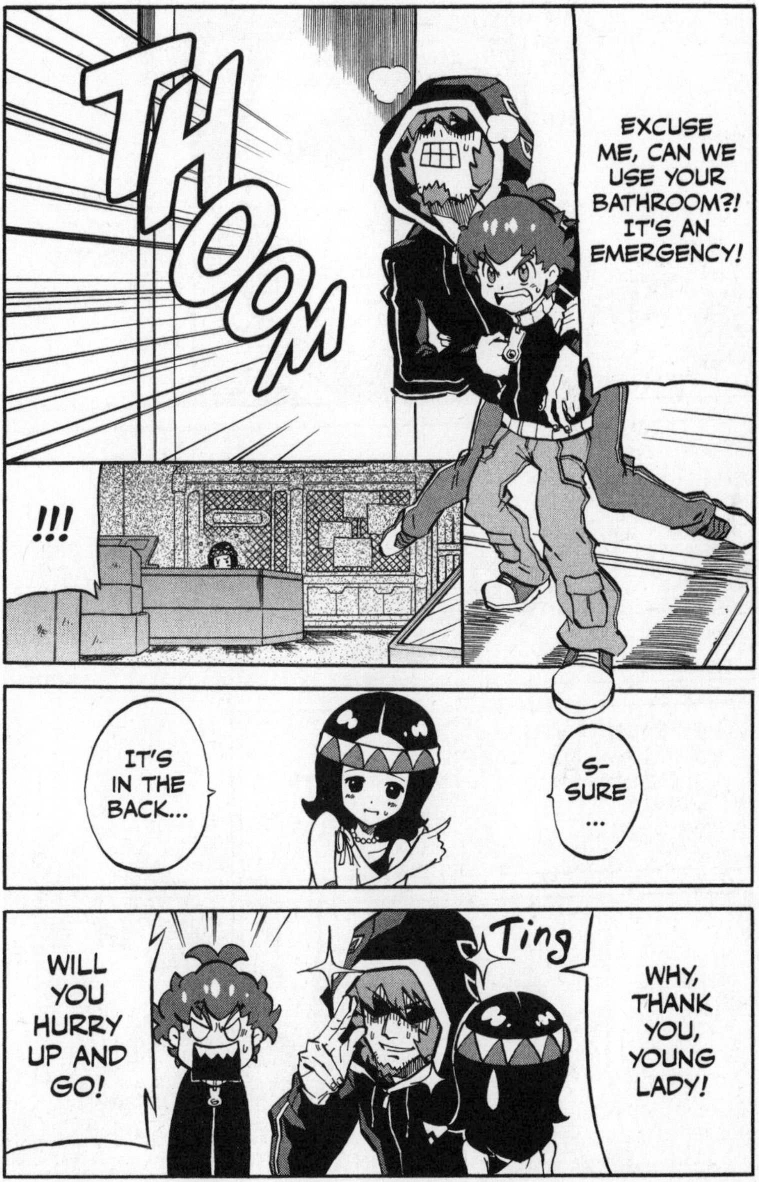
THOOM
EXCUSE ME, CAN WE USE YOUR BATHROOM?! IT'S AN EMERGENCY!
!!!
S-SURE...
IT'S IN THE BACK...
Ting
WHY, THANK YOU, YOUNG LADY!
WILL YOU HURRY UP AND GO!

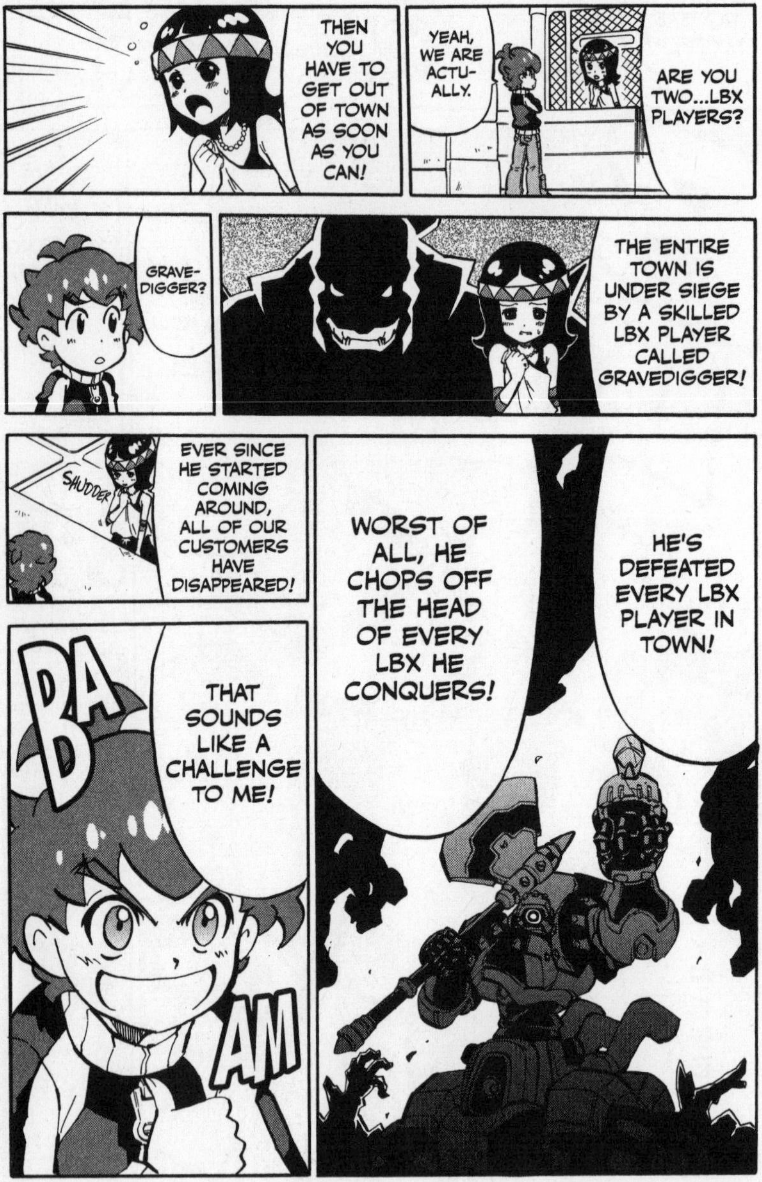
ARE YOU TWO...LBX PLAYERS?
YEAH, WE ARE ACTU-ALLY.
THEN YOU HAVE TO GET OUT OF TOWN AS SOON AS YOU CAN!
THE ENTIRE TOWN IS UNDER SIEGE BY A SKILLED LBX PLAYER CALLED GRAVEDIGGER!
GRAVE-DIGGER?
HE'S DEFEATED EVERY LBX PLAYER IN TOWN!
WORST OF ALL, HE CHOPS OFF THE HEAD OF EVERY LBX HE CONQUERS!
EVER SINCE HE STARTED COMING AROUND, ALL OF OUR CUSTOMERS HAVE DISAPPEARED!
SHUDDER
BA DAM
THAT SOUNDS LIKE A CHALLENGE TO ME!

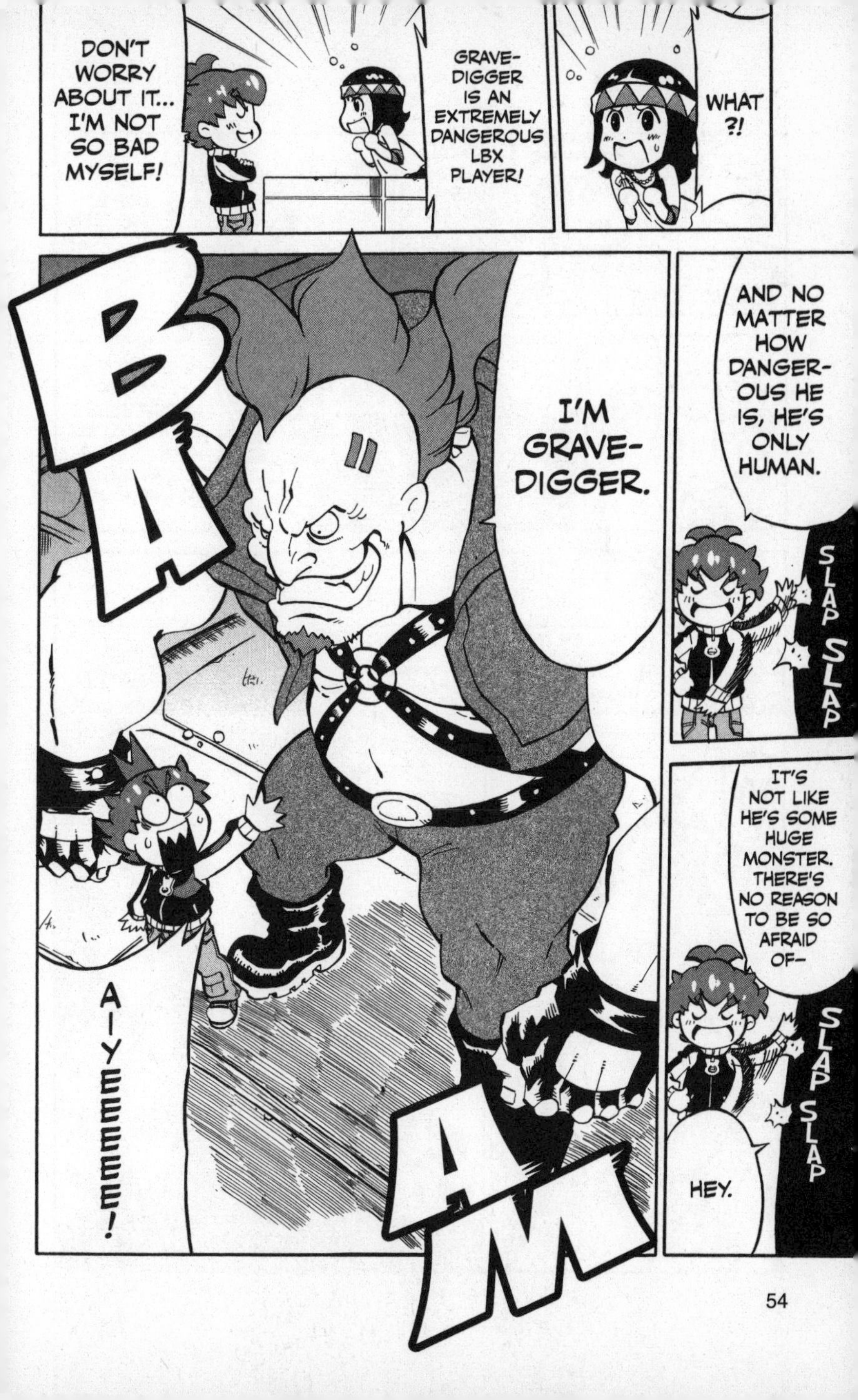
WHAT?!
GRAVE-DIGGER IS AN EXTREMELY DANGEROUS LBX PLAYER!
DON'T WORRY ABOUT IT... I'M NOT SO BAD MYSELF!
AND NO MATTER HOW DANGER-OUS HE IS, HE'S ONLY HUMAN.
SLAP SLAP SLAP
IT'S NOT LIKE HE'S SOME HUGE MONSTER. THERE'S NO REASON TO BE SO AFRAID OF-
SLAP SLAP SLAP
HEY.
BAAM
I'M GRAVE-DIGGER.
AIYEEEEEE!

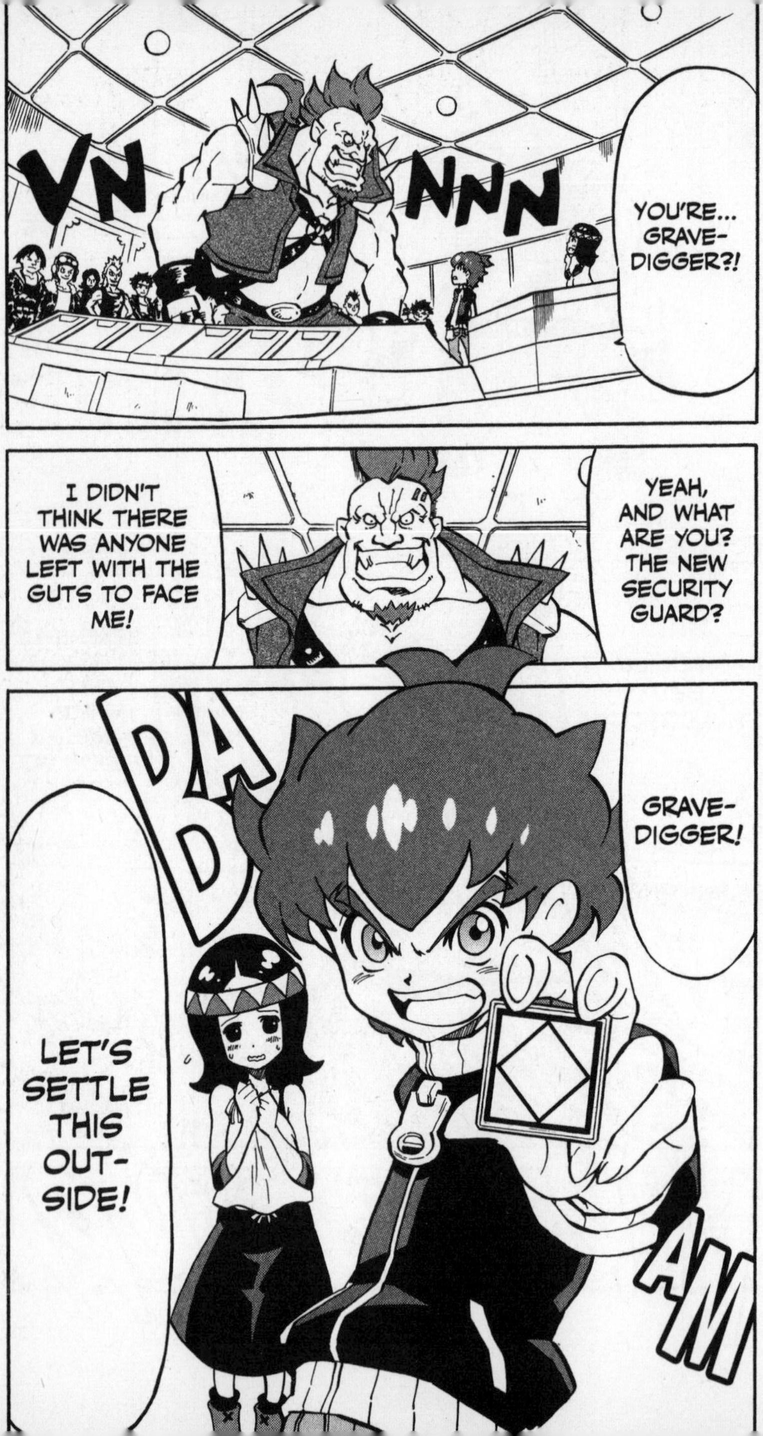
VNNNN
YOU'RE... GRAVE-DIGGER?!
YEAH, AND WHAT ARE YOU? THE NEW SECURITY GUARD?
I DIDN'T THINK THERE WAS ANYONE LEFT WITH THE GUTS TO FACE ME!
DADAM
GRAVE-DIGGER!
LET'S SETTLE THIS OUT-SIDE!

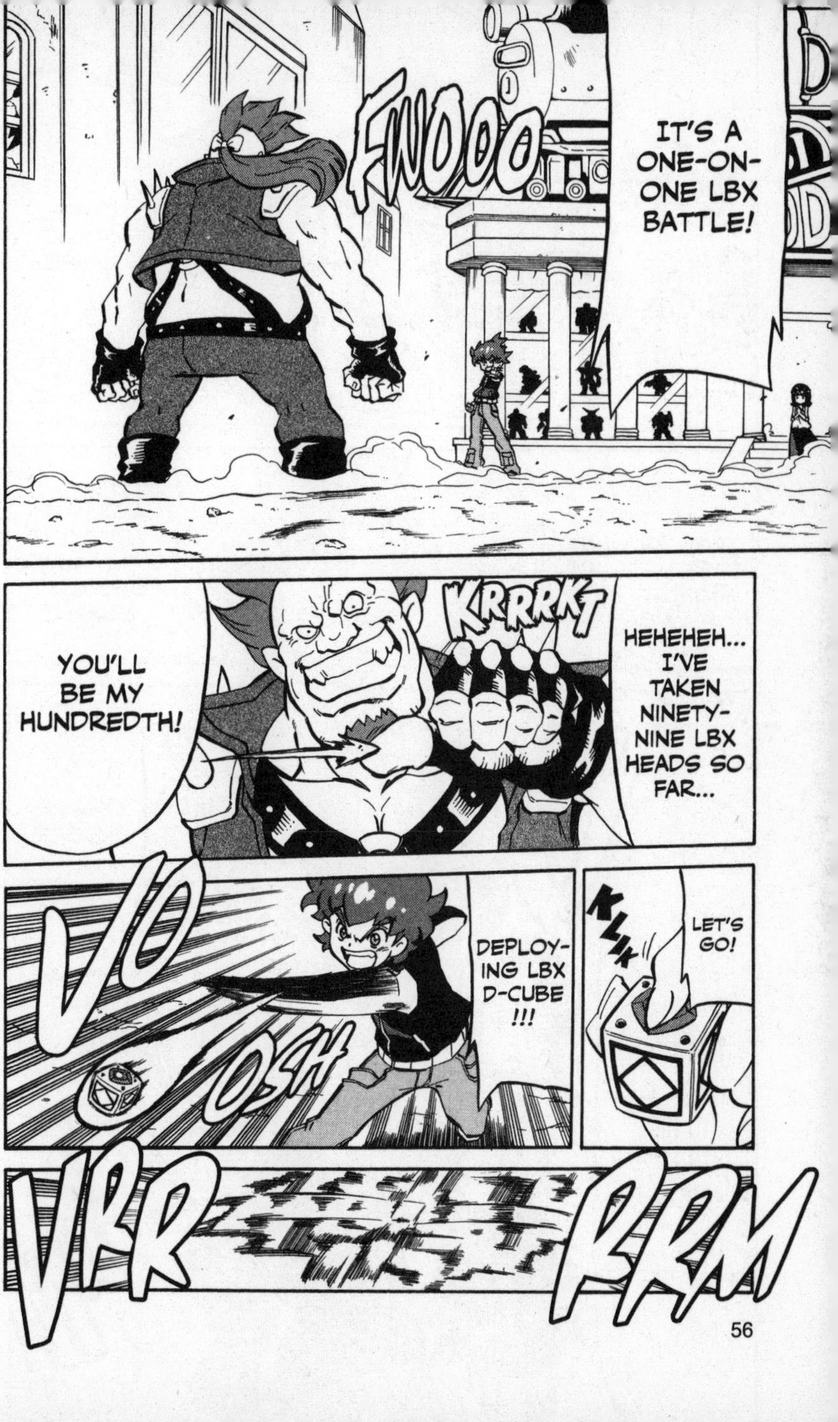
IT'S A ONE-ON-ONE LBX BATTLE!
FWOOO
HEHEHEH... I'VE TAKEN NINETY-NINE LBX HEADS SO FAR...
KRRRKT
YOU'LL BE MY HUNDREDTH!
LET'S GO!
KLIK
DEPLOYING LBX D-CUBE !!!
VOOSH
VRR
RRM

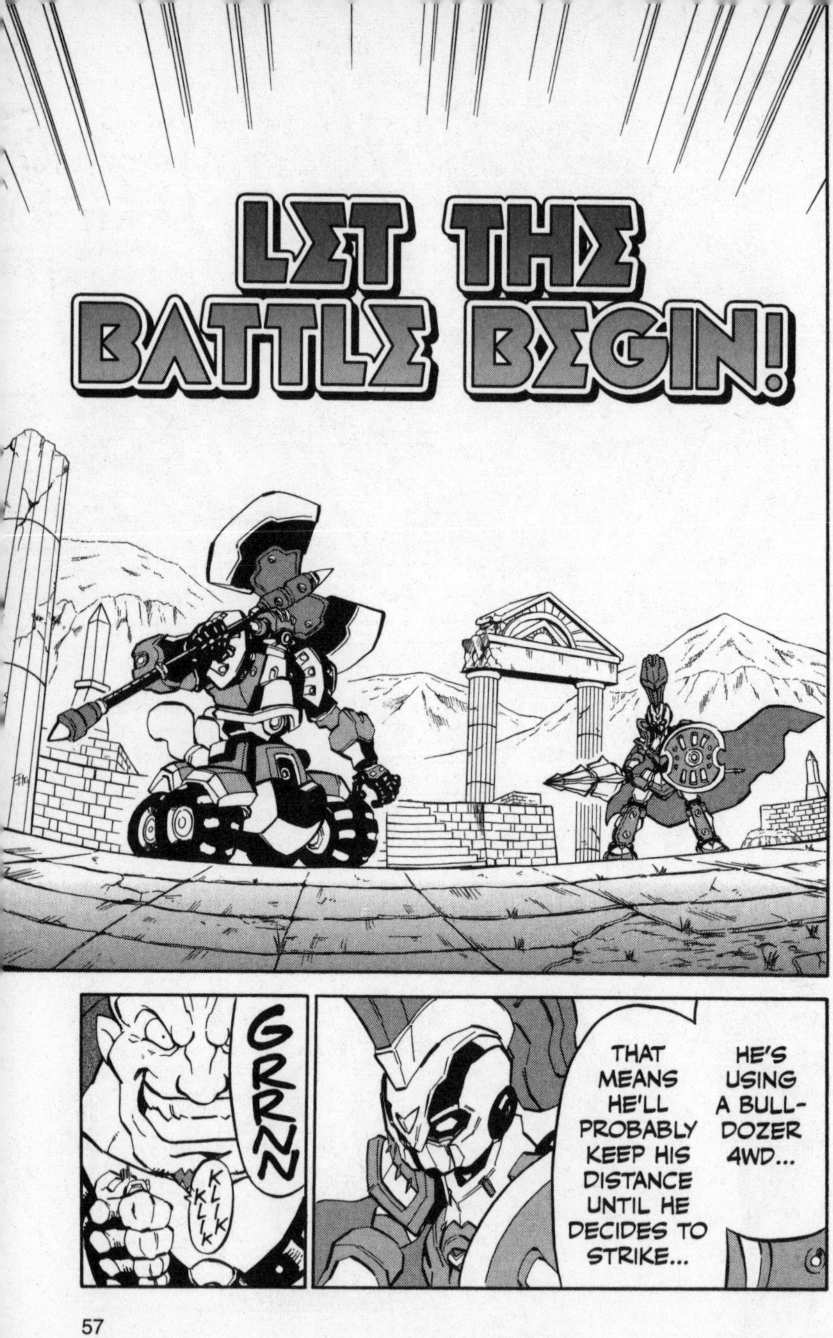
LET THE BATTLE BEGIN!
HE'S USING A BULL-DOZER 4WD...
THAT MEANS HE'LL PROBABLY KEEP HIS DISTANCE UNTIL HE DECIDES TO STRIKE...
GRRNN
KLIK KLIK

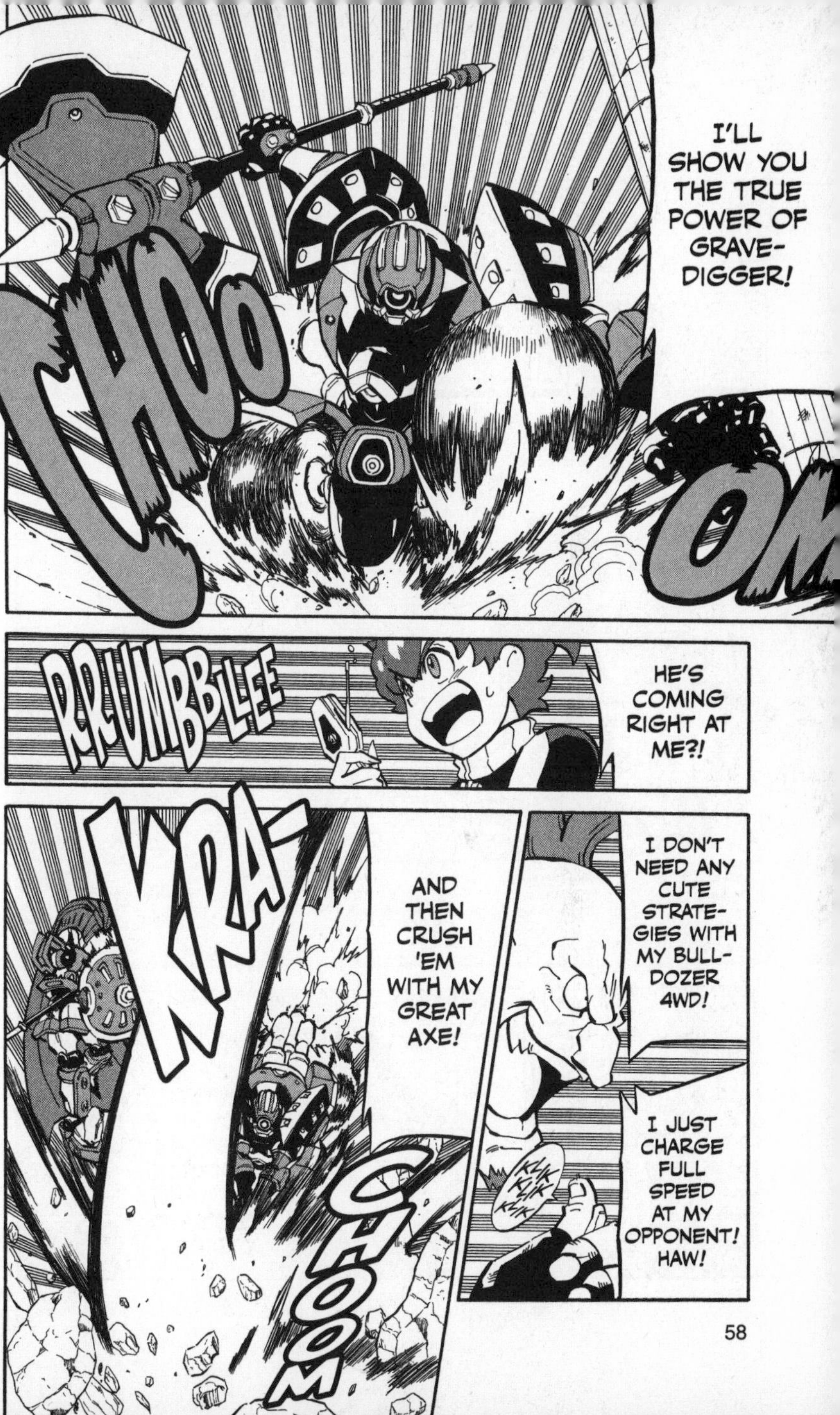
I'LL SHOW YOU THE TRUE POWER OF GRAVE-DIGGER!
CHOO
OM
RRUMBBLEE
HE'S COMING RIGHT AT ME?!
I DON'T NEED ANY CUTE STRATE-GIES WITH MY BULL-DOZER 4WD!
I JUST CHARGE FULL SPEED AT MY OPPONENT! HAW!
AND THEN CRUSH 'EM WITH MY GREAT AXE!
KRA-
CHOOOM

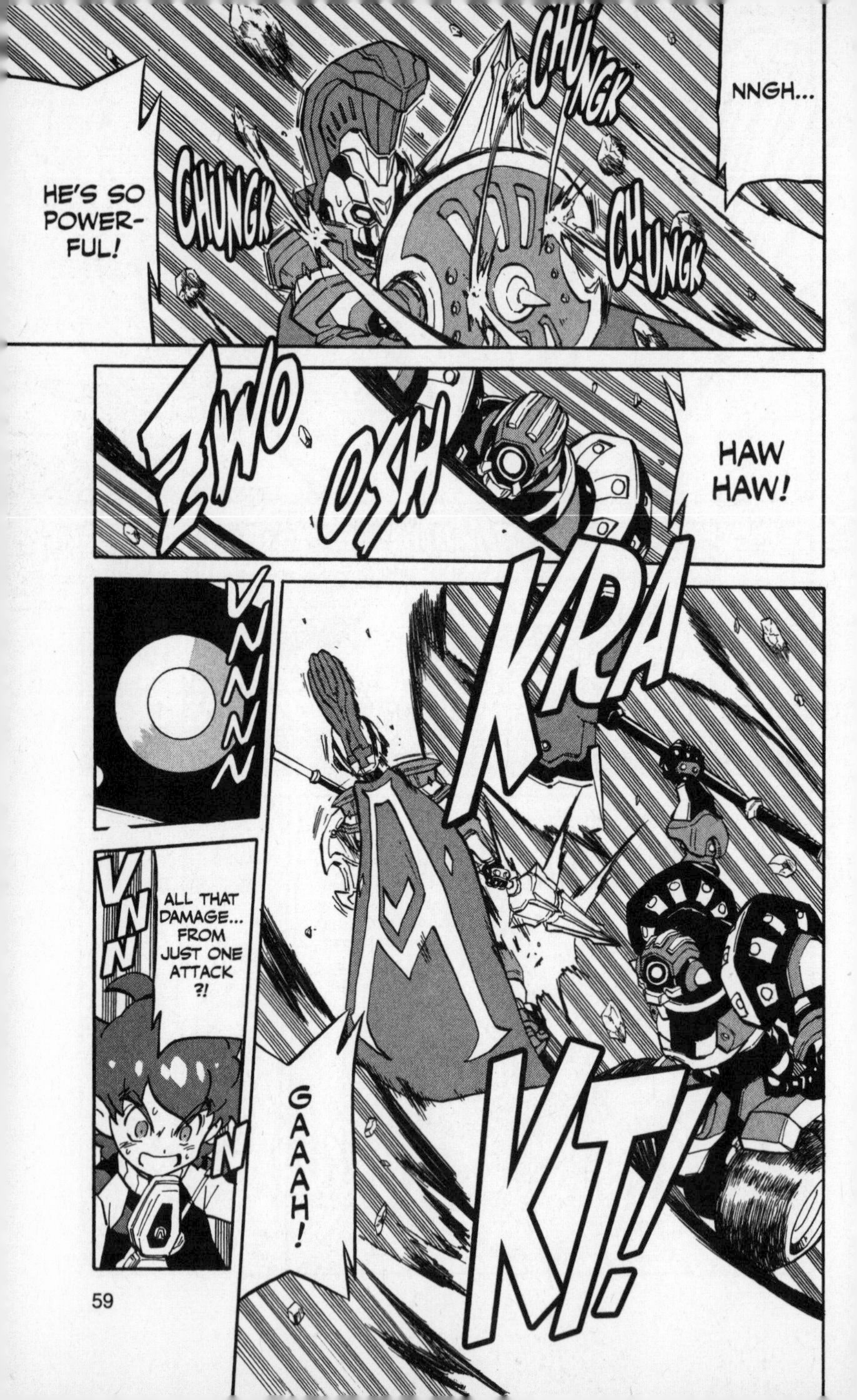
NNGH...
CHUNGK
CHUNGK
HE'S SO POWER-FUL!
CHUNGK
HAW HAW!
ZWOOSH
KRAKT!
GAAAAH!
VNNNNN
VNN
ALL THAT DAMAGE... FROM JUST ONE ATTACK ?!
N

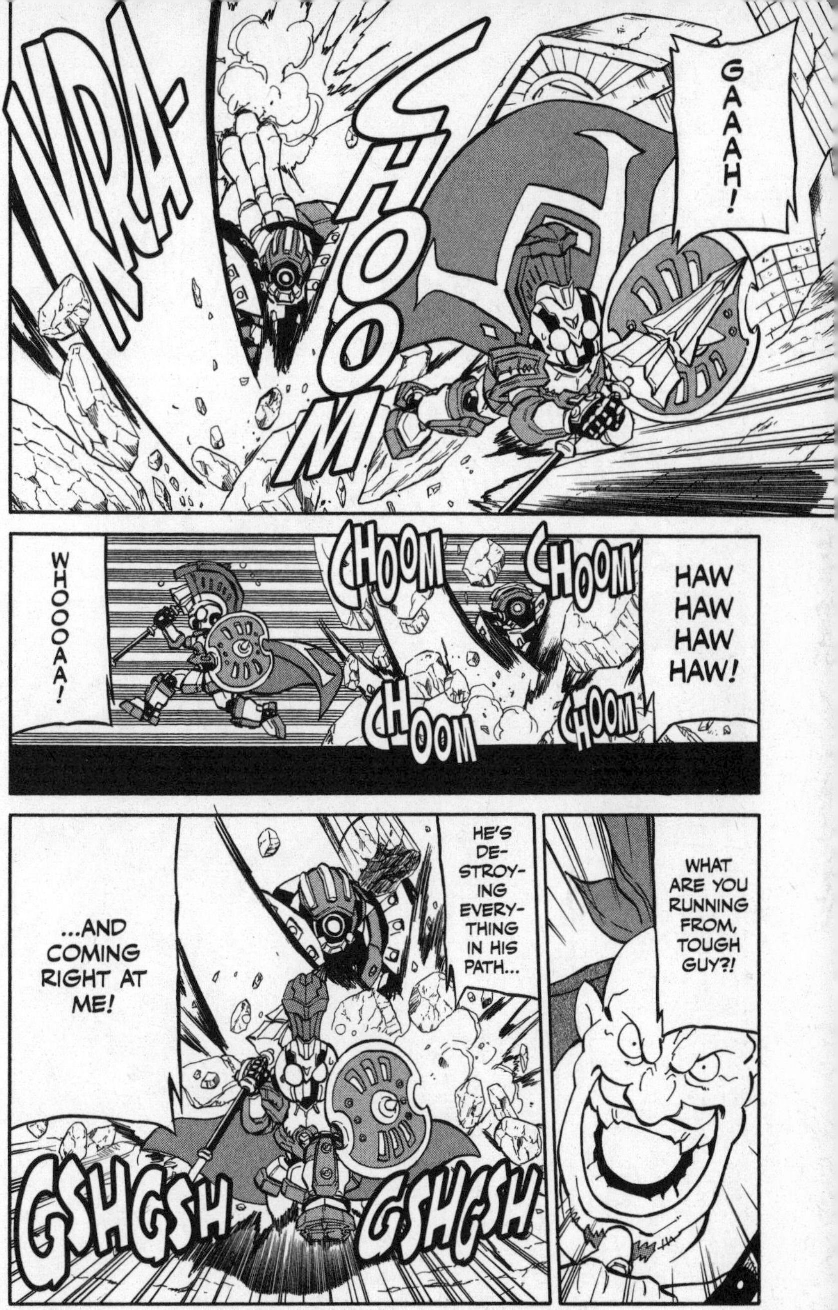
GAAAAH!
CHOOOM
HAW HAW HAW HAW!
CHOOM
CHOOM
CHOOM
CHOOM
WHOOOOAA!
WHAT ARE YOU RUNNING FROM, TOUGH GUY?!
HE'S DE-STROY-ING EVERY-THING IN HIS PATH...
...AND COMING RIGHT AT ME!
GSHGSH
GSHGSH

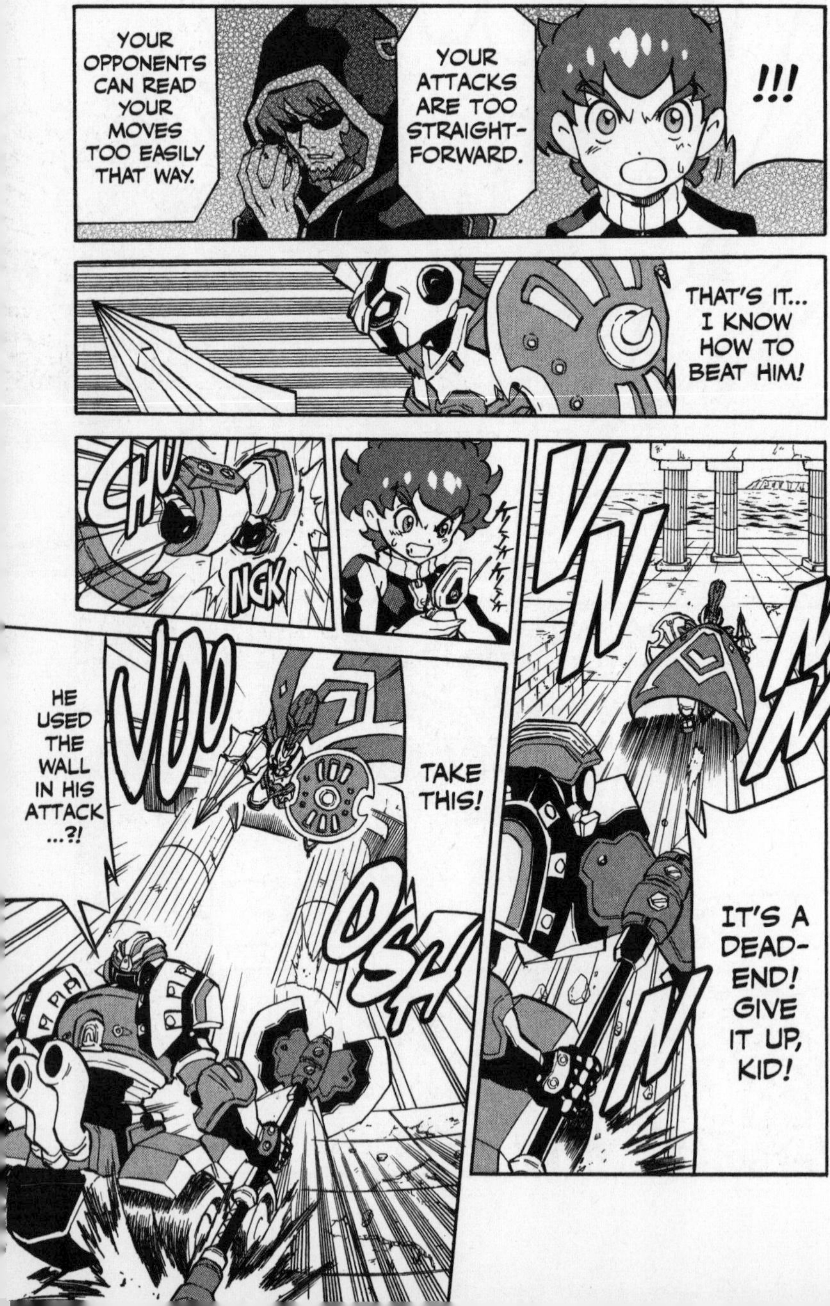
!!!
YOUR ATTACKS ARE TOO STRAIGHT-FORWARD.
YOUR OPPONENTS CAN READ YOUR MOVES TOO EASILY THAT WAY.
THAT'S IT... I KNOW HOW TO BEAT HIM!
VNNNN
CHUNGK
IT'S A DEAD-END! GIVE IT UP, KID!
TAKE THIS!
JOOOSH
HE USED THE WALL IN HIS ATTACK...?!

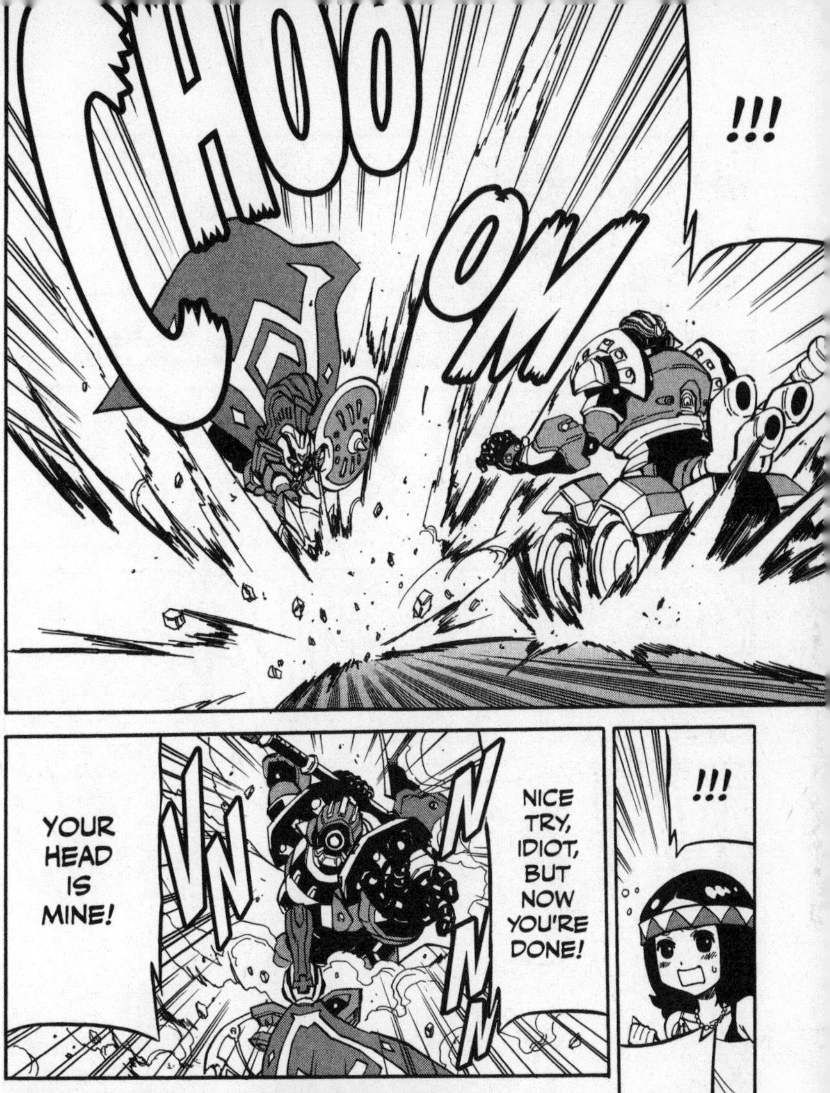
CHOOOOM
!!!
!!!
HE AT-TACKED TOO EARLY!
NICE TRY, IDIOT, BUT NOW YOU'RE DONE!
VWNNNNN
YOUR HEAD IS MINE!
YOU'RE THE IDIOT!
WHAT?!

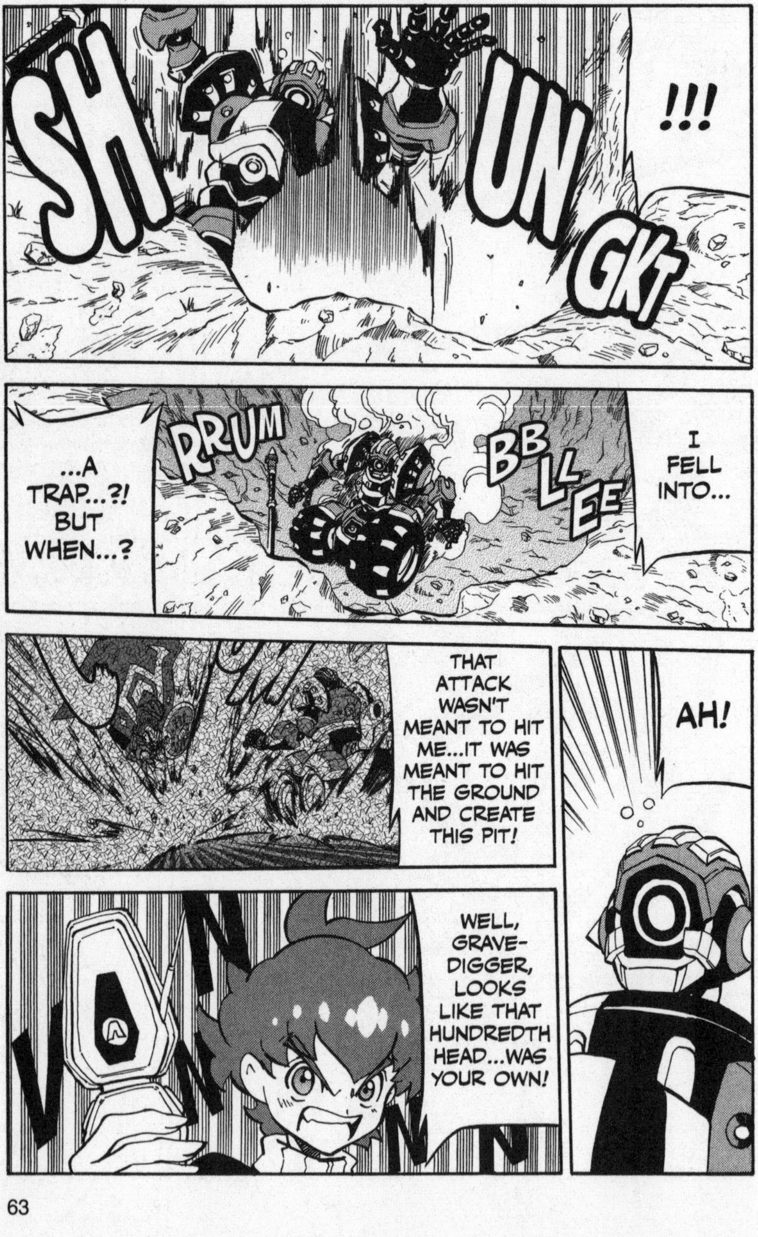
SH UN GKT!!!
I FELL INTO...
BBLLEE
RRUM
...A TRAP...?! BUT WHEN...?
AH!
THAT ATTACK WASN'T MEANT TO HIT ME...IT WAS MEANT TO HIT THE GROUND AND CREATE THIS PIT!
WELL, GRAVE-DIGGER, LOOKS LIKE THAT HUNDREDTH HEAD...WAS YOUR OWN!
VNNNN

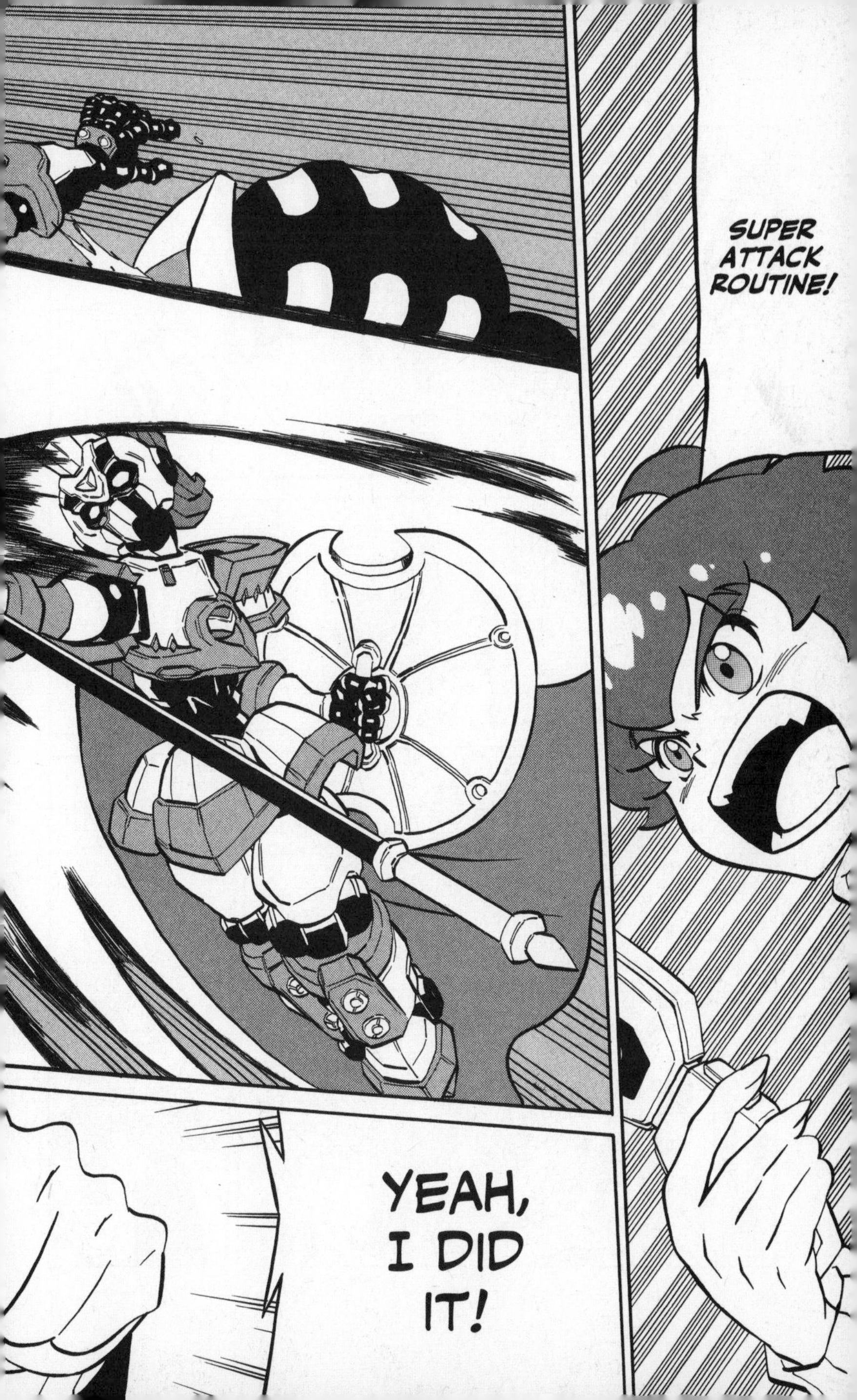
SUPER ATTACK ROUTINE!
YEAH, I DID IT!

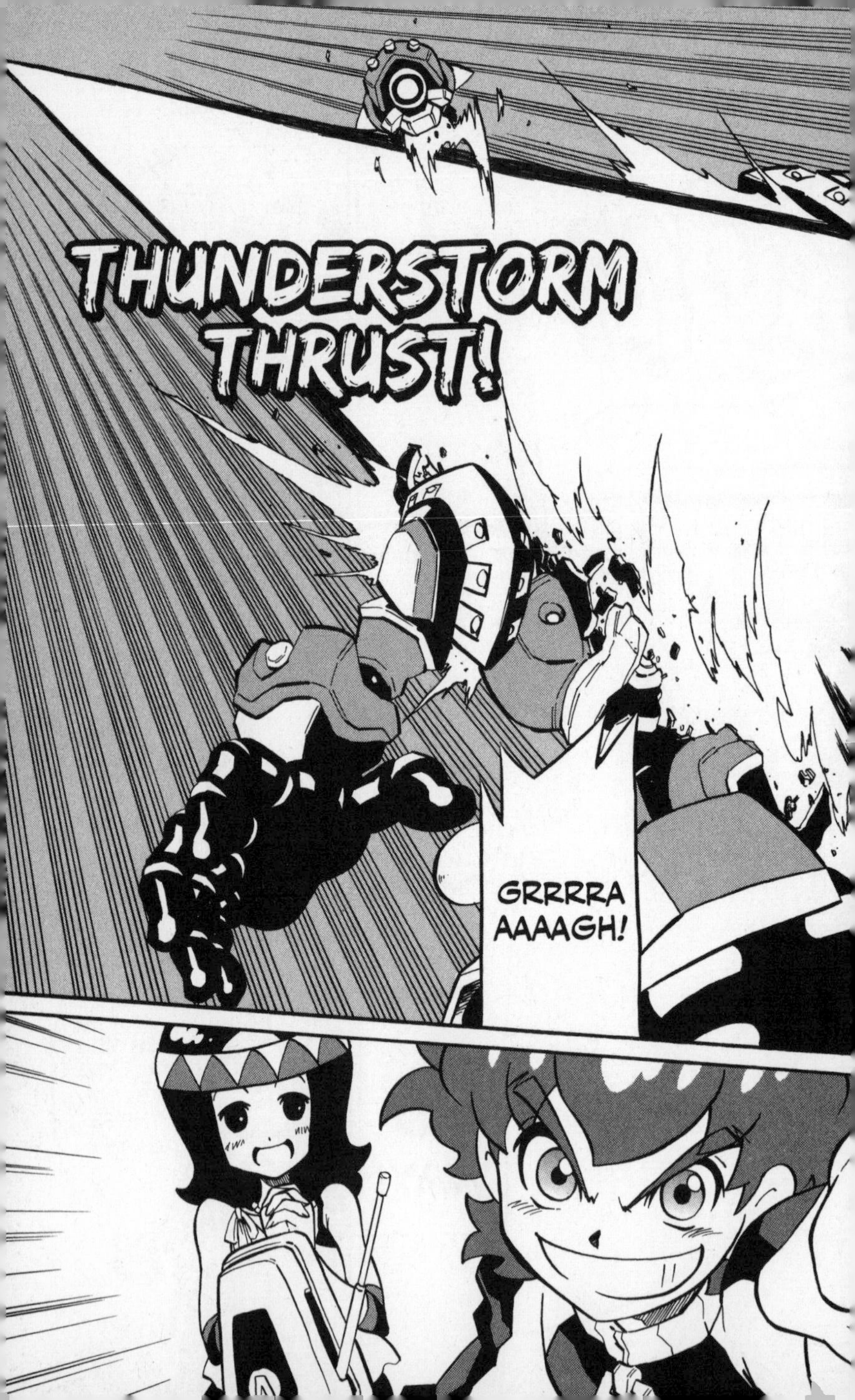
THUNDERSTORM THRUST!
GRRRRA AAAAGH!

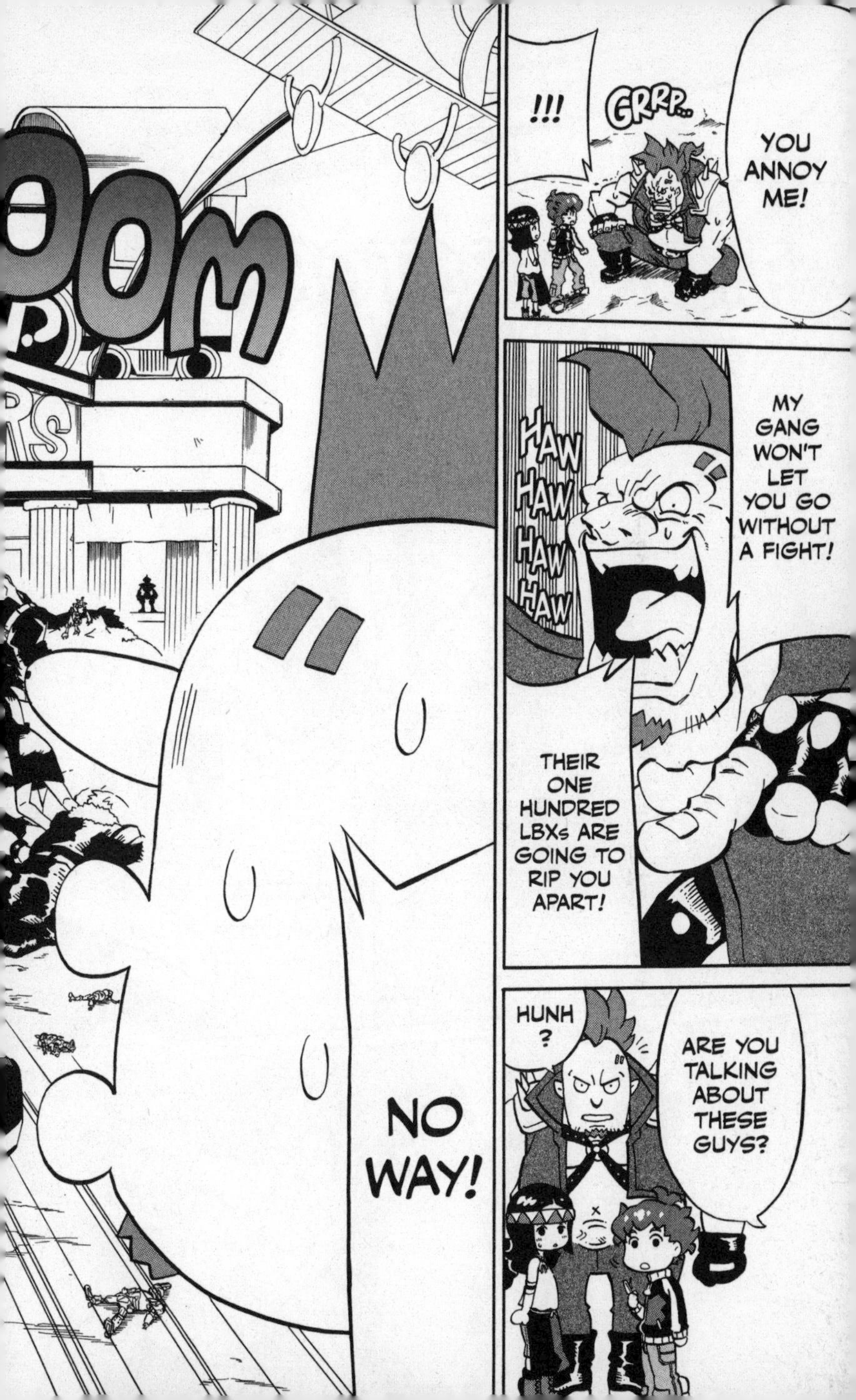
YOU ANNOY ME!
GRRR...
!!!
MY GANG WON'T LET YOU GO WITHOUT A FIGHT!
HAW HAW HAW HAW
THEIR ONE HUNDRED LBXs ARE GOING TO RIP YOU APART!
ARE YOU TALKING ABOUT THESE GUYS?
HUNH?
OOM
NO WAY!

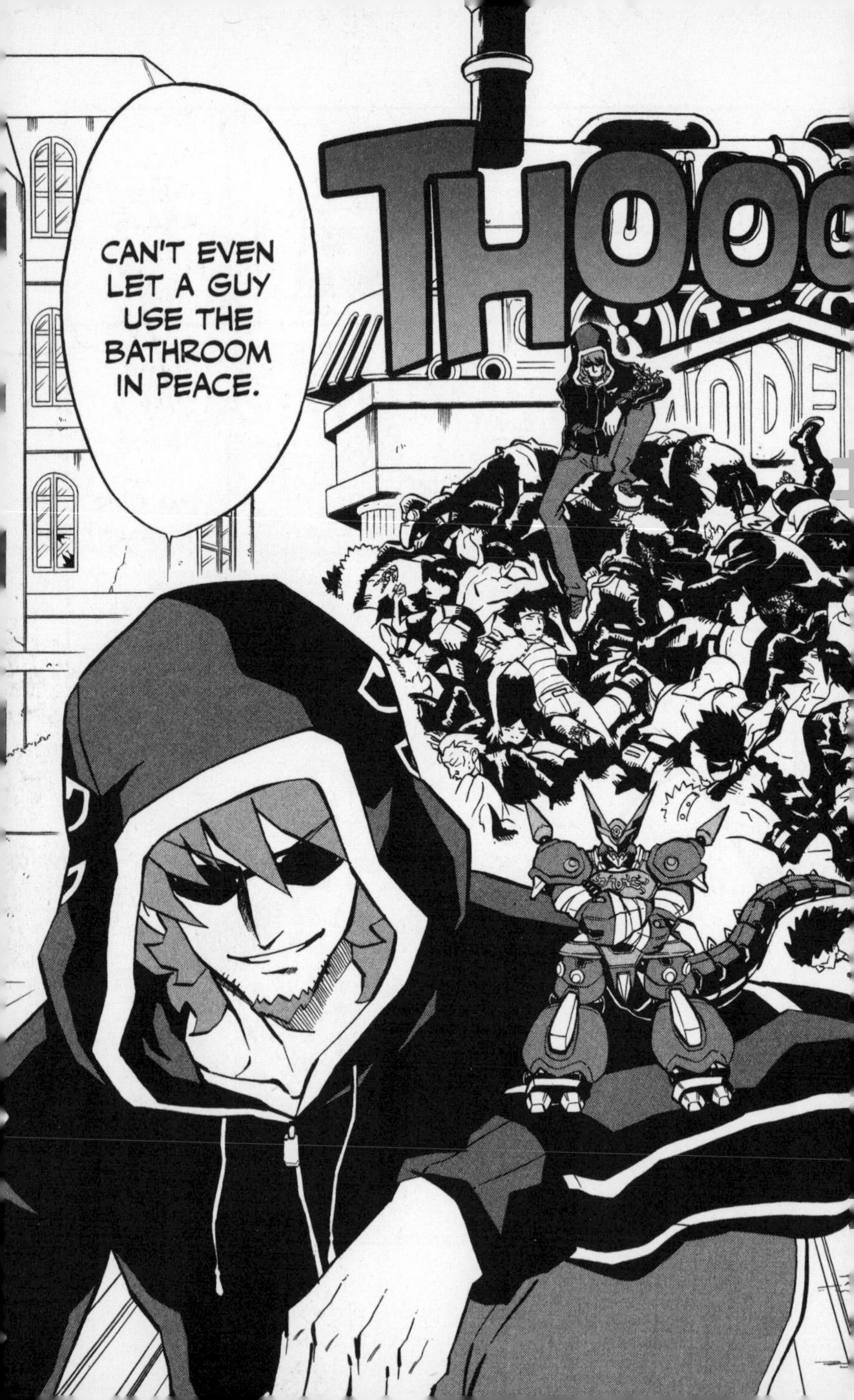
THOOO
CAN'T EVEN LET A GUY USE THE BATHROOM IN PEACE.

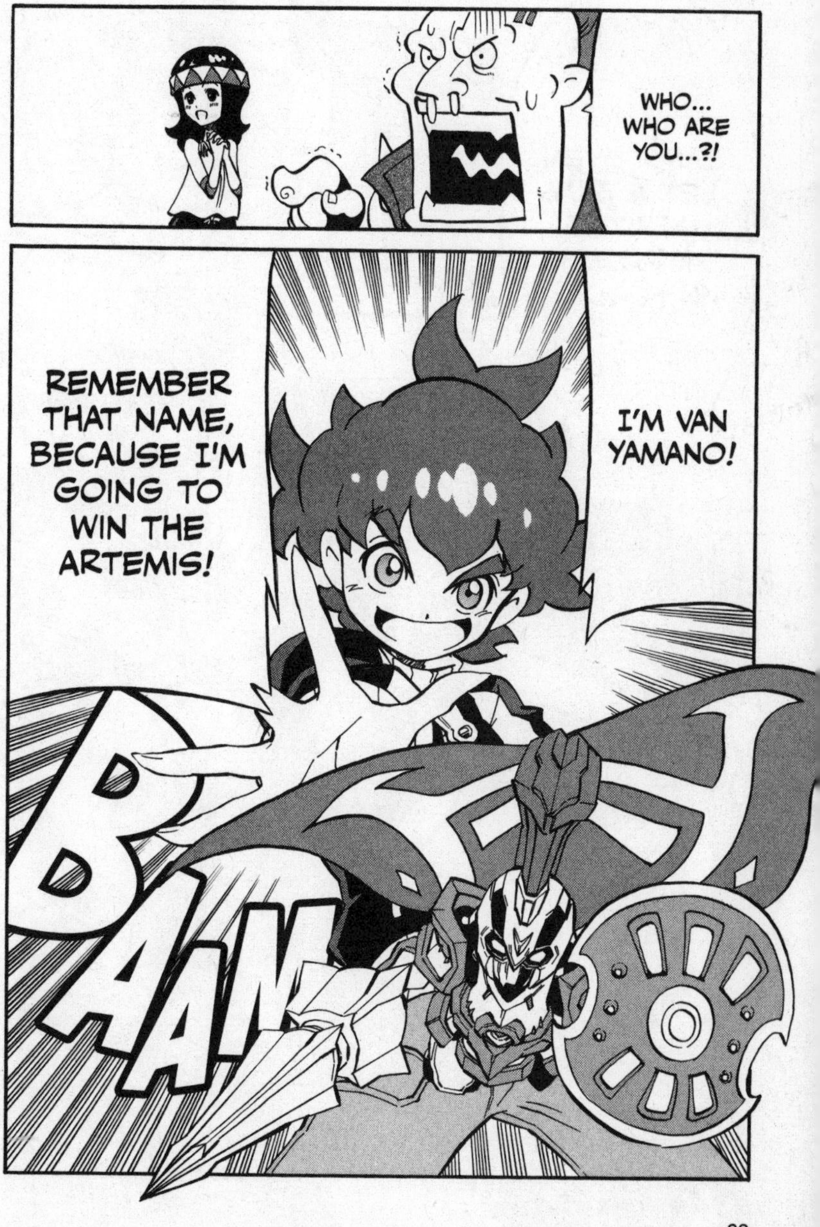
WHO... WHO ARE YOU...?!
I'M VAN YAMANO!
REMEMBER THAT NAME, BECAUSE I'M GOING TO WIN THE ARTEMIS!
BAAM

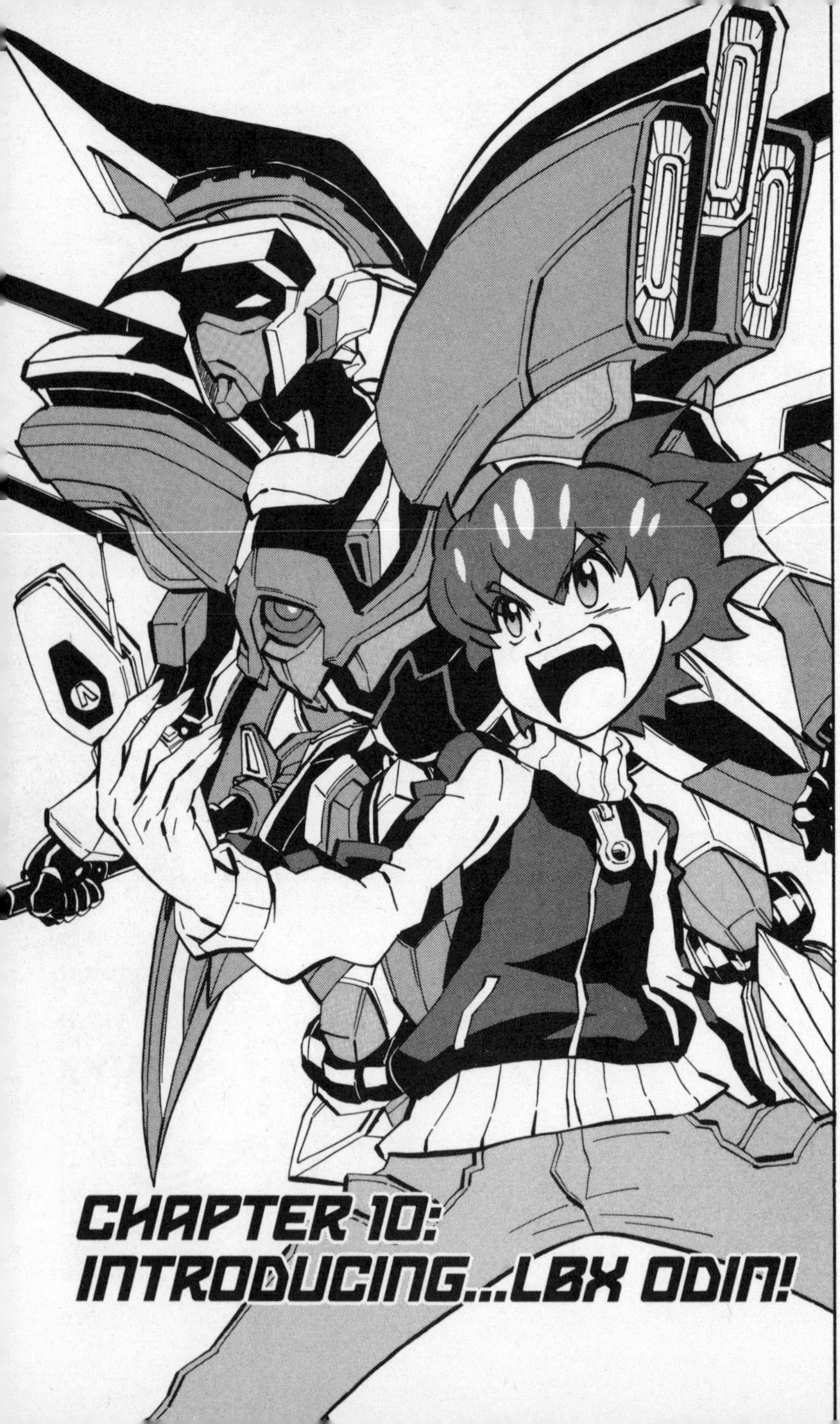
CHAPTER 10:
INTRODUCING...LBX ODIN!

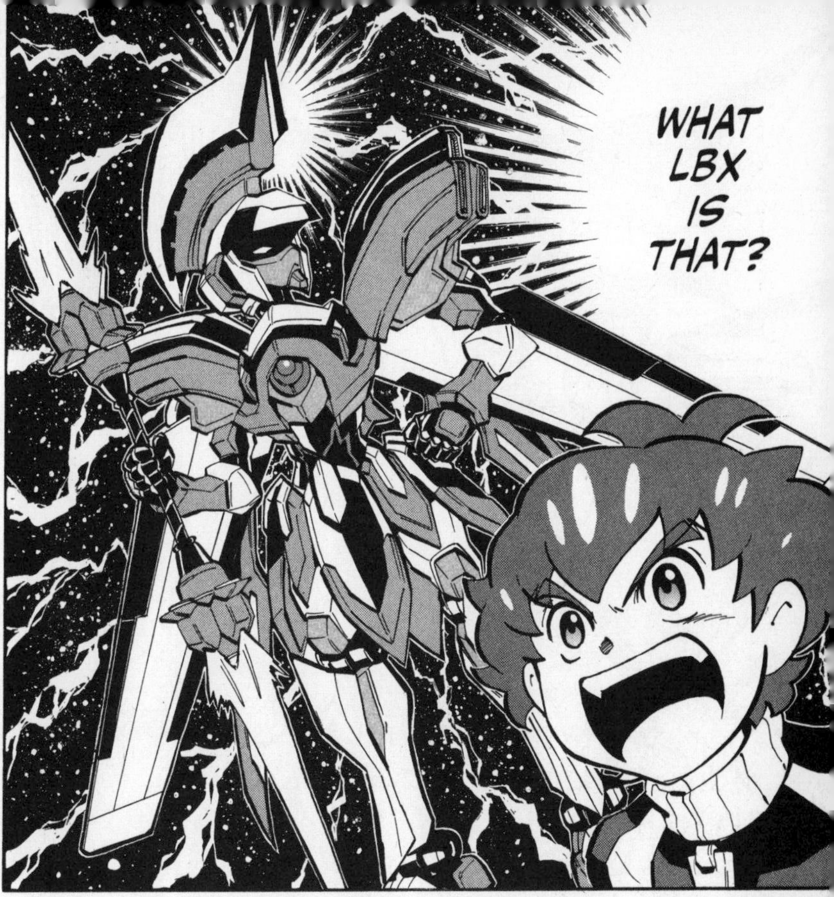
WHAT LBX IS THAT?

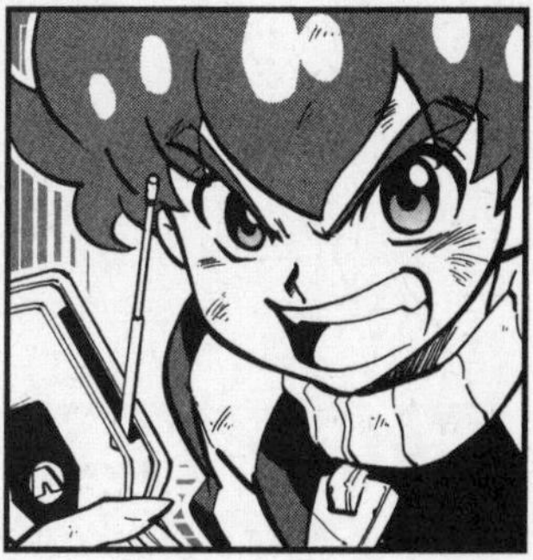

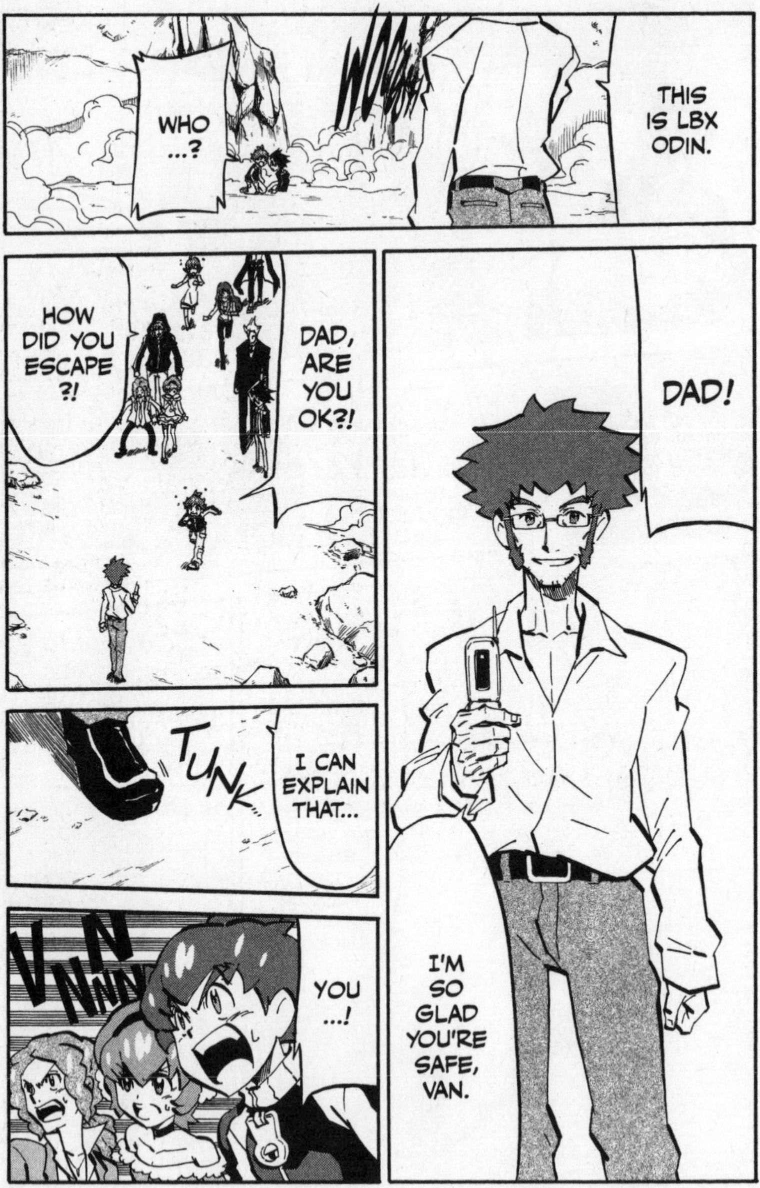
THIS IS LBX ODIN.
WHO ...?
DAD!
I'M SO GLAD YOU'RE SAFE, VAN.
DAD, ARE YOU OK?!
HOW DID YOU ESCAPE ?!
I CAN EXPLAIN THAT...
TUNK...
YOU ...!
VNNNNN

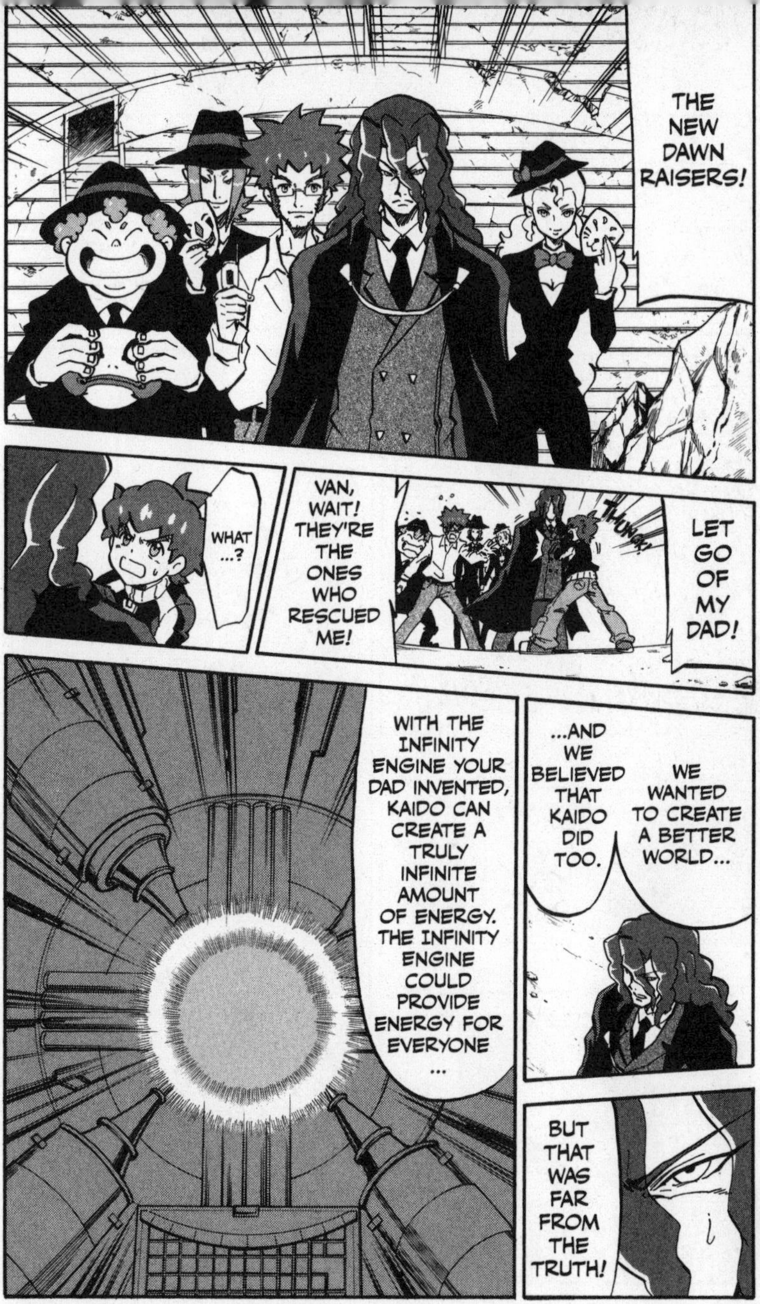
THE NEW DAWN RAISERS!
LET GO OF MY DAD!
THUNK!
VAN, WAIT! THEY'RE THE ONES WHO RESCUED ME!
WHAT ...?
WE WANTED TO CREATE A BETTER WORLD...
...AND WE BELIEVED THAT KAIDO DID TOO.
BUT THAT WAS FAR FROM THE TRUTH!
WITH THE INFINITY ENGINE YOUR DAD INVENTED, KAIDO CAN CREATE A TRULY INFINITE AMOUNT OF ENERGY. THE INFINITY ENGINE COULD PROVIDE ENERGY FOR EVERYONE ...

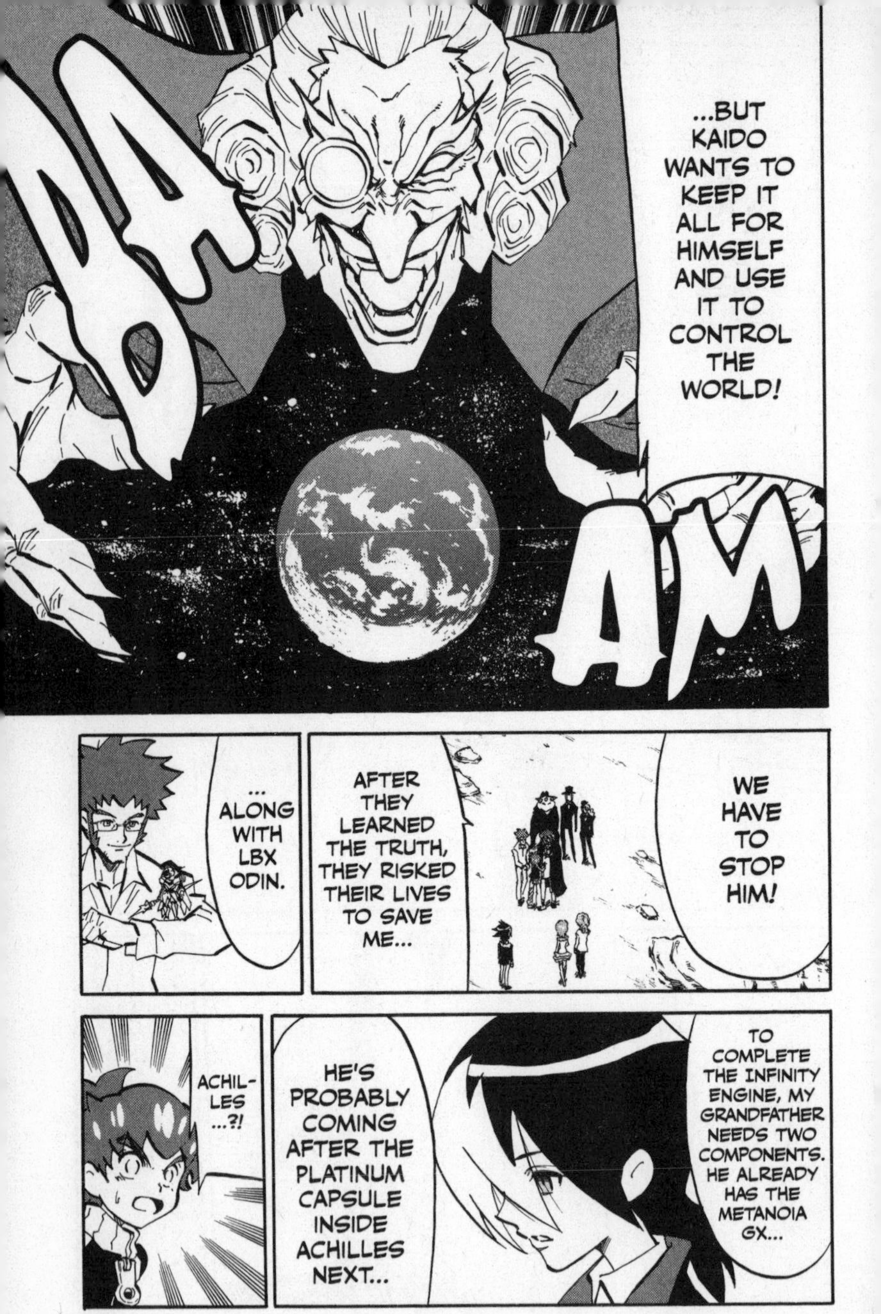
...BUT KAIDO WANTS TO KEEP IT ALL FOR HIMSELF AND USE IT TO CONTROL THE WORLD!
WE HAVE TO STOP HIM!
AFTER THEY LEARNED THE TRUTH, THEY RISKED THEIR LIVES TO SAVE ME...
... ALONG WITH LBX ODIN.
TO COMPLETE THE INFINITY ENGINE, MY GRANDFATHER NEEDS TWO COMPONENTS. HE ALREADY HAS THE METANOIA GX...
HE'S PROBABLY COMING AFTER THE PLATINUM CAPSULE INSIDE ACHILLES NEXT...
ACHIL-LES ...?!

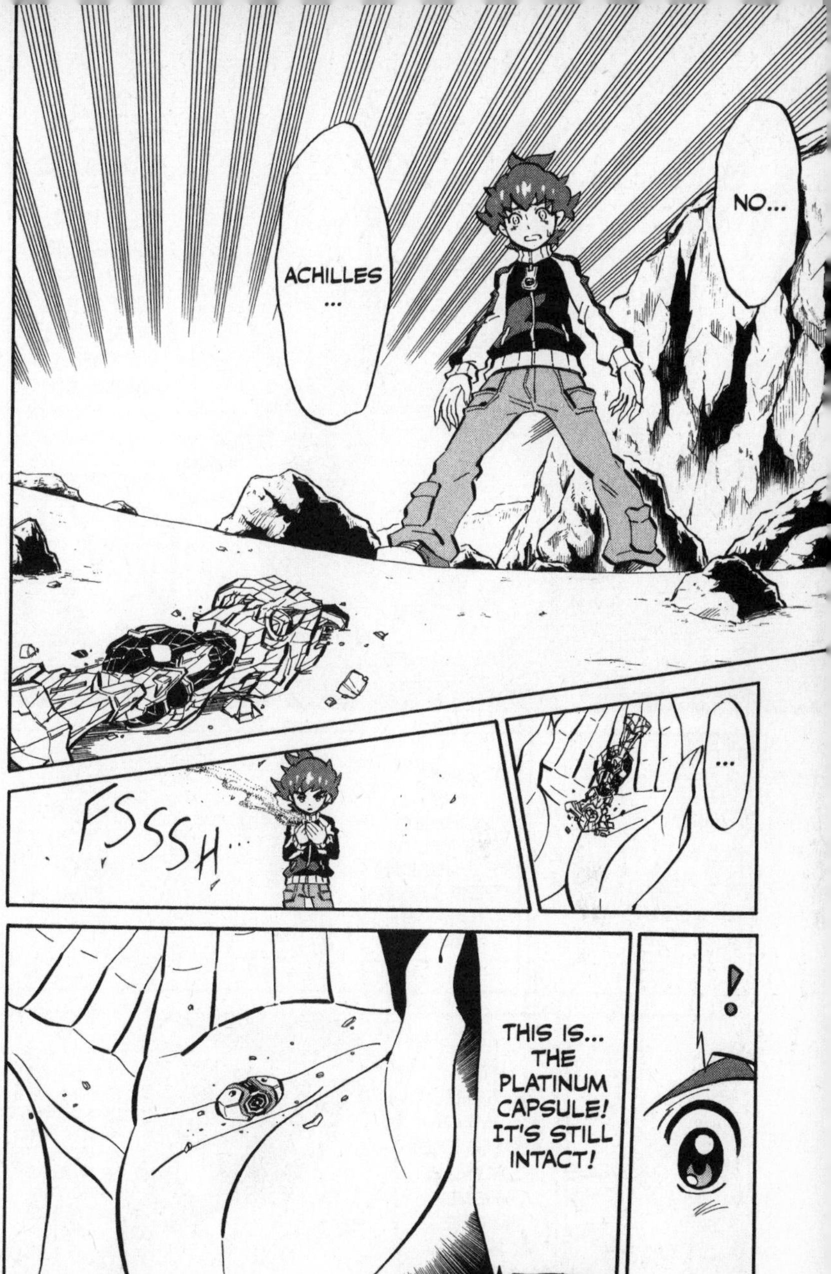
NO...
ACHILLES ...
...
FSSSH...
!
THIS IS... THE PLATINUM CAPSULE! IT'S STILL INTACT!

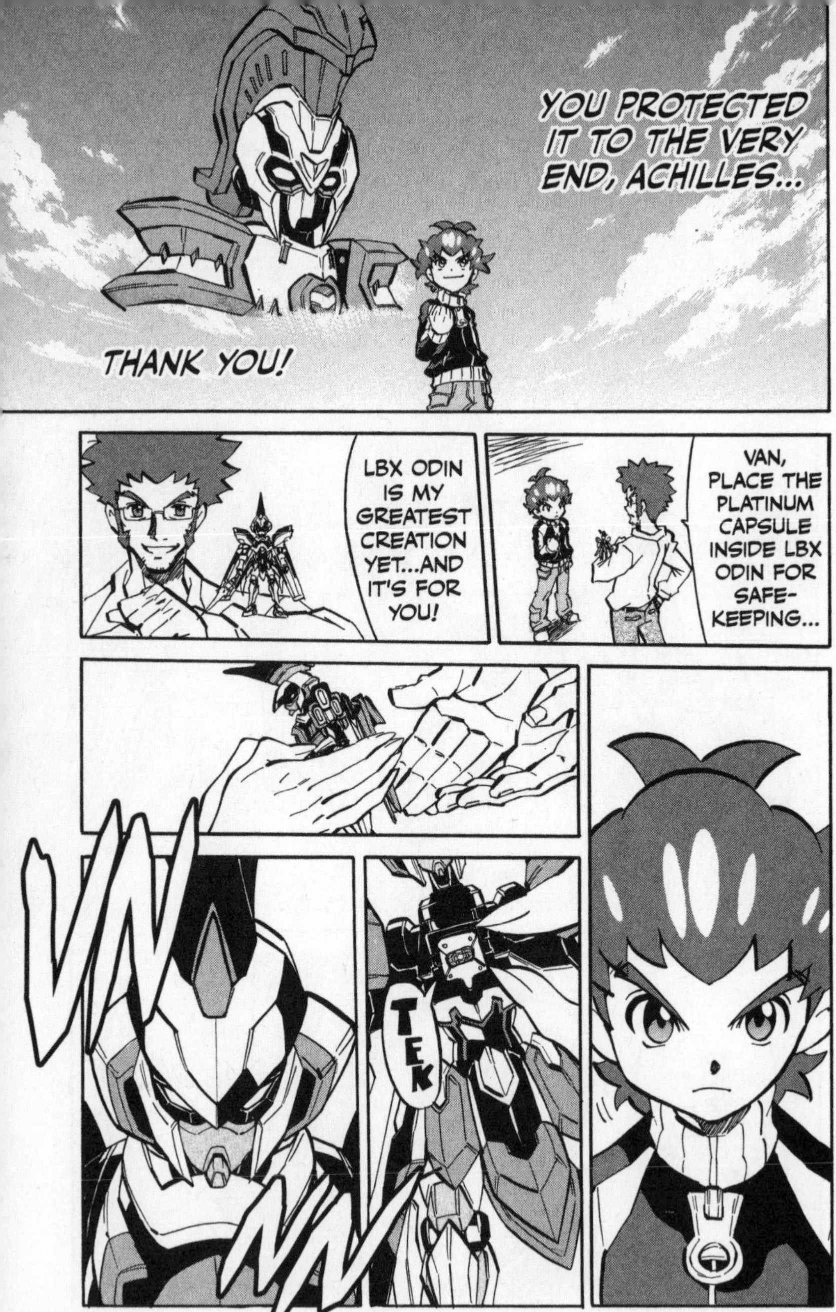
YOU PROTECTED IT TO THE VERY END, ACHILLES...
THANK YOU!
VAN, PLACE THE PLATINUM CAPSULE INSIDE LBX ODIN FOR SAFE-KEEPING...
LBX ODIN IS MY GREATEST CREATION YET...AND IT'S FOR YOU!
TEK
VNNNN

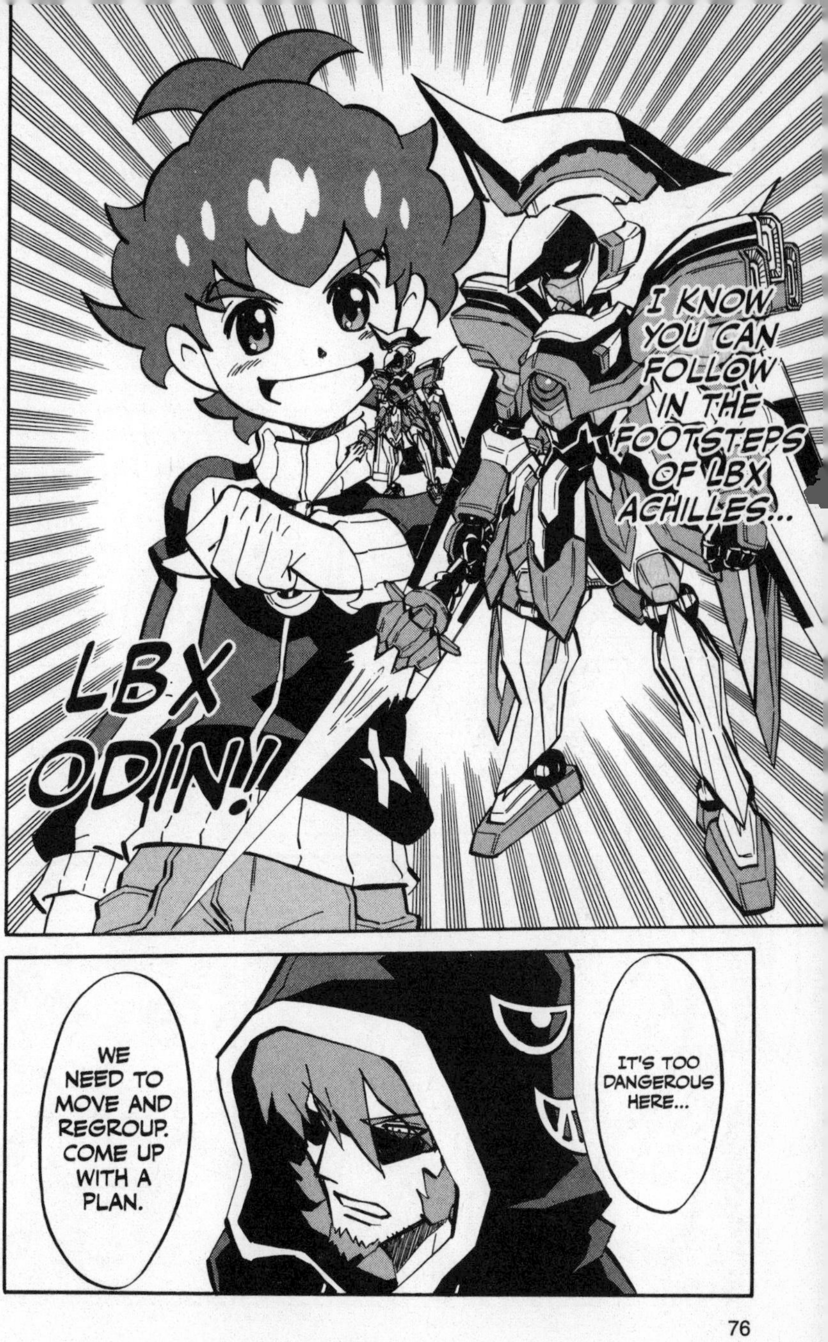
I KNOW YOU CAN FOLLOW IN THE FOOTSTEPS OF LBX ACHILLES...
LBX ODIN!!
IT'S TOO DANGEROUS HERE...
WE NEED TO MOVE AND REGROUP. COME UP WITH A PLAN.

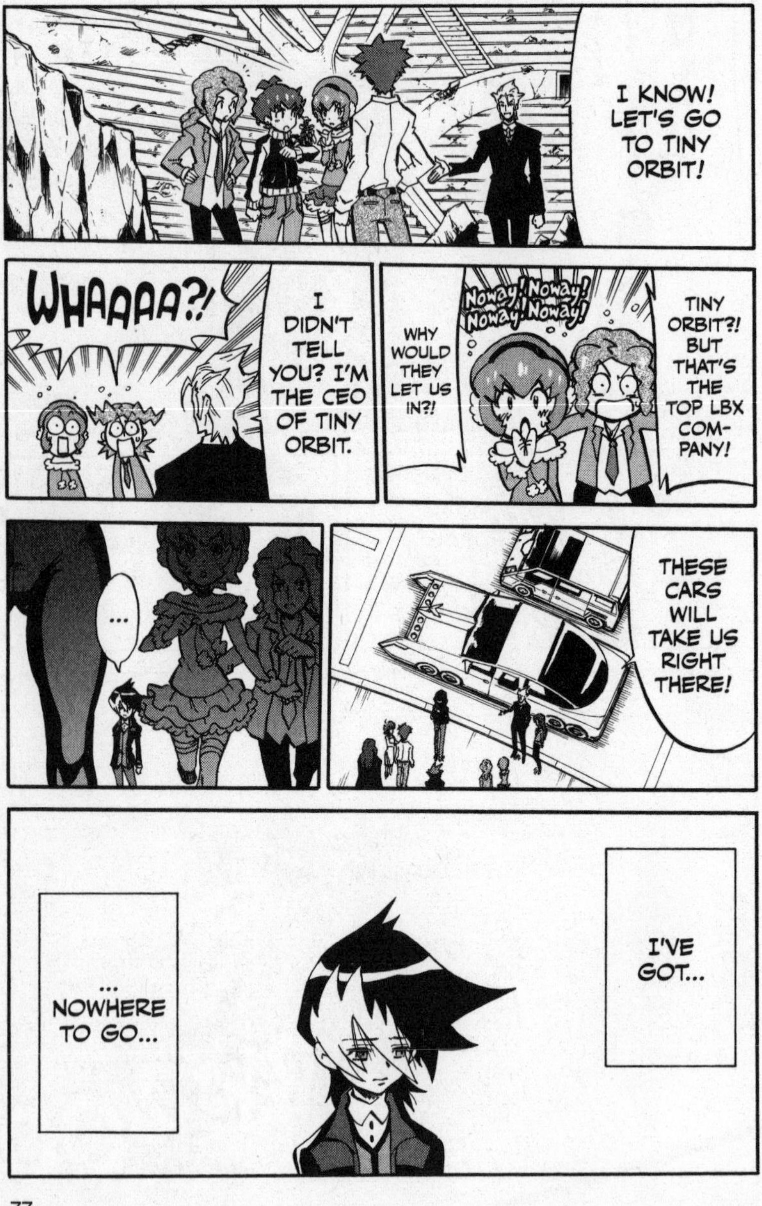
I KNOW! LET'S GO TO TINY ORBIT!
TINY ORBIT?! BUT THAT'S THE TOP LBX COMPANY!
Noway! Noway! Noway! Noway!
WHY WOULD THEY LET US IN?!
I DIDN'T TELL YOU? I'M THE CEO OF TINY ORBIT.
WHAAAA?!
THESE CARS WILL TAKE US RIGHT THERE!
...
I'VE GOT...
... NOWHERE TO GO...

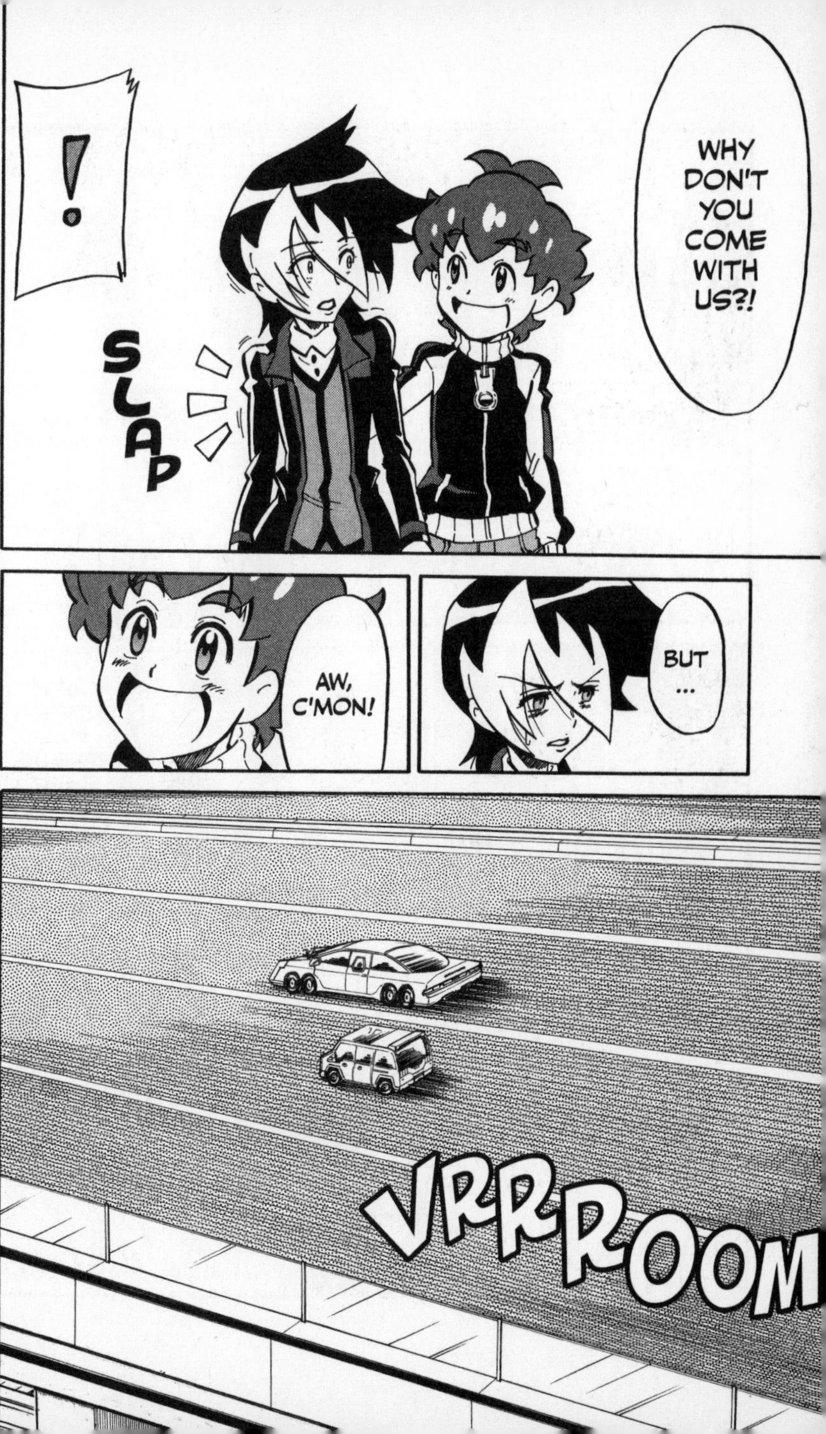
WHY DON'T YOU COME WITH US?!
!
SLAP
BUT ...
AW, C'MON!
VRRROOM

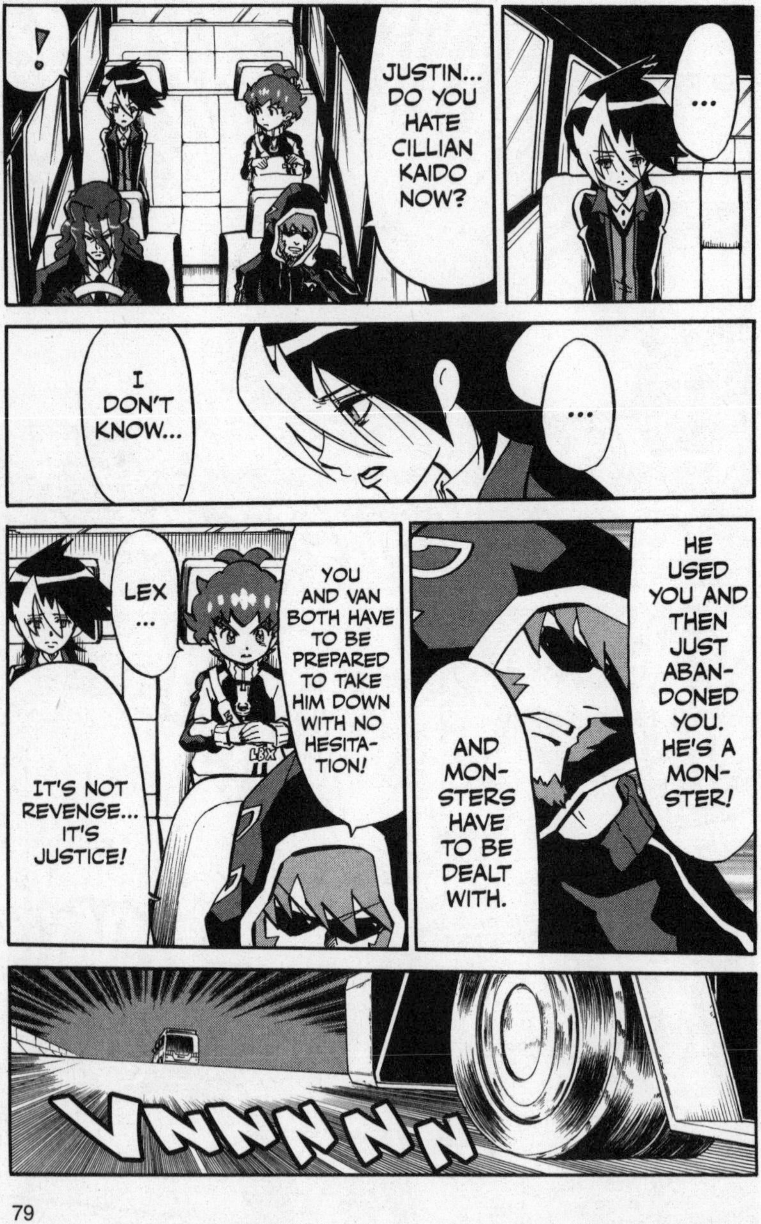
...
JUSTIN... DO YOU HATE CILLIAN KAIDO NOW?
!
...
I DON'T KNOW...
HE USED YOU AND THEN JUST ABANDONED YOU. HE'S A MONSTER!
AND MONSTERS HAVE TO BE DEALT WITH.
YOU AND VAN BOTH HAVE TO BE PREPARED TO TAKE HIM DOWN WITH NO HESITATION!
LEX...
IT'S NOT REVENGE... IT'S JUSTICE!
LBX
VNNNNN

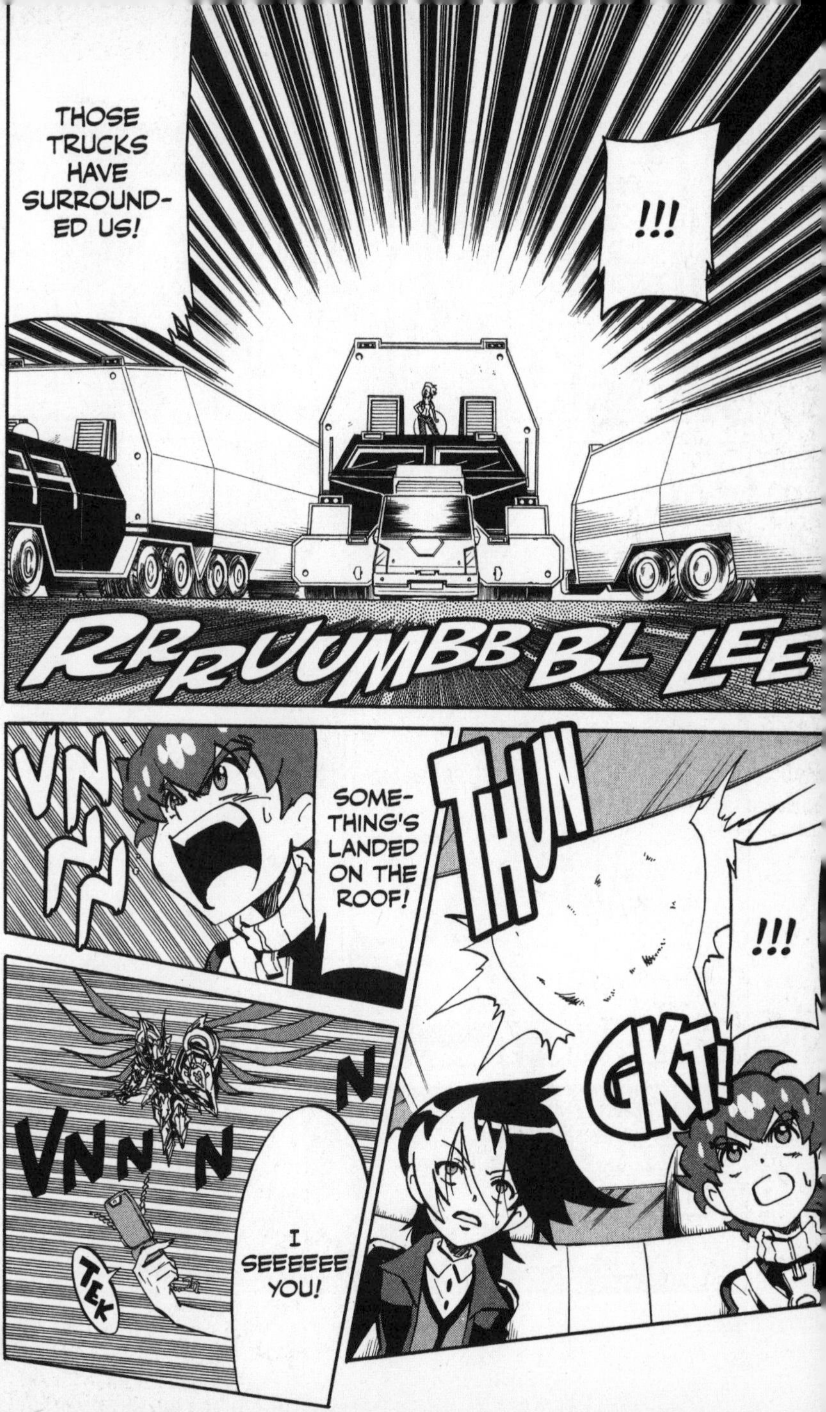
!!!
THOSE TRUCKS HAVE SURROUND-ED US!
RRRUUMBB BL LEE
THUN
!!!
GKT!
SOME-THING'S LANDED ON THE ROOF!
VN
VNNNN
I SEEEEEE YOU!
TEK

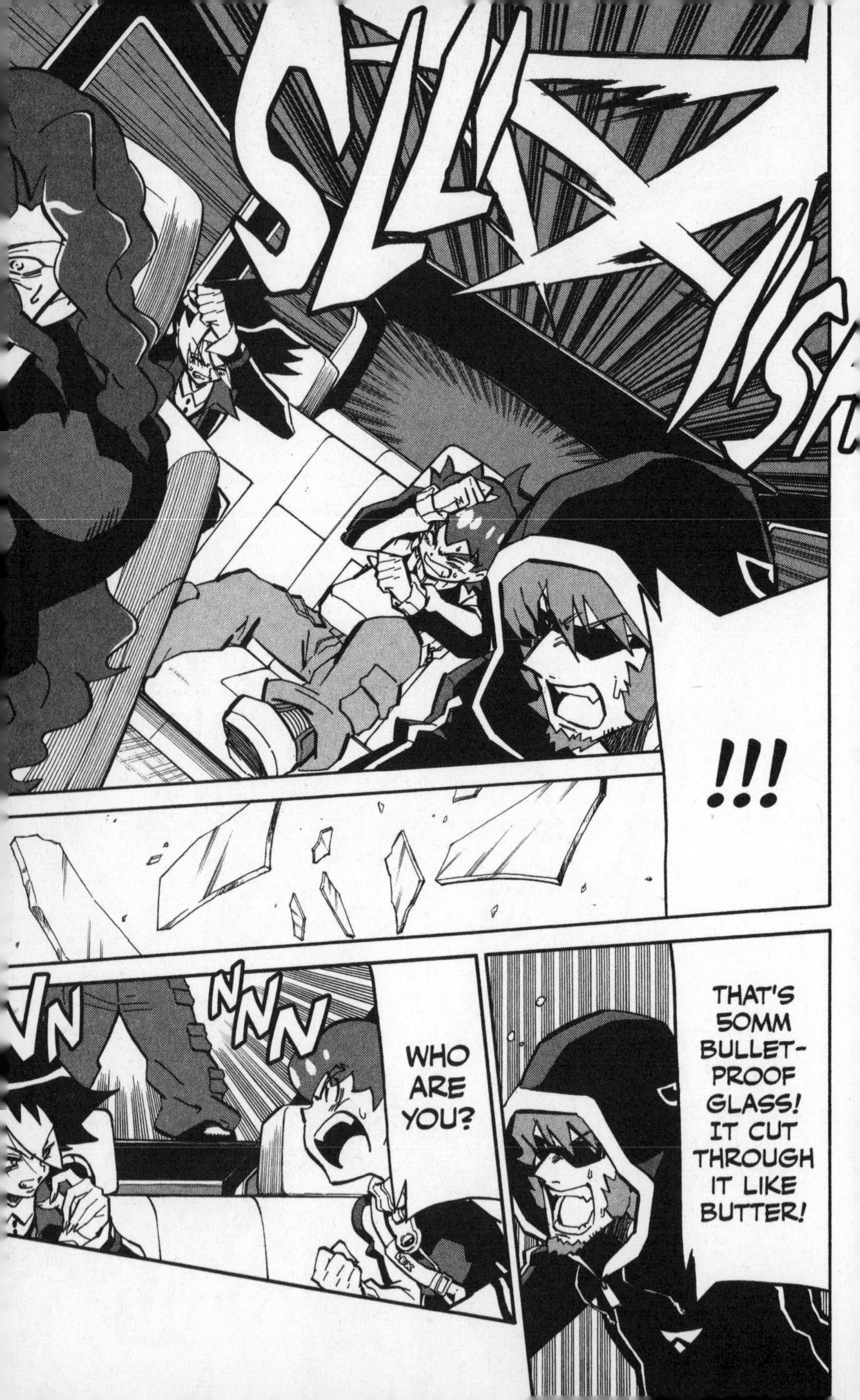
!!!
THAT'S 50MM BULLET-PROOF GLASS! IT CUT THROUGH IT LIKE BUTTER!
WHO ARE YOU?
NNN

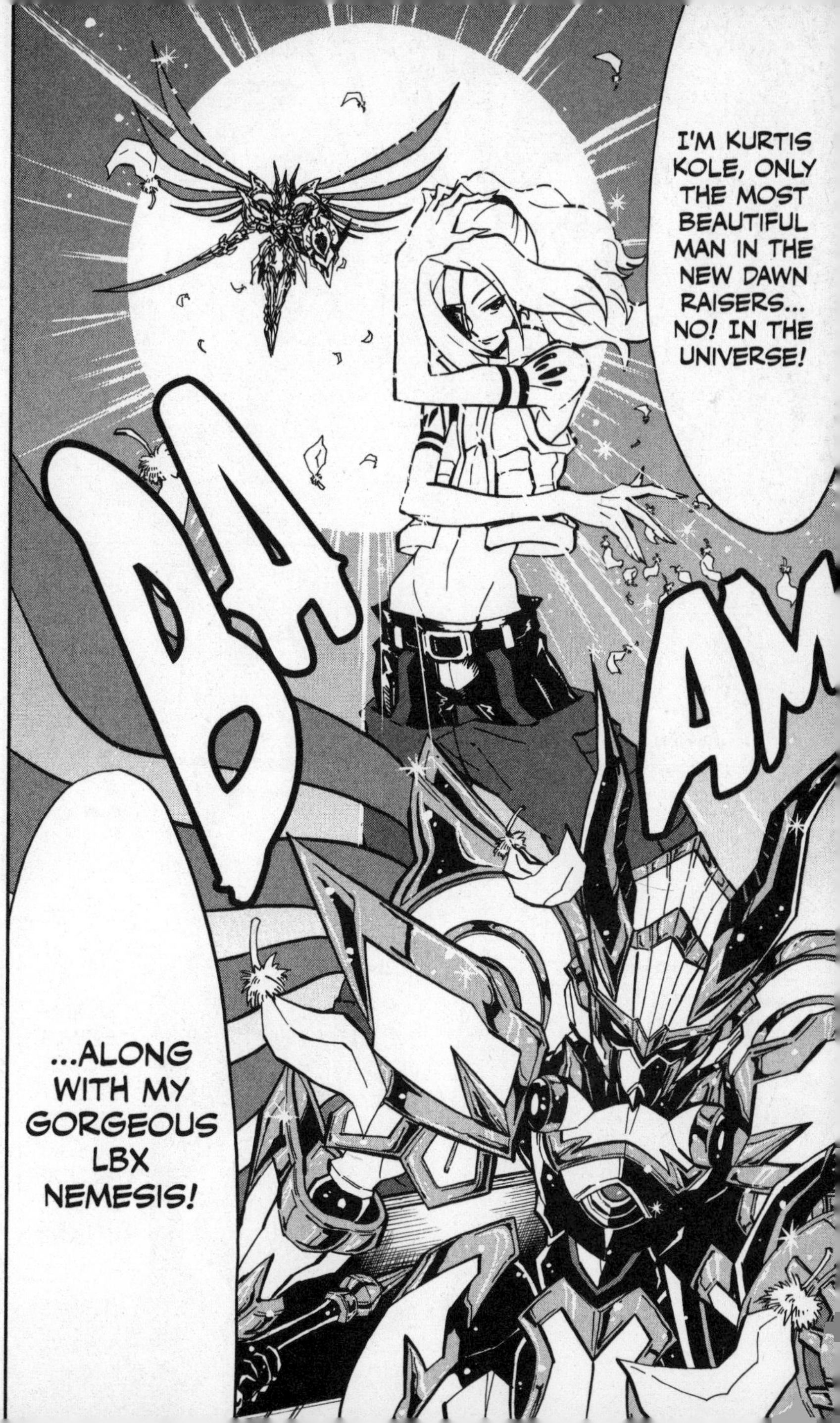
I'M KURTIS KOLE, ONLY THE MOST BEAUTIFUL MAN IN THE NEW DAWN RAISERS... NO! IN THE UNIVERSE!
...ALONG WITH MY GORGEOUS LBX NEMESIS!

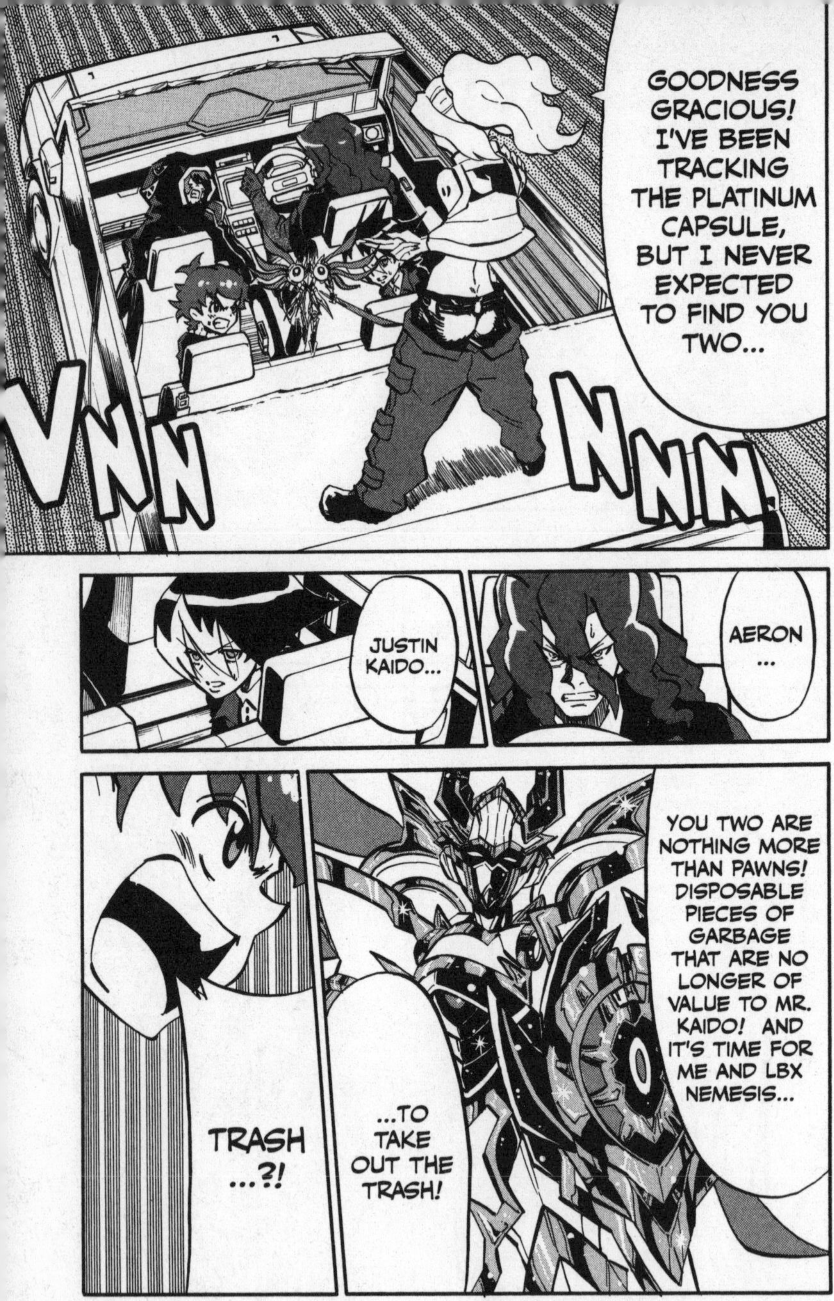
GOODNESS GRACIOUS! I'VE BEEN TRACKING THE PLATINUM CAPSULE, BUT I NEVER EXPECTED TO FIND YOU TWO...
VNN NNNN
AERON ...
JUSTIN KAIDO...
YOU TWO ARE NOTHING MORE THAN PAWNS! DISPOSABLE PIECES OF GARBAGE THAT ARE NO LONGER OF VALUE TO MR. KAIDO! AND IT'S TIME FOR ME AND LBX NEMESIS...
...TO TAKE OUT THE TRASH!
TRASH ...?!

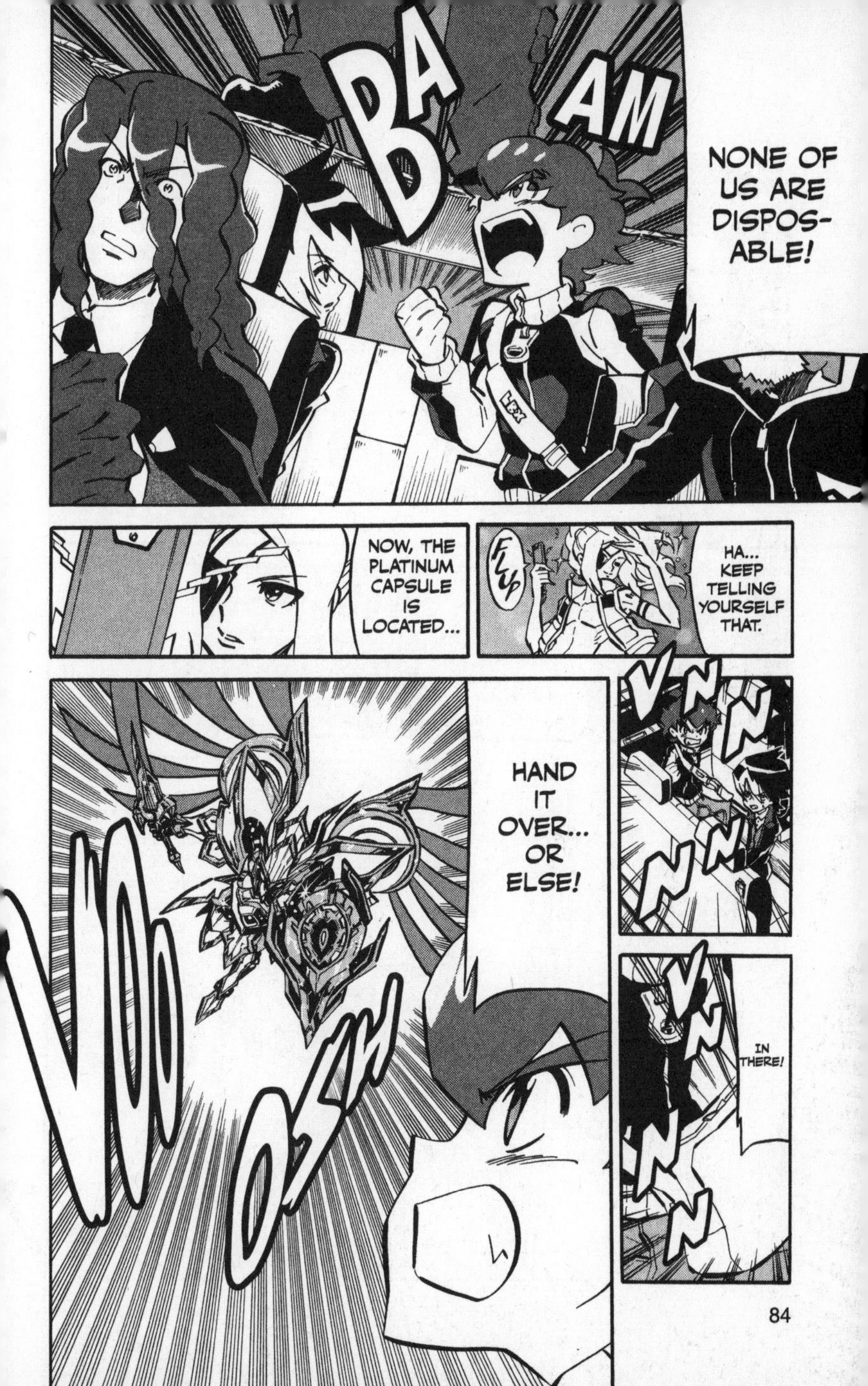
BAAM
NONE OF US ARE DISPOS-ABLE!
FLIP
HA... KEEP TELLING YOURSELF THAT.
NOW, THE PLATINUM CAPSULE IS LOCATED...
VNNNN
VNNNN
IN THERE!
HAND IT OVER... OR ELSE!
VOOOSH

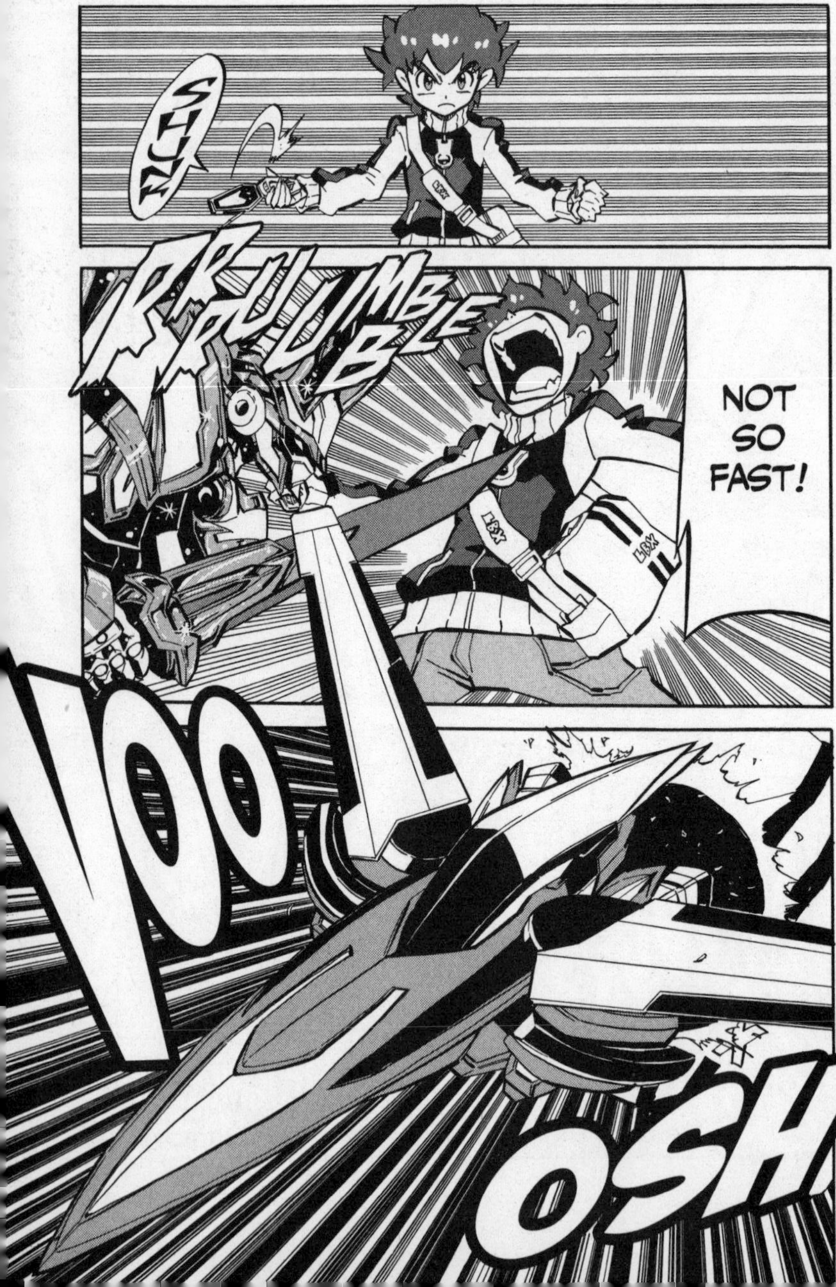
SHUN
NOT SO FAST!
RUMBLE
RUMBLE
VOO
OSH

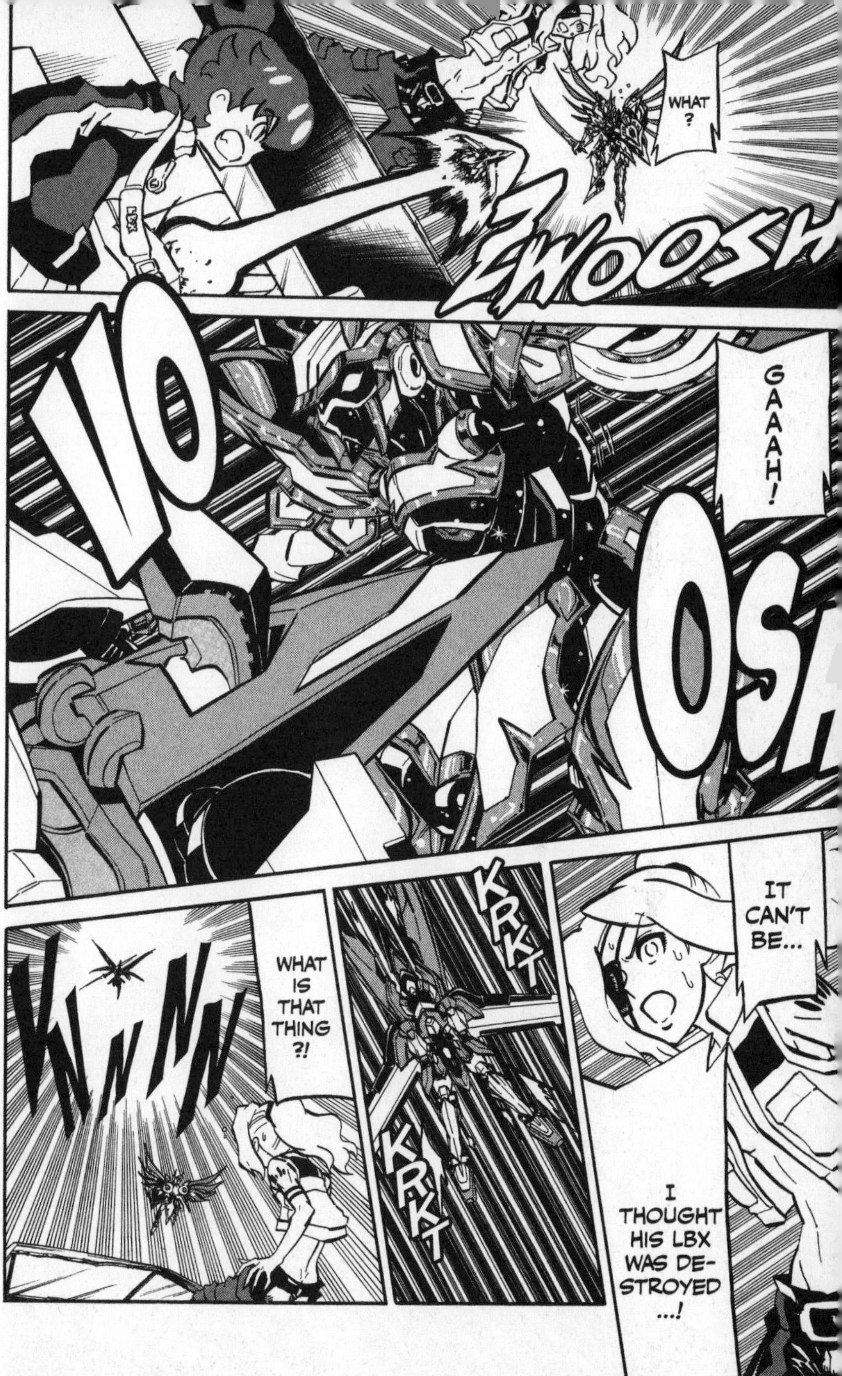
WHAT ?
WOOSH
GAAAH!
VO
OS
IT CAN'T BE...
I THOUGHT HIS LBX WAS DE-STROYED ...!
KRKT
KRKT
WHAT IS THAT THING ?!
KNNNN

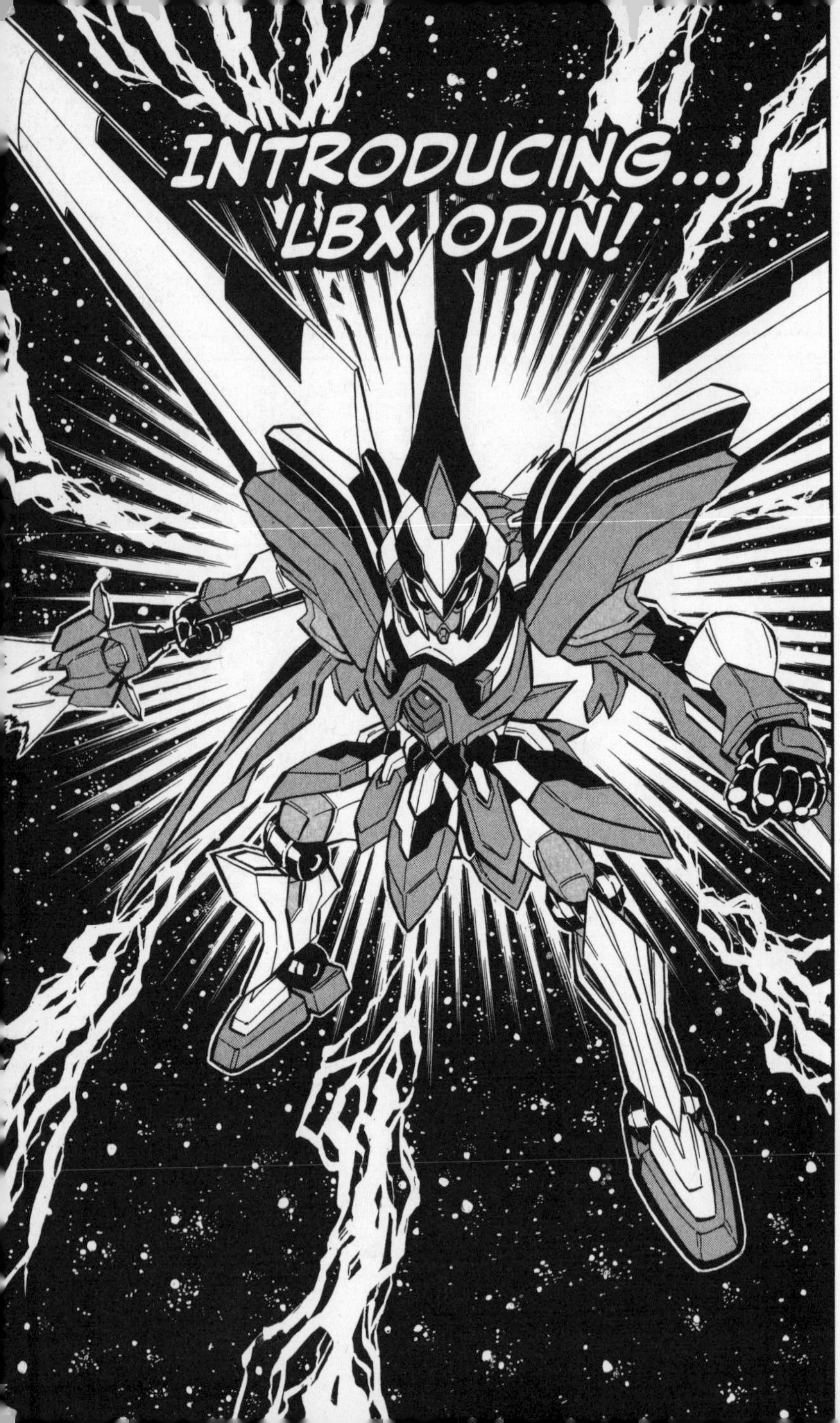
INTRODUCING... LBX ODIN!

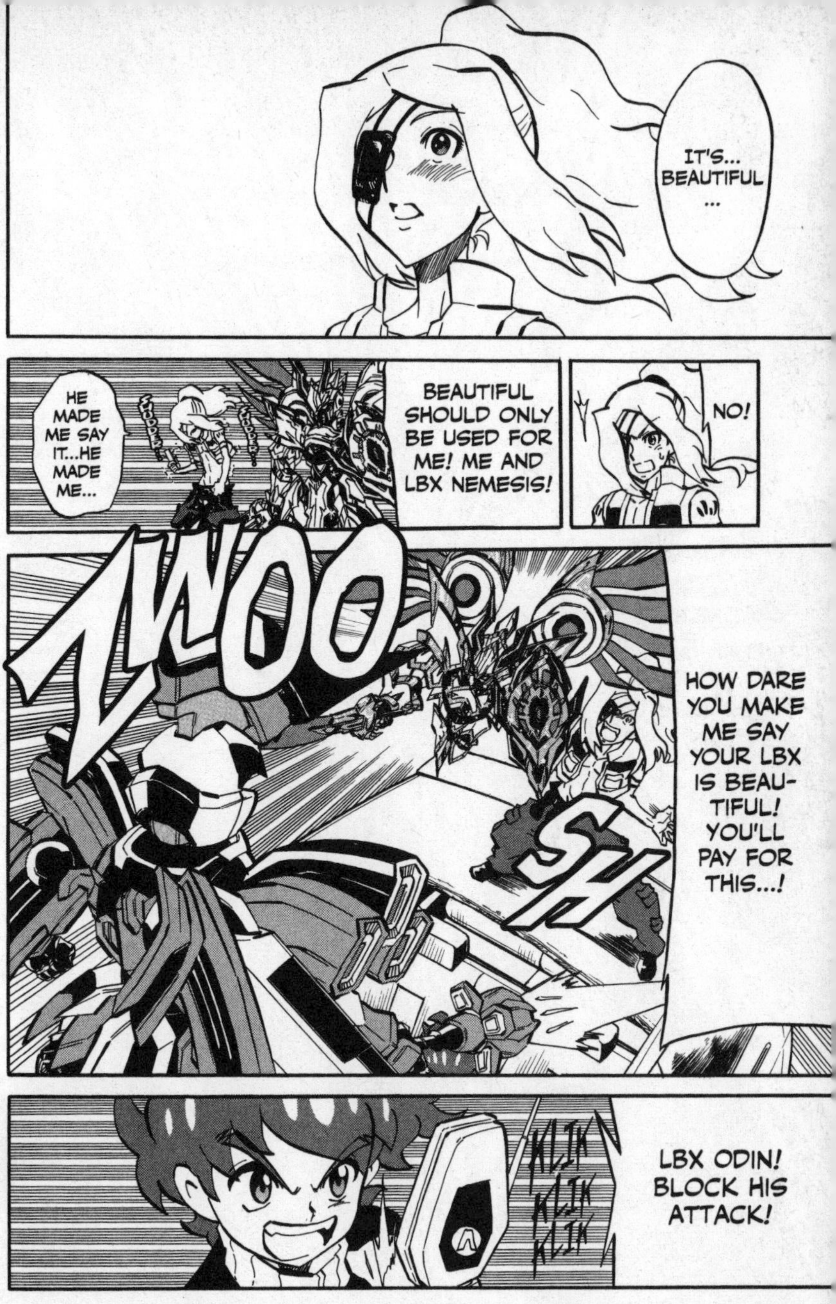
IT'S... BEAUTIFUL ...
NO!
BEAUTIFUL SHOULD ONLY BE USED FOR ME! ME AND LBX NEMESIS!
HE MADE ME SAY IT...HE MADE ME...
HOW DARE YOU MAKE ME SAY YOUR LBX IS BEAU-TIFUL! YOU'LL PAY FOR THIS...!
ZWOO
SH
LBX ODIN! BLOCK HIS ATTACK!
KLIK KLIK KLIK

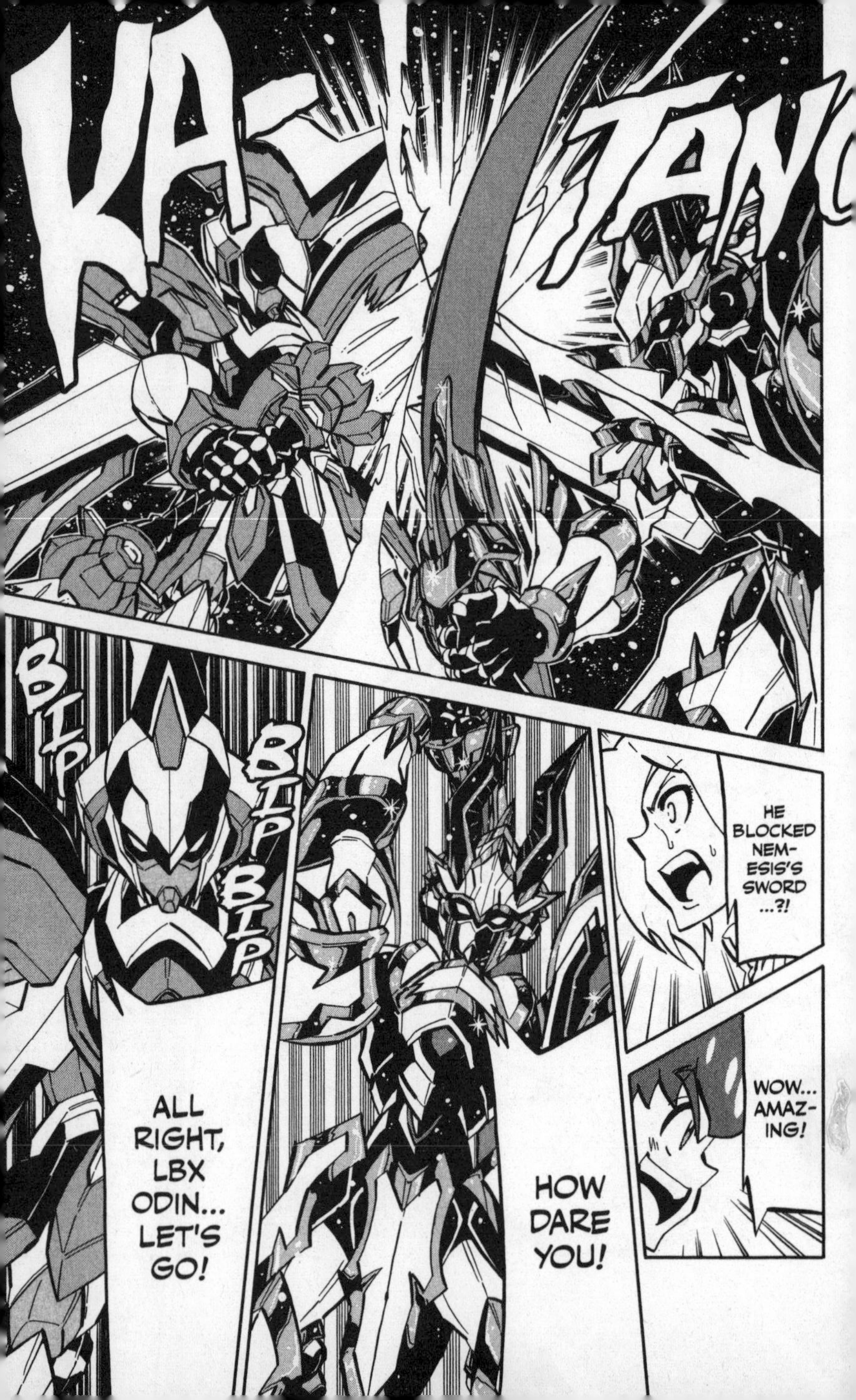
KA-TAN
HE BLOCKED NEM-ESIS'S SWORD ...?!
WOW... AMAZ-ING!
HOW DARE YOU!
BIP
BIP
BIP
BIP
ALL RIGHT, LBX ODIN... LET'S GO!

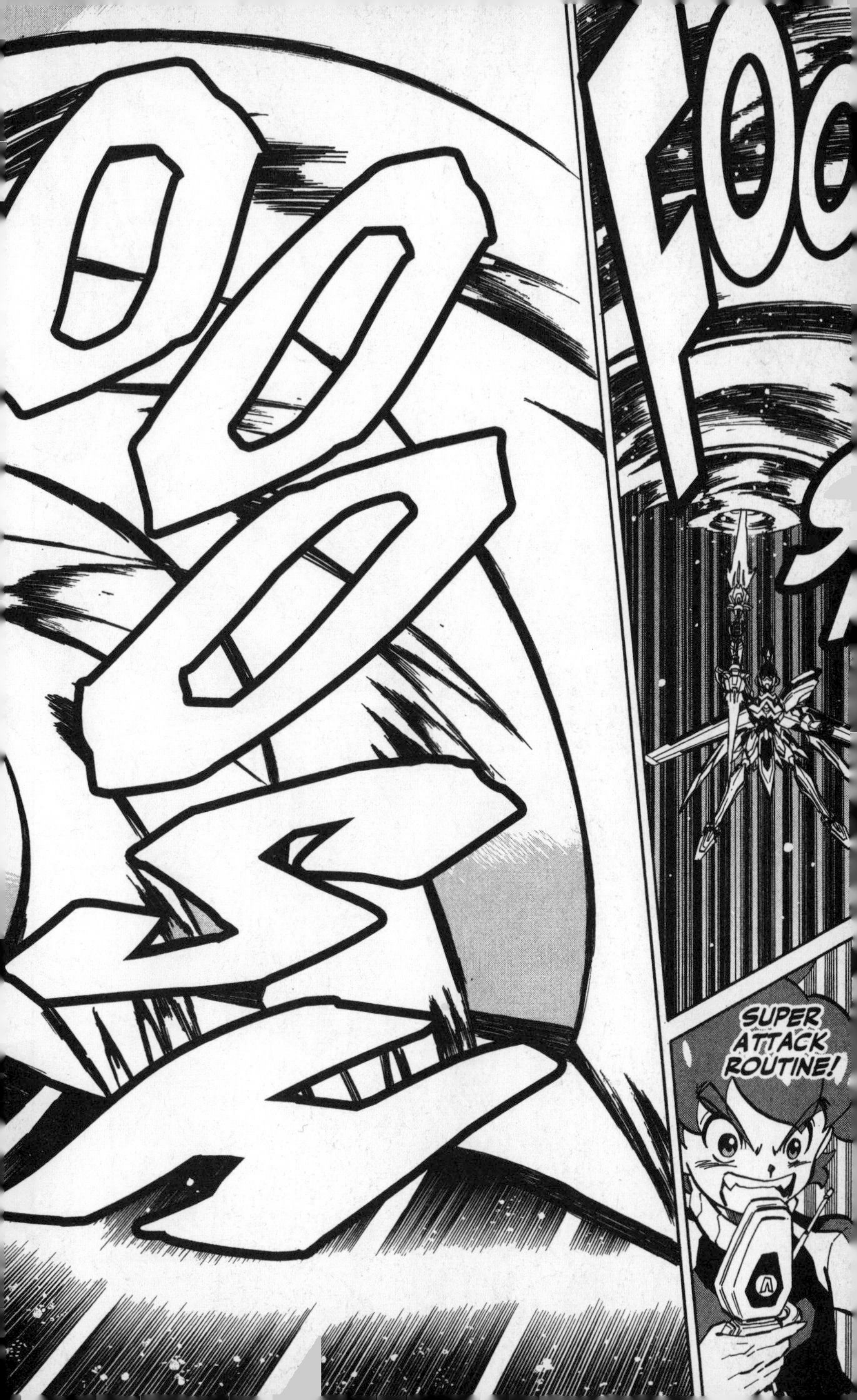
SUPER ATTACK ROUTINE!

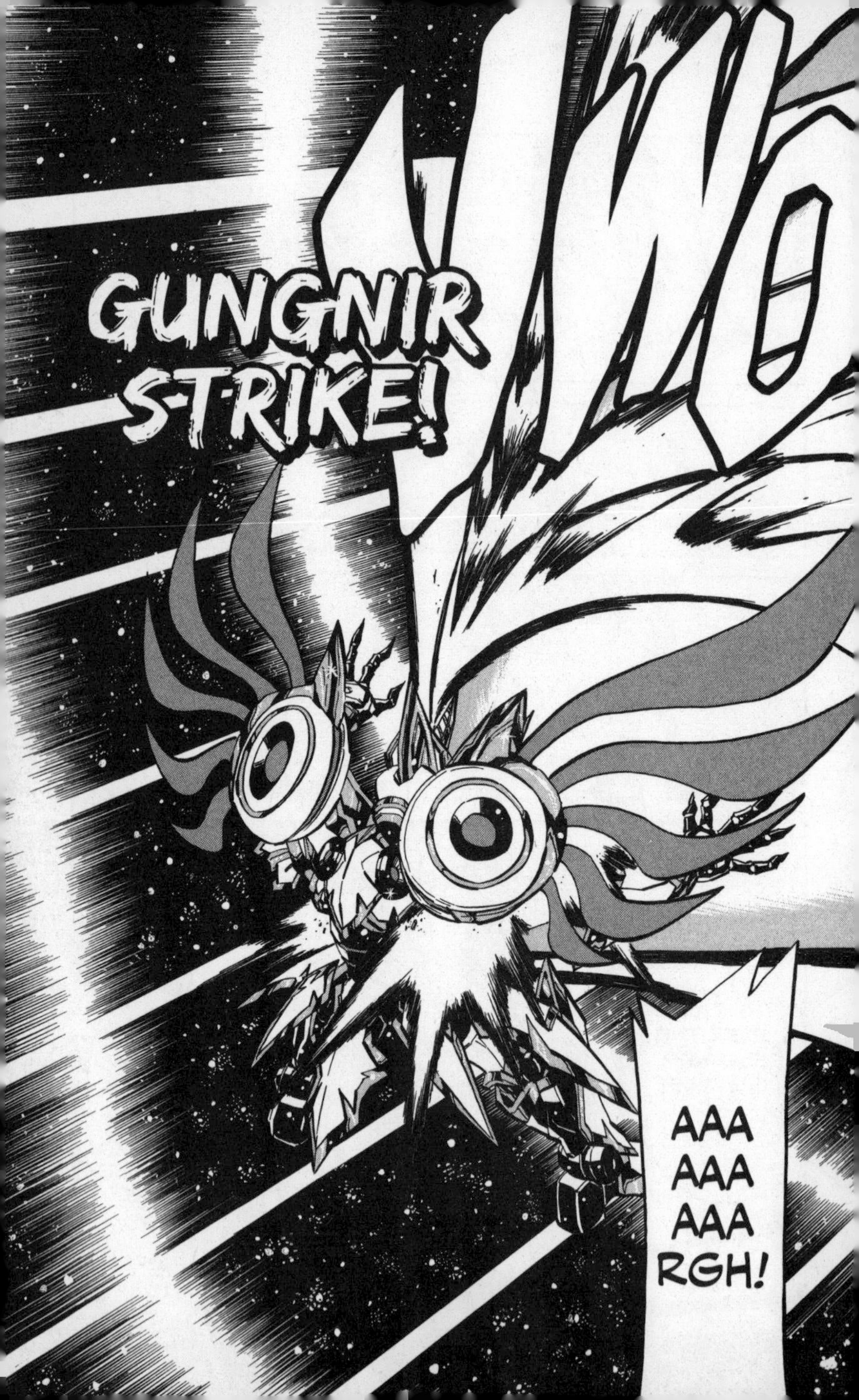
GUNGNIR STRIKE!
AAAAAAAAARGH!

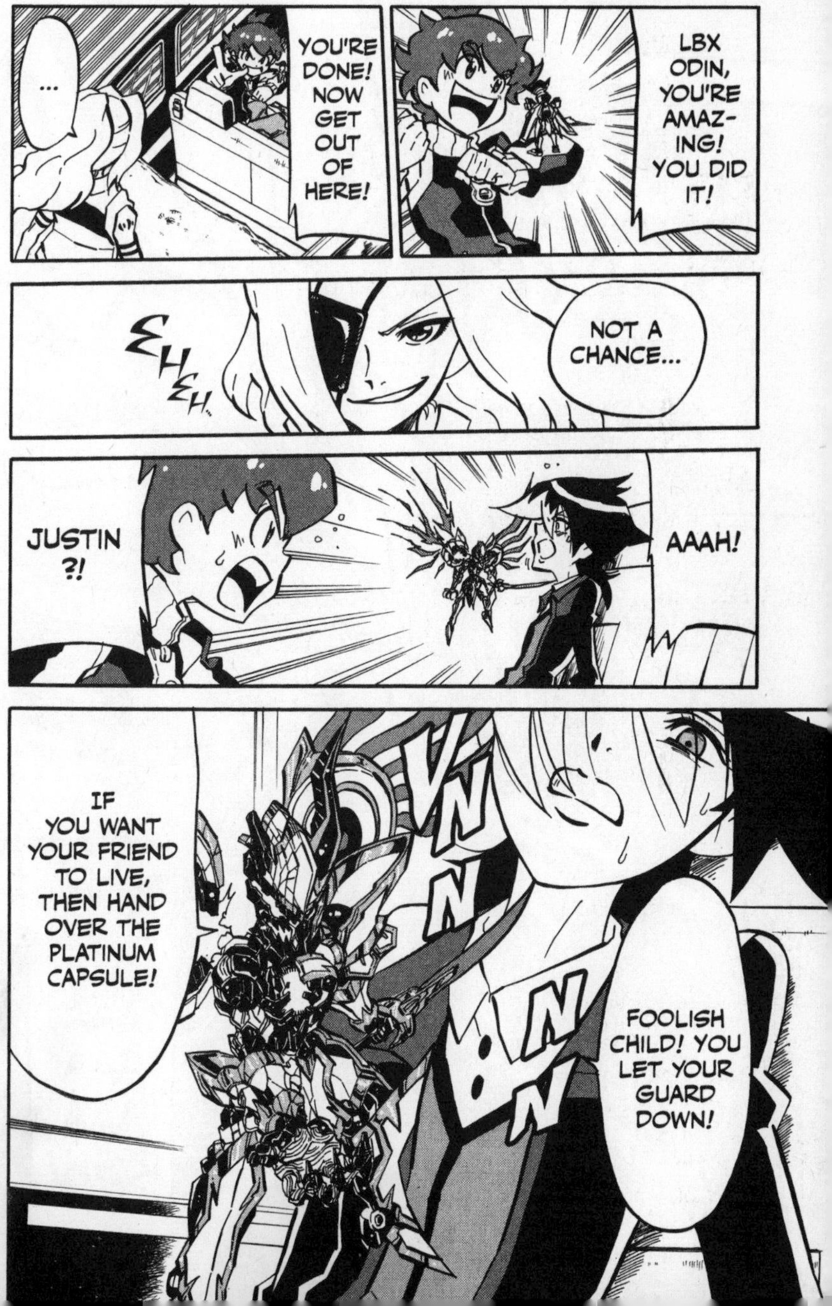
LBX ODIN, YOU'RE AMAZ-ING! YOU DID IT!
YOU'RE DONE! NOW GET OUT OF HERE!
...
NOT A CHANCE...
EHEH...
AAAH!
JUSTIN?!
VNNN
NNN
FOOLISH CHILD! YOU LET YOUR GUARD DOWN!
IF YOU WANT YOUR FRIEND TO LIVE, THEN HAND OVER THE PLATINUM CAPSULE!

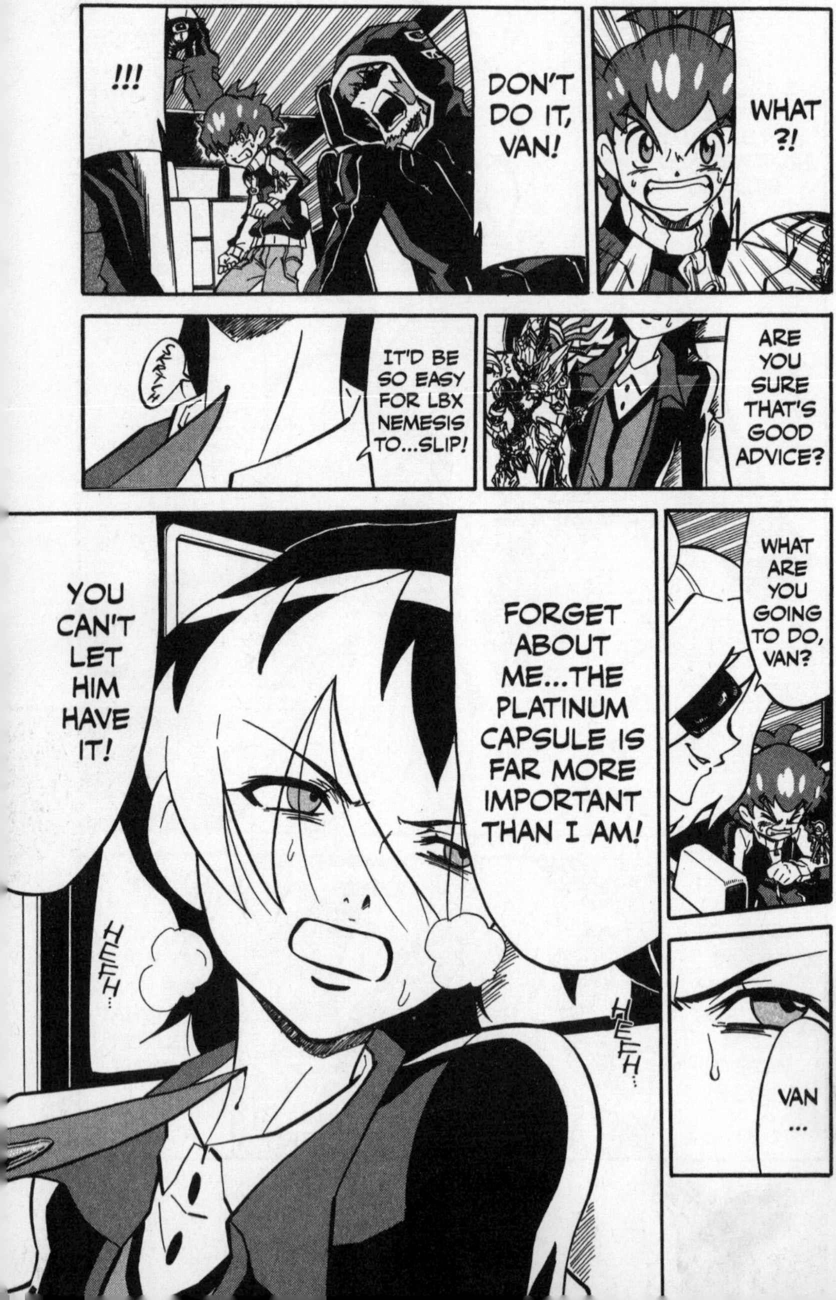
WHAT ?!
DON'T DO IT, VAN!
!!!
ARE YOU SURE THAT'S GOOD ADVICE?
IT'D BE SO EASY FOR LBX NEMESIS TO...SLIP!
WHAT ARE YOU GOING TO DO, VAN?
VAN...
FORGET ABOUT ME...THE PLATINUM CAPSULE IS FAR MORE IMPORTANT THAN I AM!
YOU CAN'T LET HIM HAVE IT!
HEFH...
HEFH...

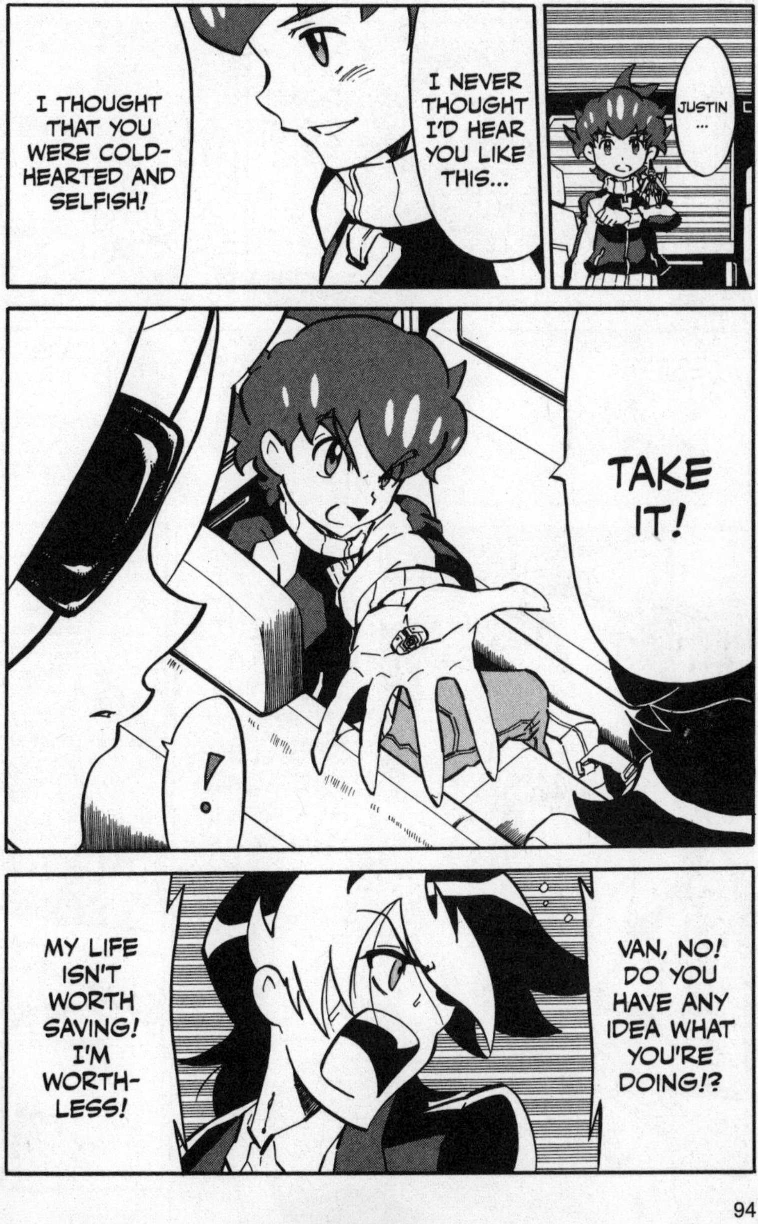
JUSTIN ...
I NEVER THOUGHT I'D HEAR YOU LIKE THIS...
I THOUGHT THAT YOU WERE COLD-HEARTED AND SELFISH!
TAKE IT!
!
VAN, NO! DO YOU HAVE ANY IDEA WHAT YOU'RE DOING!?
MY LIFE ISN'T WORTH SAVING! I'M WORTH-LESS!

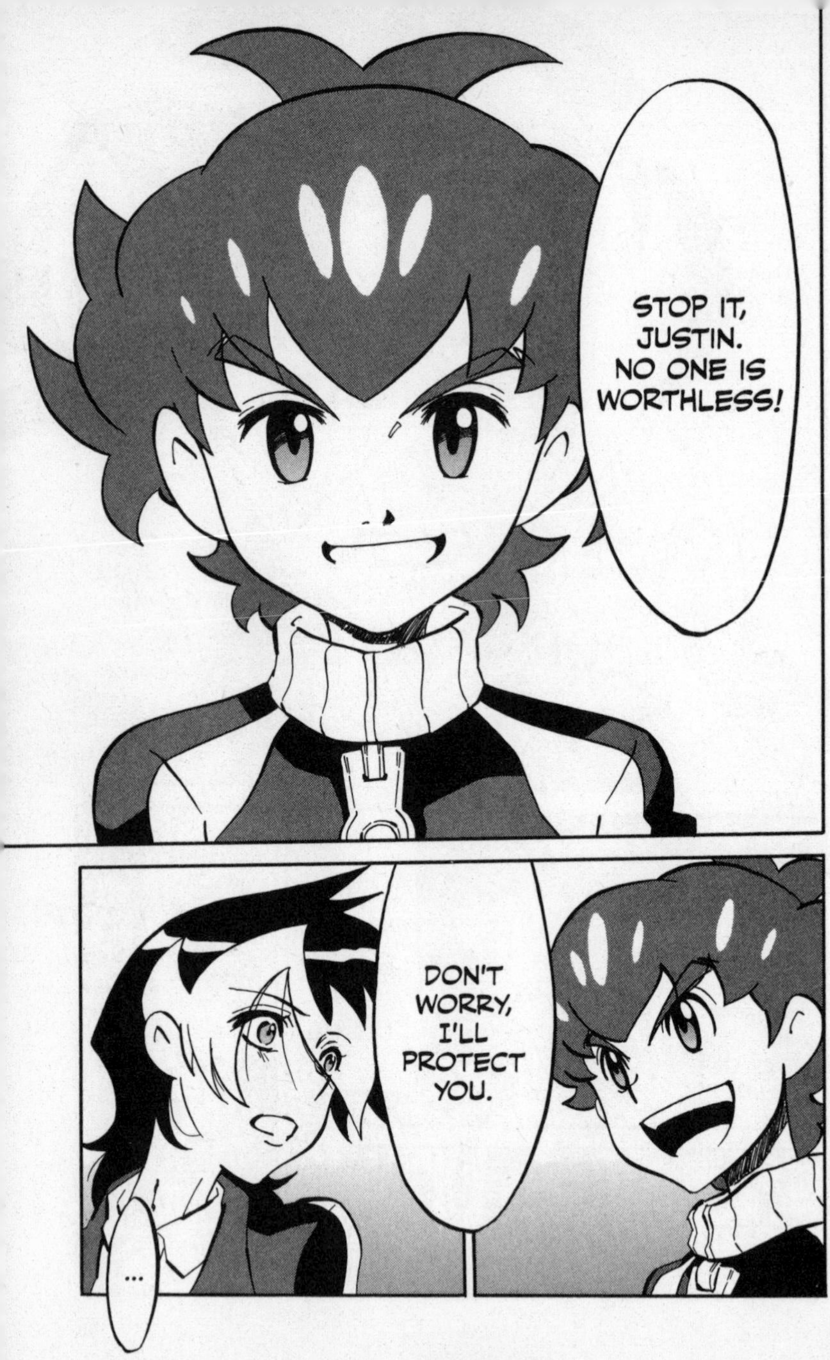
STOP IT, JUSTIN. NO ONE IS WORTHLESS!
DON'T WORRY, I'LL PROTECT YOU.
...

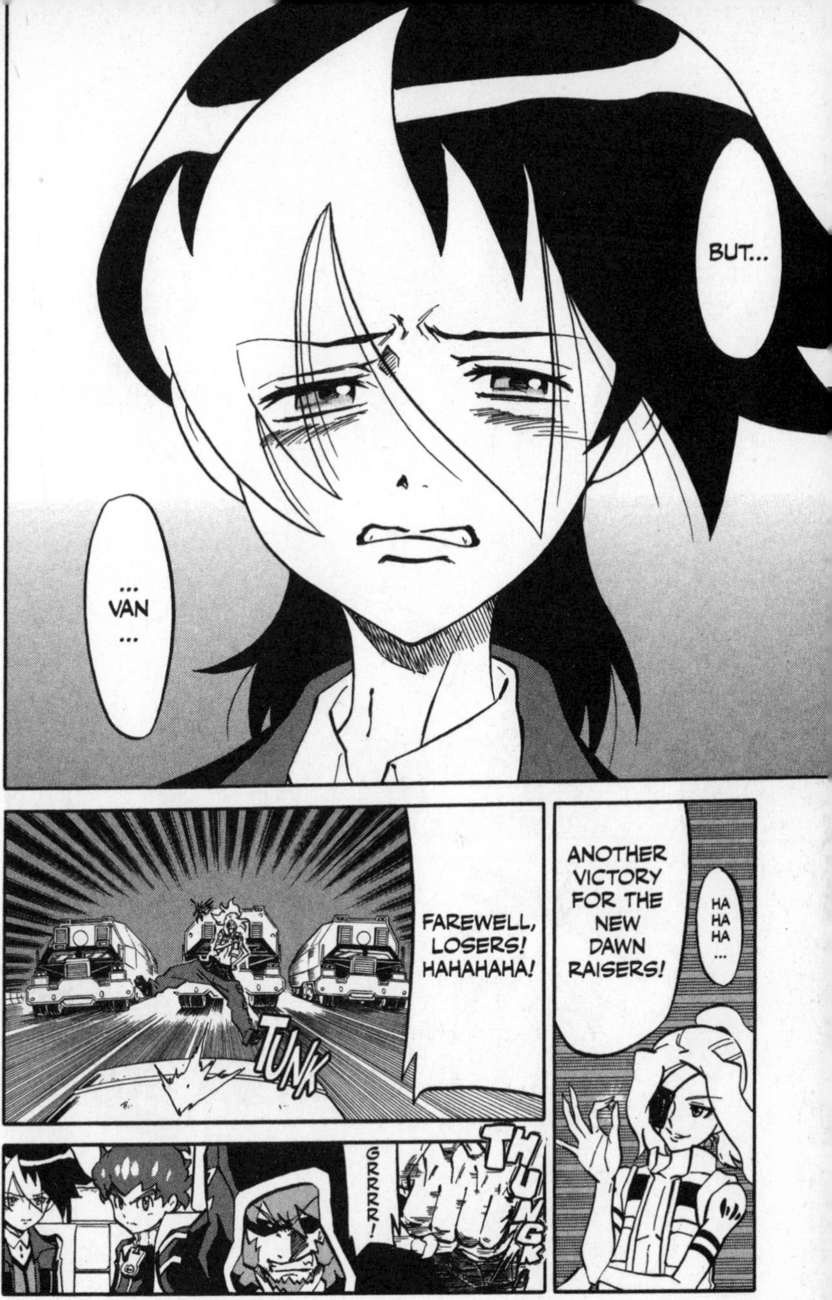
BUT...
...VAN...
ANOTHER VICTORY FOR THE NEW DAWN RAISERS!
HA HA HA...
FAREWELL, LOSERS! HAHAHAHA!
TUNK
THUNK
GRRRR!

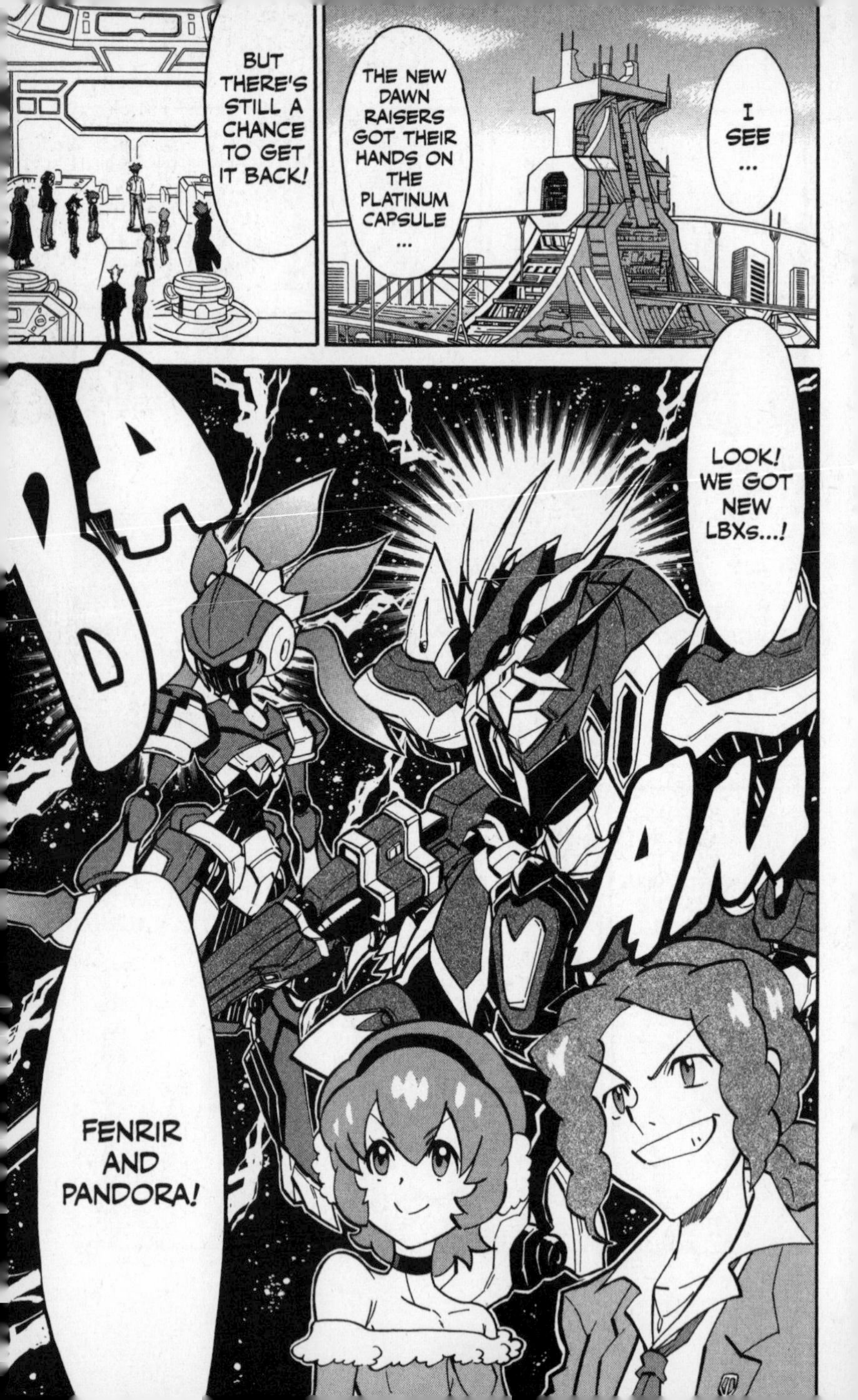
I SEE ...
THE NEW DAWN RAISERS GOT THEIR HANDS ON THE PLATINUM CAPSULE ...
BUT THERE'S STILL A CHANCE TO GET IT BACK!
LOOK! WE GOT NEW LBXs...!
FENRIR AND PANDORA!

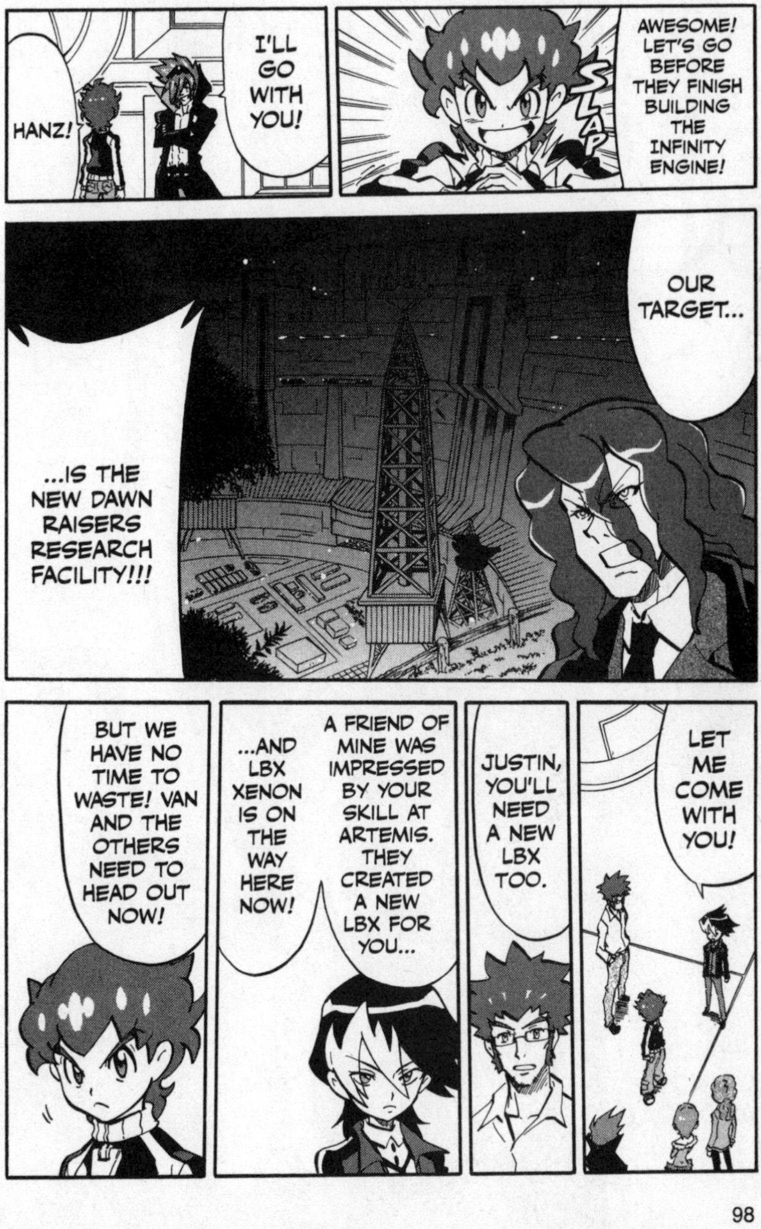
AWESOME! LET'S GO BEFORE THEY FINISH BUILDING THE INFINITY ENGINE!
SLAP
I'LL GO WITH YOU!
HANZ!
OUR TARGET...
...IS THE NEW DAWN RAISERS RESEARCH FACILITY!!!
LET ME COME WITH YOU!
JUSTIN, YOU'LL NEED A NEW LBX TOO.
A FRIEND OF MINE WAS IMPRESSED BY YOUR SKILL AT ARTEMIS. THEY CREATED A NEW LBX FOR YOU...
...AND LBX XENON IS ON THE WAY HERE NOW!
BUT WE HAVE NO TIME TO WASTE! VAN AND THE OTHERS NEED TO HEAD OUT NOW!

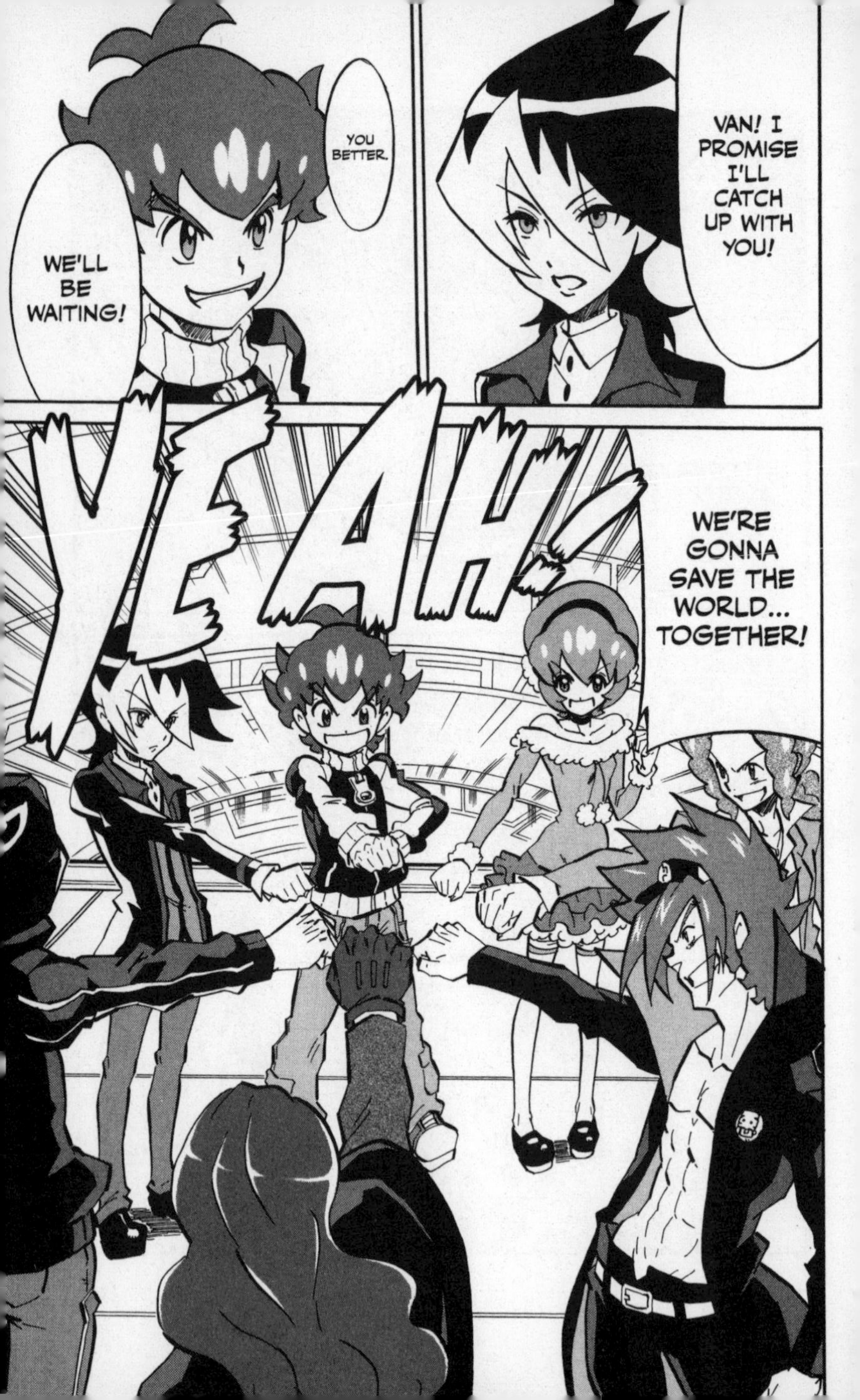
VAN! I PROMISE I'LL CATCH UP WITH YOU!
YOU BETTER.
WE'LL BE WAITING!
WE'RE GONNA SAVE THE WORLD... TOGETHER!
YEAH!

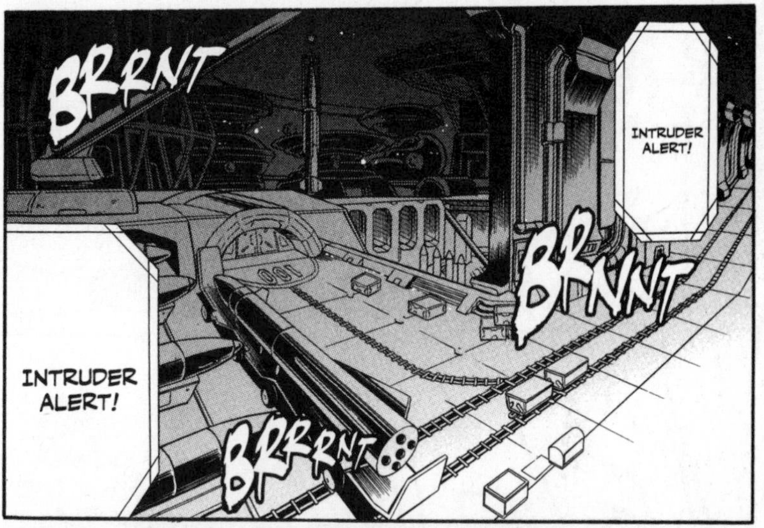
INTRUDER ALERT!
BRRNT
BRNNNT
INTRUDER ALERT!
BRRRRNT
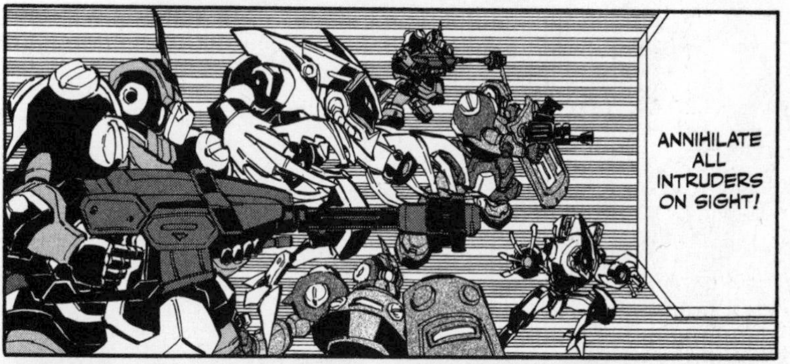
ANNIHILATE ALL INTRUDERS ON SIGHT!
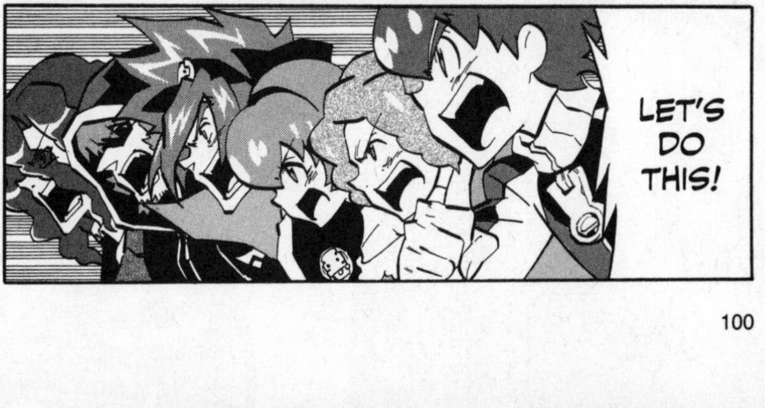
LET'S DO THIS!

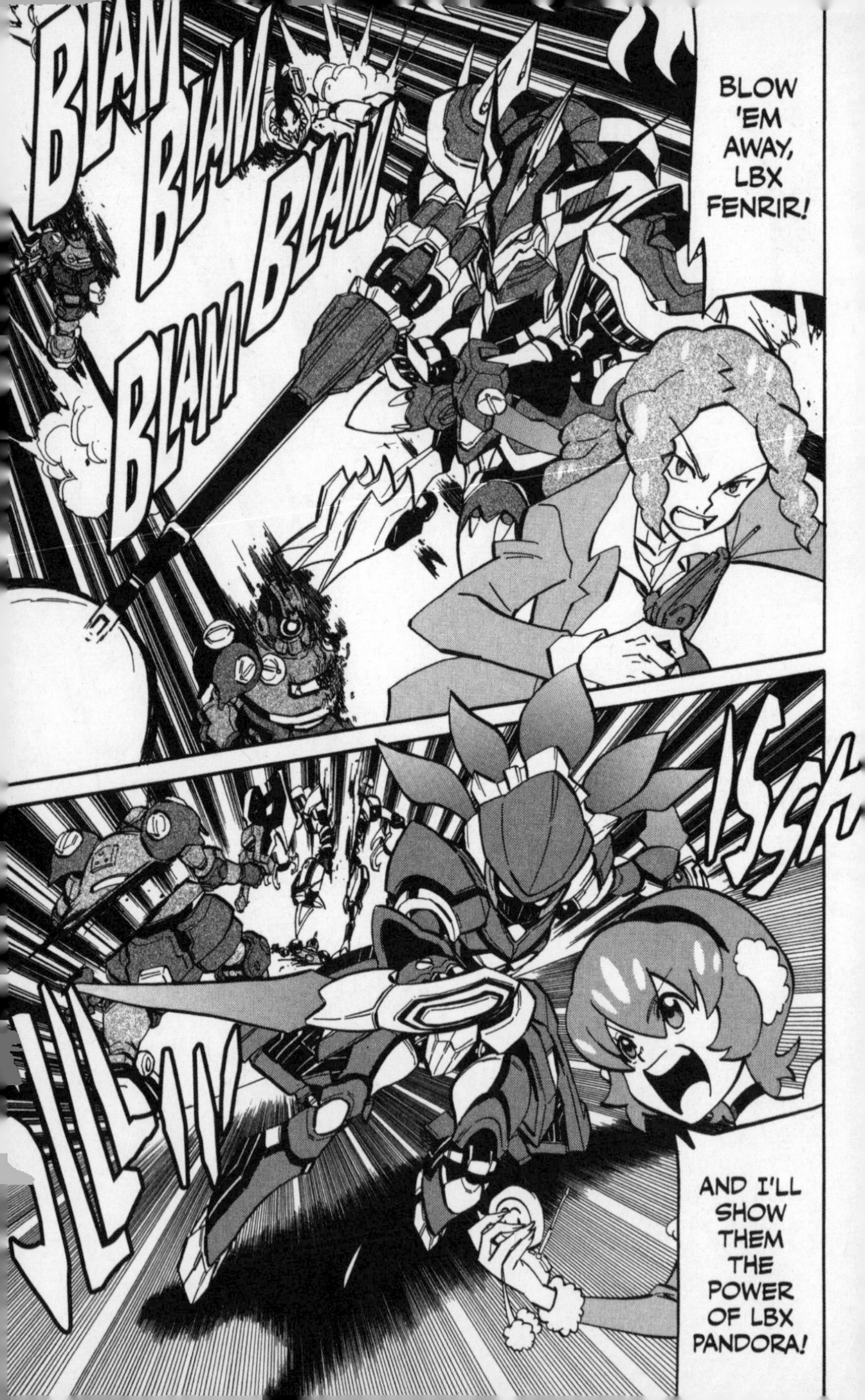
BLOW 'EM AWAY, LBX FENRIR!
BLAM
BLAM
BLAM
BLAM
AND I'LL SHOW THEM THE POWER OF LBX PANDORA!

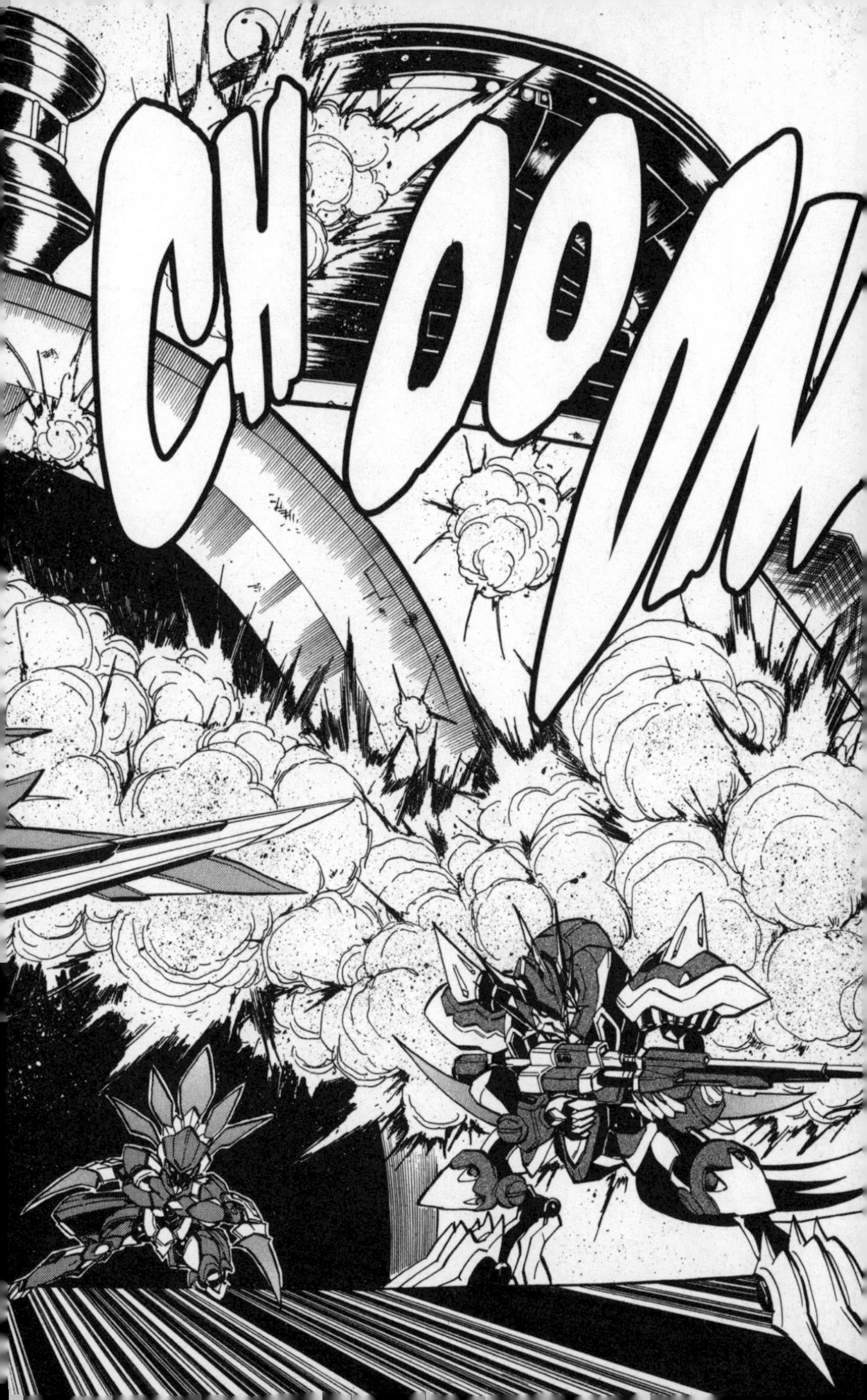
CHOOM

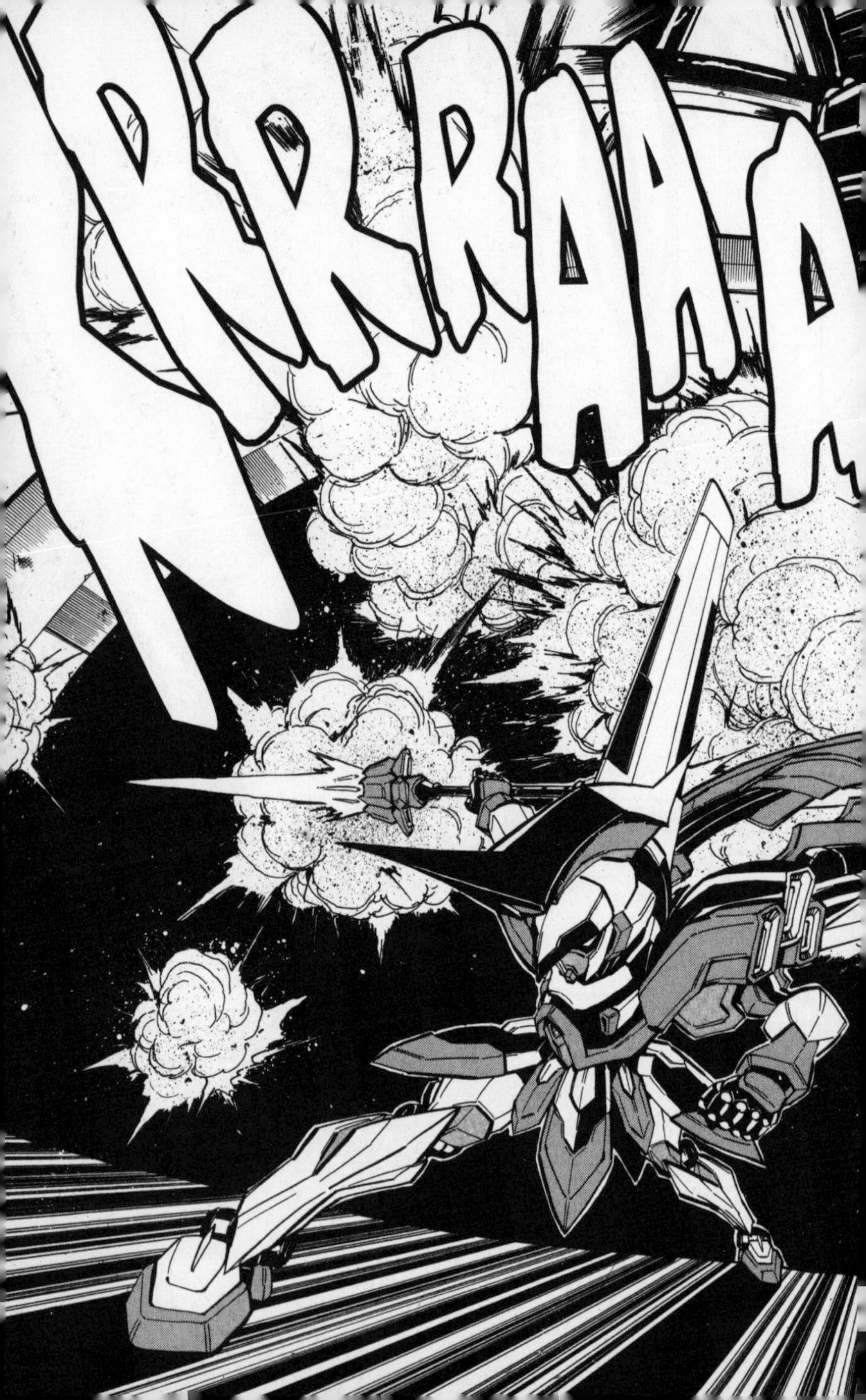

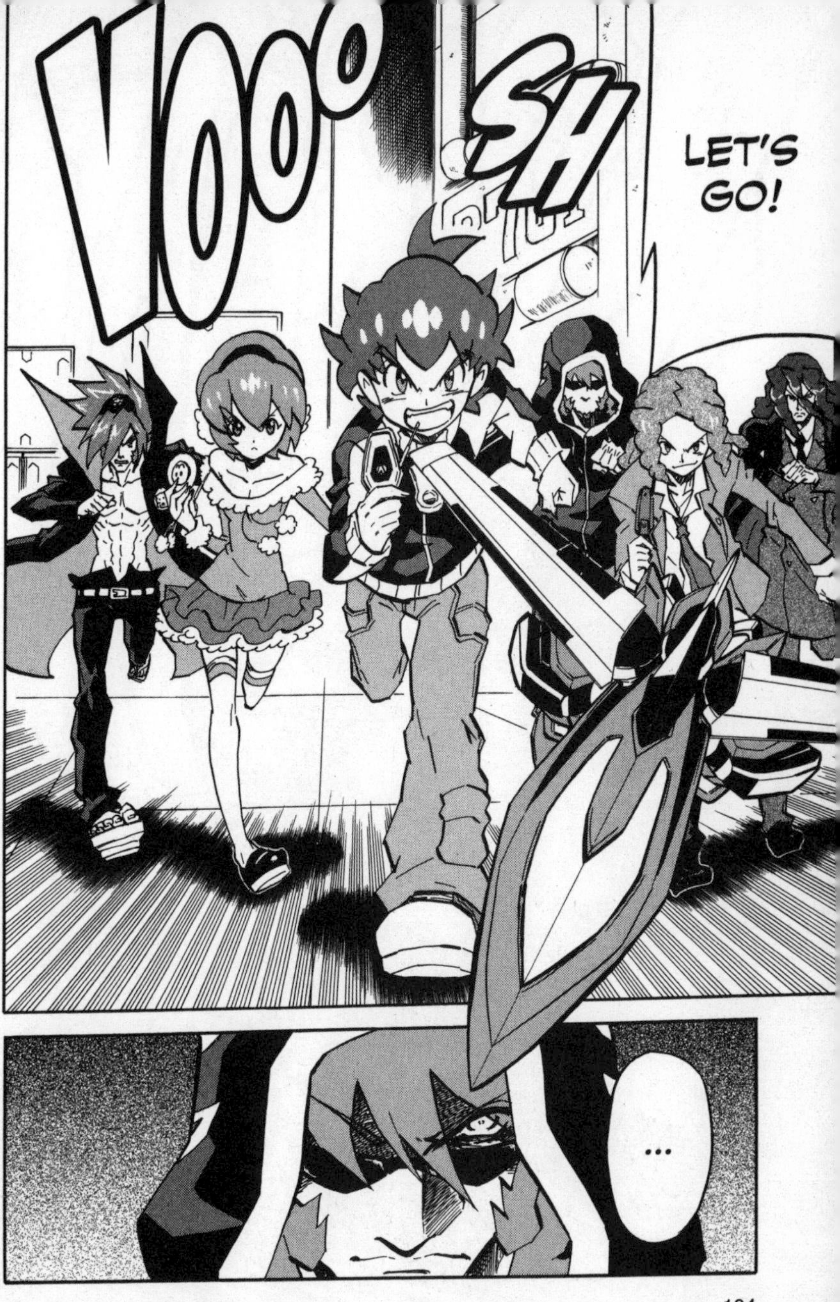
VOOOSH
LET'S GO!
...

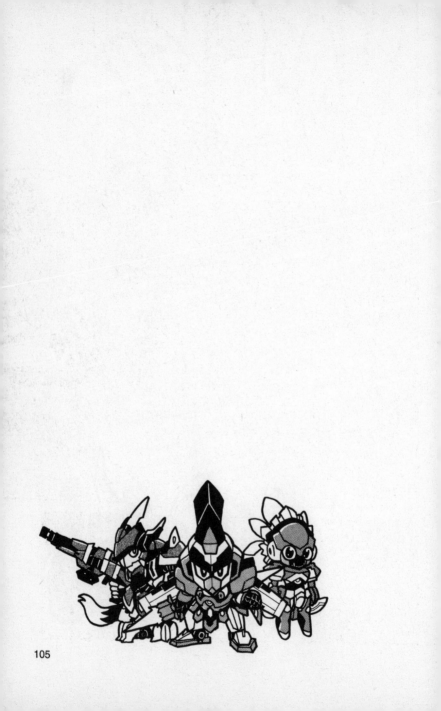

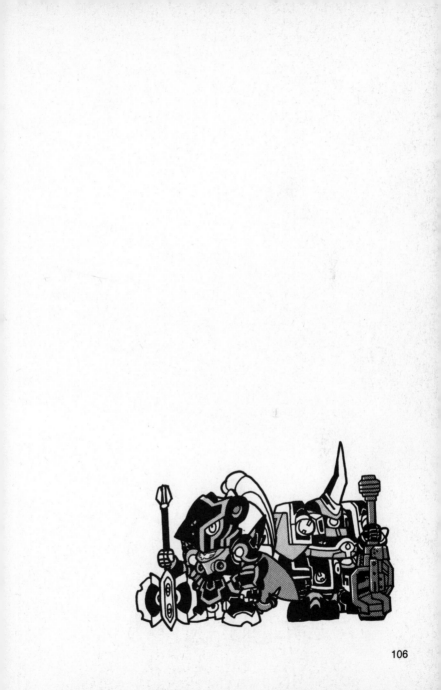

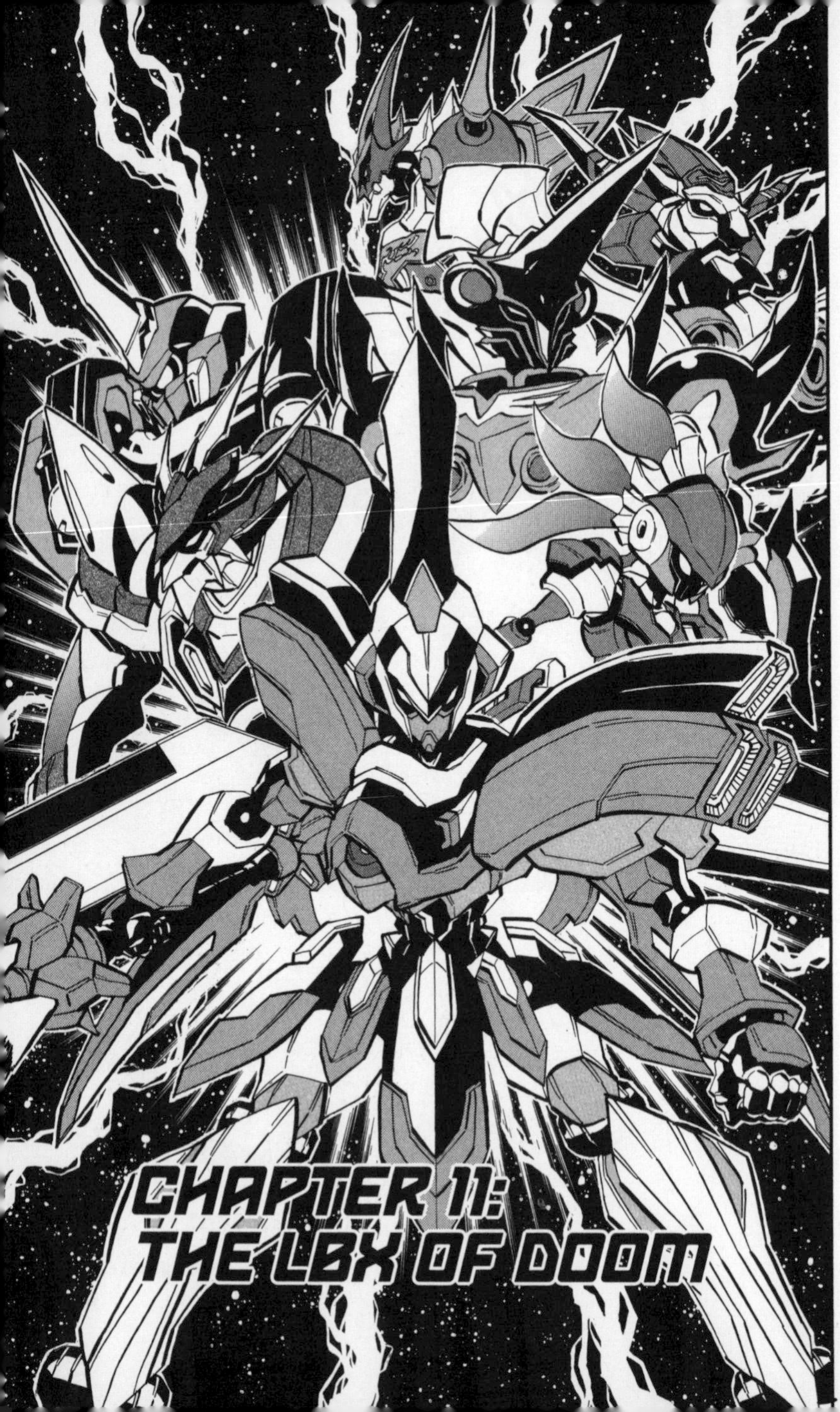
CHAPTER 11:
THE LBX OF DOOM

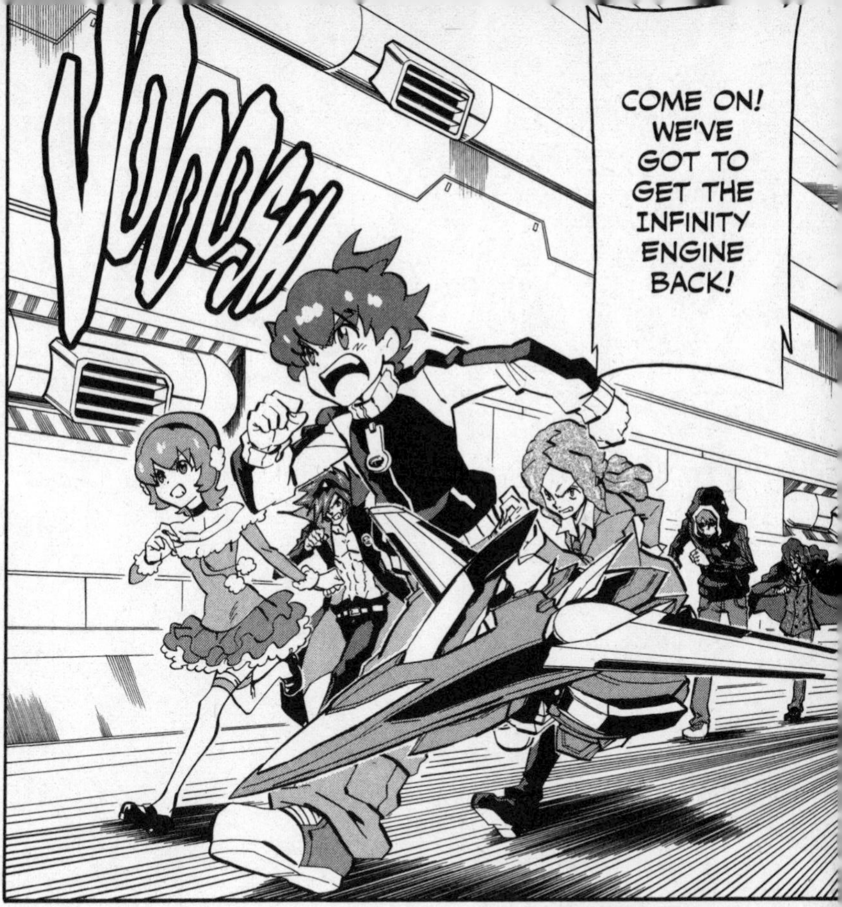
COME ON! WE'VE GOT TO GET THE INFINITY ENGINE BACK!

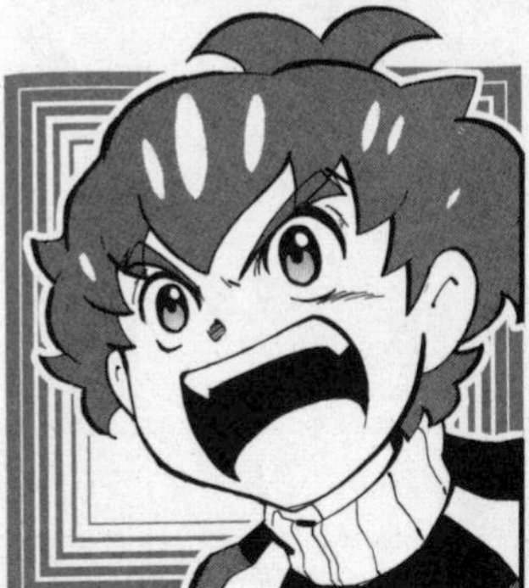

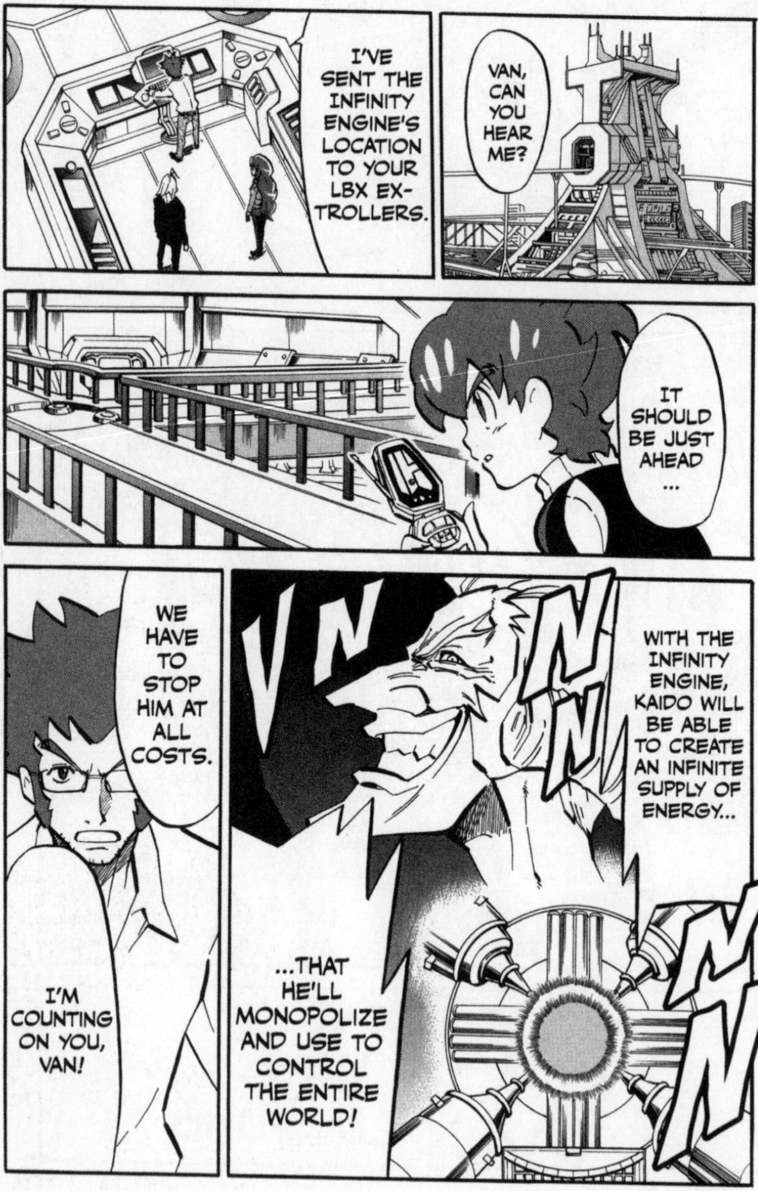
VAN, CAN YOU HEAR ME?
I'VE SENT THE INFINITY ENGINE'S LOCATION TO YOUR LBX EX-TROLLERS.
IT SHOULD BE JUST AHEAD...
VNNN
WITH THE INFINITY ENGINE, KAIDO WILL BE ABLE TO CREATE AN INFINITE SUPPLY OF ENERGY...
NNN
...THAT HE'LL MONOPOLIZE AND USE TO CONTROL THE ENTIRE WORLD!
WE HAVE TO STOP HIM AT ALL COSTS.
I'M COUNTING ON YOU, VAN!

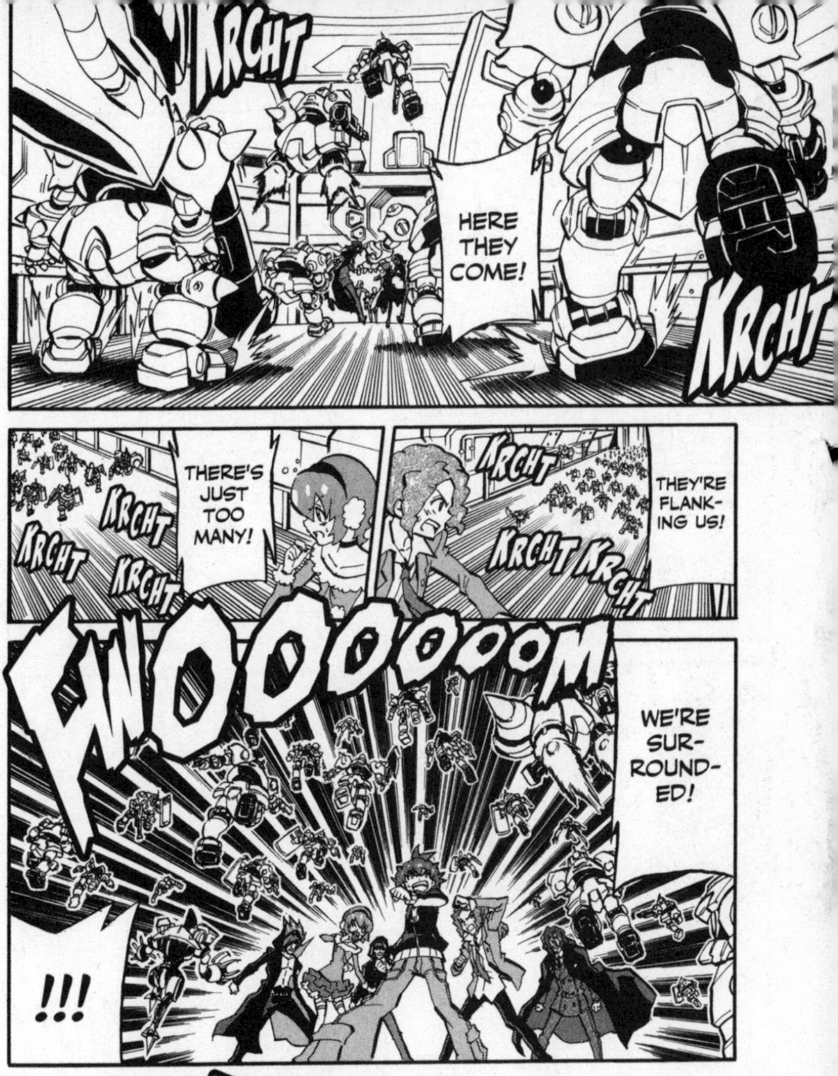
HERE THEY COME!
KRCHT
KRCHT
THEY'RE FLANK-ING US!
KRCHT
KRCHT KRCHT
THERE'S JUST TOO MANY!
KRCHT
KRCHT
KRCHT
WE'RE SUR-ROUND-ED!
FWOOOOOOM
!!!
KRA...

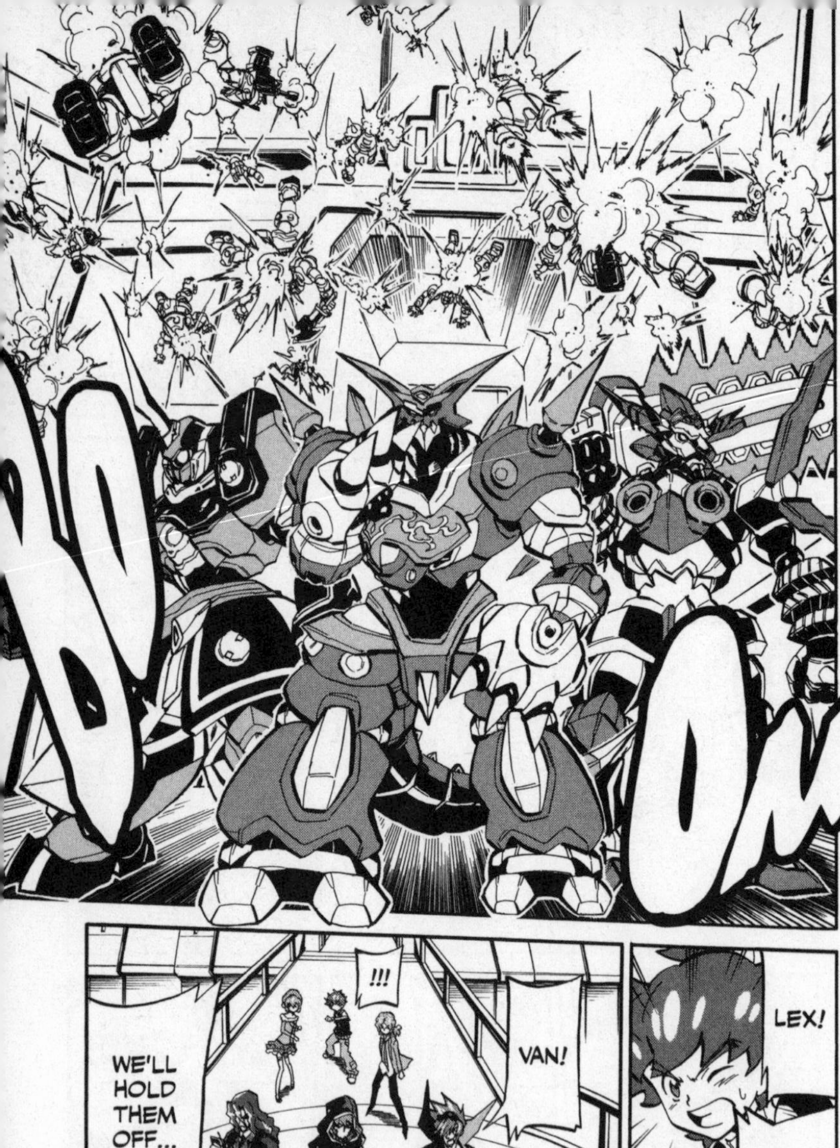
LEX!
HANZ! MR. AERON!
!!!
VAN!
WE'LL HOLD THEM OFF... YOU GO AHEAD!

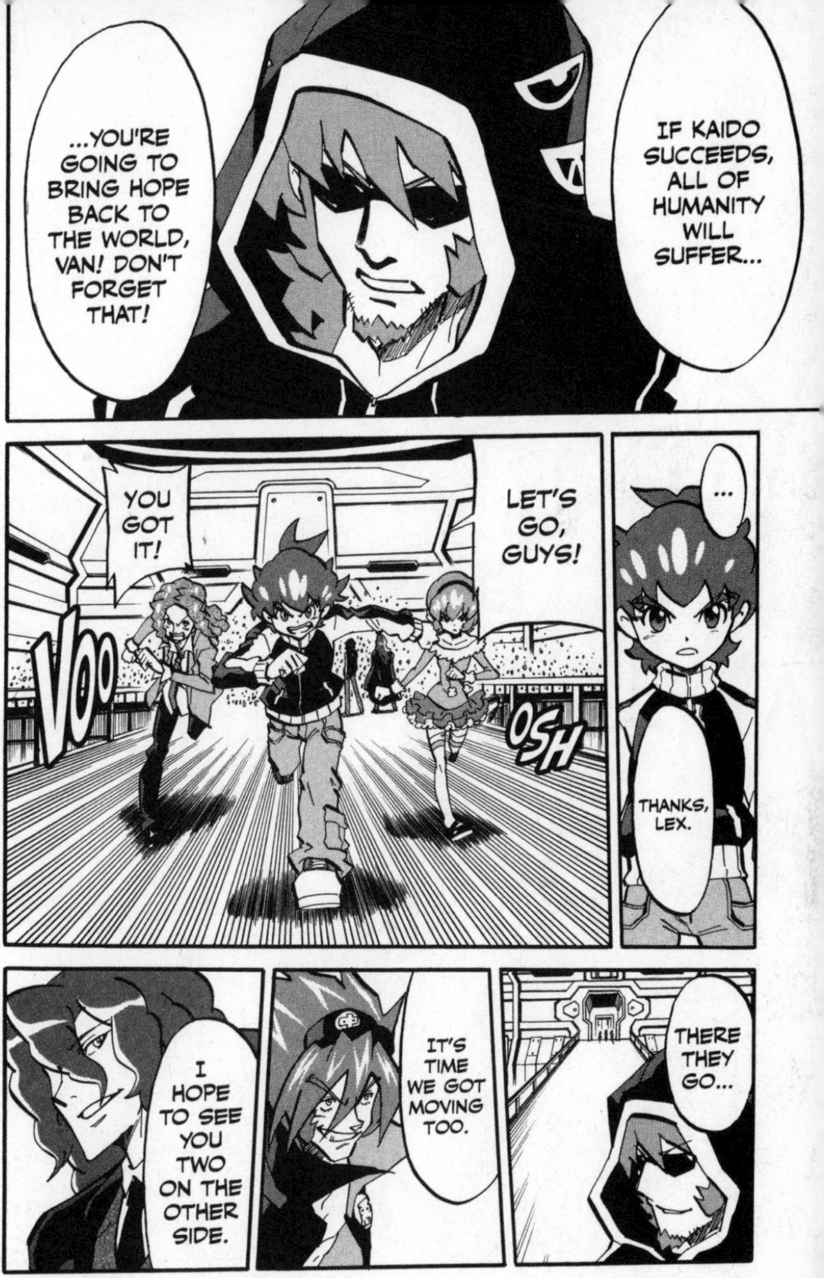
IF KAIDO SUCCEEDS, ALL OF HUMANITY WILL SUFFER...
...YOU'RE GOING TO BRING HOPE BACK TO THE WORLD, VAN! DON'T FORGET THAT!
...
THANKS, LEX.
LET'S GO, GUYS!
YOU GOT IT!
VOO
OSH
THERE THEY GO...
IT'S TIME WE GOT MOVING TOO.
I HOPE TO SEE YOU TWO ON THE OTHER SIDE.

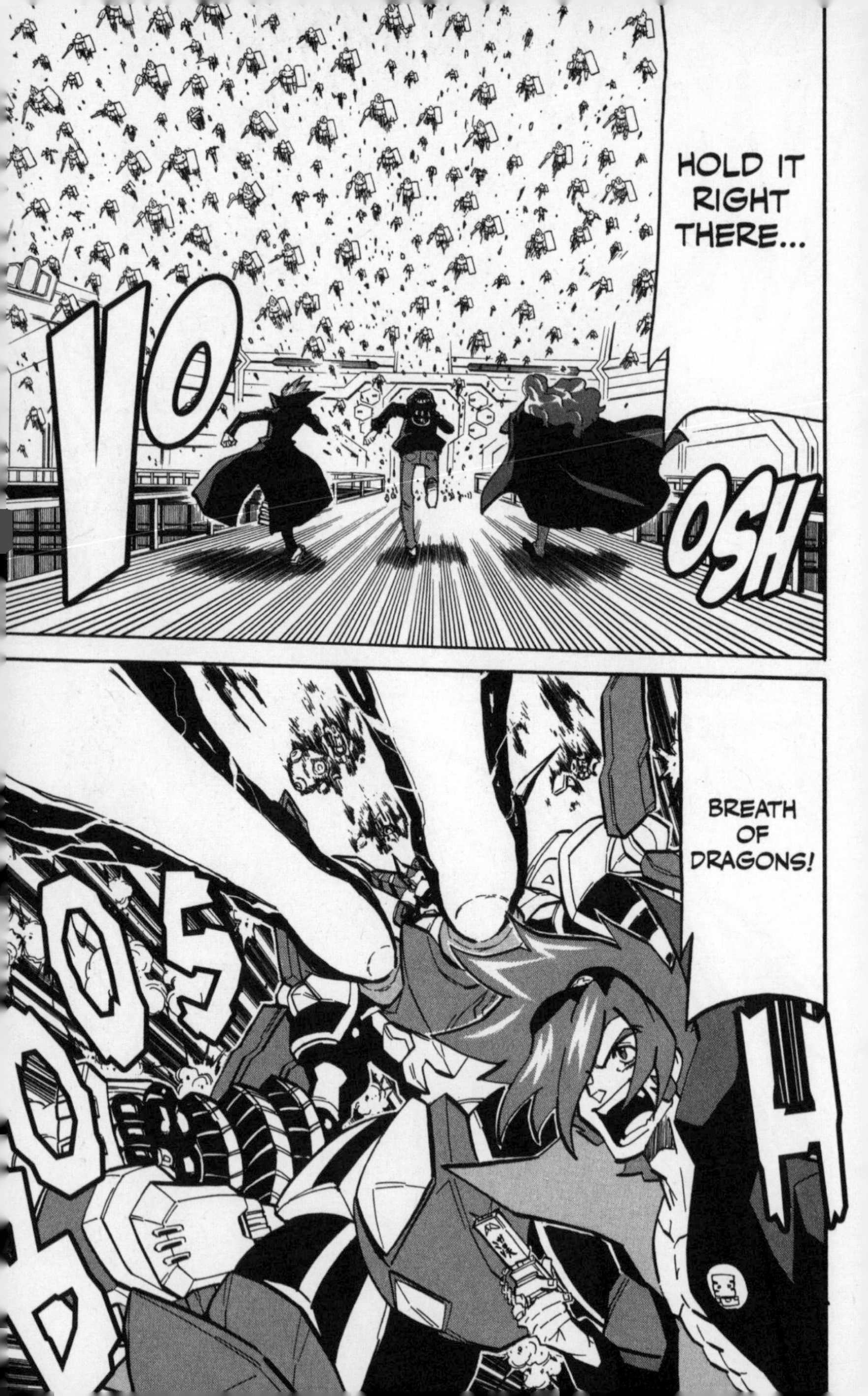
HOLD IT RIGHT THERE...
VO
OSH
BREATH OF DRAGONS!

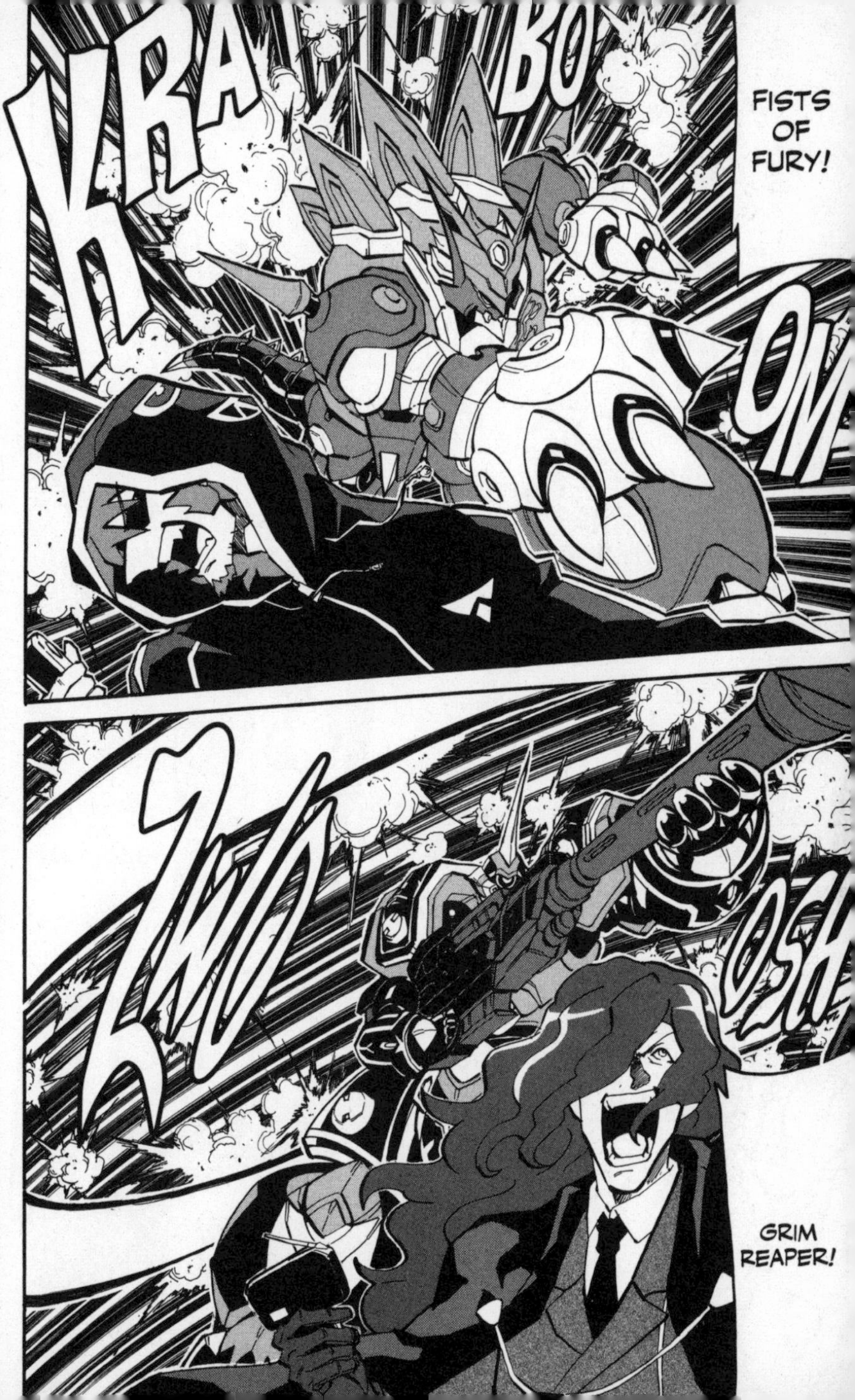
FISTS OF FURY!
KRA
BO
OM
ZWO
OSH
GRIM REAPER!

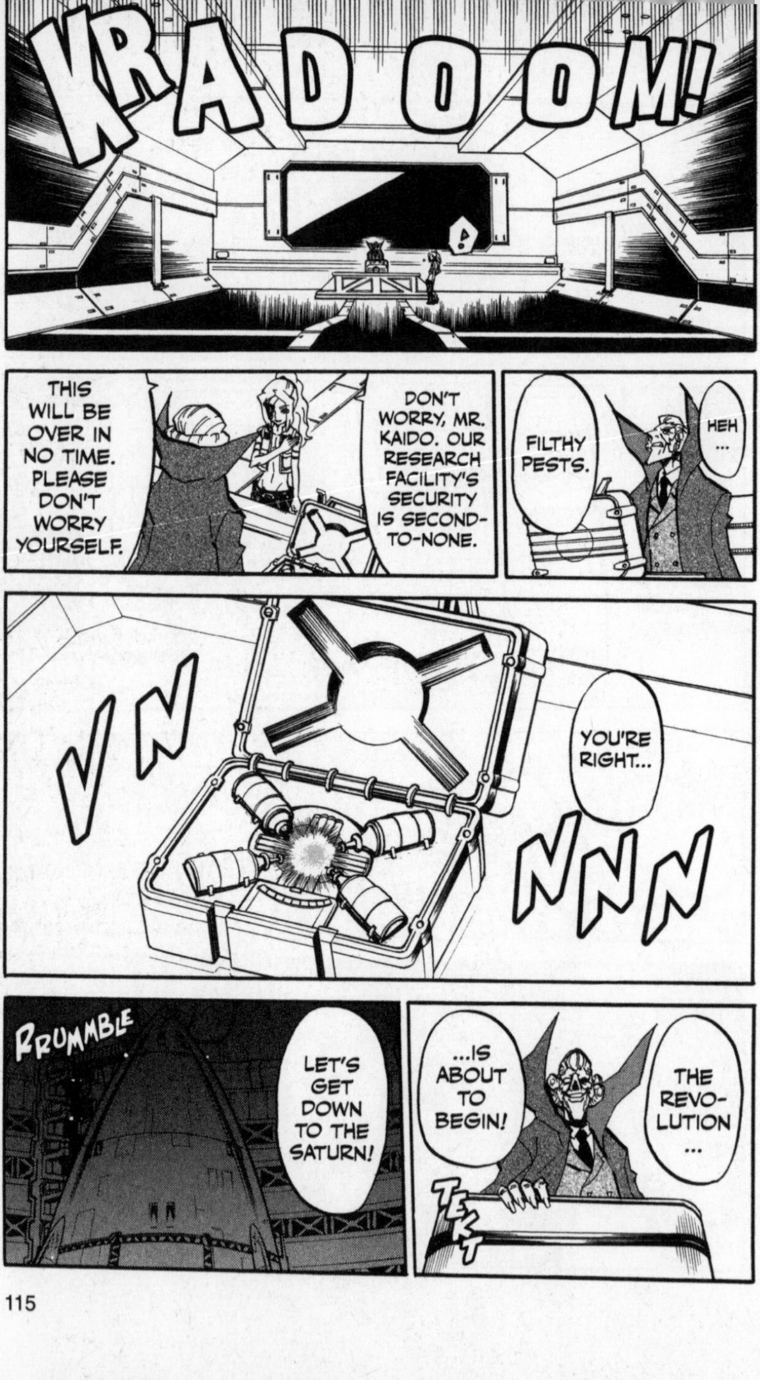
KRADOOM!
HEH...
FILTHY PESTS.
DON'T WORRY, MR. KAIDO. OUR RESEARCH FACILITY'S SECURITY IS SECOND-TO-NONE.
THIS WILL BE OVER IN NO TIME. PLEASE DON'T WORRY YOURSELF.
YOU'RE RIGHT...
VNNNN
THE REVO-LUTION...
...IS ABOUT TO BEGIN!
TEKT
LET'S GET DOWN TO THE SATURN!
RRUMBLE

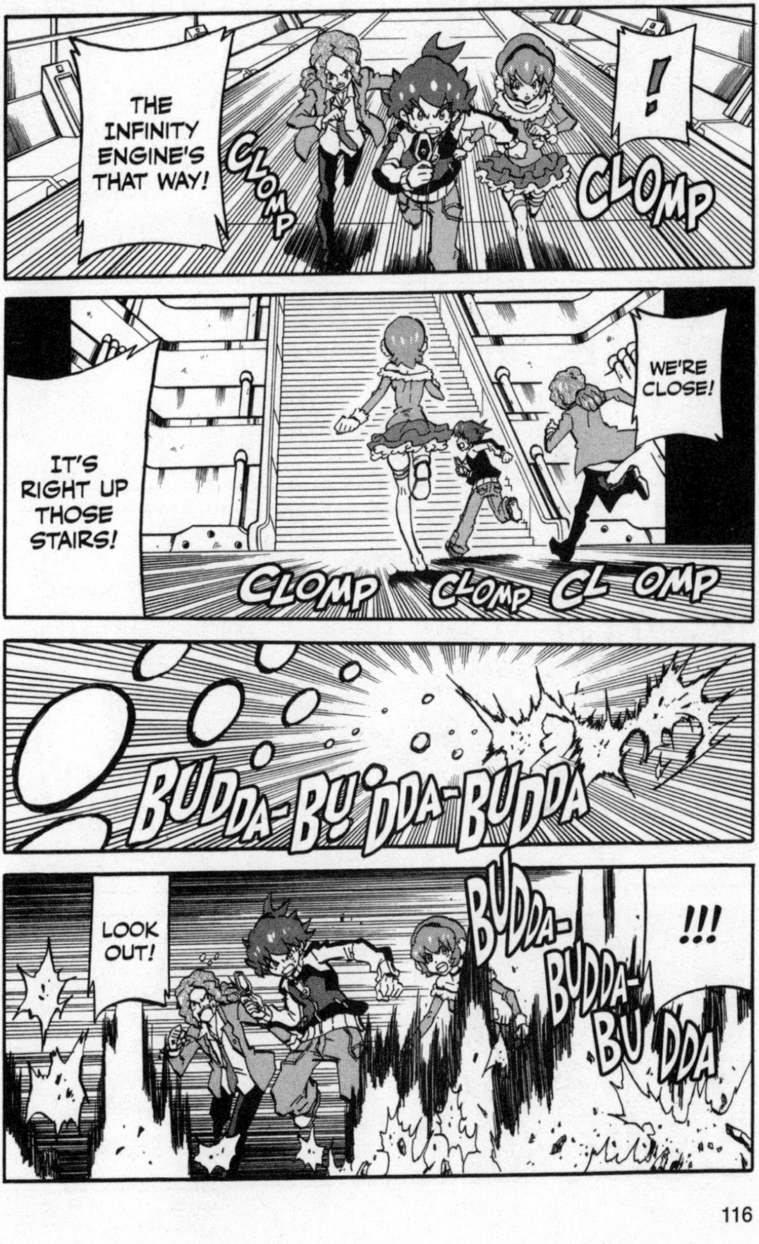
!
CLOMP
CLOMP
THE INFINITY ENGINE'S THAT WAY!
WE'RE CLOSE!
IT'S RIGHT UP THOSE STAIRS!
CLOMP
CLOMP
CLOMP
BUDDA-BUDDA-BUDDA
!!!
BUDDA-BUDDA-BUDDA
LOOK OUT!

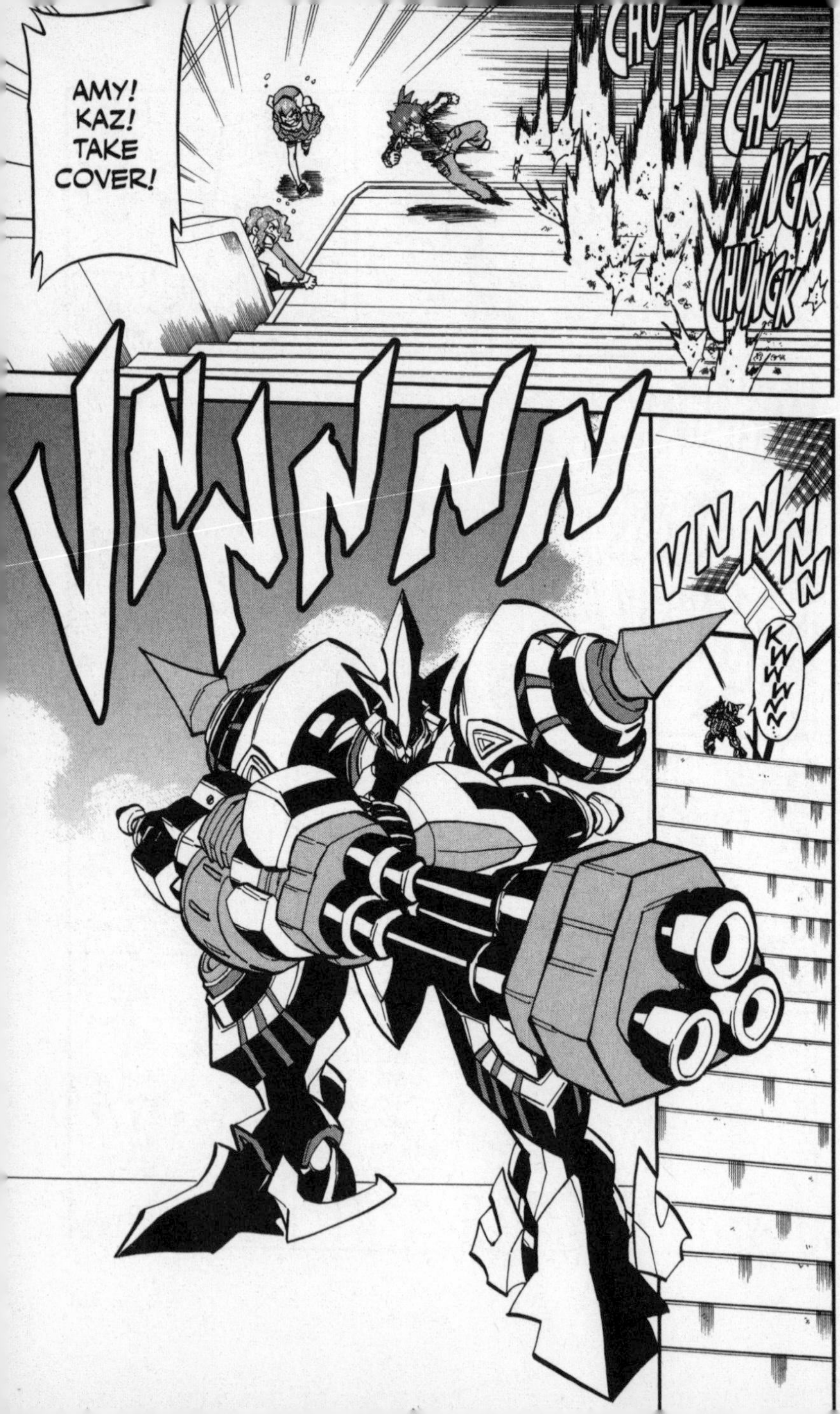
CHUNGK CHUNGK CHUNGK
AMY! KAZ! TAKE COVER!
VNNNN
KWWWN
VNNNNN

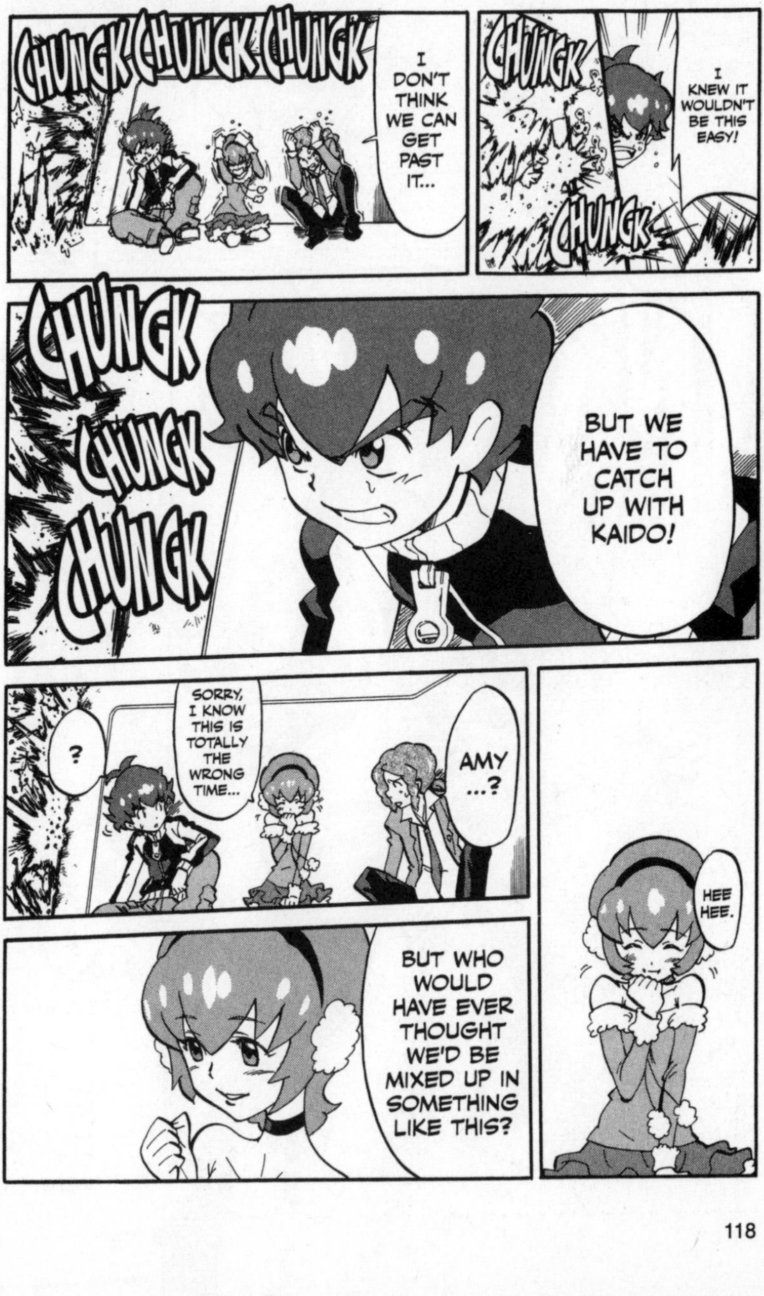
I KNEW IT WOULDN'T BE THIS EASY!
CHUNGK
CHUNGK
I DON'T THINK WE CAN GET PAST IT...
CHUNGK CHUNGK CHUNGK
BUT WE HAVE TO CATCH UP WITH KAIDO!
CHUNGK
CHUNGK
CHUNGK
HEE HEE.
AMY ...?
SORRY, I KNOW THIS IS TOTALLY THE WRONG TIME...
?
BUT WHO WOULD HAVE EVER THOUGHT WE'D BE MIXED UP IN SOMETHING LIKE THIS?

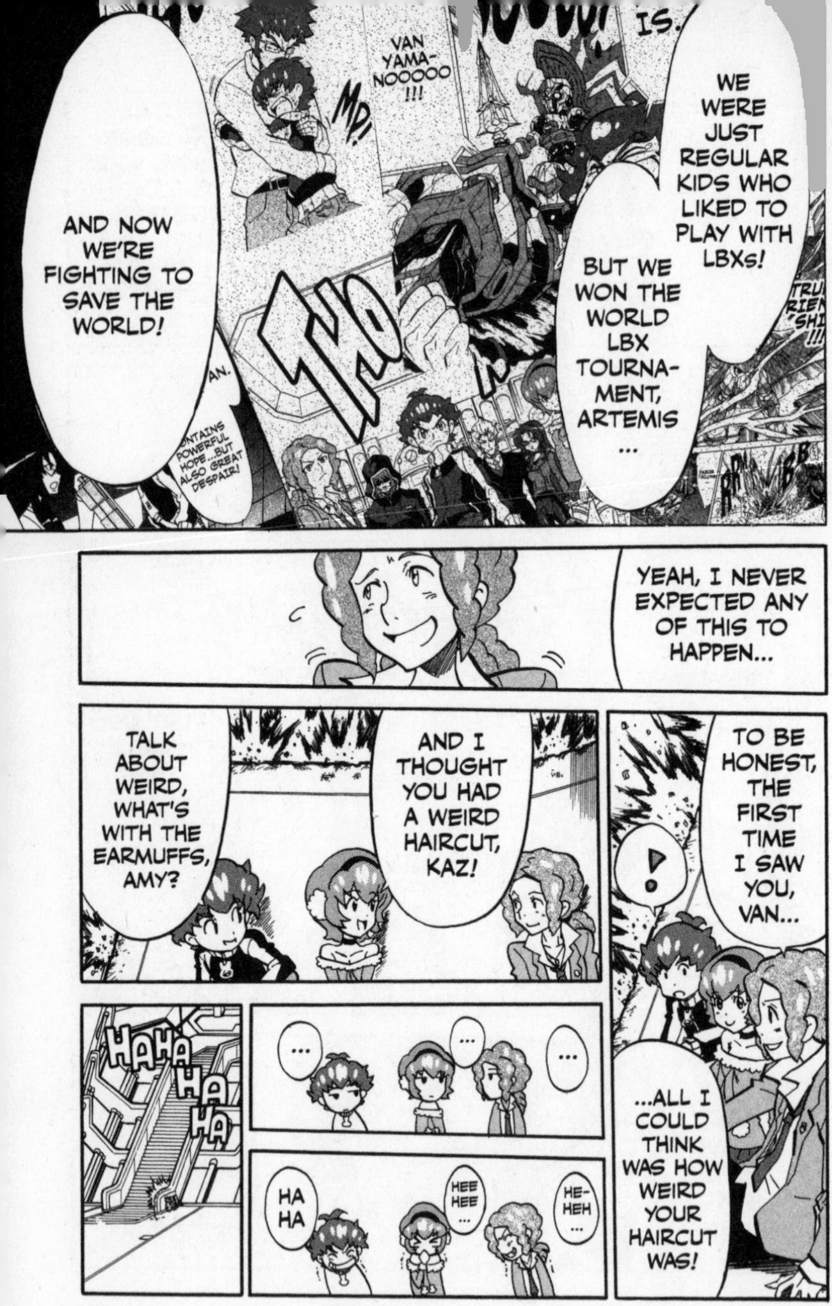
IS.
WE WERE JUST REGULAR KIDS WHO LIKED TO PLAY WITH LBXs!
BUT WE WON THE WORLD LBX TOURNAMENT, ARTEMIS ...
VAN YAMA-NOOOOO !!!
AND NOW WE'RE FIGHTING TO SAVE THE WORLD!
AN.
ONTAINS POWERFUL HOPE...BUT ALSO GREAT DESPAIR!
YEAH, I NEVER EXPECTED ANY OF THIS TO HAPPEN...
TO BE HONEST, THE FIRST TIME I SAW YOU, VAN...
!
...ALL I COULD THINK WAS HOW WEIRD YOUR HAIRCUT WAS!
AND I THOUGHT YOU HAD A WEIRD HAIRCUT, KAZ!
TALK ABOUT WEIRD, WHAT'S WITH THE EARMUFFS, AMY?
...
...
...
HE-HEH ...
HEE HEE ...
HA HA
HAHA HA HA

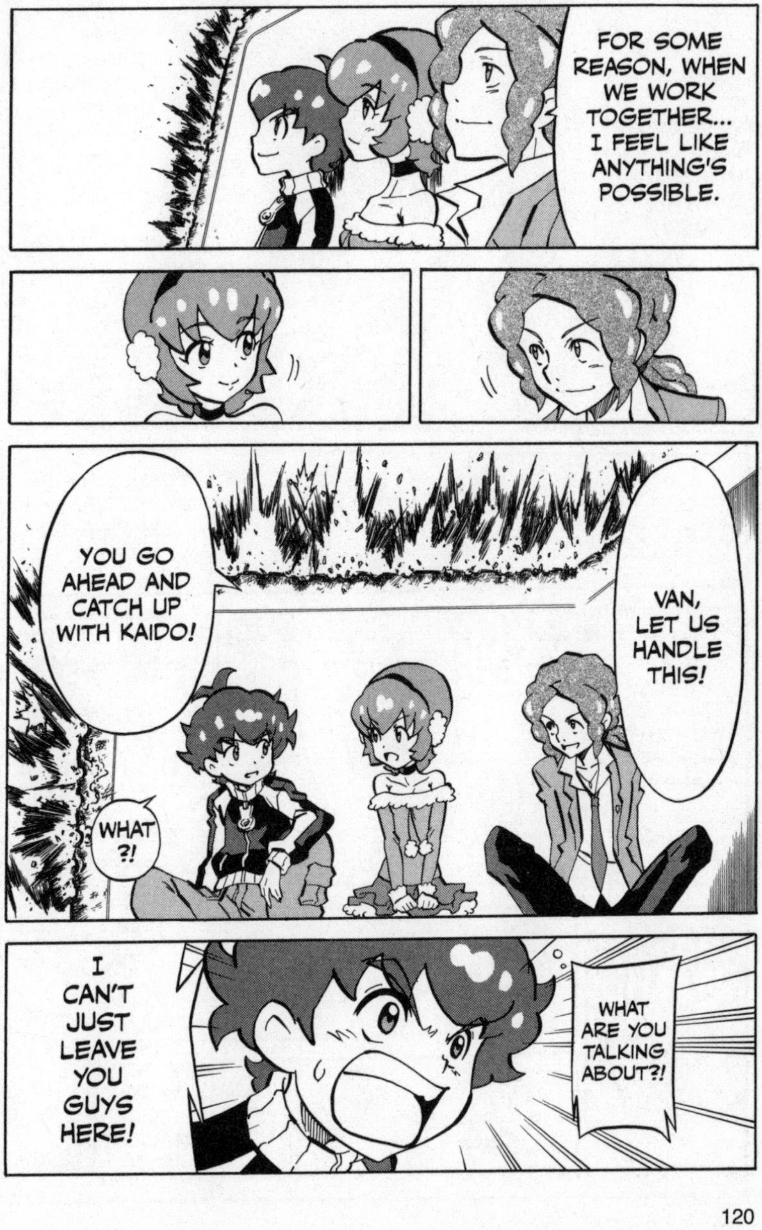
FOR SOME REASON, WHEN WE WORK TOGETHER... I FEEL LIKE ANYTHING'S POSSIBLE.
VAN, LET US HANDLE THIS!
YOU GO AHEAD AND CATCH UP WITH KAIDO!
WHAT?!
WHAT ARE YOU TALKING ABOUT?!
I CAN'T JUST LEAVE YOU GUYS HERE!

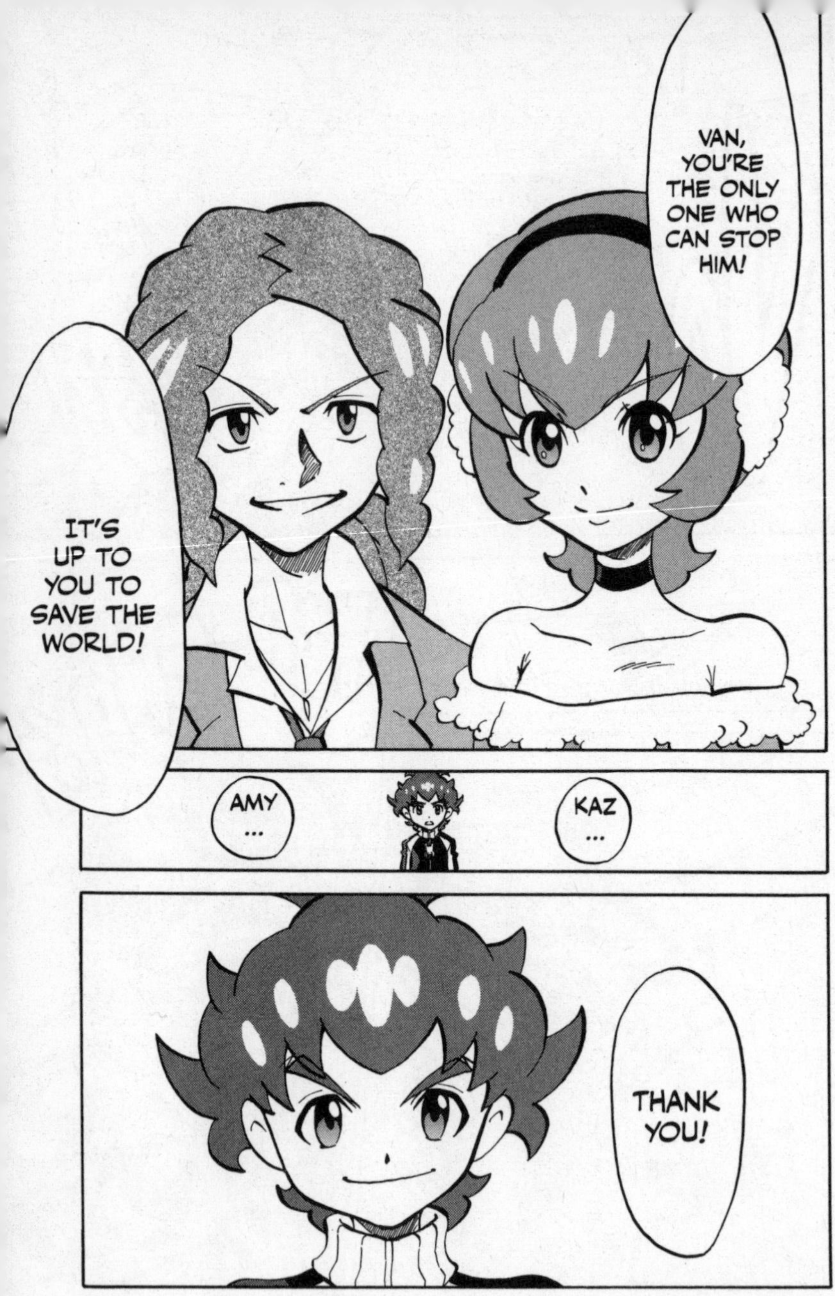
VAN, YOU'RE THE ONLY ONE WHO CAN STOP HIM!
IT'S UP TO YOU TO SAVE THE WORLD!
KAZ ...
AMY ...
THANK YOU!

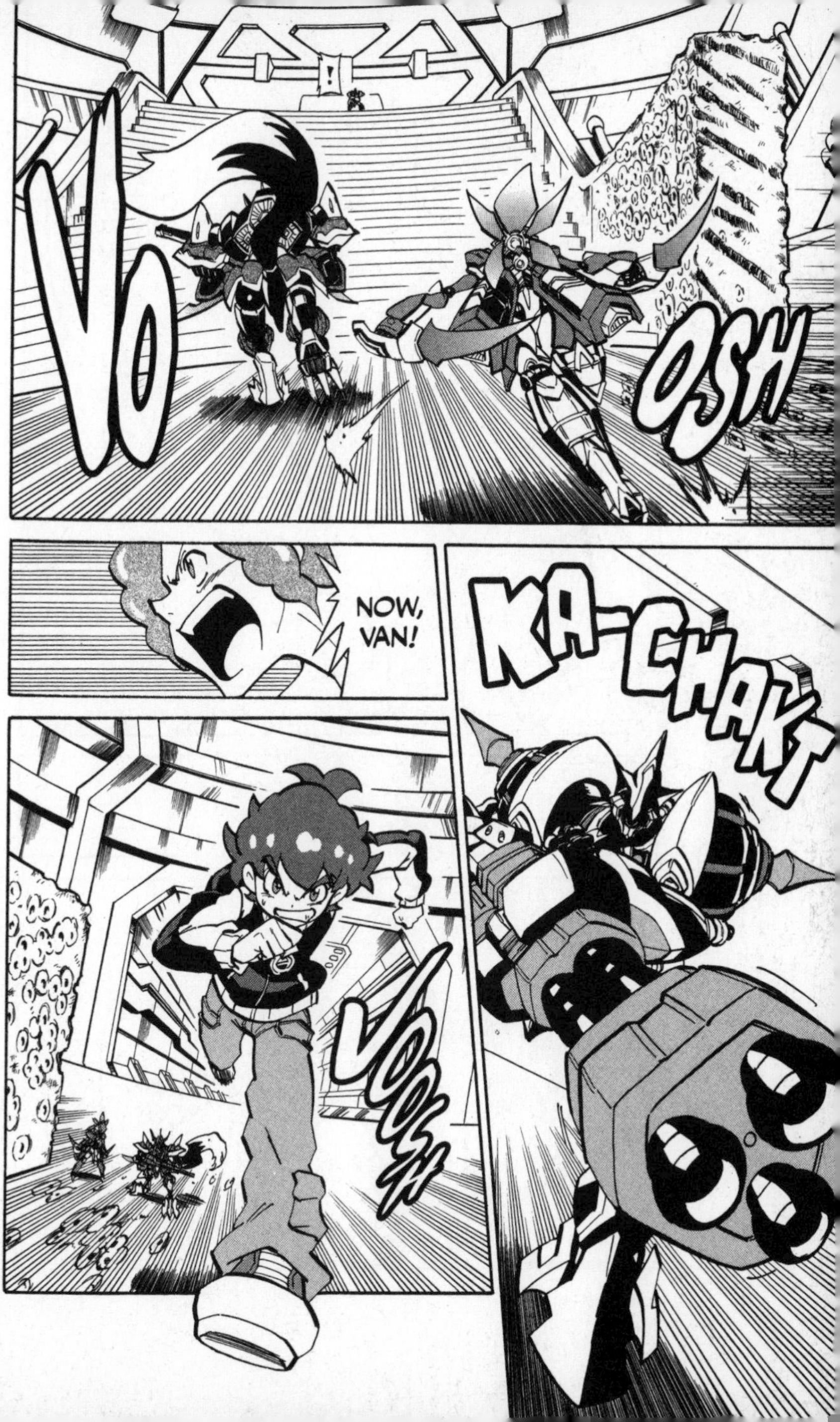
VO
OSH
KA-CHAKT
NOW, VAN!
VOOOM

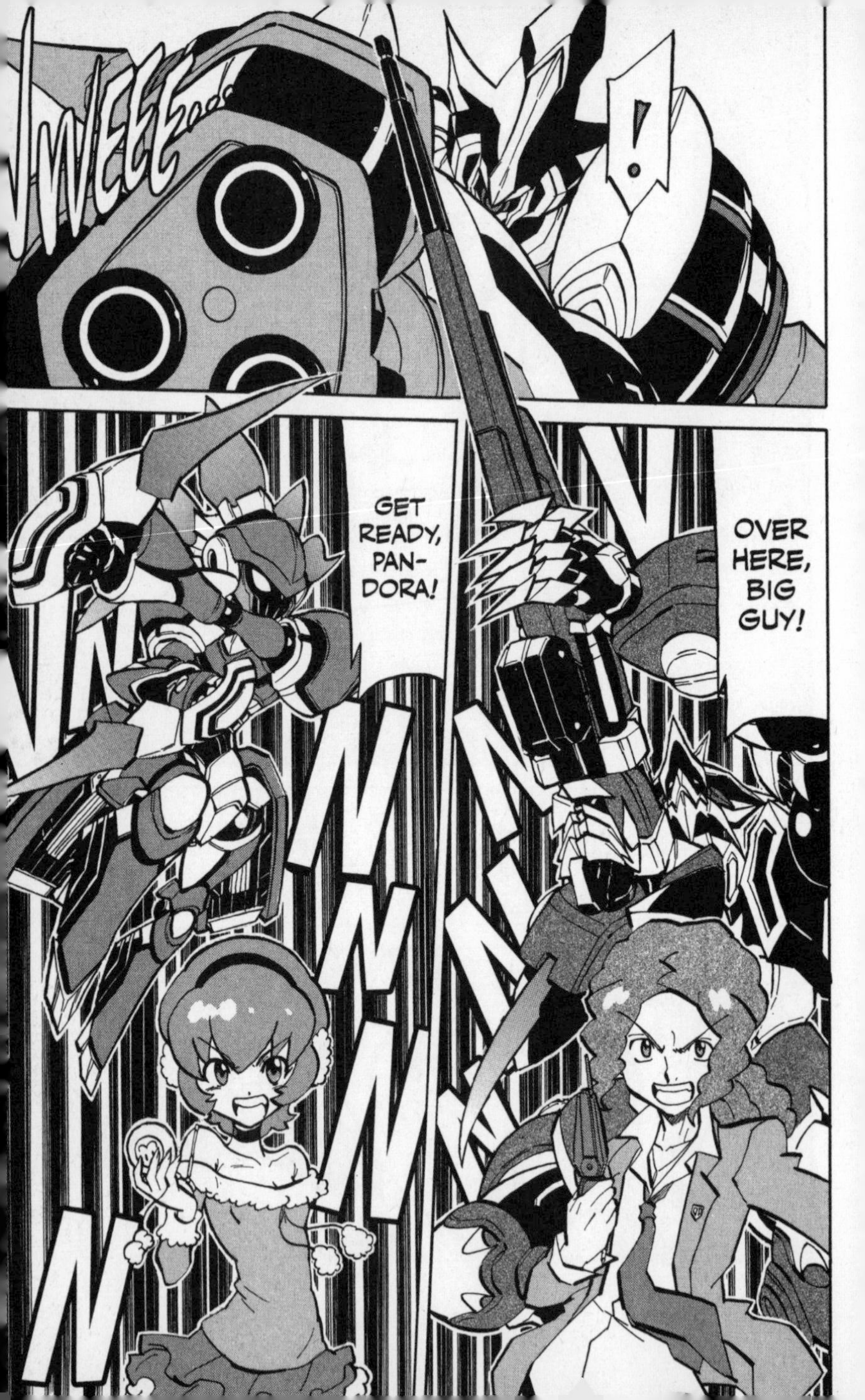
!
VWEEE...
OVER HERE, BIG GUY!
GET READY, PAN-DORA!

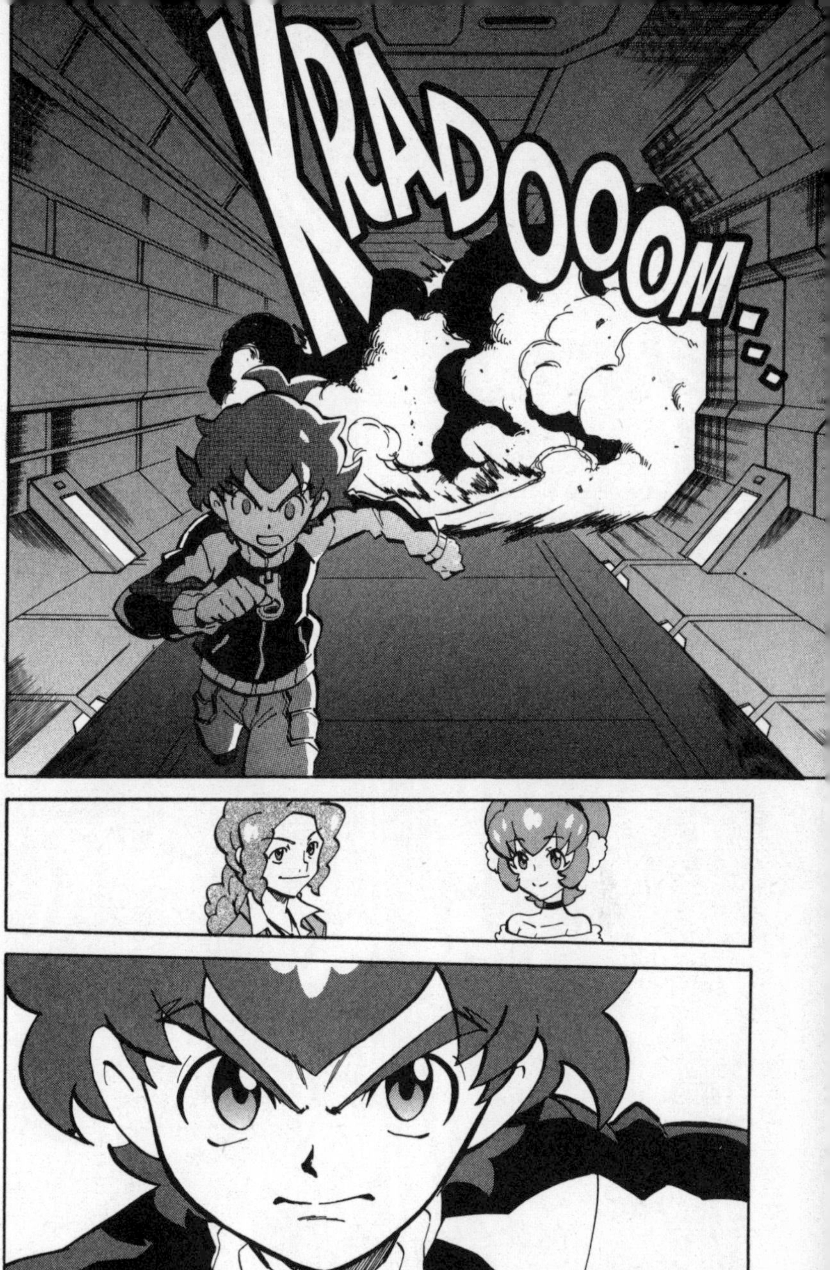
KRADOOOM...

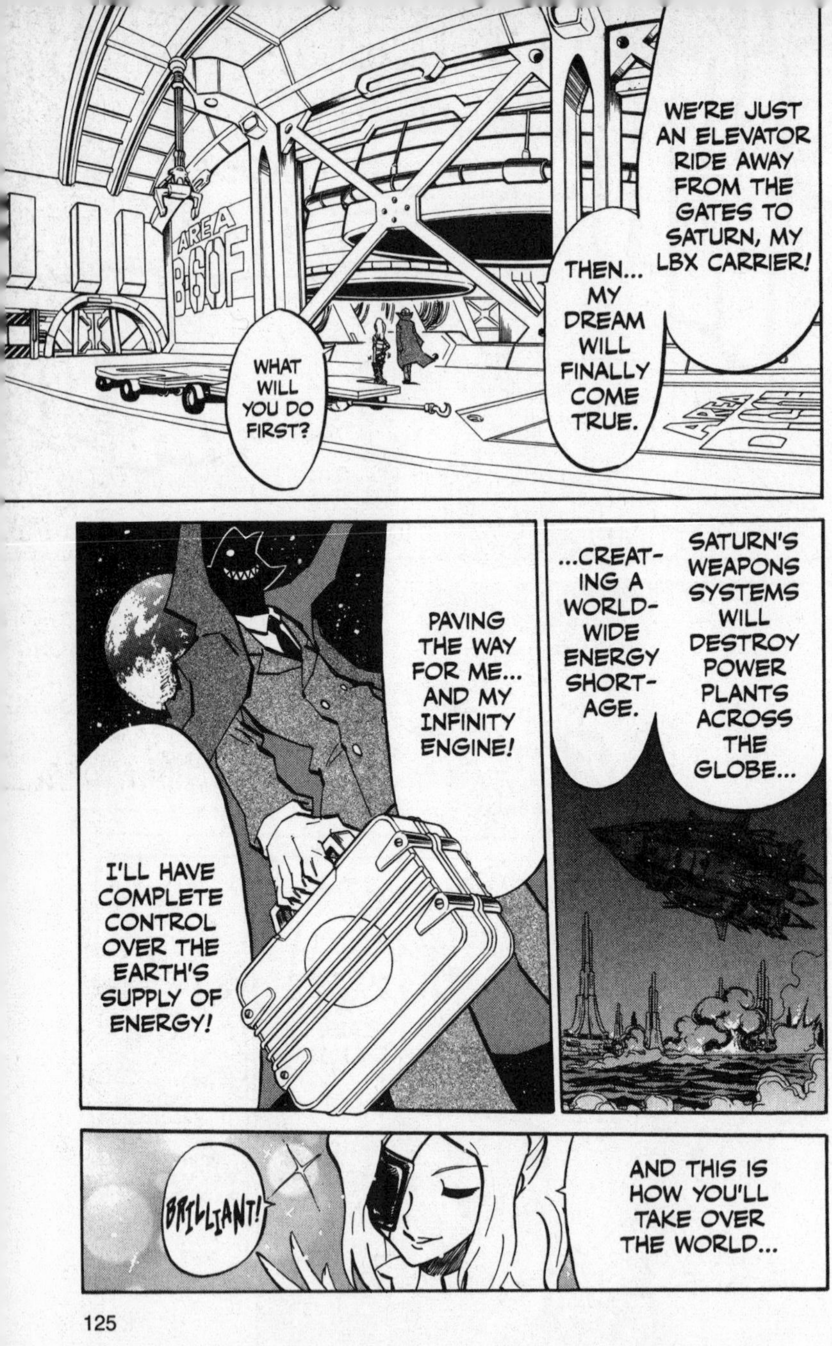
WE'RE JUST AN ELEVATOR RIDE AWAY FROM THE GATES TO SATURN, MY LBX CARRIER!
THEN... MY DREAM WILL FINALLY COME TRUE.
WHAT WILL YOU DO FIRST?
SATURN'S WEAPONS SYSTEMS WILL DESTROY POWER PLANTS ACROSS THE GLOBE...
...CREATING A WORLD-WIDE ENERGY SHORTAGE.
PAVING THE WAY FOR ME... AND MY INFINITY ENGINE!
I'LL HAVE COMPLETE CONTROL OVER THE EARTH'S SUPPLY OF ENERGY!
AND THIS IS HOW YOU'LL TAKE OVER THE WORLD...
BRILLIANT!

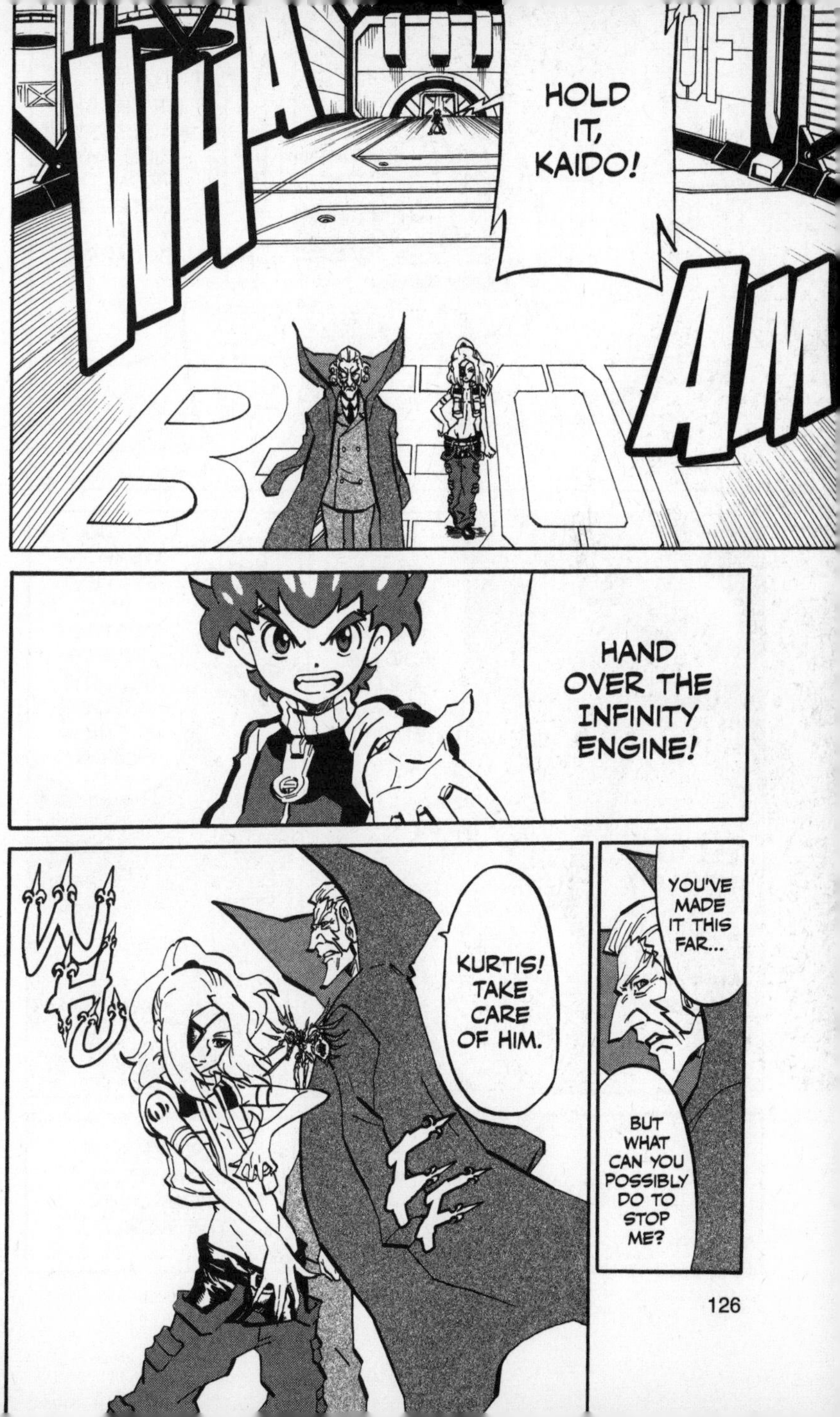
HOLD IT, KAIDO!
HAND OVER THE INFINITY ENGINE!
YOU'VE MADE IT THIS FAR...
BUT WHAT CAN YOU POSSIBLY DO TO STOP ME?
KURTIS! TAKE CARE OF HIM.

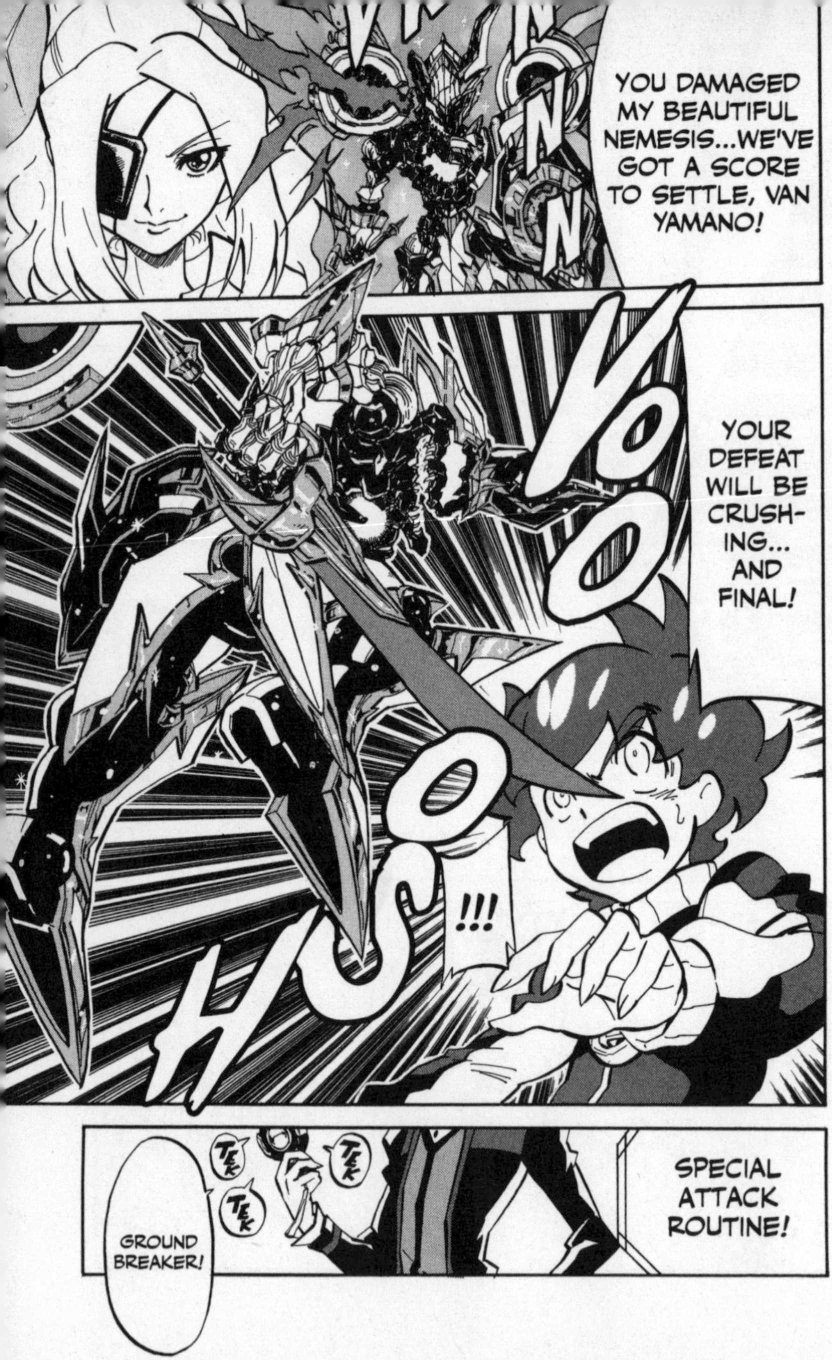
YOU DAMAGED MY BEAUTIFUL NEMESIS...WE'VE GOT A SCORE TO SETTLE, VAN YAMANO!
YOUR DEFEAT WILL BE CRUSH-ING... AND FINAL!
!!!
SPECIAL ATTACK ROUTINE!
TEK
TEK
TEK
GROUND BREAKER!

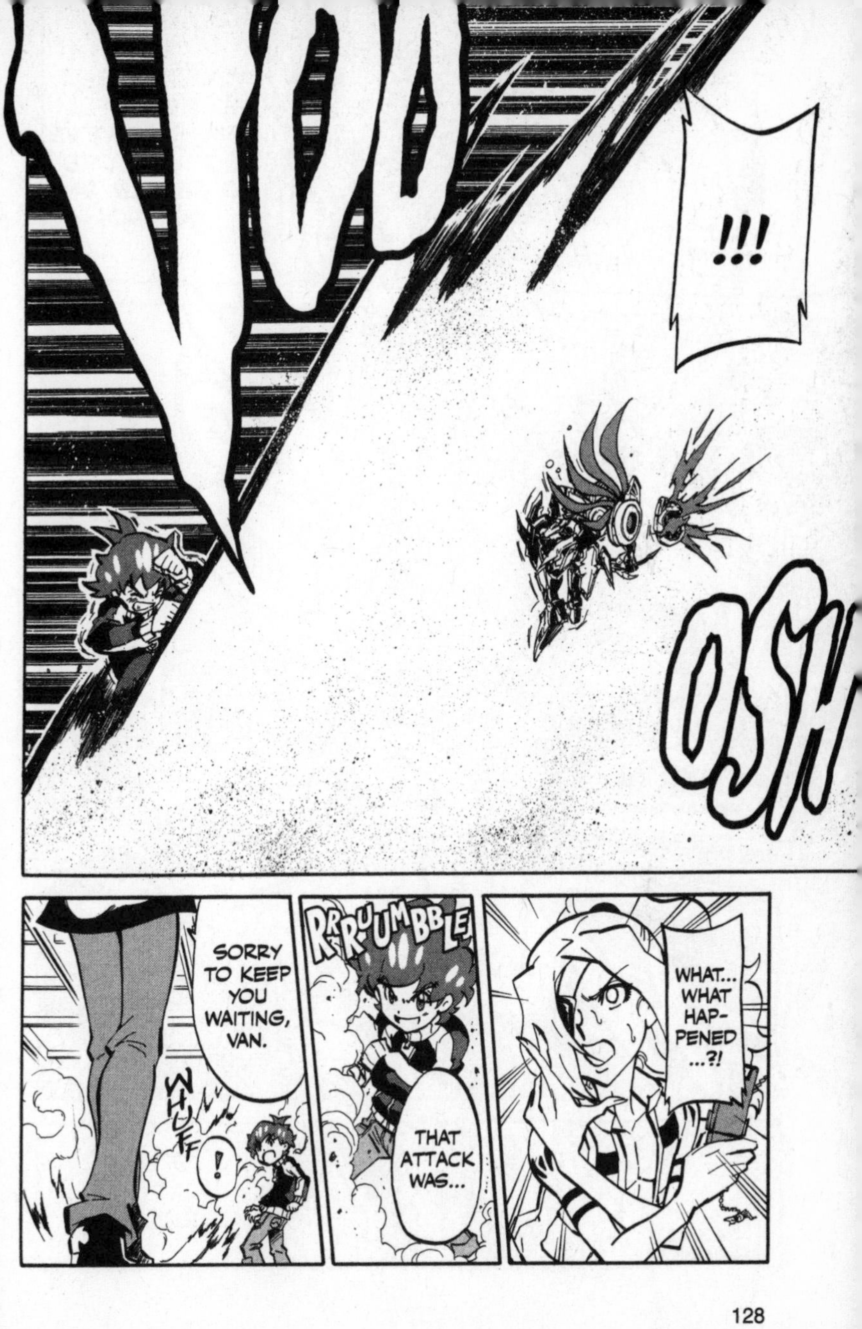
!!!
OSH
WHAT... WHAT HAP-PENED ...?!
RRRUUMBBLE
THAT ATTACK WAS...
SORRY TO KEEP YOU WAITING, VAN.
WHUFF
!

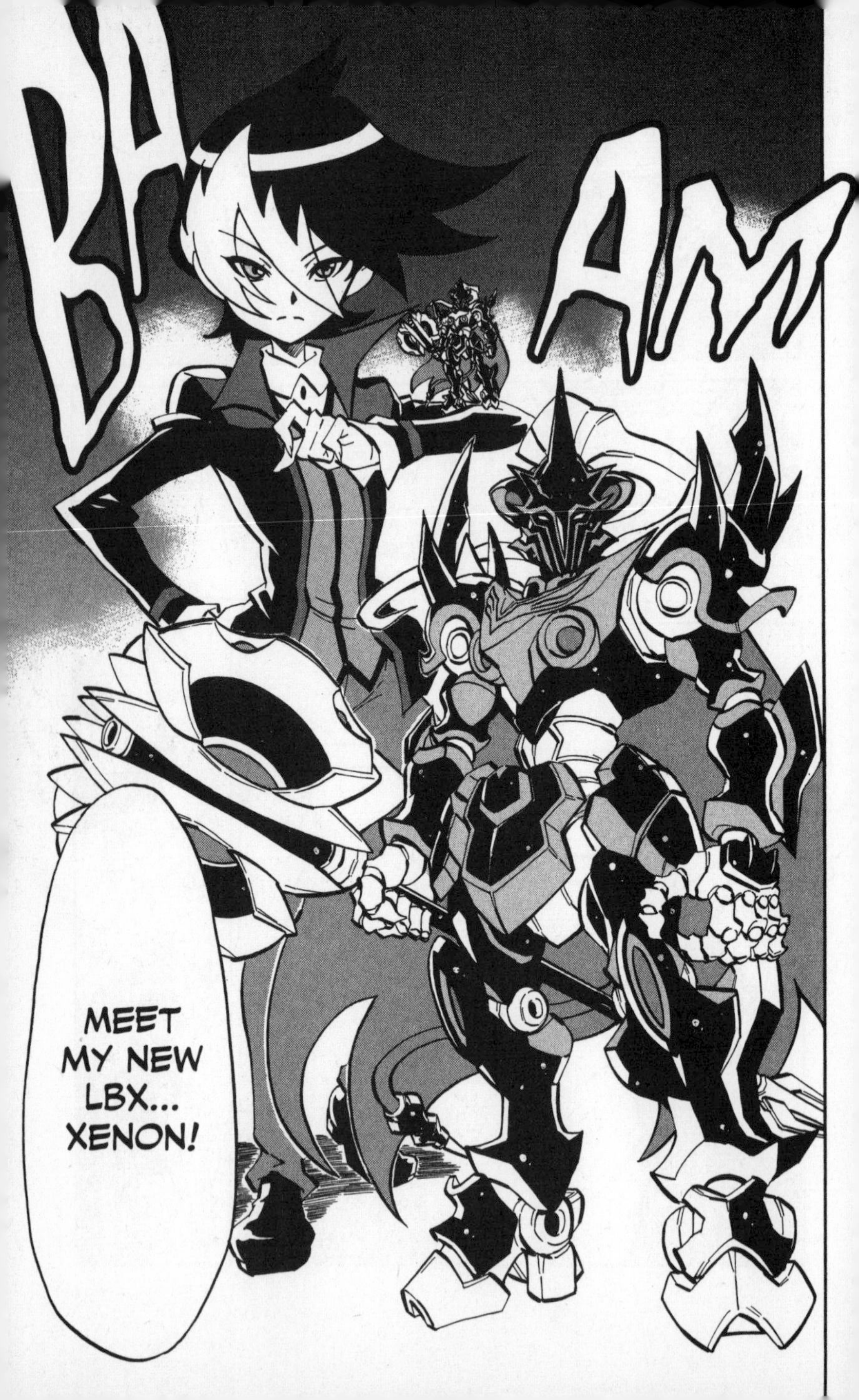
BAAM
MEET MY NEW LBX... XENON!

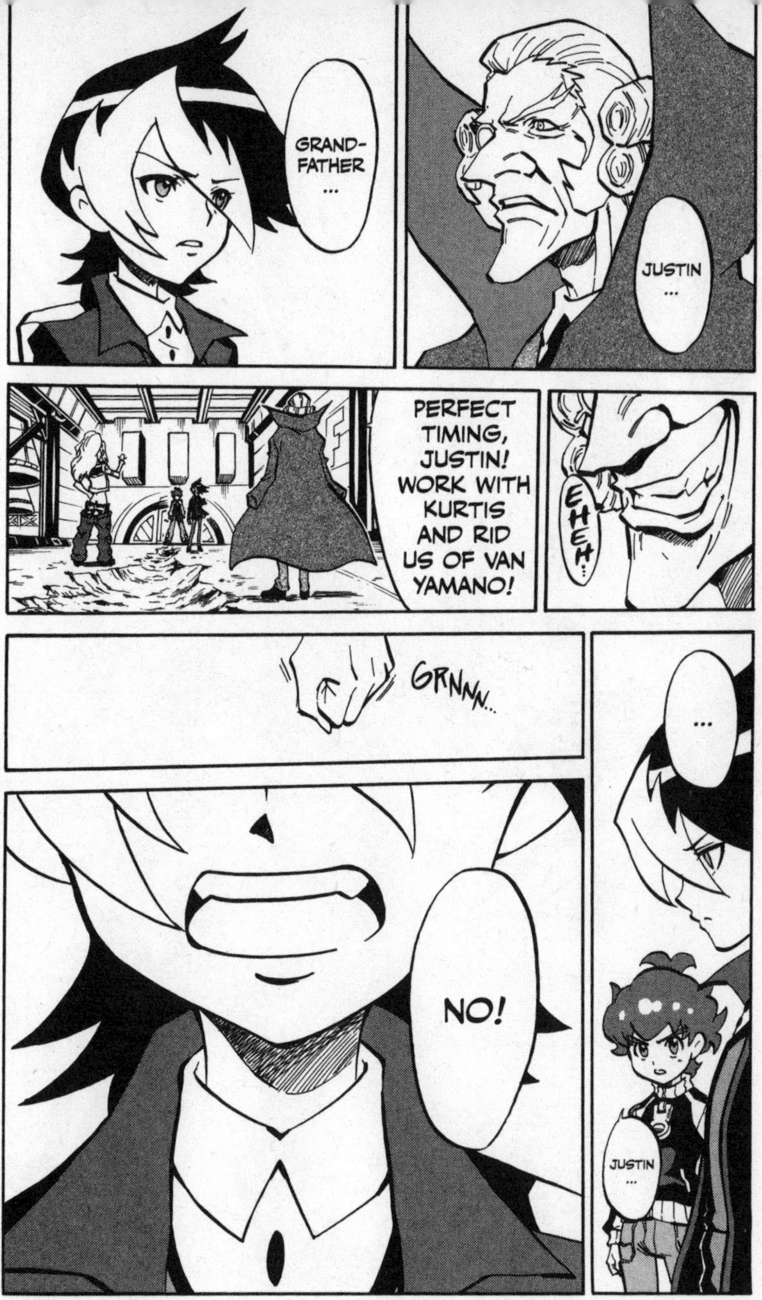
JUSTIN ...
GRAND-FATHER ...
EHEH...
PERFECT TIMING, JUSTIN! WORK WITH KURTIS AND RID US OF VAN YAMANO!
...
JUSTIN ...
GRNNN...
NO!

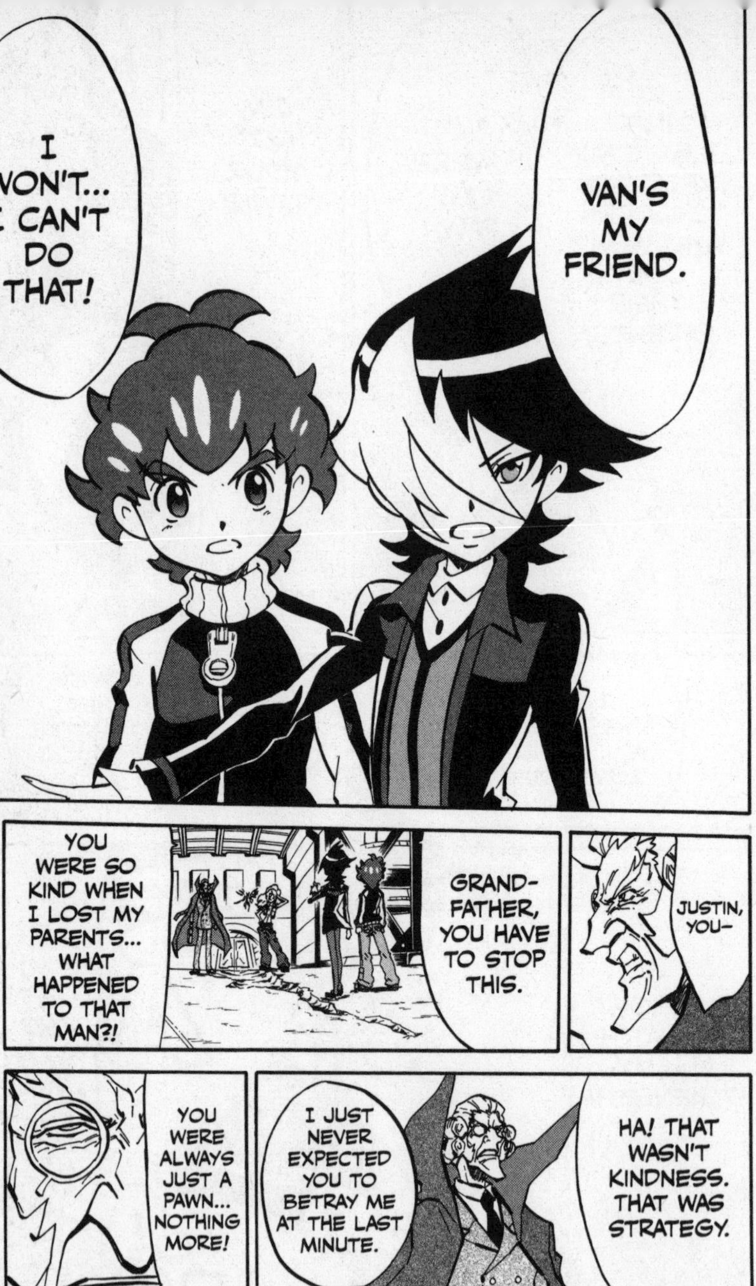
VAN'S MY FRIEND.
I WON'T... I CAN'T DO THAT!
JUSTIN, YOU-
GRAND-FATHER, YOU HAVE TO STOP THIS.
YOU WERE SO KIND WHEN I LOST MY PARENTS... WHAT HAPPENED TO THAT MAN?!
HA! THAT WASN'T KINDNESS. THAT WAS STRATEGY.
I JUST NEVER EXPECTED YOU TO BETRAY ME AT THE LAST MINUTE.
YOU WERE ALWAYS JUST A PAWN... NOTHING MORE!

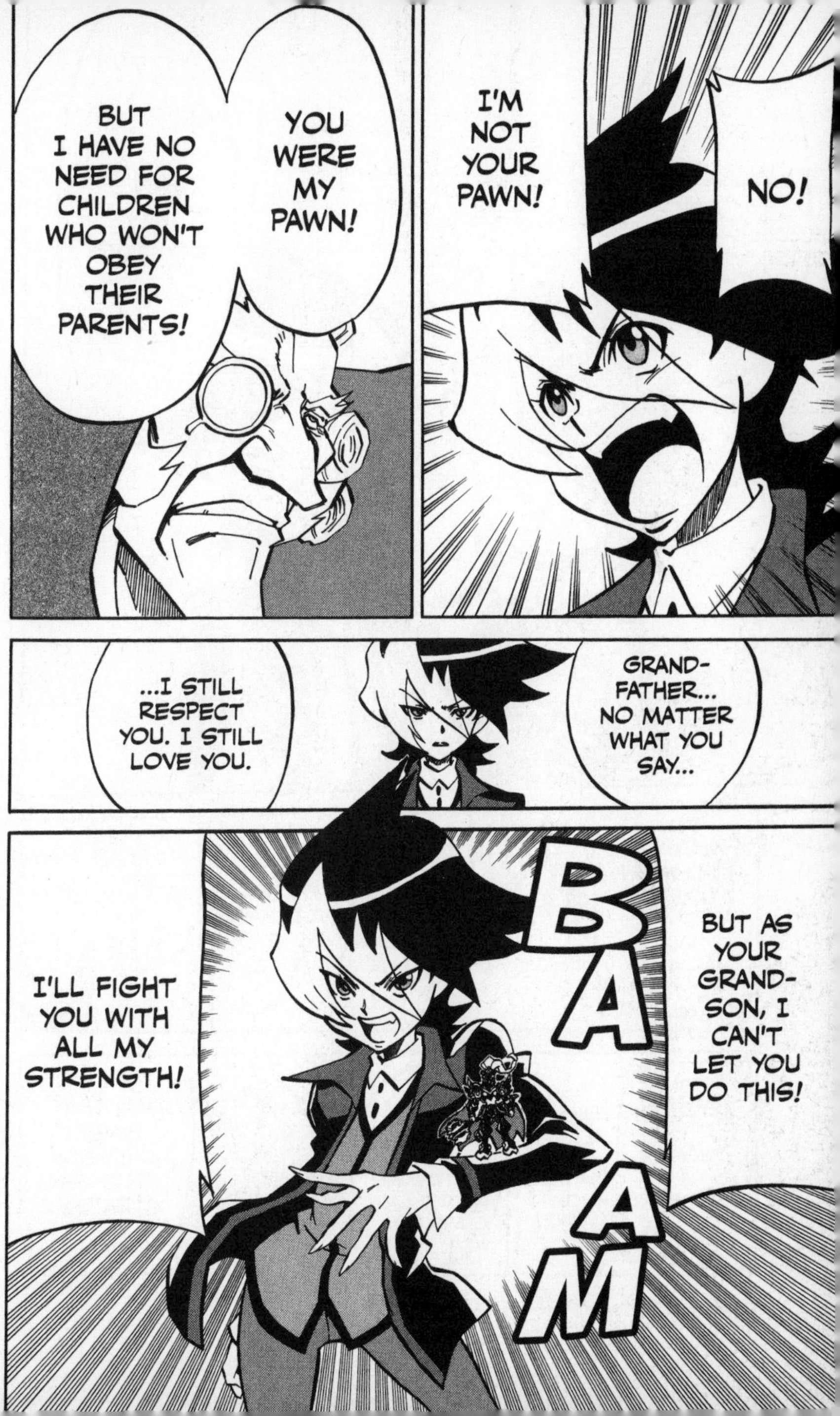
NO!
I'M NOT YOUR PAWN!
YOU WERE MY PAWN!
BUT I HAVE NO NEED FOR CHILDREN WHO WON'T OBEY THEIR PARENTS!
GRAND-FATHER... NO MATTER WHAT YOU SAY...
...I STILL RESPECT YOU. I STILL LOVE YOU.
BUT AS YOUR GRAND-SON, I CAN'T LET YOU DO THIS!
BAAM
I'LL FIGHT YOU WITH ALL MY STRENGTH!

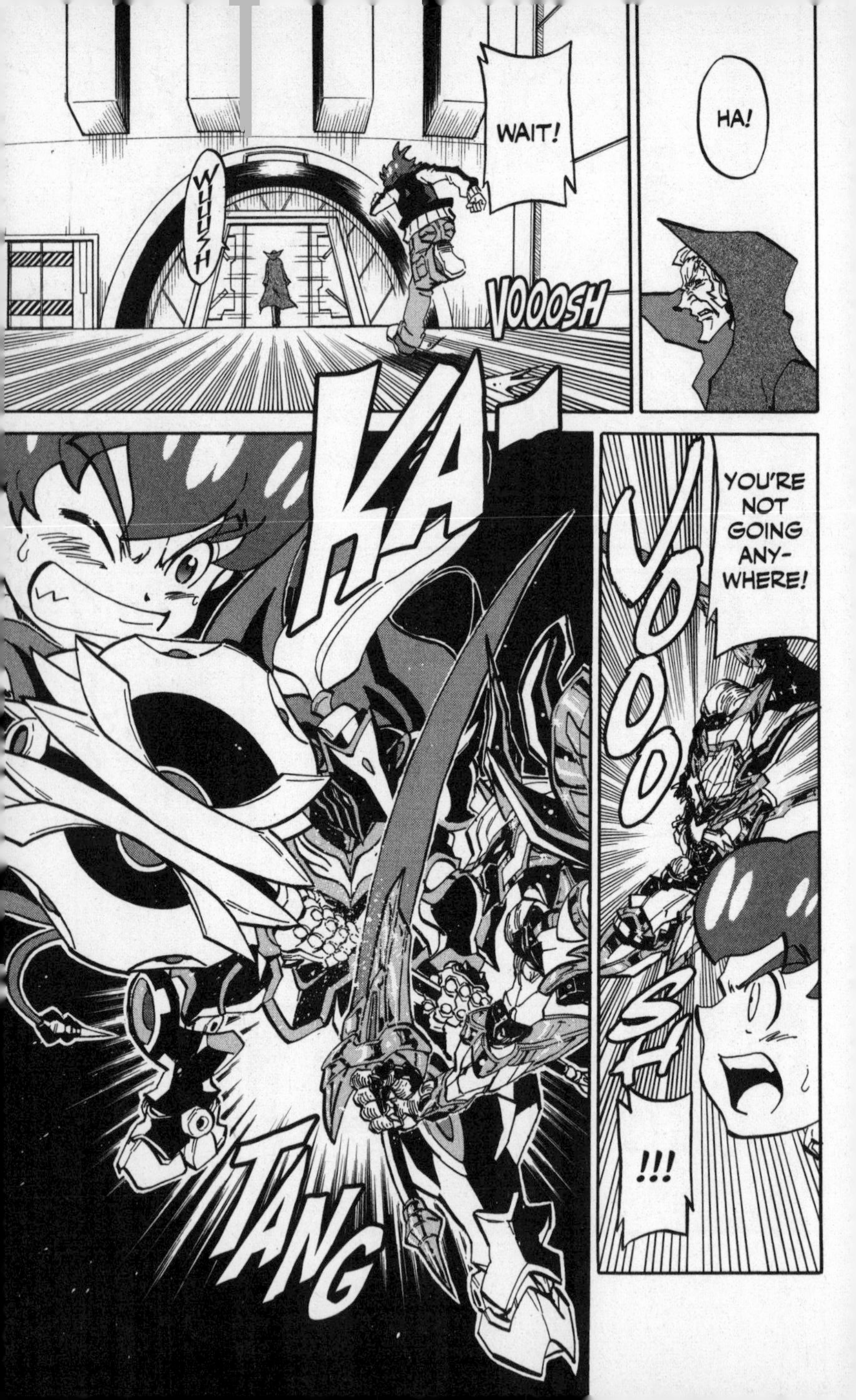
HA!
WAIT!
WUUUSH
VOOOSH
YOU'RE NOT GOING ANY-WHERE!
VOOOOSH
!!!
KA-
TANG

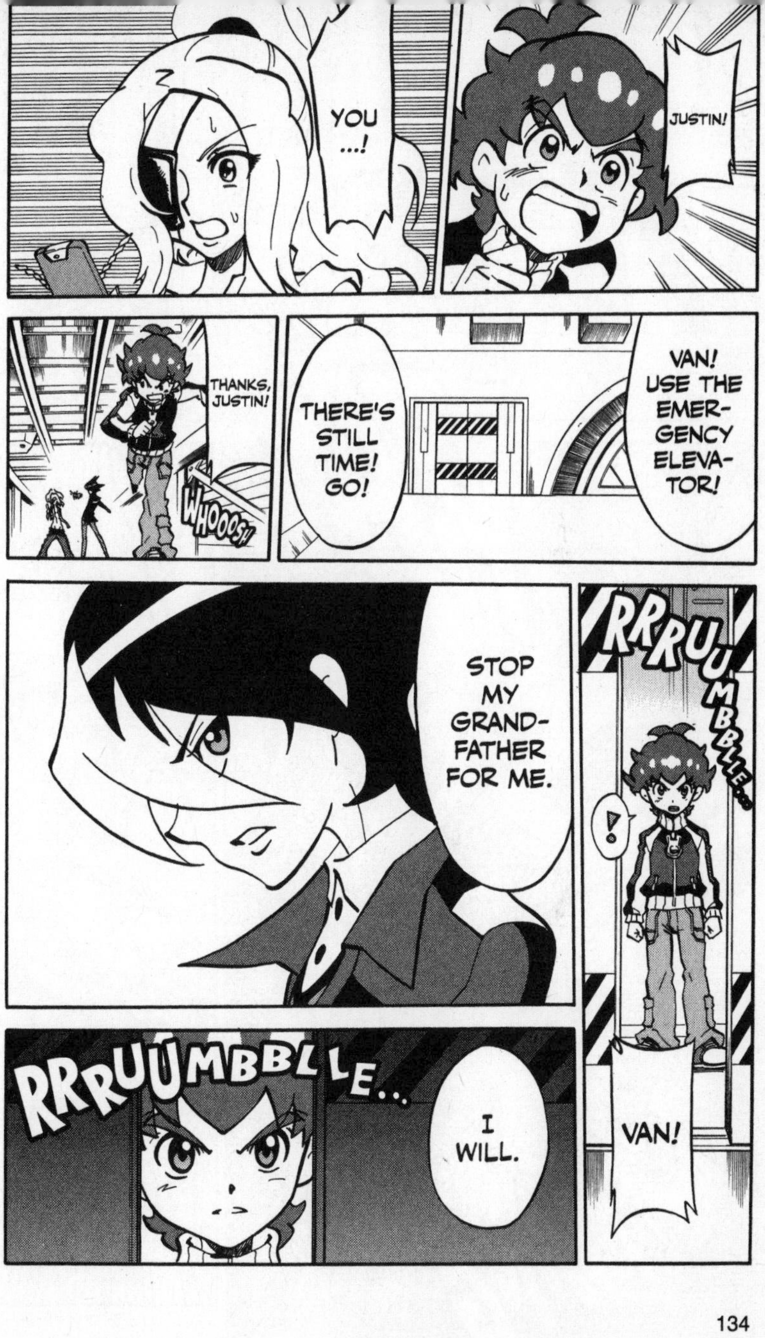
JUSTIN!
YOU ...!
VAN! USE THE EMERGENCY ELEVATOR!
THERE'S STILL TIME! GO!
THANKS, JUSTIN!
WHOOOSH
RRRUUMBBLE...
!
VAN!
STOP MY GRANDFATHER FOR ME.
RRRUUMBBLLE...
I WILL.

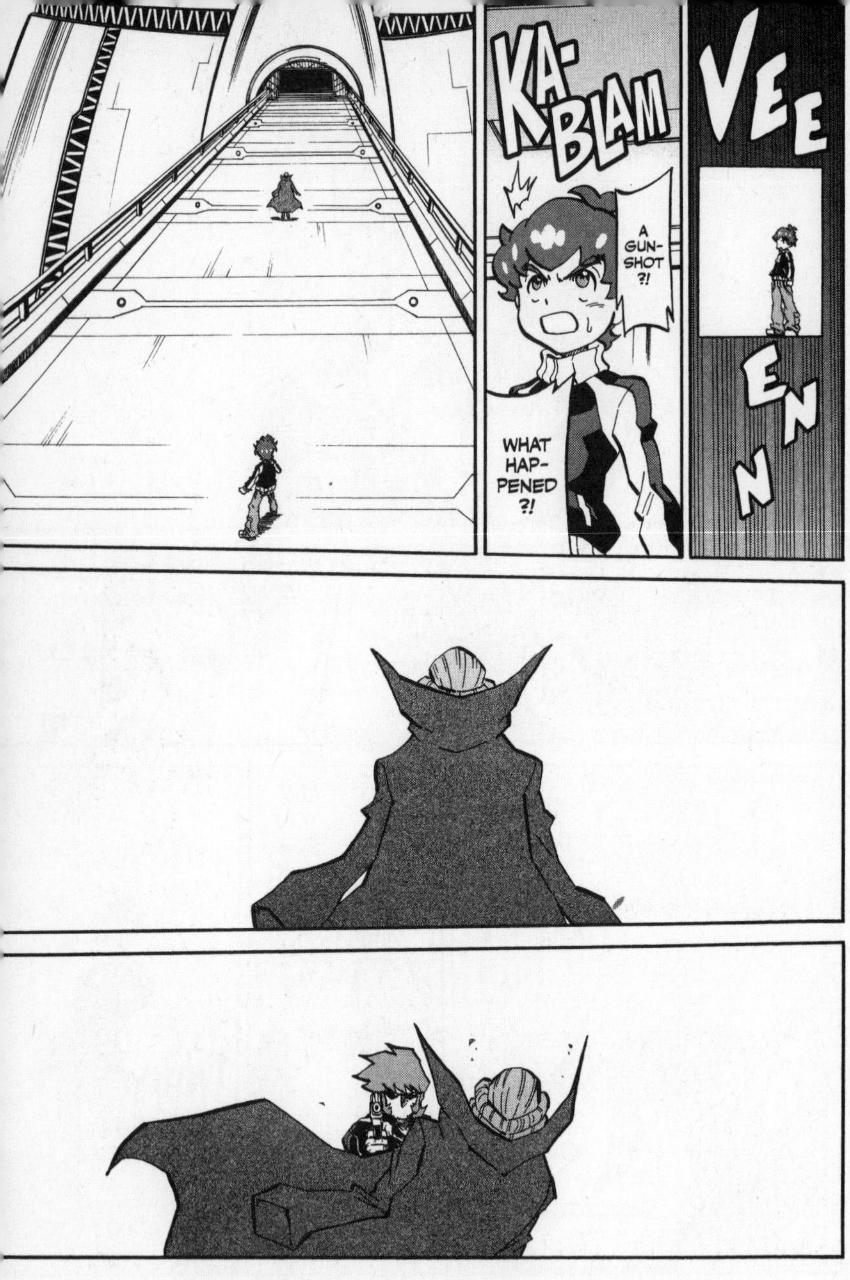
VEE
ENN
KA-BLAM
A GUN-SHOT ?!
WHAT HAP-PENED ?!

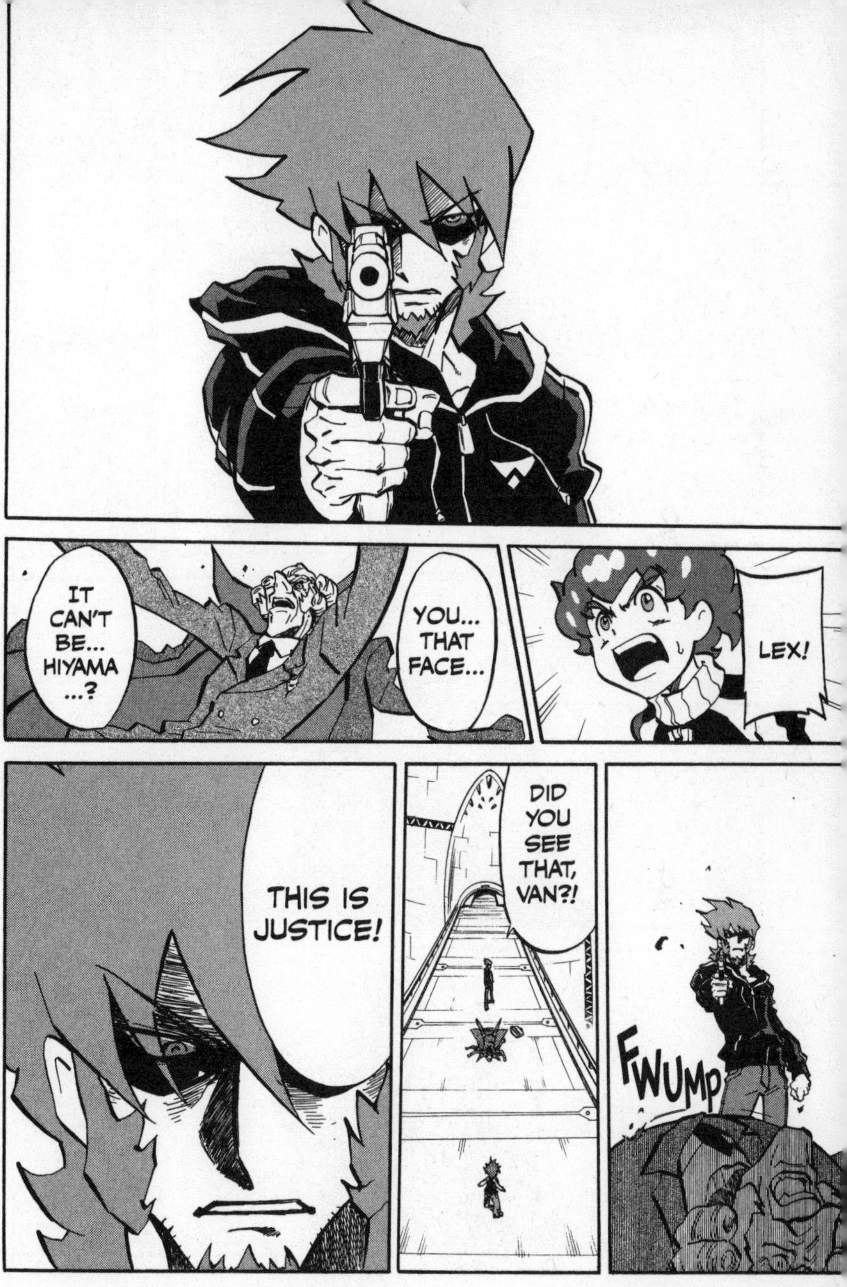
LEX!
YOU... THAT FACE...
IT CAN'T BE... HIYAMA ...?
FWUMP
DID YOU SEE THAT, VAN?!
THIS IS JUSTICE!

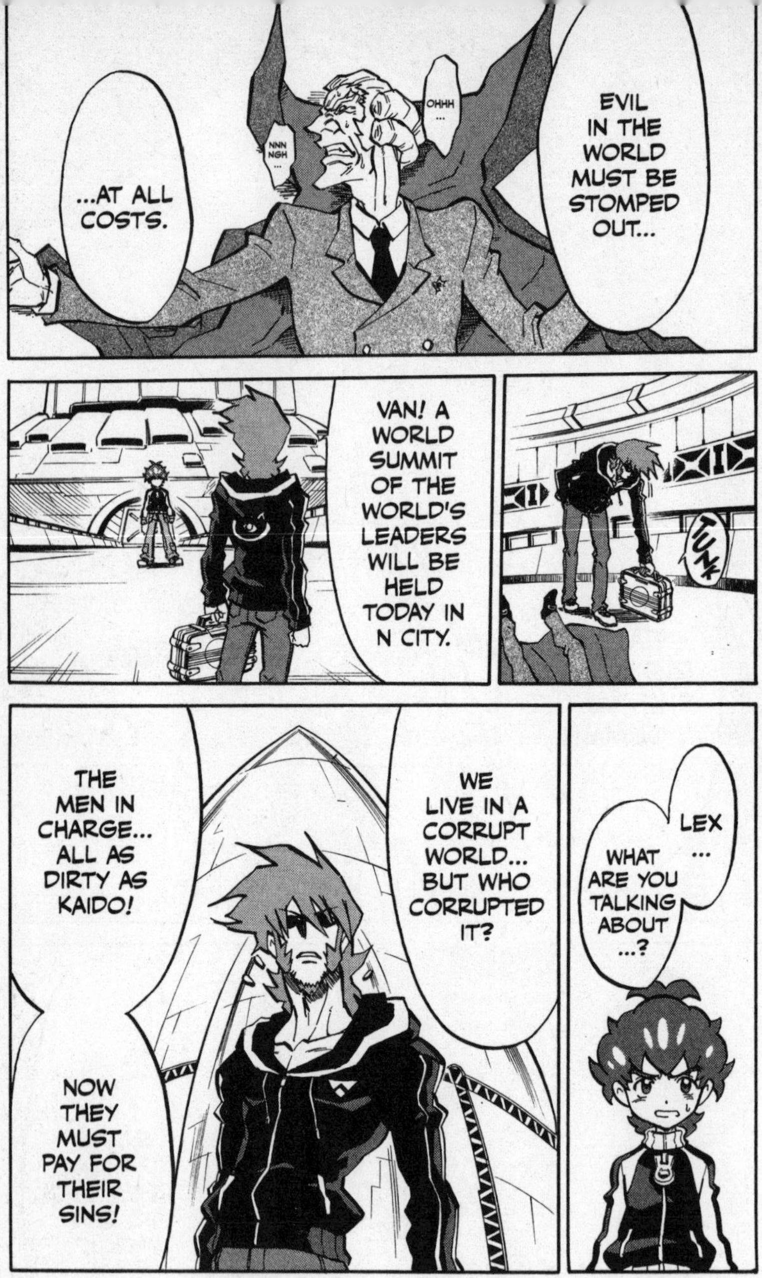
EVIL IN THE WORLD MUST BE STOMPED OUT...
OHHH...
NNNNGH...
...AT ALL COSTS.
TUNK
VAN! A WORLD SUMMIT OF THE WORLD'S LEADERS WILL BE HELD TODAY IN N CITY.
LEX...
WHAT ARE YOU TALKING ABOUT...?
WE LIVE IN A CORRUPT WORLD... BUT WHO CORRUPTED IT?
THE MEN IN CHARGE... ALL AS DIRTY AS KAIDO!
NOW THEY MUST PAY FOR THEIR SINS!

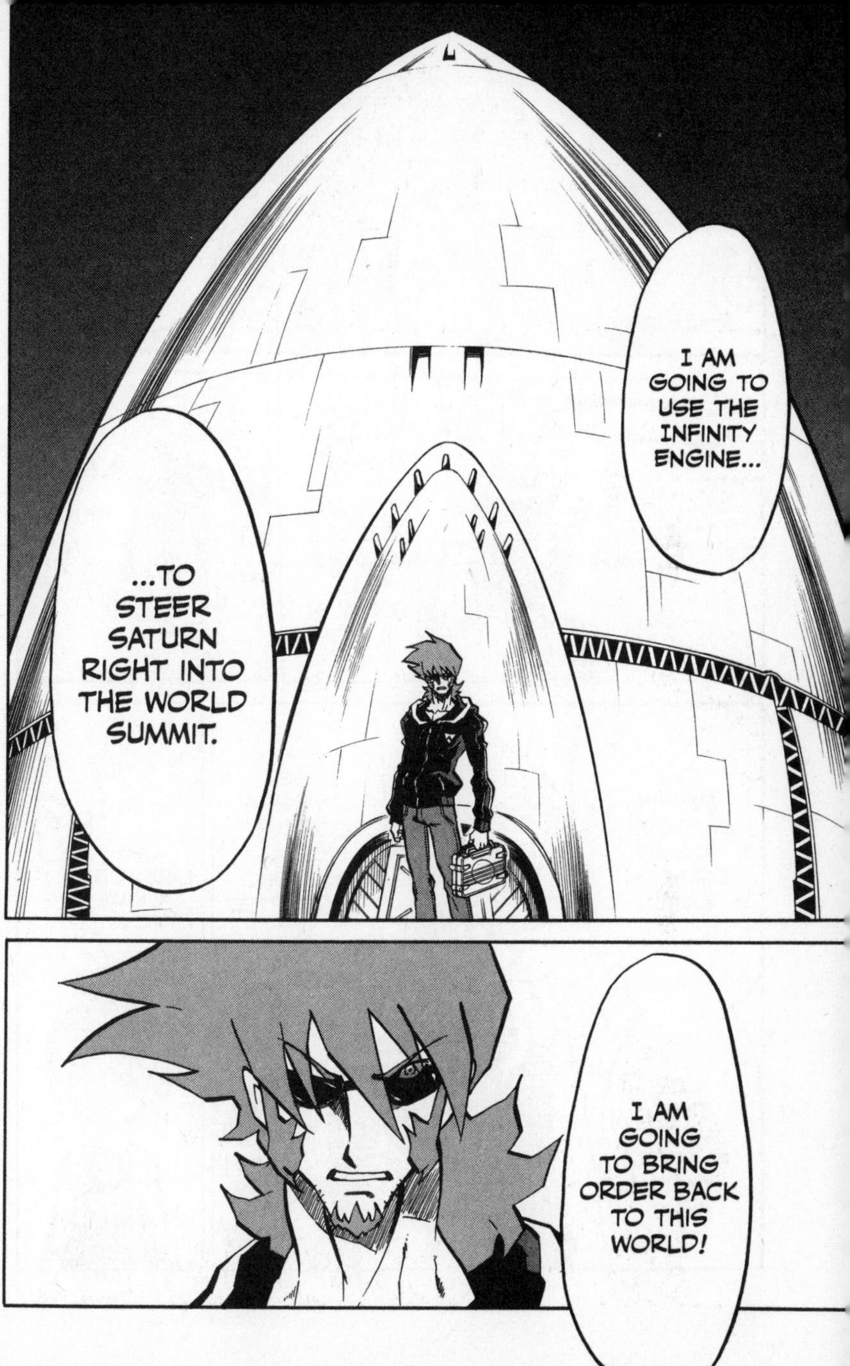
I AM GOING TO USE THE INFINITY ENGINE...
...TO STEER SATURN RIGHT INTO THE WORLD SUMMIT.
I AM GOING TO BRING ORDER BACK TO THIS WORLD!

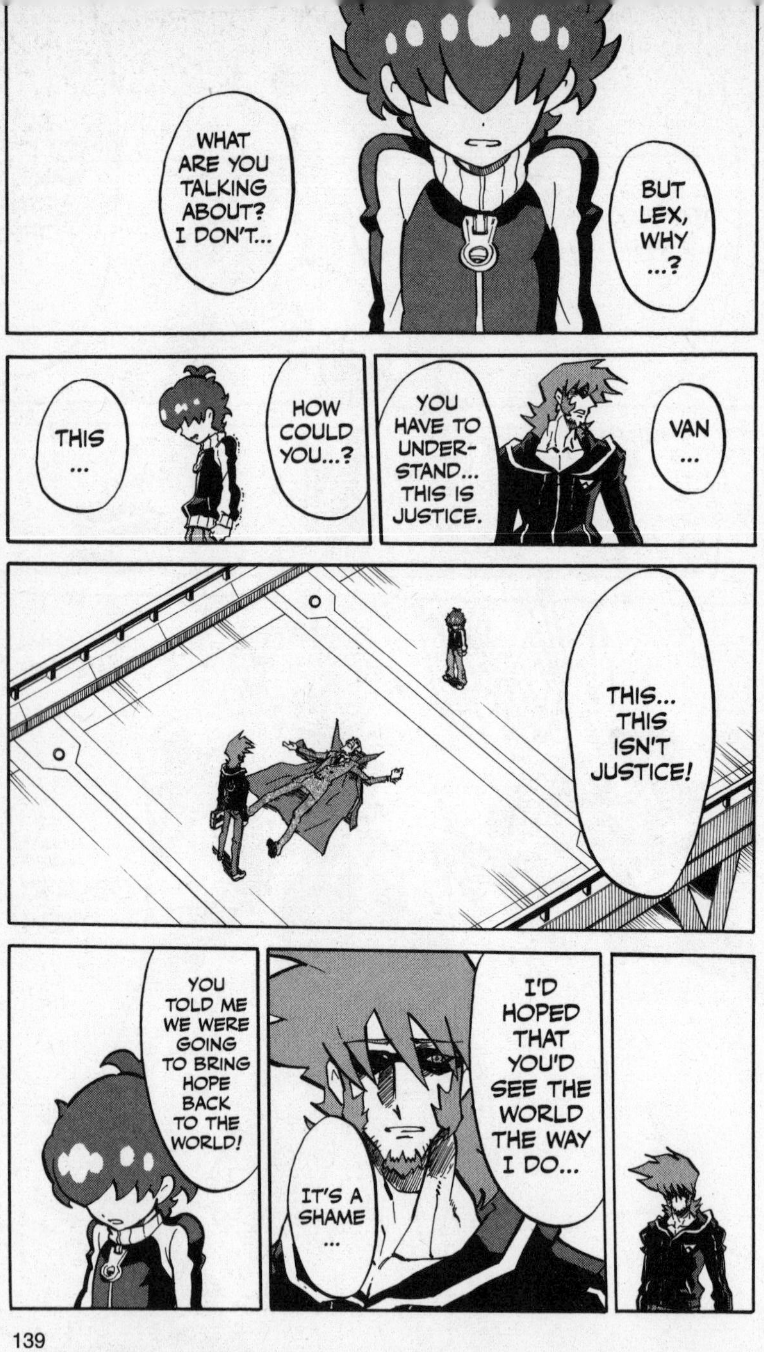
BUT LEX, WHY ...?
WHAT ARE YOU TALKING ABOUT? I DON'T...
VAN ...
YOU HAVE TO UNDER-STAND... THIS IS JUSTICE.
HOW COULD YOU...?
THIS ...
THIS... THIS ISN'T JUSTICE!
I'D HOPED THAT YOU'D SEE THE WORLD THE WAY I DO...
IT'S A SHAME ...
YOU TOLD ME WE WERE GOING TO BRING HOPE BACK TO THE WORLD!

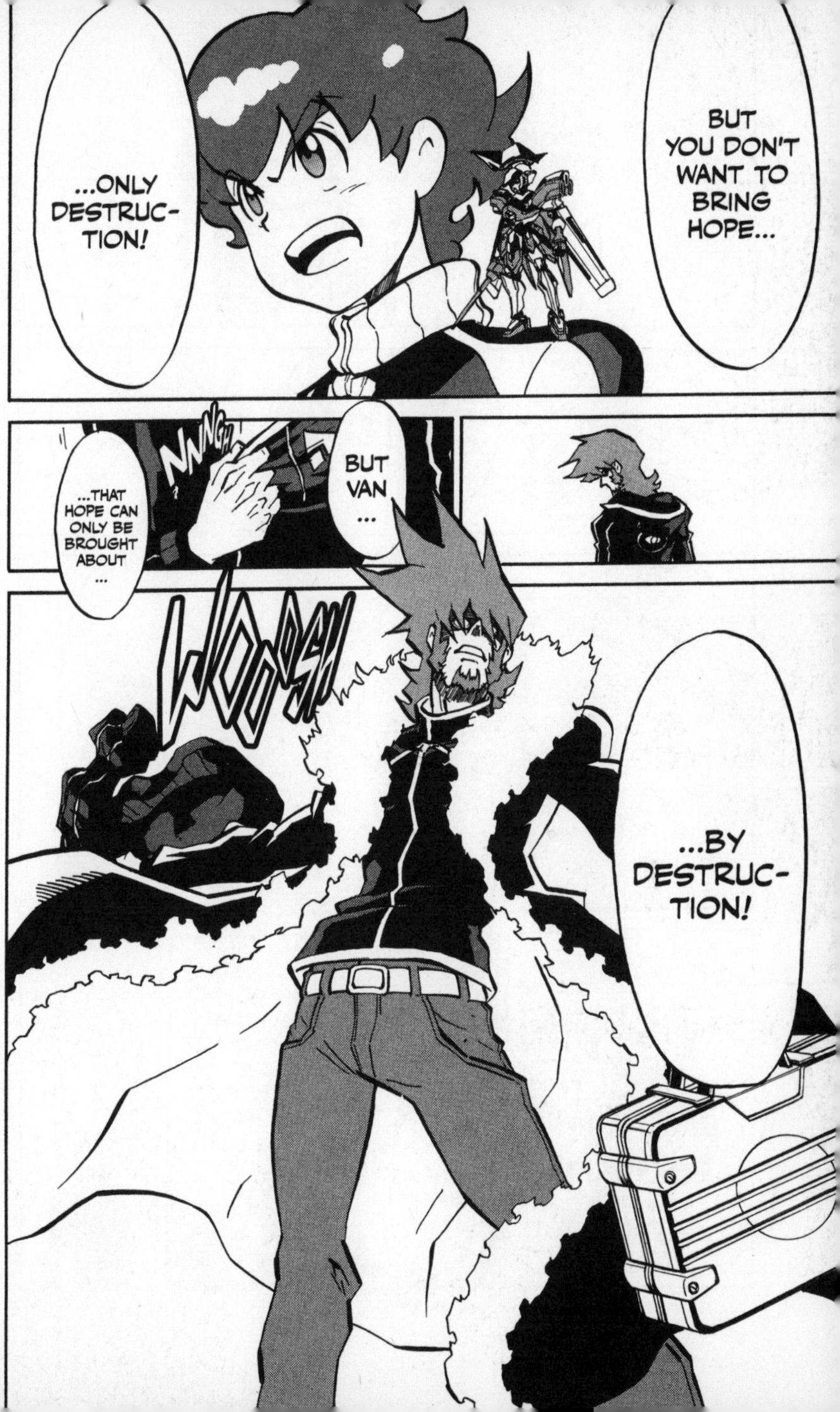
BUT YOU DON'T WANT TO BRING HOPE...
...ONLY DESTRUCTION!
BUT VAN ...
NNNGH!
...THAT HOPE CAN ONLY BE BROUGHT ABOUT ...
WOOOSH!
...BY DESTRUCTION!

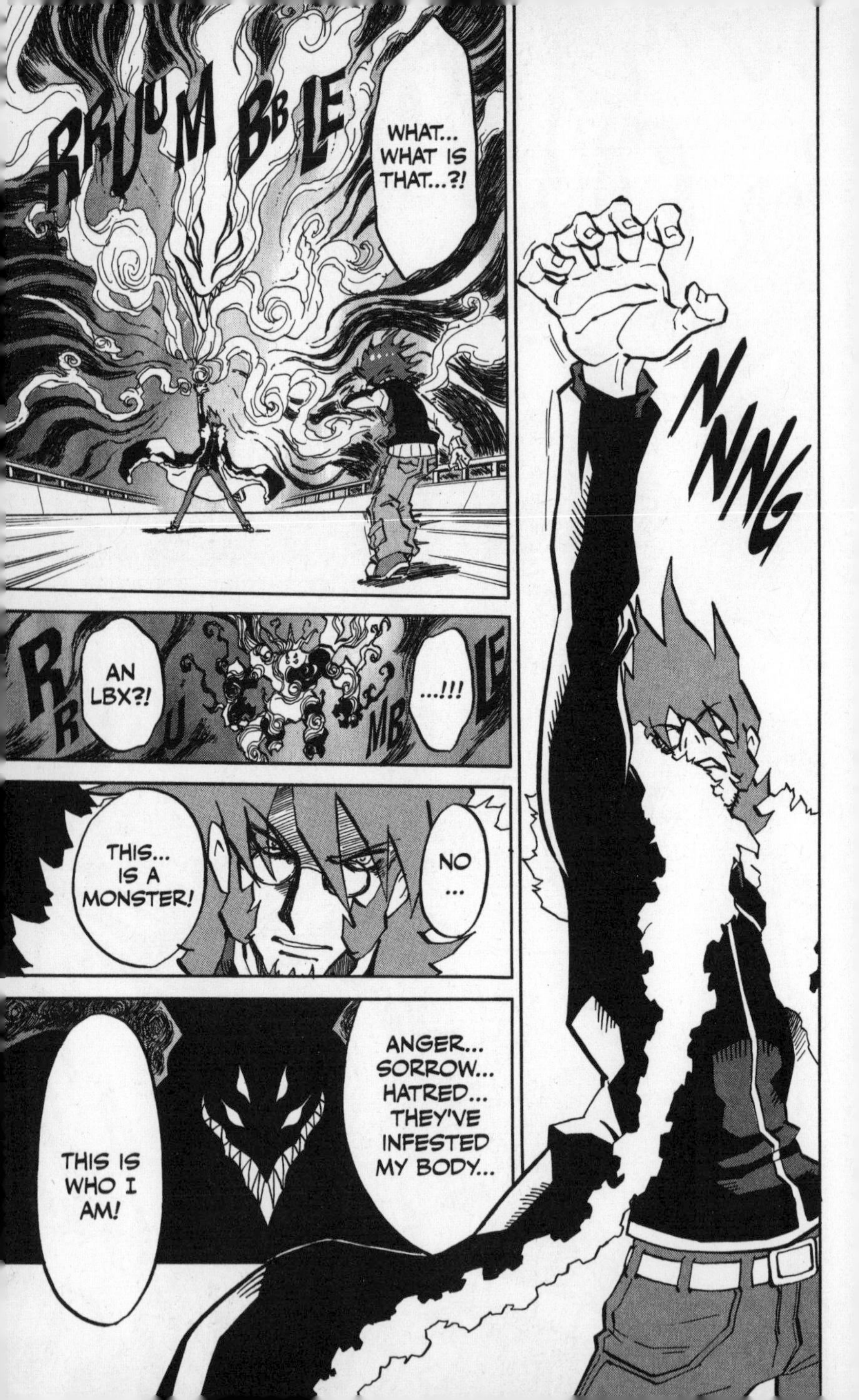
NNNG
WHAT... WHAT IS THAT...?!
RRUUMBBLE
...!!!
RRUMBLE
AN LBX?!
NO...
THIS... IS A MONSTER!
ANGER... SORROW... HATRED... THEY'VE INFESTED MY BODY...
THIS IS WHO I AM!

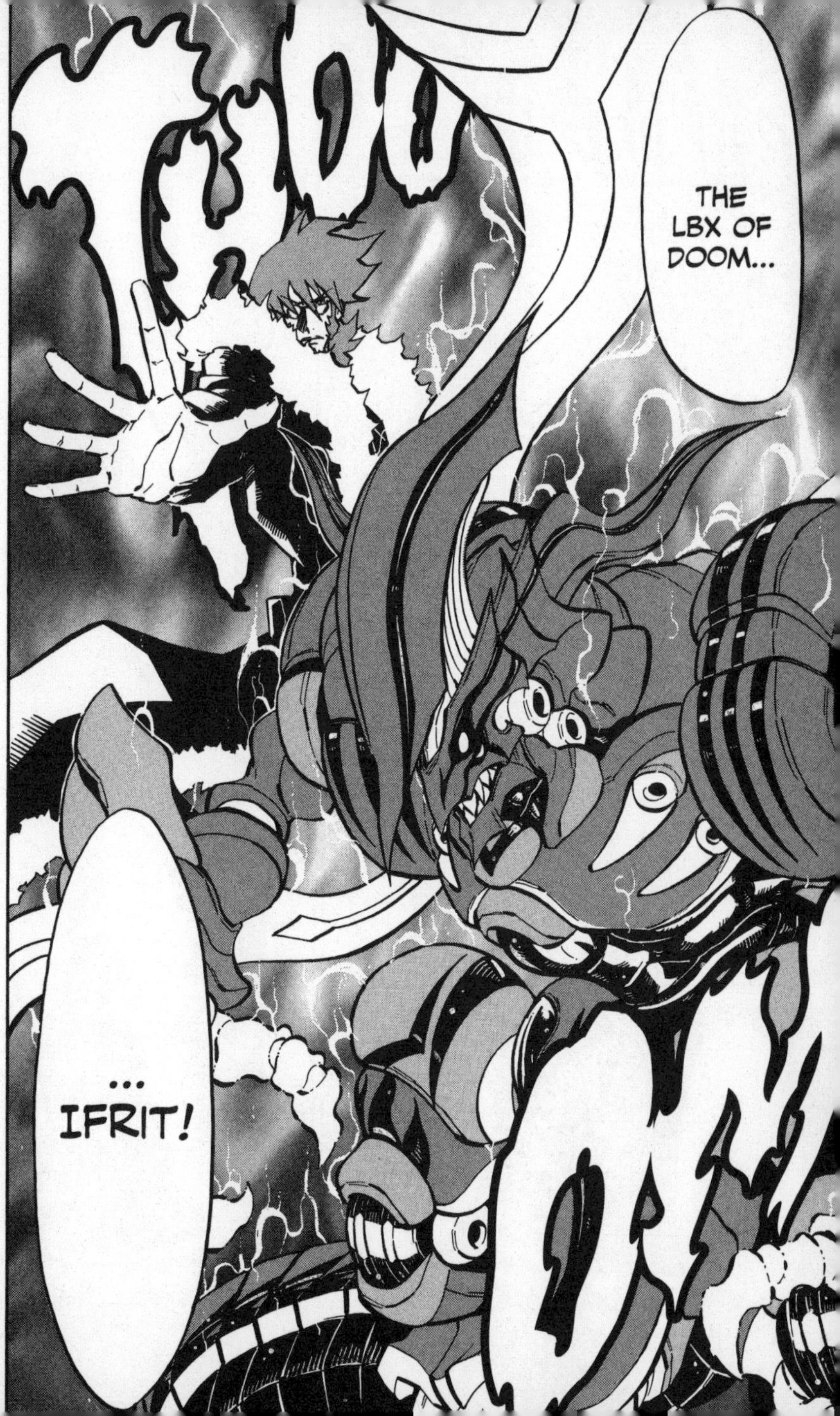
THE LBX OF DOOM...
... IFRIT!

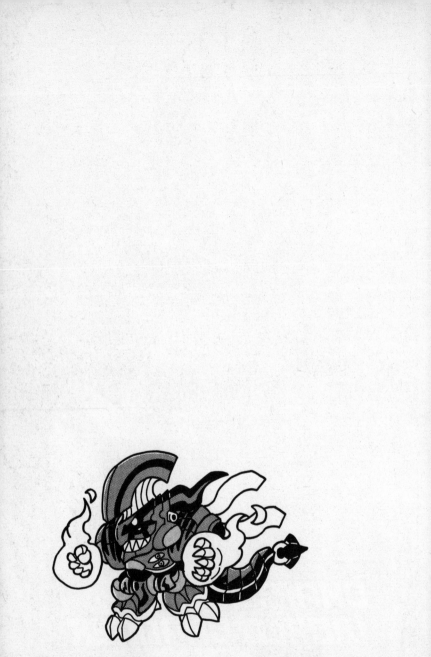

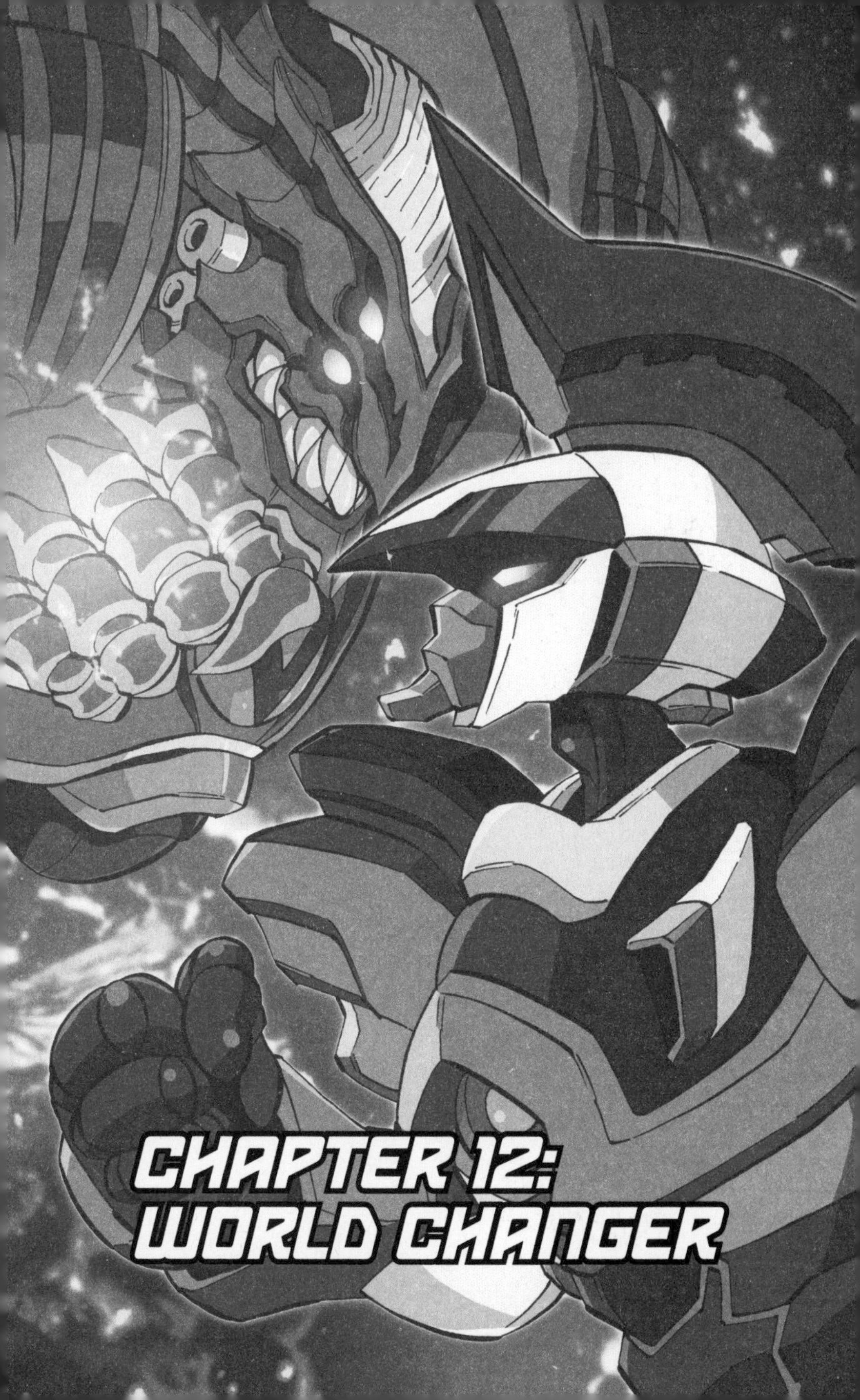
CHAPTER 12:
WORLD CHANGER

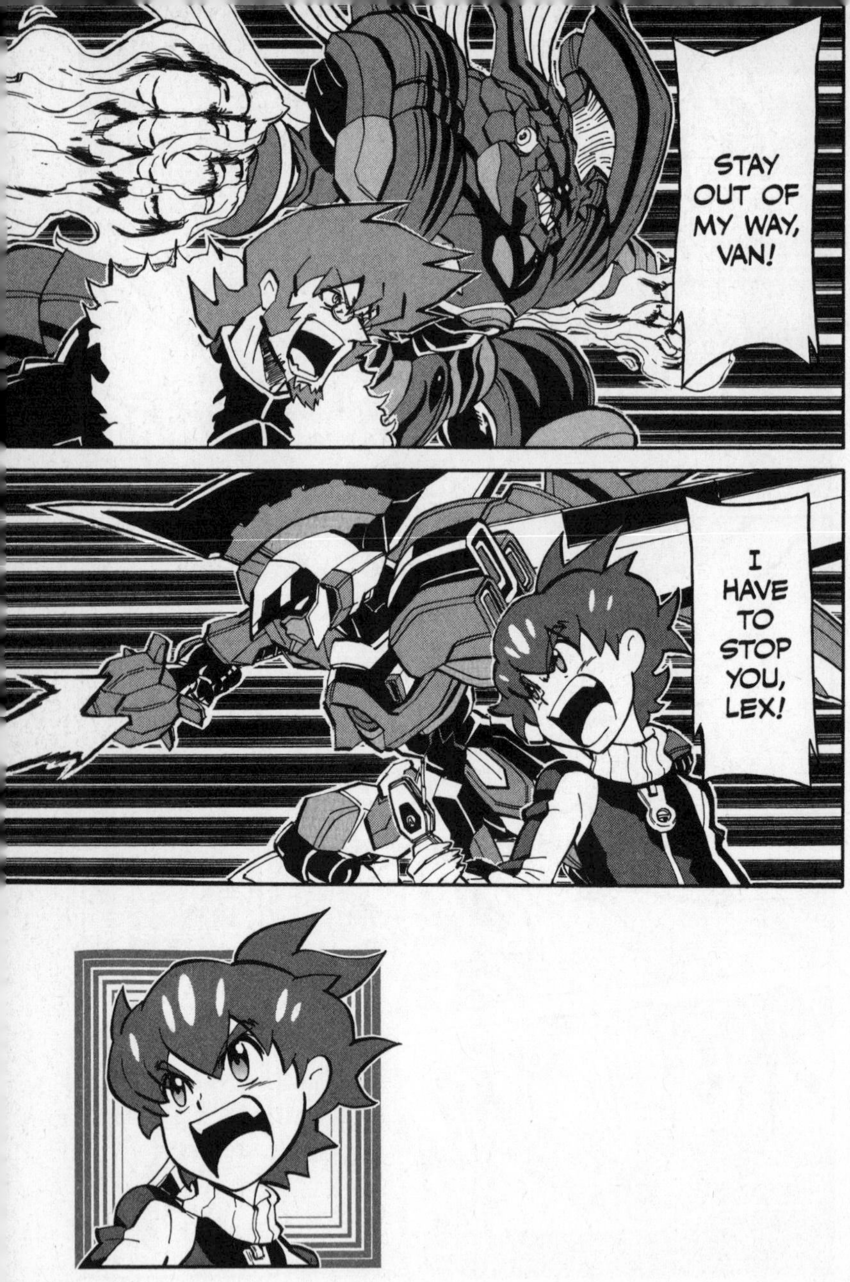
STAY OUT OF MY WAY, VAN!
I HAVE TO STOP YOU, LEX!

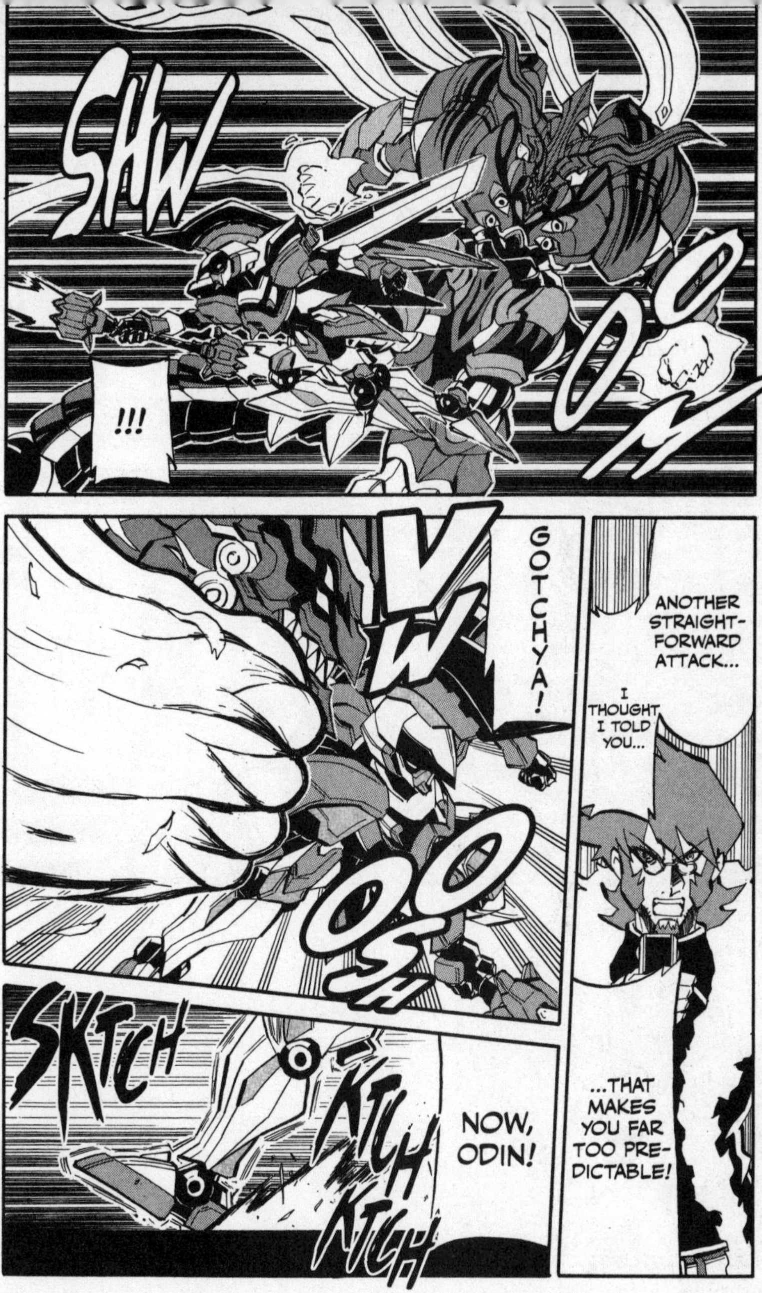
DOOM
SHAW
!!!
ANOTHER STRAIGHT-FORWARD ATTACK...
I THOUGHT I TOLD YOU...
...THAT MAKES YOU FAR TOO PRE-DICTABLE!
GOTCHYA!
VWOOOSH
NOW, ODIN!
KTCH KTCH
SKTCH

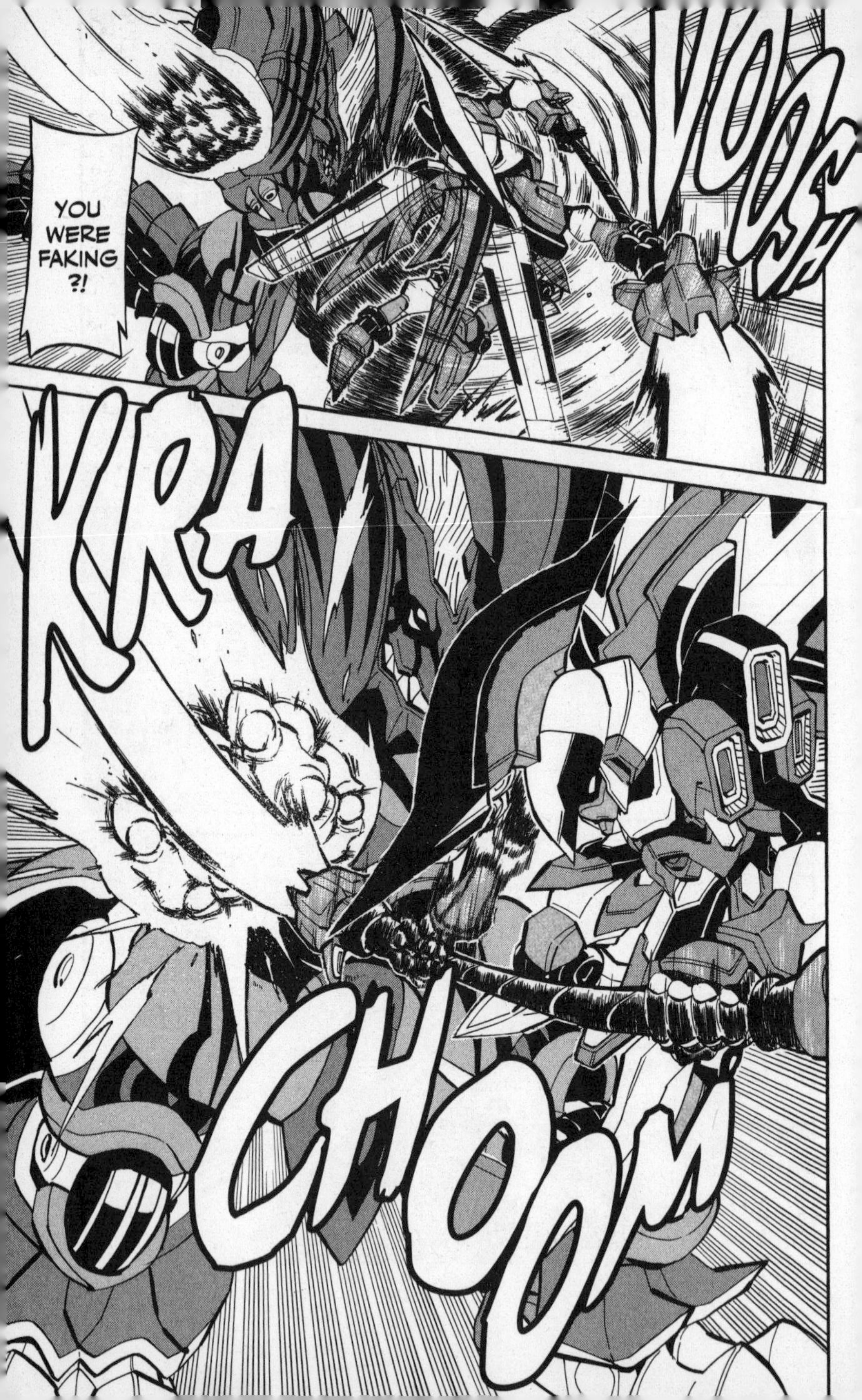
VOOSH
YOU WERE FAKING ?!
KRA
CHOOM

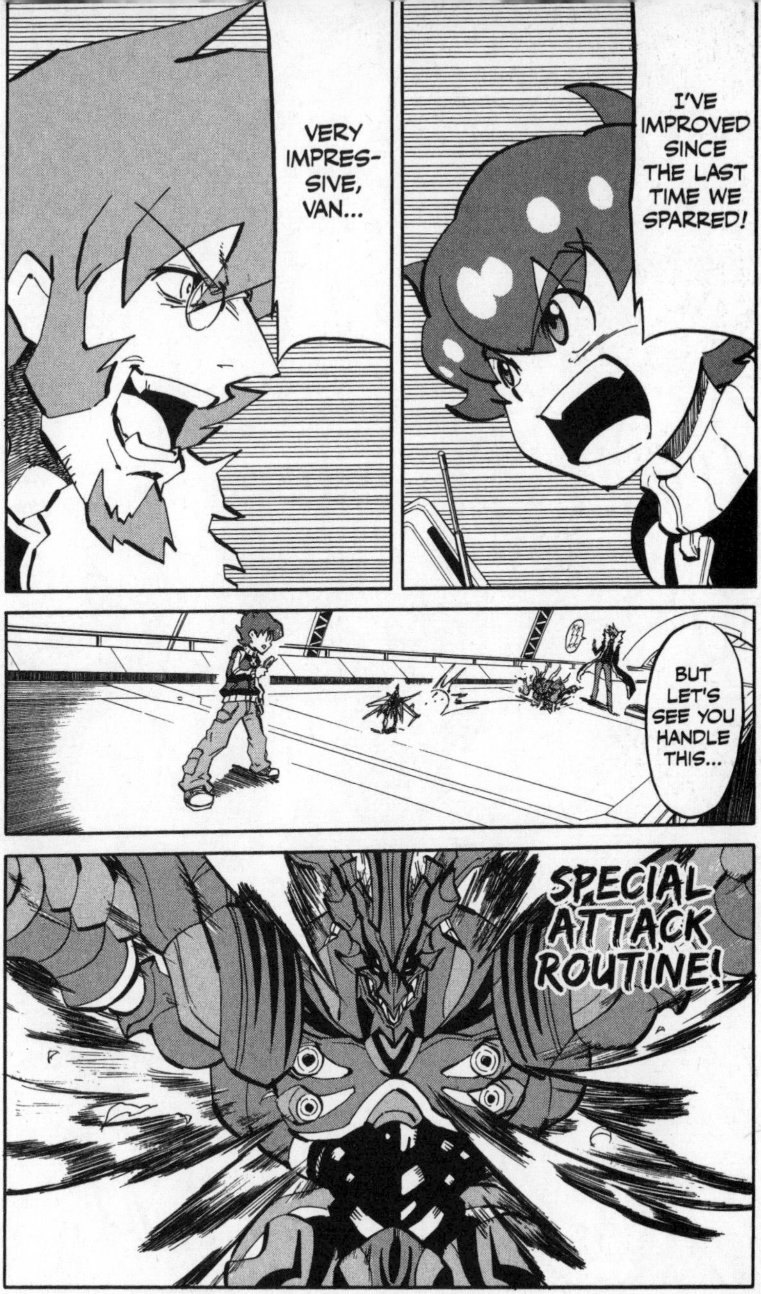
I'VE IMPROVED SINCE THE LAST TIME WE SPARRED!
VERY IMPRES-SIVE, VAN...
BUT LET'S SEE YOU HANDLE THIS...
SPECIAL ATTACK ROUTINE!

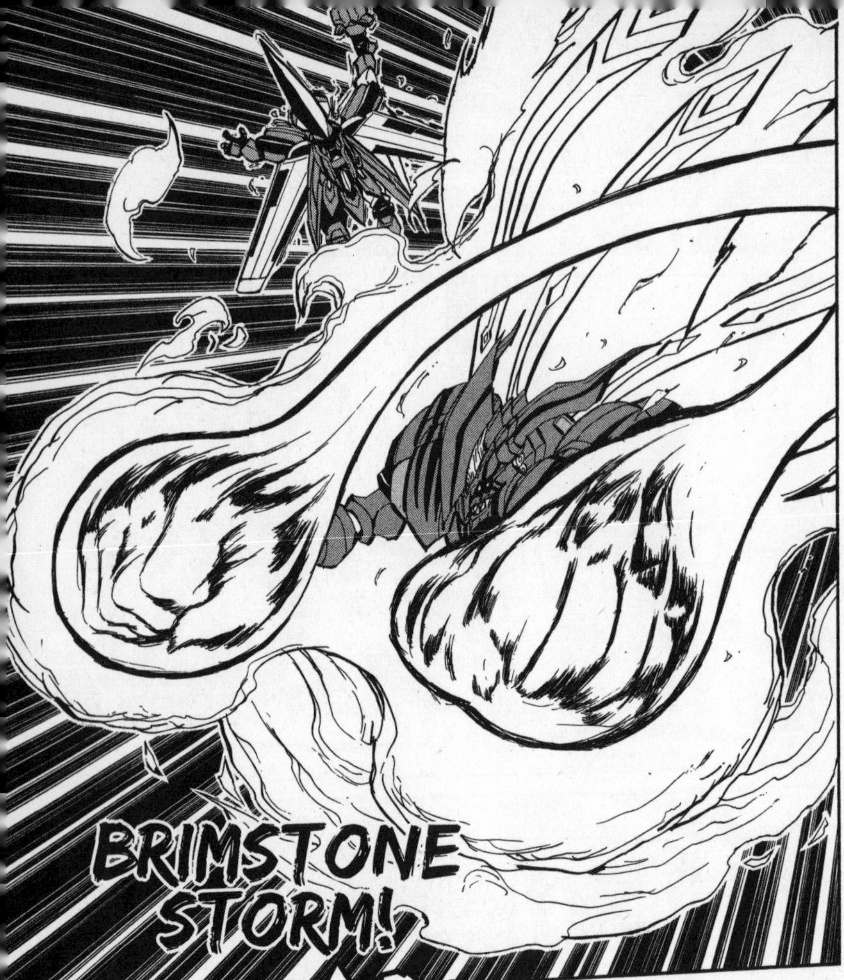
BRIMSTONE STORM!
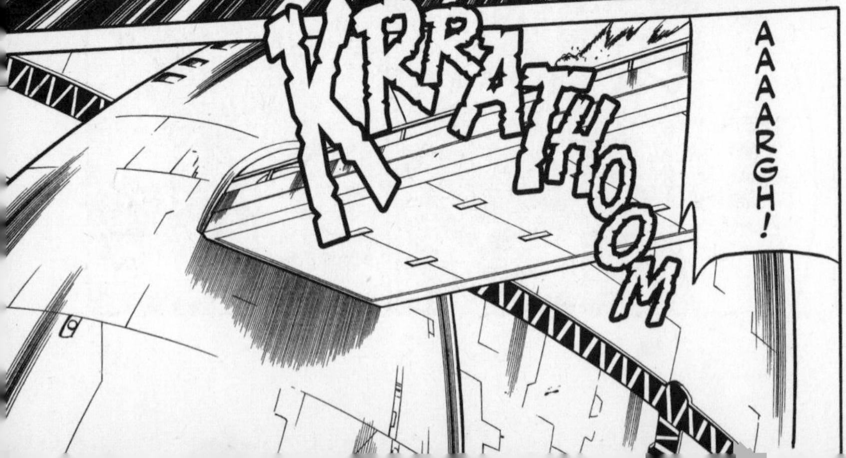
KRRATHOOM
AAAARGH!

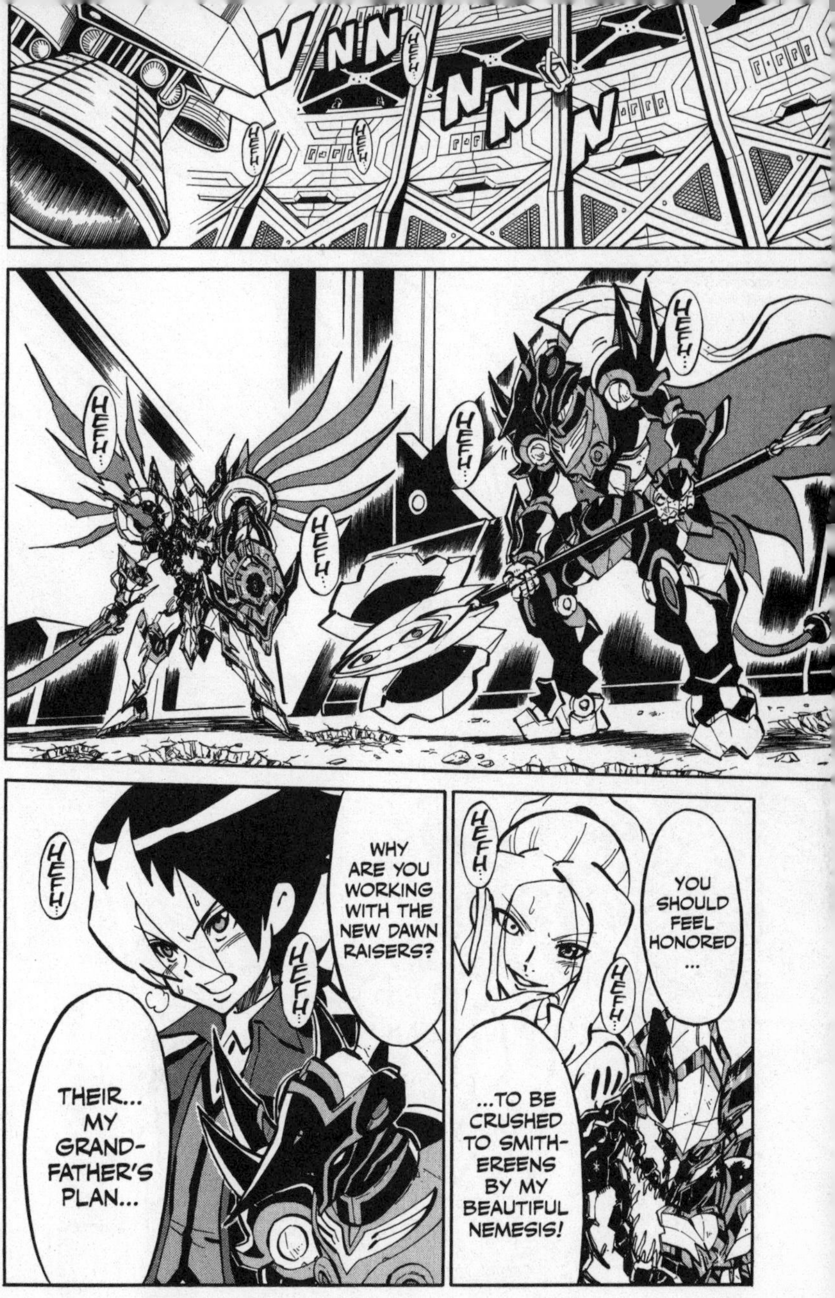
VNNNNN
HEFH...
HEFH...
HEFH...
HEFH...
HEFH...
HEFH...
HEFH...
HEFH...
HEFH...
YOU SHOULD FEEL HONORED...
...TO BE CRUSHED TO SMITHEREENS BY MY BEAUTIFUL NEMESIS!
HEFH...
HEFH...
WHY ARE YOU WORKING WITH THE NEW DAWN RAISERS?
THEIR... MY GRANDFATHER'S PLAN...

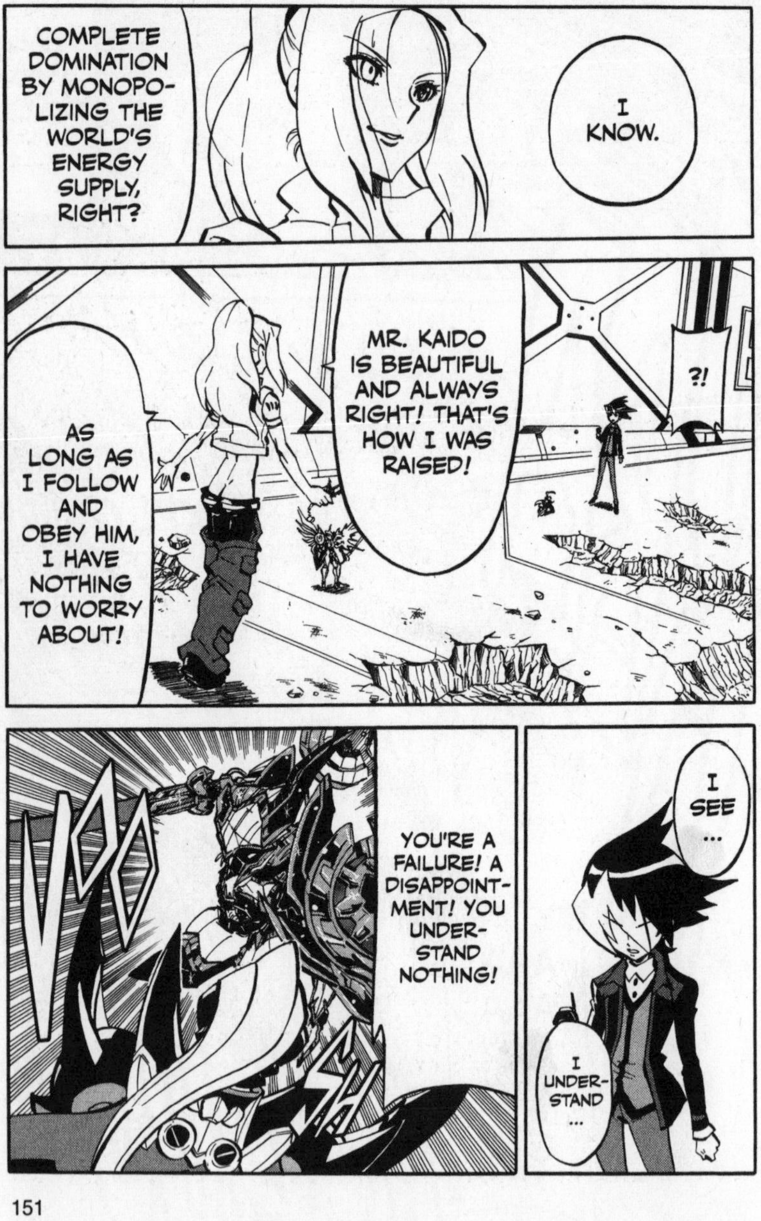
I KNOW.
COMPLETE DOMINATION BY MONOPO-LIZING THE WORLD'S ENERGY SUPPLY, RIGHT?
?!
MR. KAIDO IS BEAUTIFUL AND ALWAYS RIGHT! THAT'S HOW I WAS RAISED!
AS LONG AS I FOLLOW AND OBEY HIM, I HAVE NOTHING TO WORRY ABOUT!
I SEE ...
I UNDER-STAND ...
YOU'RE A FAILURE! A DISAPPOINT-MENT! YOU UNDER-STAND NOTHING!

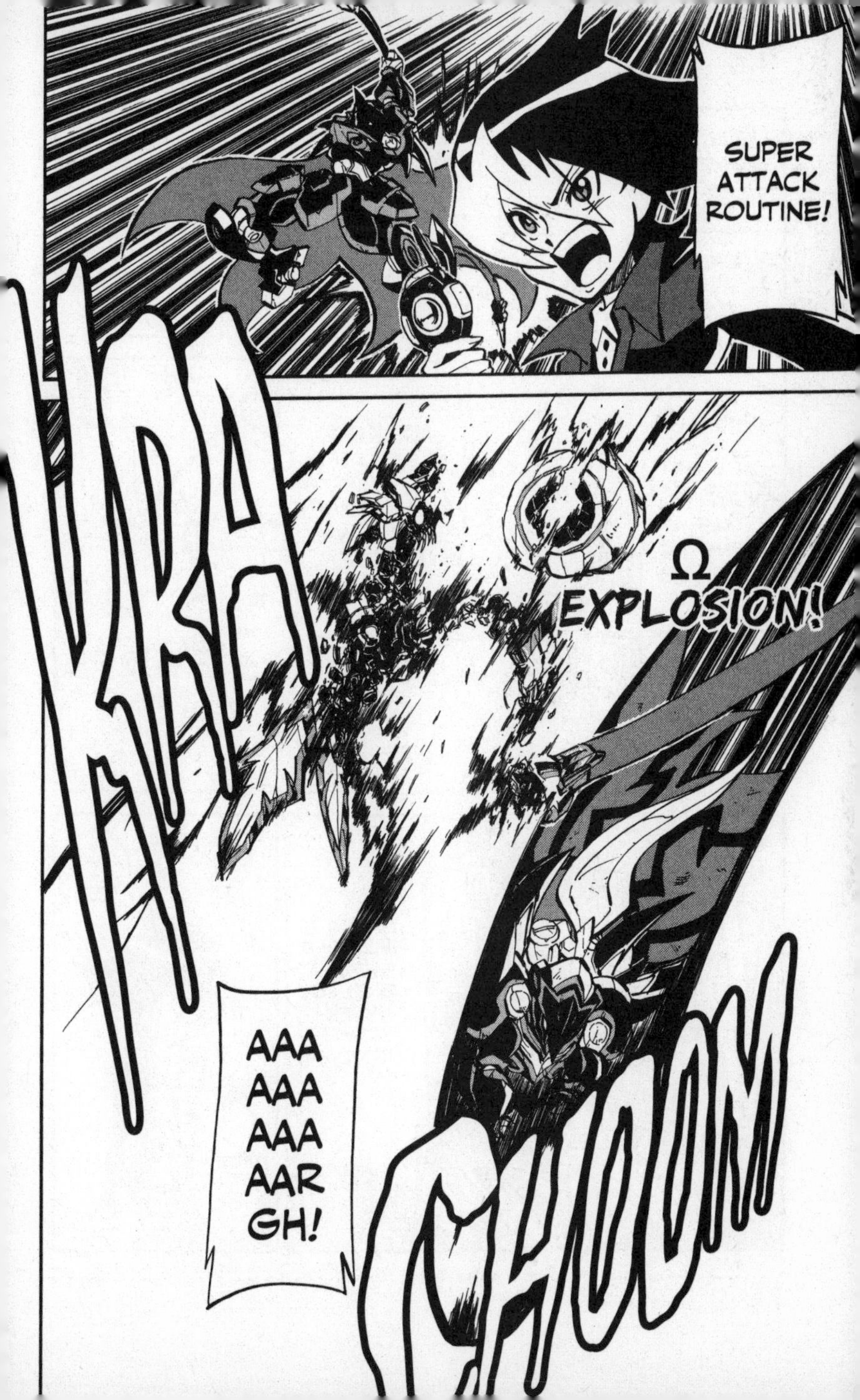
SUPER ATTACK ROUTINE!
Ω EXPLOSION!
AAAAAAAAAAAARGH!

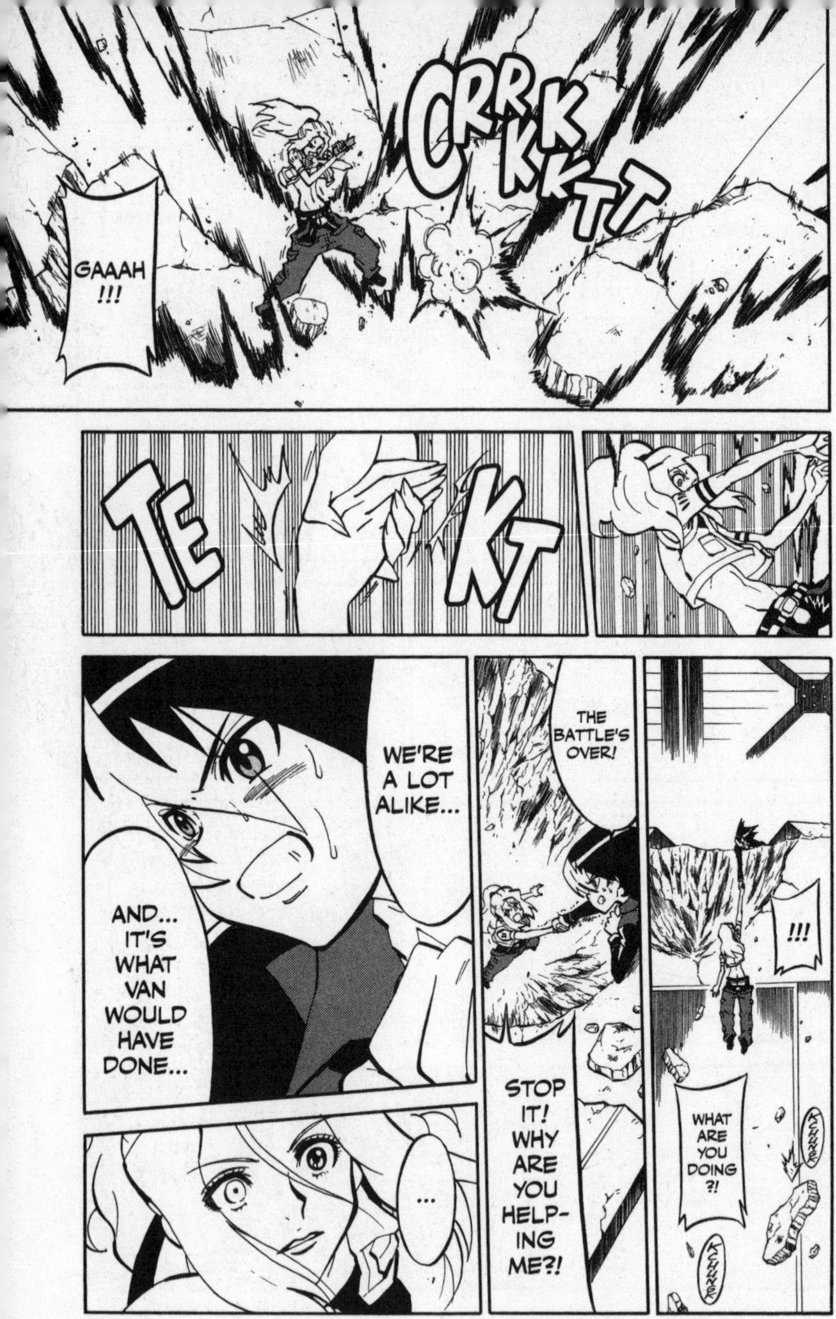
CRRKKKTT
GAAAH!!!
TEKT
!!!
WHAT ARE YOU DOING?!
KCHNNK
KCHNNK
THE BATTLE'S OVER!
STOP IT! WHY ARE YOU HELPING ME?!
WE'RE A LOT ALIKE...
AND... IT'S WHAT VAN WOULD HAVE DONE...
...

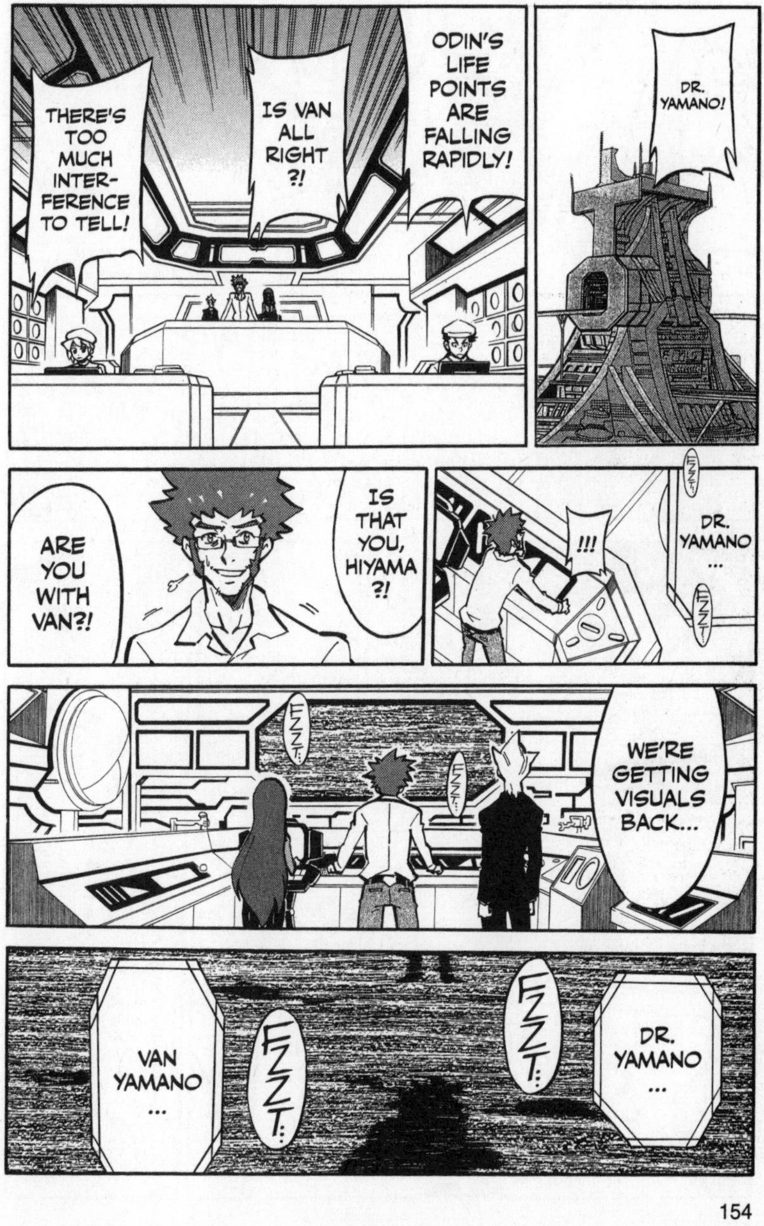
DR. YAMANO!
ODIN'S LIFE POINTS ARE FALLING RAPIDLY!
IS VAN ALL RIGHT?!
THERE'S TOO MUCH INTERFERENCE TO TELL!
FZZT...
DR. YAMANO ...
FZZT...
!!!
IS THAT YOU, HIYAMA?!
ARE YOU WITH VAN?!
WE'RE GETTING VISUALS BACK...
FZZT...
FZZT...
DR. YAMANO ...
FZZT...
FZZT...
VAN YAMANO ...

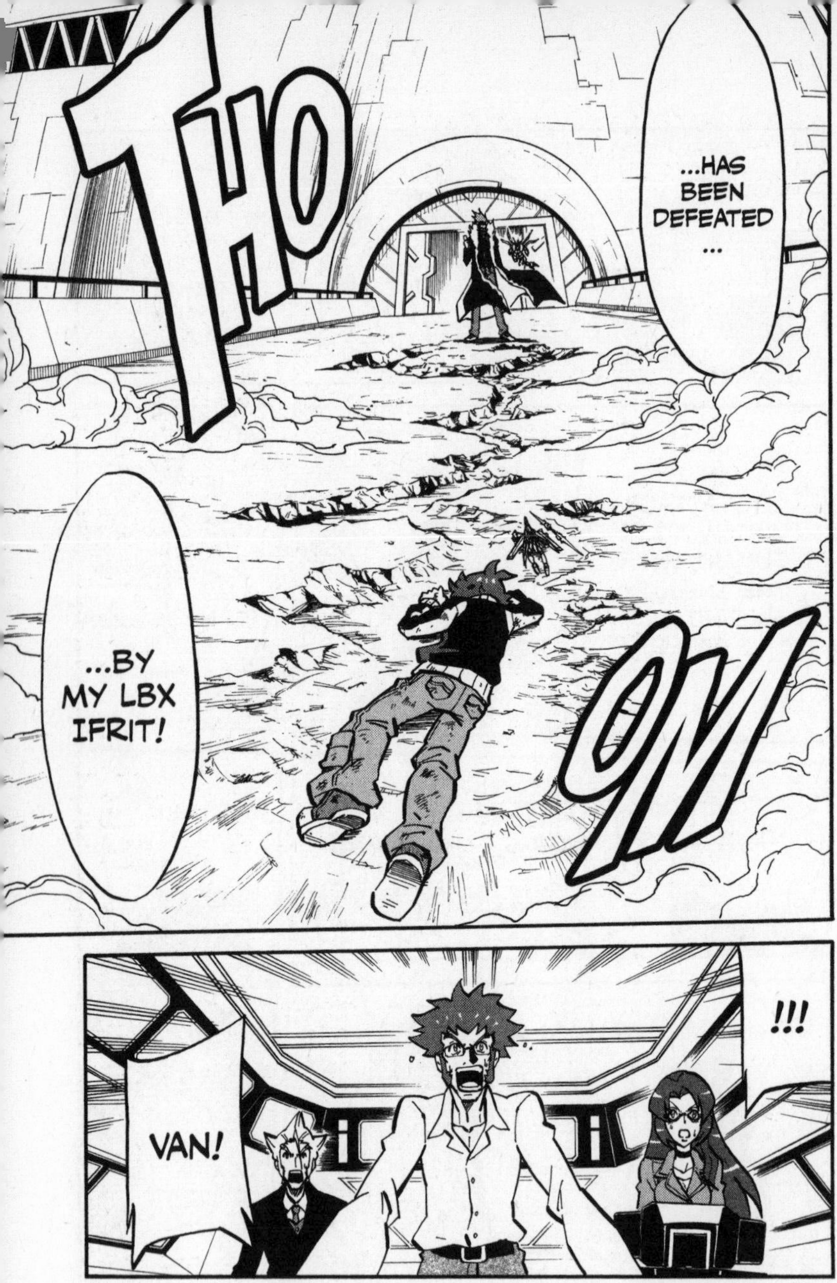
...HAS BEEN DEFEATED ...
THO
OM
...BY MY LBX IFRIT!
!!!
VAN!

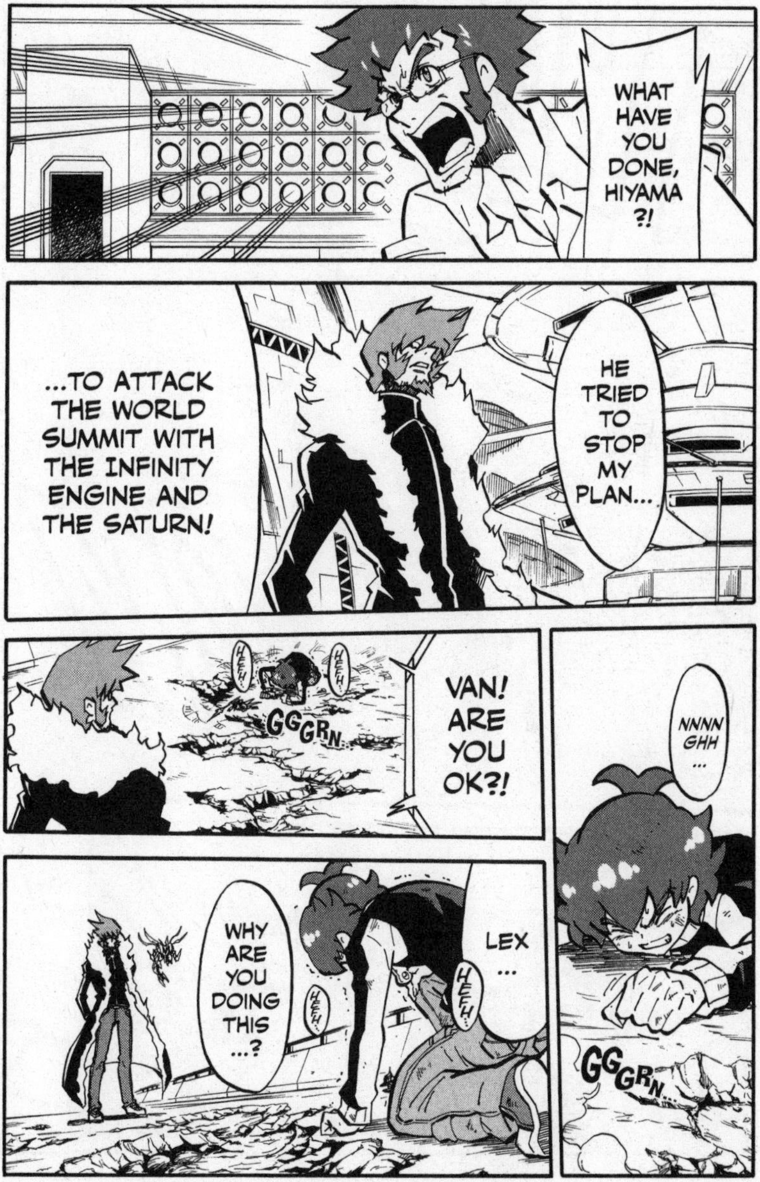
WHAT HAVE YOU DONE, HIYAMA?!
HE TRIED TO STOP MY PLAN...
...TO ATTACK THE WORLD SUMMIT WITH THE INFINITY ENGINE AND THE SATURN!
NNNNGHH...
GGGRN...
VAN! ARE YOU OK?!
HEFH
HEFH
GGGRN...
LEX...
HEFH...
HEFH...
WHY ARE YOU DOING THIS...?

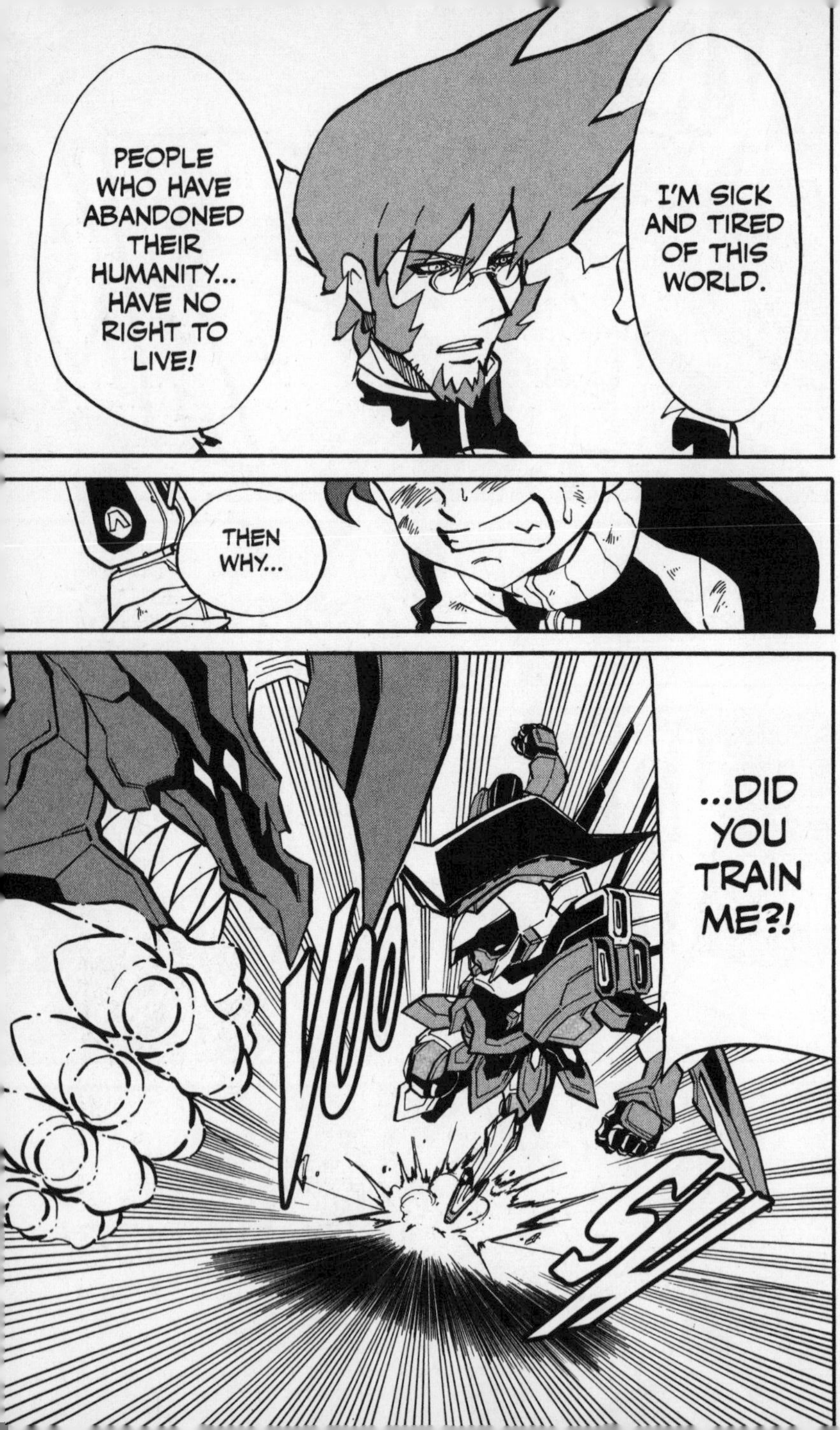
I'M SICK AND TIRED OF THIS WORLD.
PEOPLE WHO HAVE ABANDONED THEIR HUMANITY... HAVE NO RIGHT TO LIVE!
THEN WHY...
...DID YOU TRAIN ME?!

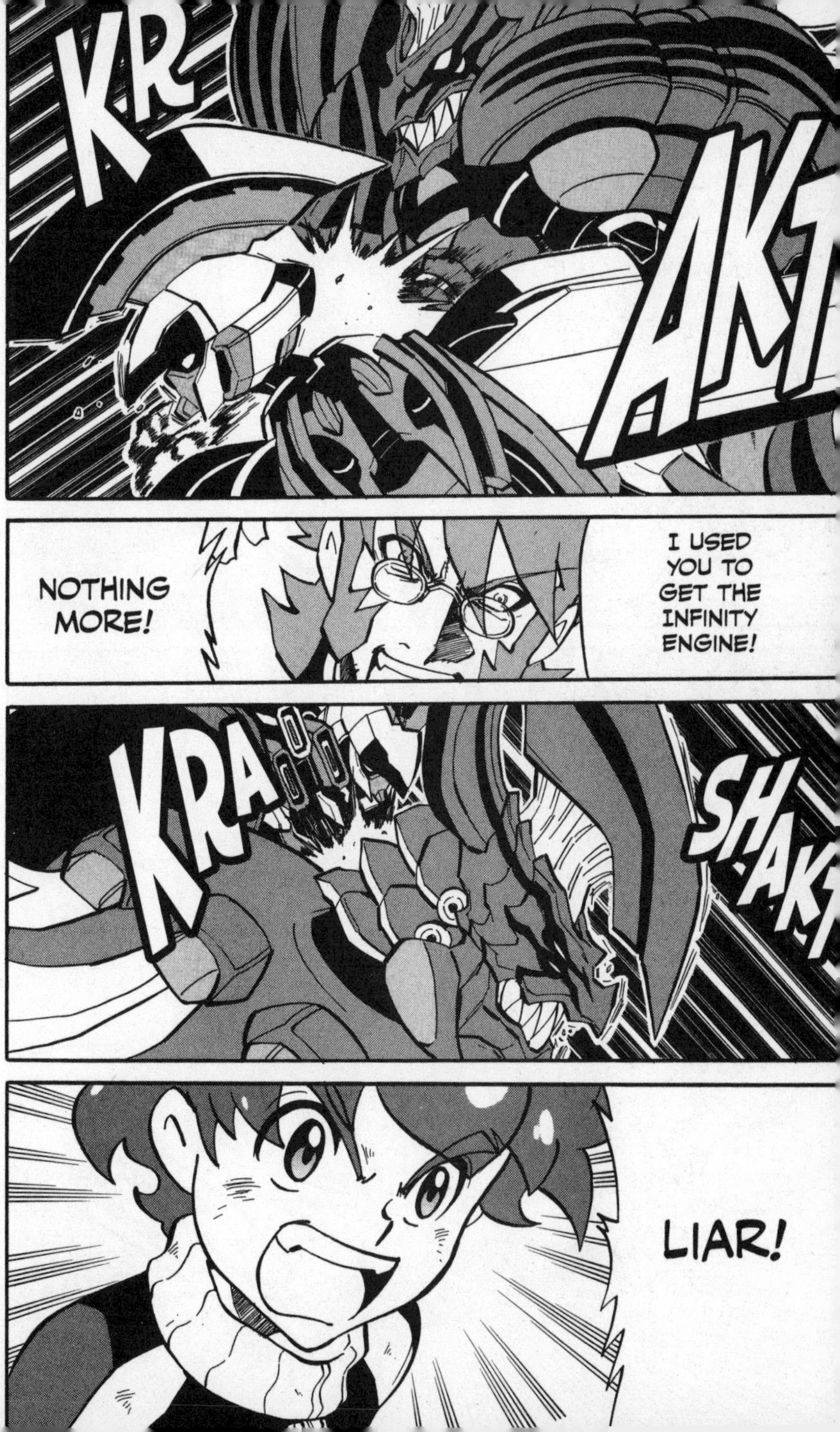
KR-
AKT
I USED YOU TO GET THE INFINITY ENGINE!
NOTHING MORE!
SHAKT
KRA
LIAR!

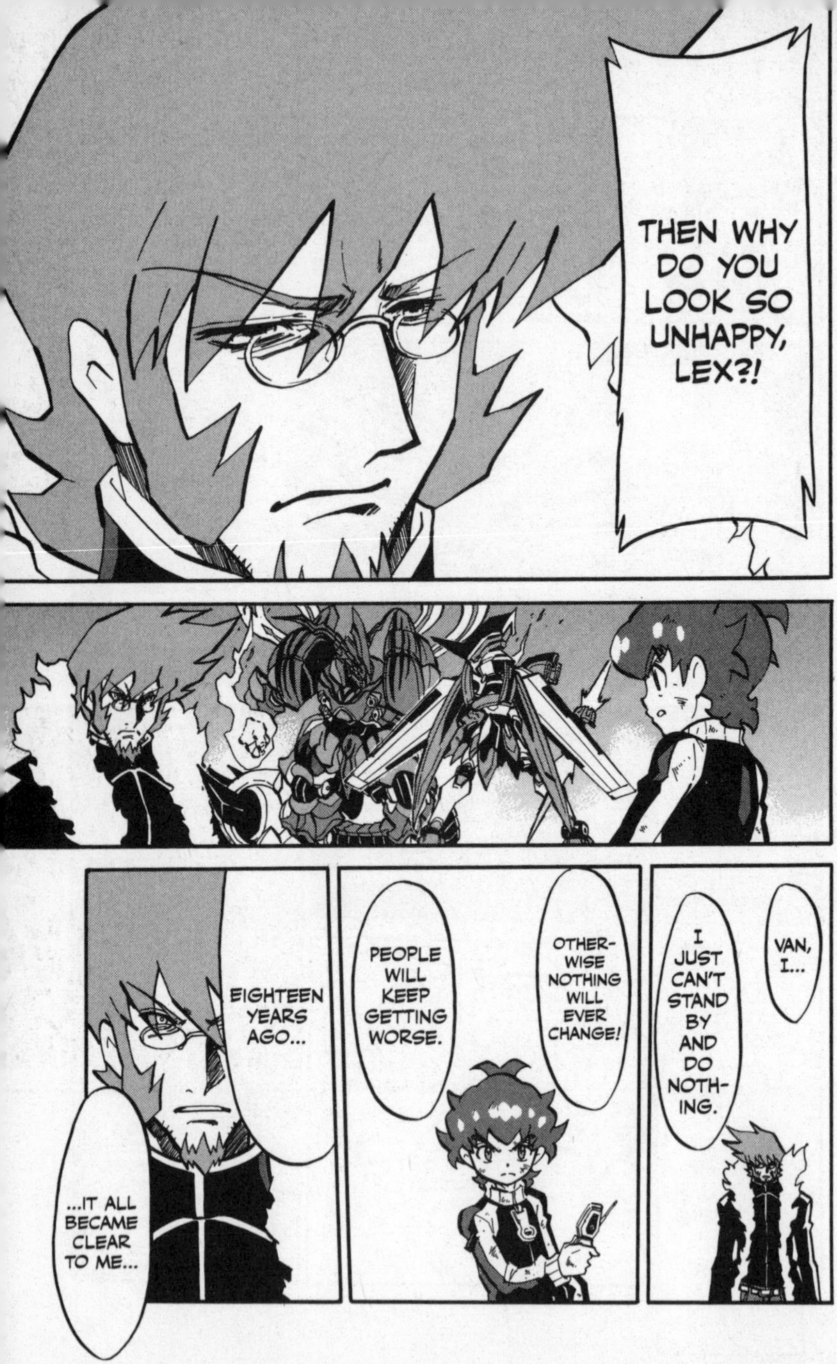
THEN WHY DO YOU LOOK SO UNHAPPY, LEX?!
VAN, I...
I JUST CAN'T STAND BY AND DO NOTHING.
OTHER-WISE NOTHING WILL EVER CHANGE!
PEOPLE WILL KEEP GETTING WORSE.
EIGHTEEN YEARS AGO...
...IT ALL BECAME CLEAR TO ME...

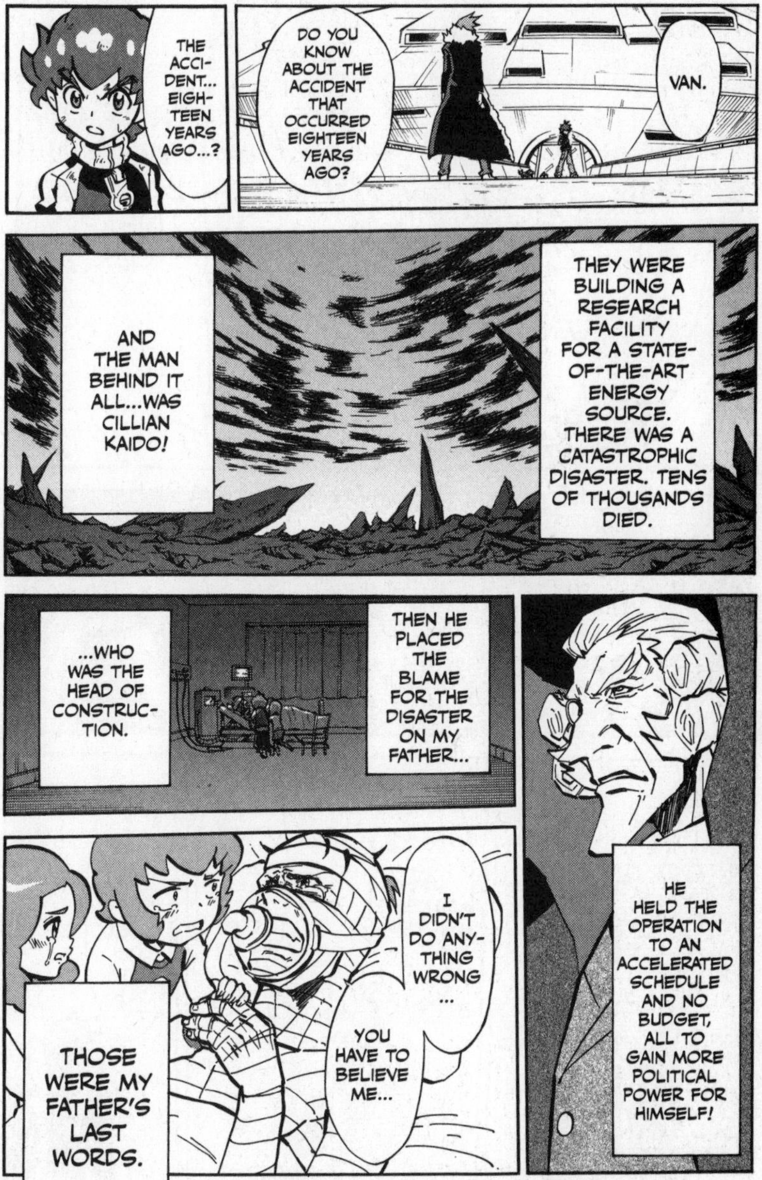
VAN.
DO YOU KNOW ABOUT THE ACCIDENT THAT OCCURRED EIGHTEEN YEARS AGO?
THE ACCI-DENT... EIGH-TEEN YEARS AGO...?
THEY WERE BUILDING A RESEARCH FACILITY FOR A STATE-OF-THE-ART ENERGY SOURCE. THERE WAS A CATASTROPHIC DISASTER. TENS OF THOUSANDS DIED.
AND THE MAN BEHIND IT ALL...WAS CILLIAN KAIDO!
HE HELD THE OPERATION TO AN ACCELERATED SCHEDULE AND NO BUDGET, ALL TO GAIN MORE POLITICAL POWER FOR HIMSELF!
THEN HE PLACED THE BLAME FOR THE DISASTER ON MY FATHER...
...WHO WAS THE HEAD OF CONSTRUC-TION.
I DIDN'T DO ANY-THING WRONG...
YOU HAVE TO BELIEVE ME...
THOSE WERE MY FATHER'S LAST WORDS.

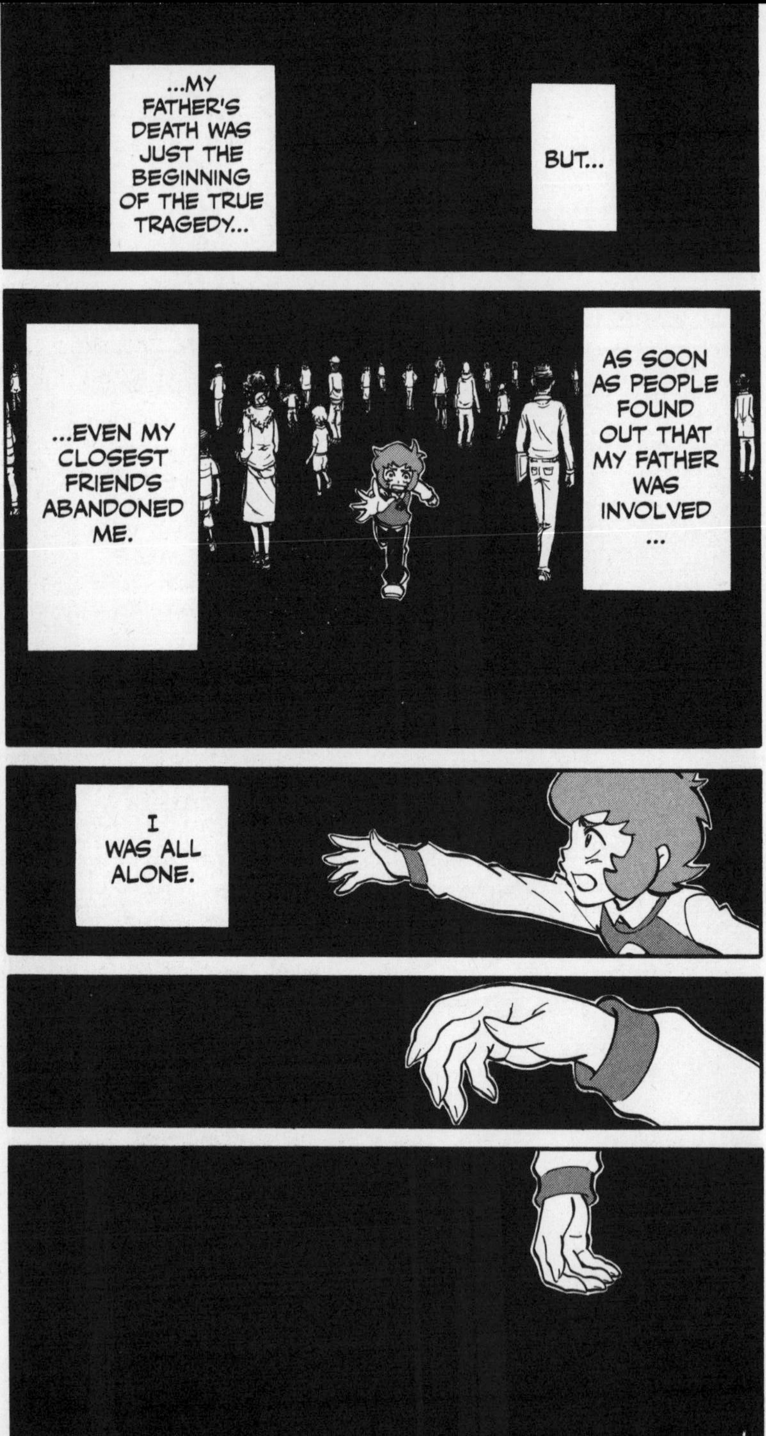
BUT...
...MY FATHER'S DEATH WAS JUST THE BEGINNING OF THE TRUE TRAGEDY...
AS SOON AS PEOPLE FOUND OUT THAT MY FATHER WAS INVOLVED...
...EVEN MY CLOSEST FRIENDS ABANDONED ME.
I WAS ALL ALONE.

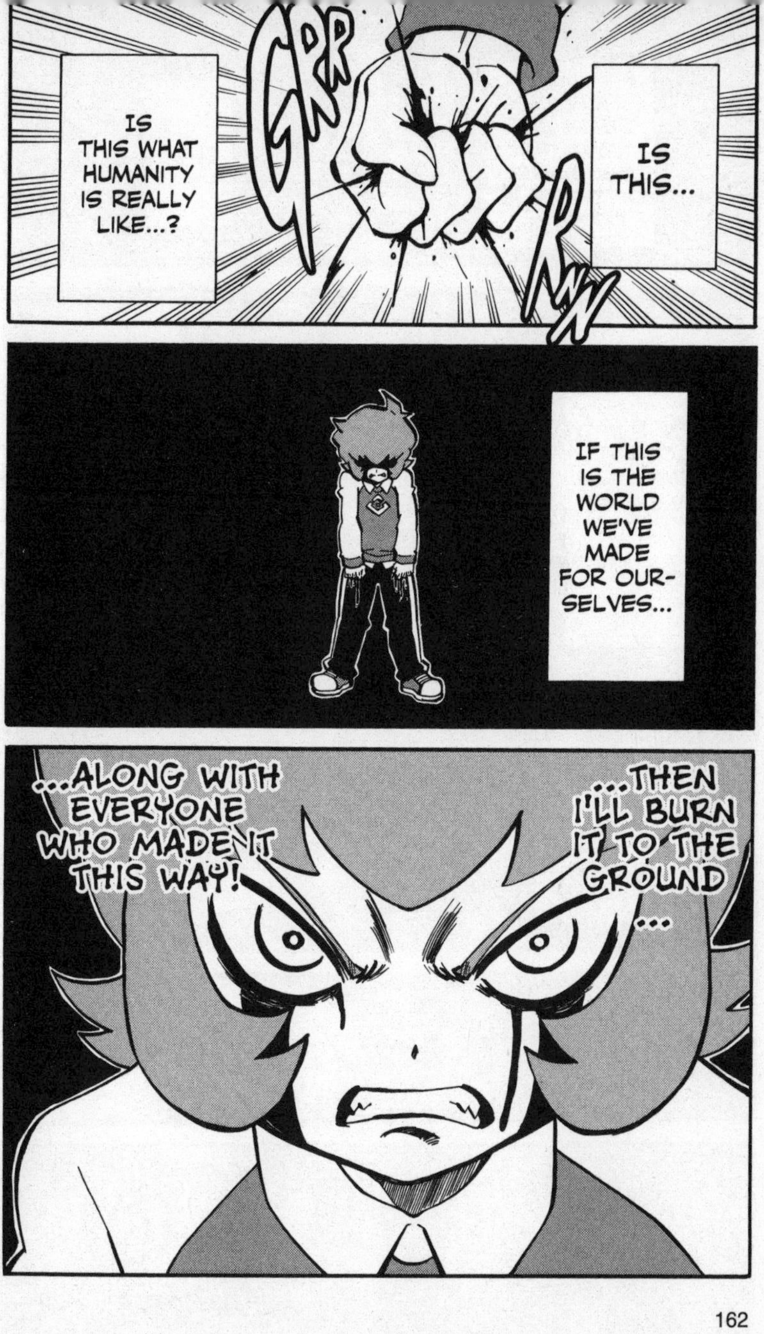
IS THIS...
GRRRNN
IS THIS WHAT HUMANITY IS REALLY LIKE...?
IF THIS IS THE WORLD WE'VE MADE FOR OURSELVES...
...THEN I'LL BURN IT TO THE GROUND...
...ALONG WITH EVERYONE WHO MADE IT THIS WAY!

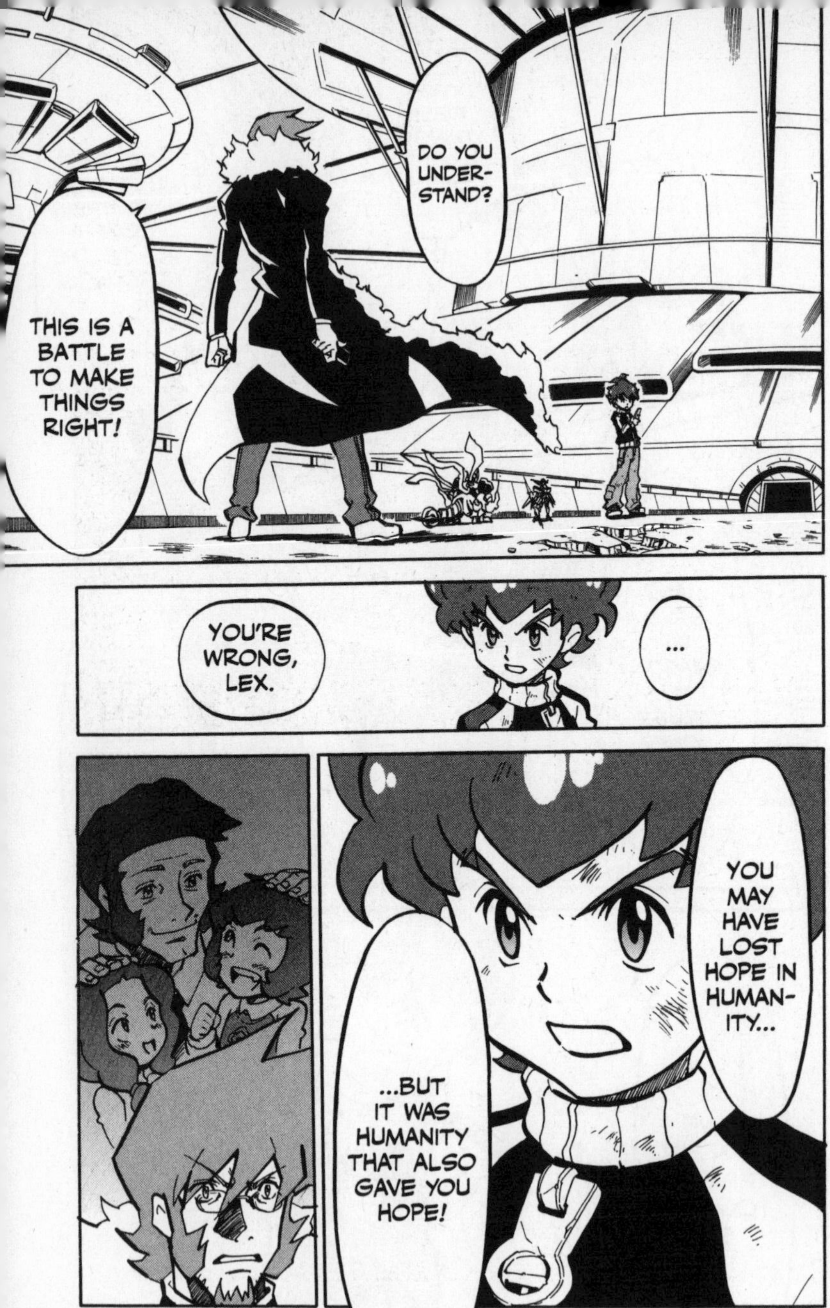
DO YOU UNDER-STAND?
THIS IS A BATTLE TO MAKE THINGS RIGHT!
...
YOU'RE WRONG, LEX.
YOU MAY HAVE LOST HOPE IN HUMAN-ITY...
...BUT IT WAS HUMANITY THAT ALSO GAVE YOU HOPE!

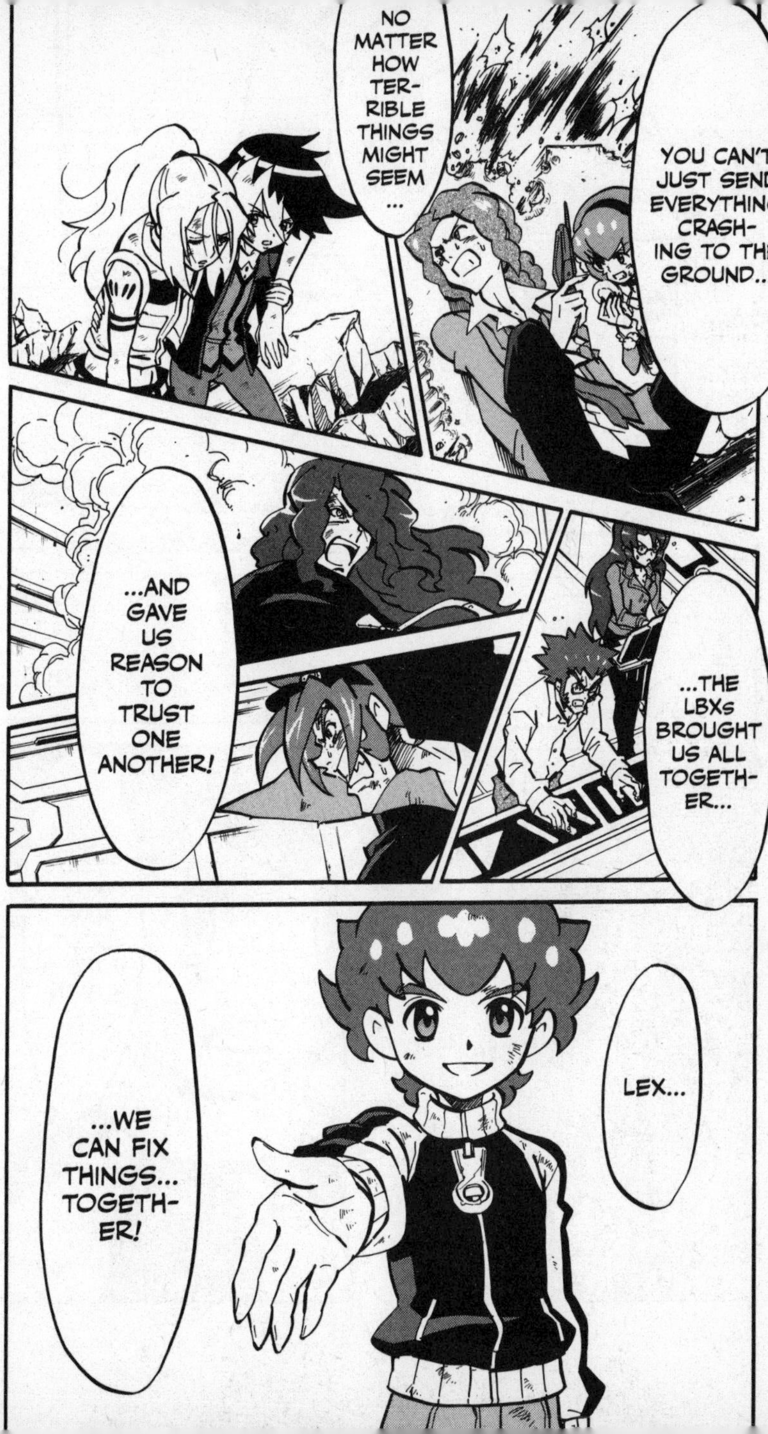
YOU CAN'T JUST SEND EVERYTHING CRASHING TO THE GROUND...
NO MATTER HOW TERRIBLE THINGS MIGHT SEEM...
...THE LBXs BROUGHT US ALL TOGETHER...
...AND GAVE US REASON TO TRUST ONE ANOTHER!
LEX...
...WE CAN FIX THINGS... TOGETHER!

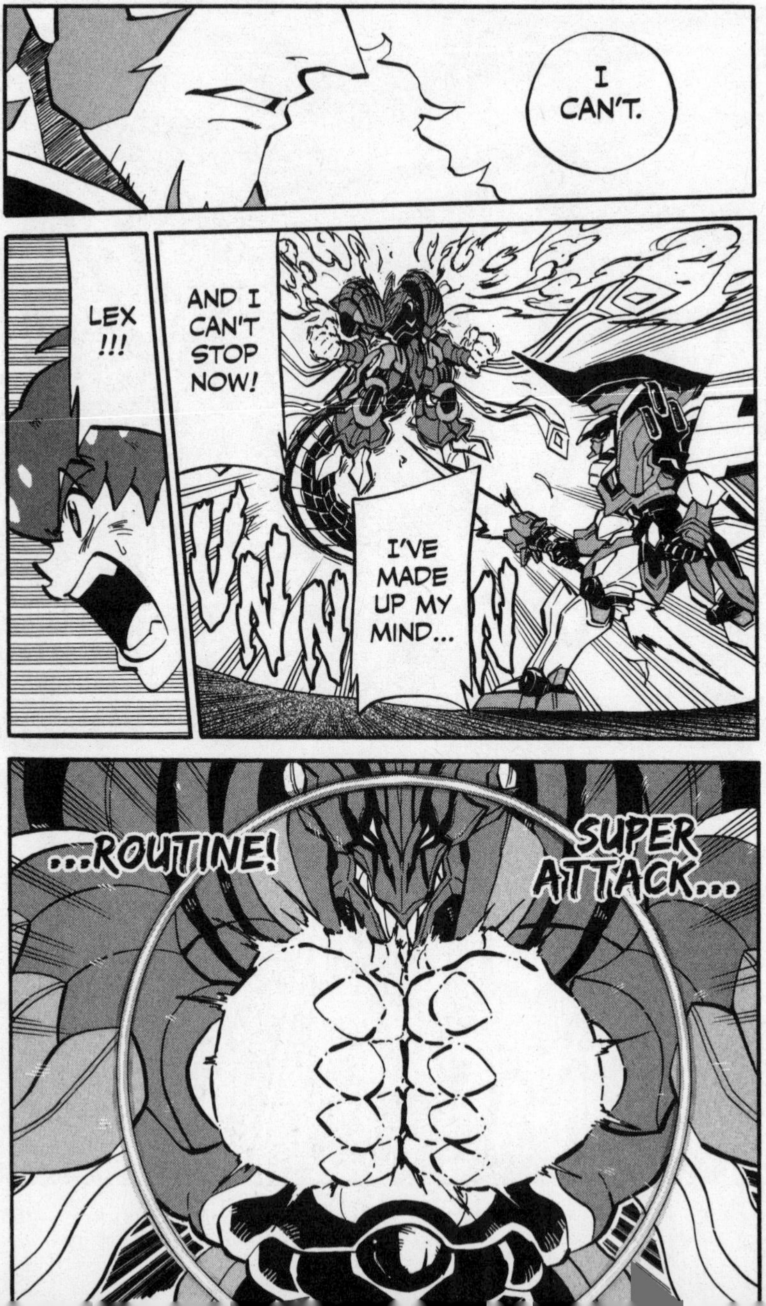
I CAN'T.
AND I CAN'T STOP NOW!
I'VE MADE UP MY MIND...
LEX !!!
SUPER ATTACK...
...ROUTINE!

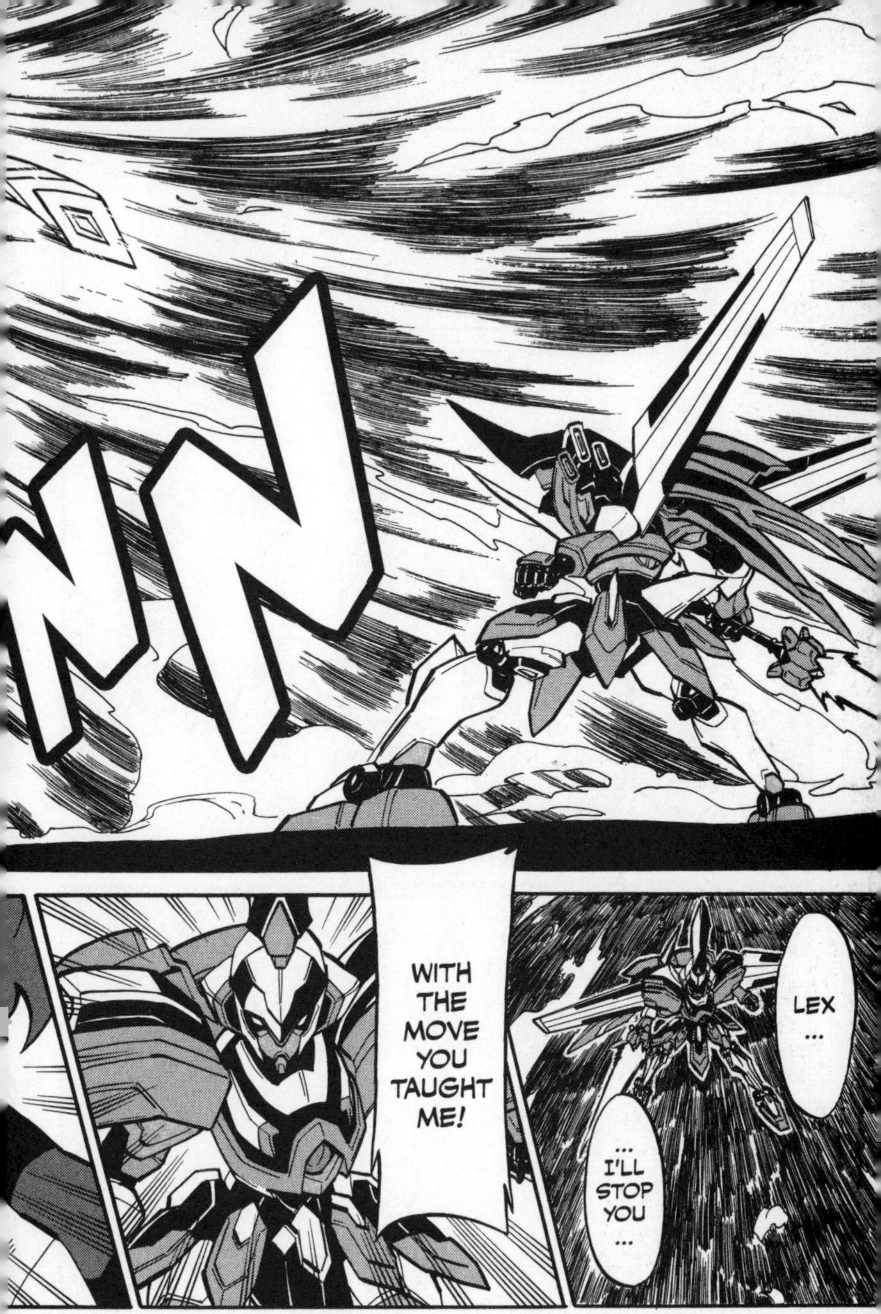
LEX ...
... I'LL STOP YOU ...
WITH THE MOVE YOU TAUGHT ME!

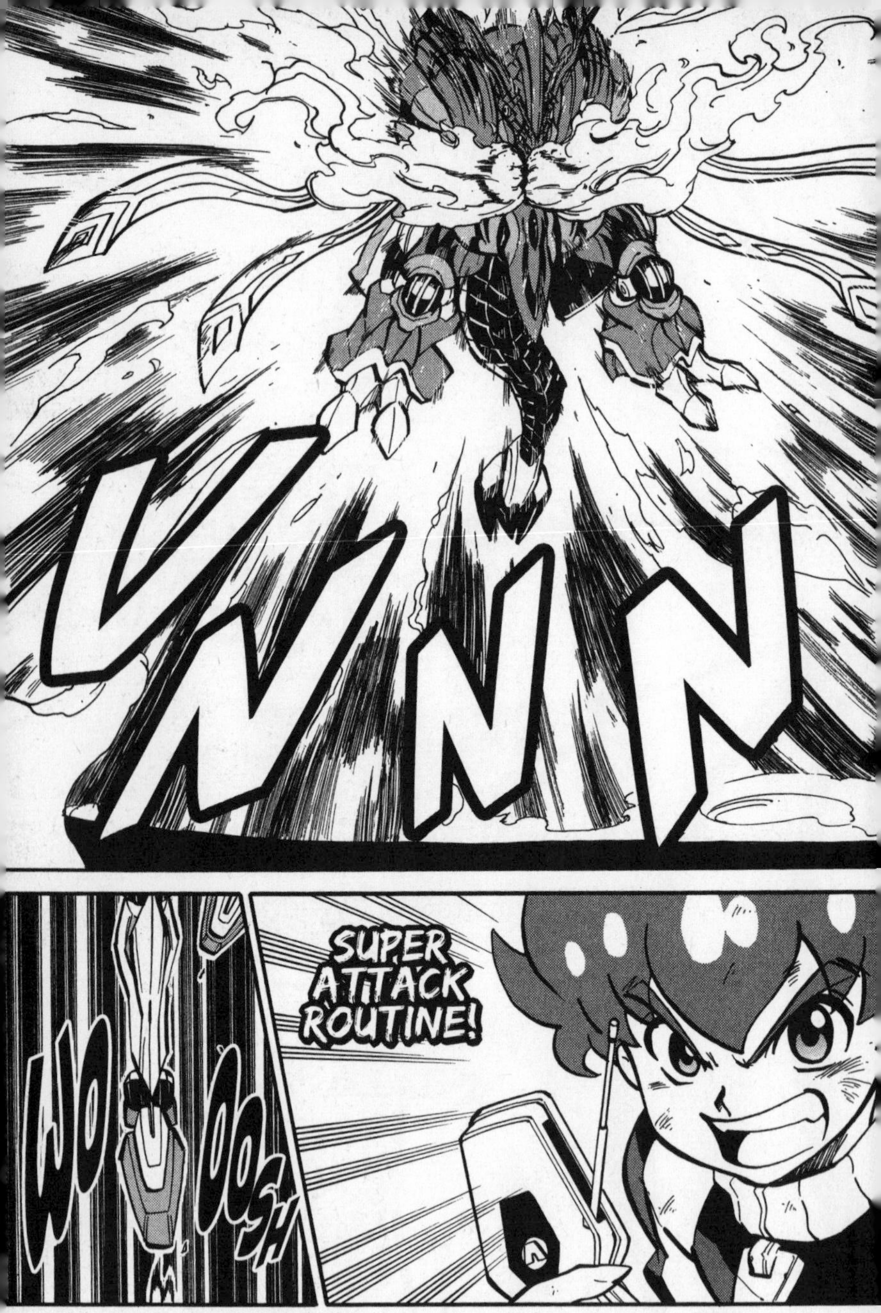
SUPER ATTACK ROUTINE!
WOOOSH

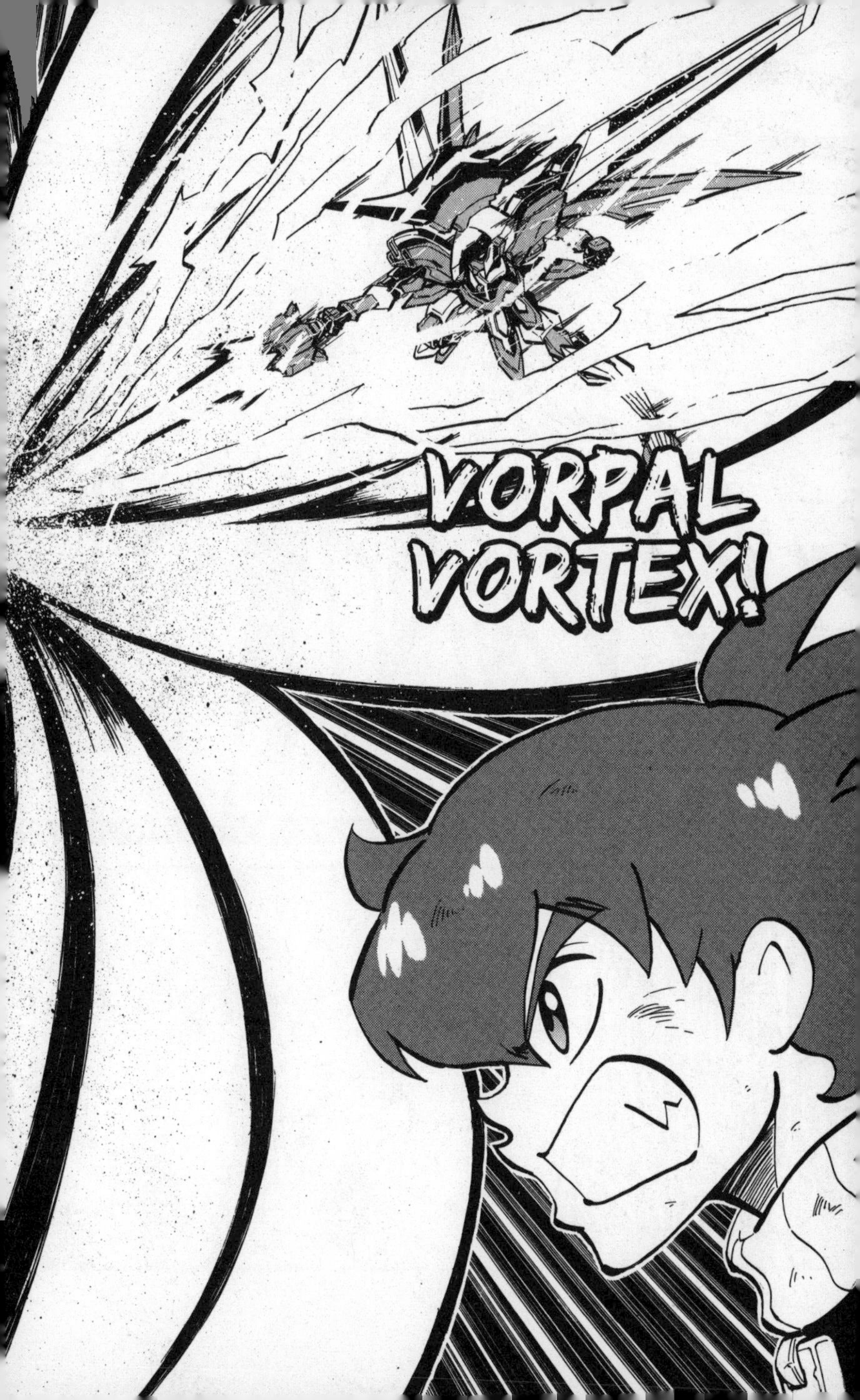
VORPAL VORTEX!

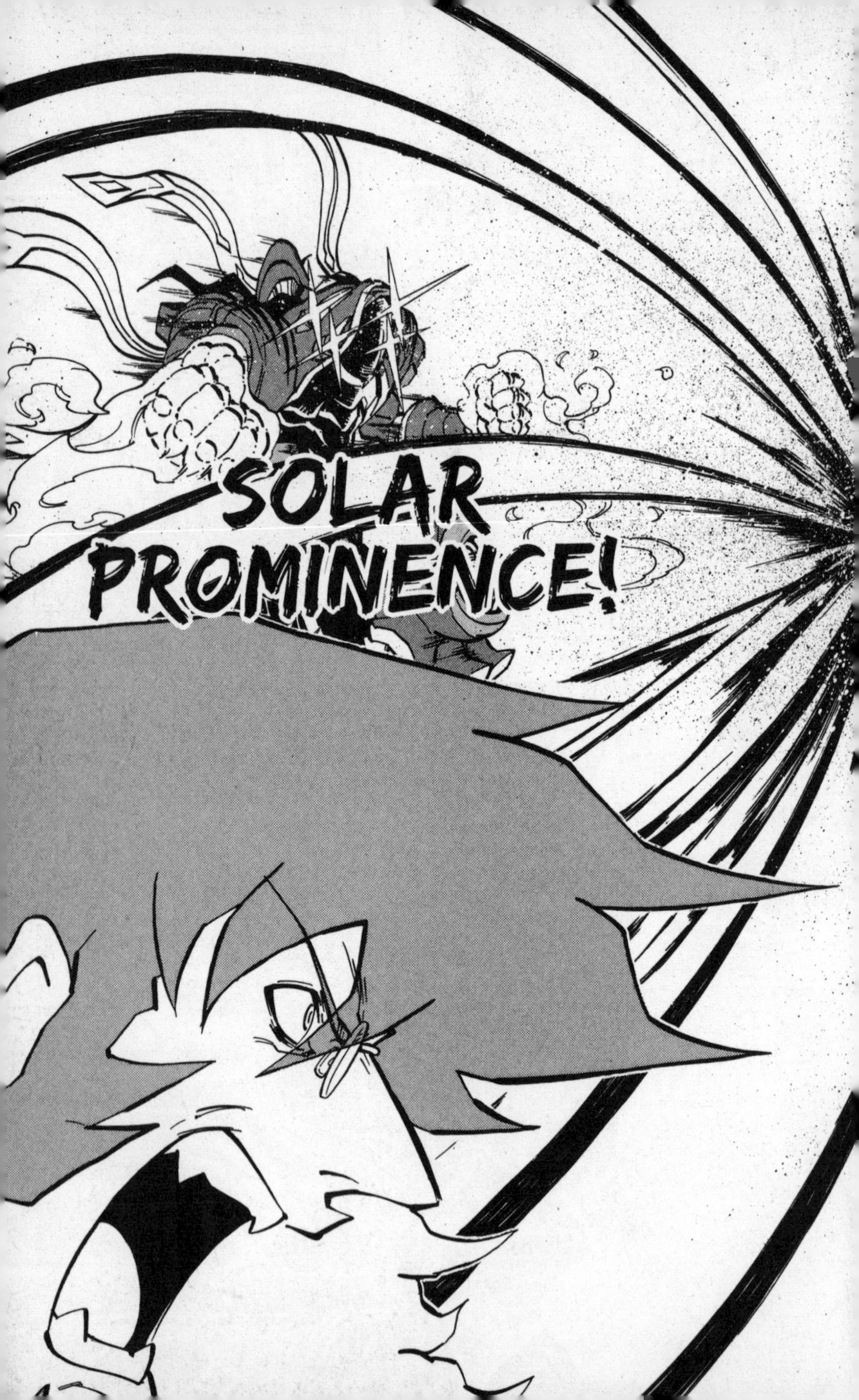
SOLAR PROMINENCE!

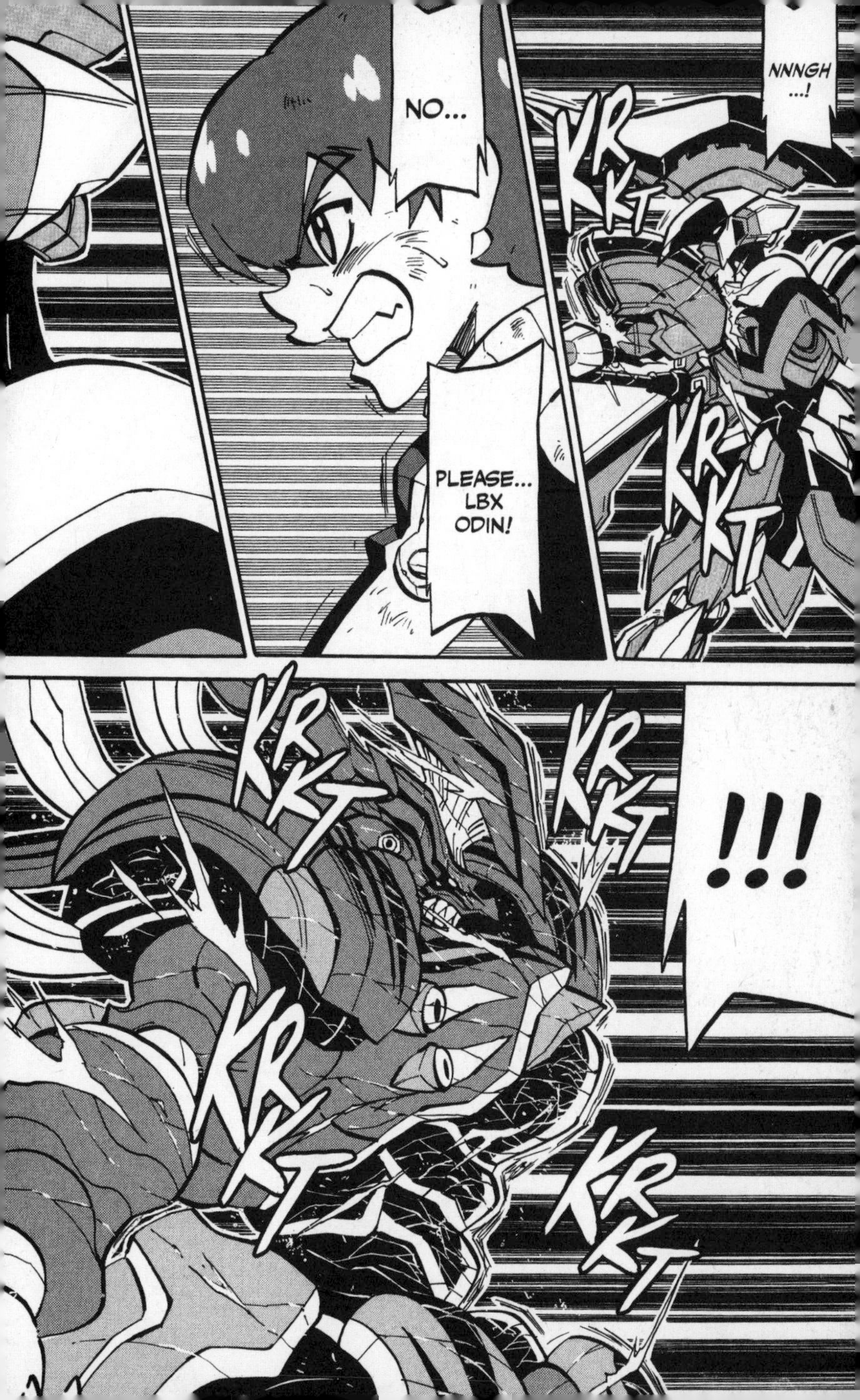
NNNGH ...!
KRKT
KRKT
NO...
PLEASE... LBX ODIN!
!!!
KRKT
KRKT
KRKT
KRKT

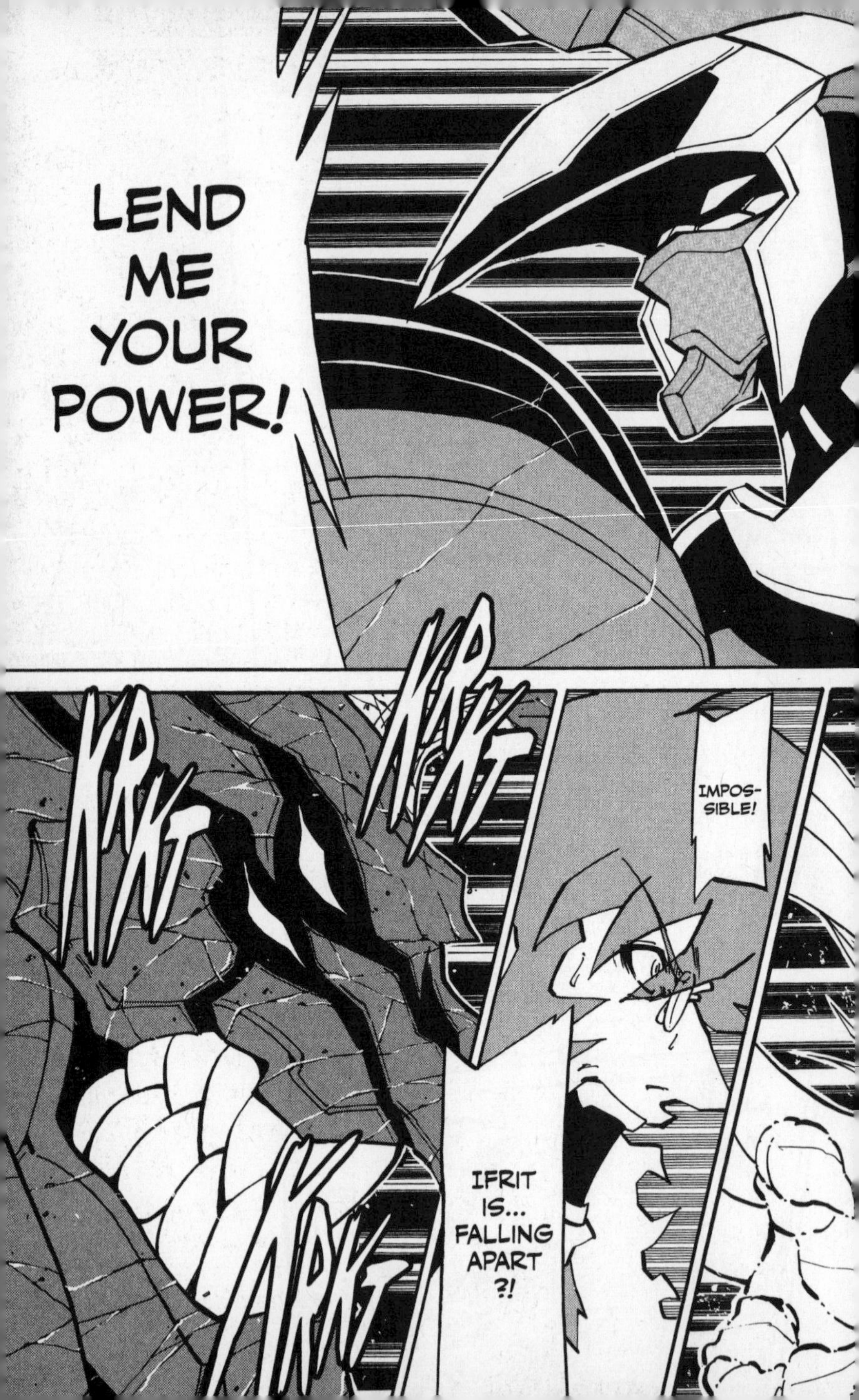
LEND ME YOUR POWER!
IMPOS-SIBLE!
KRAKT
KRAKT
IFRIT IS... FALLING APART ?!
KRAKT

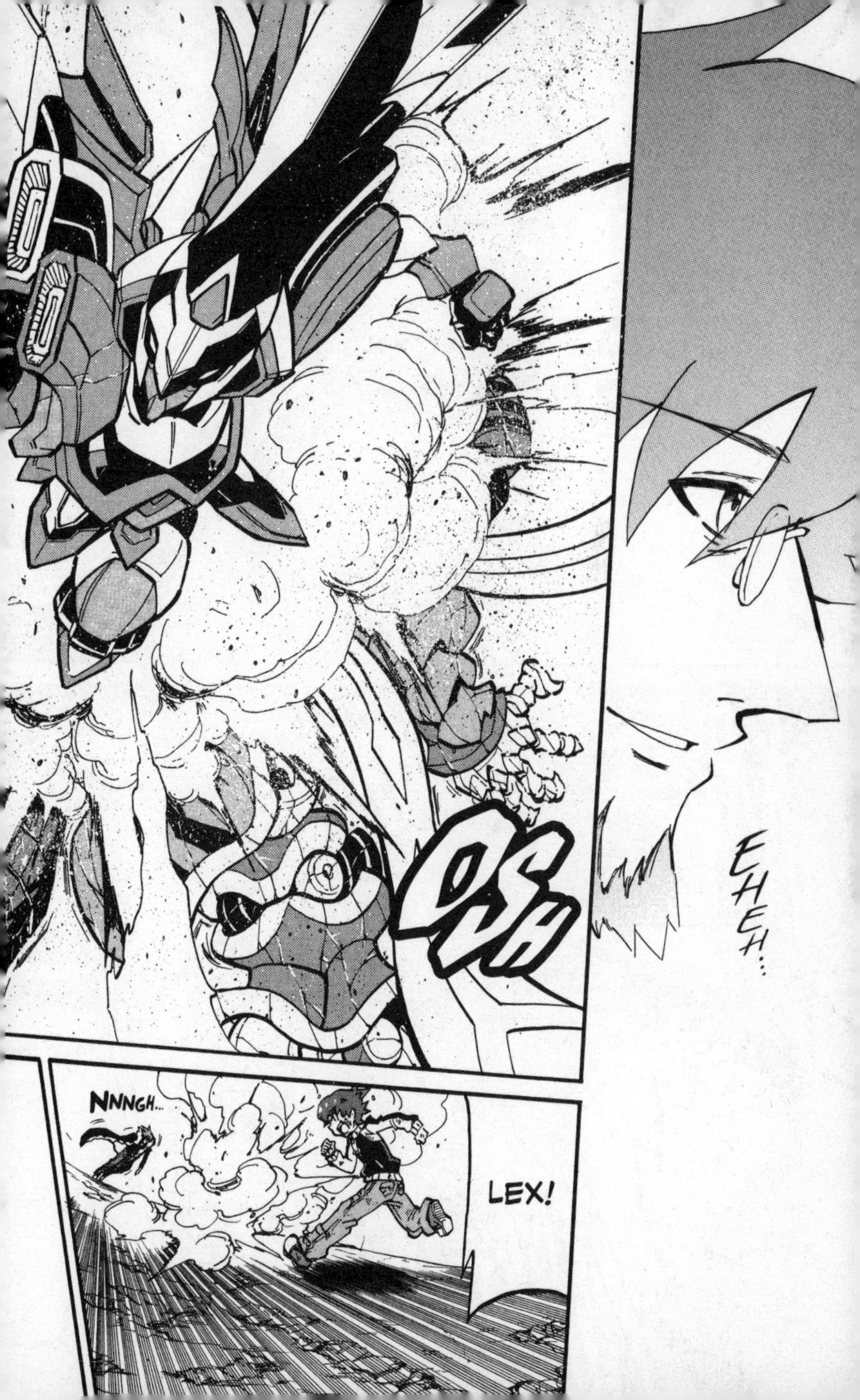
EHEH...
NNNGH...
LEX!

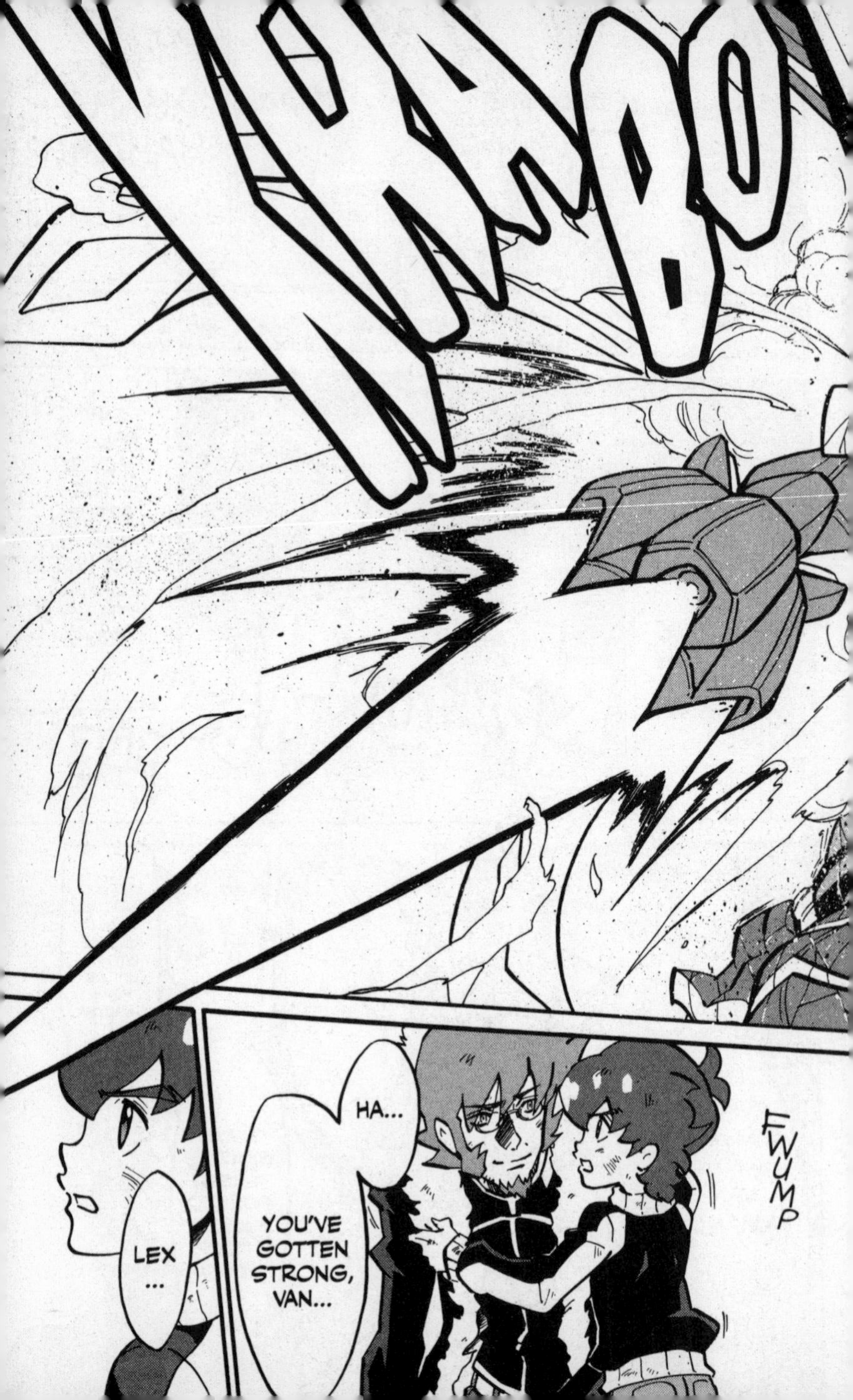
FWUMP
HA...
YOU'VE GOTTEN STRONG, VAN...
LEX ...

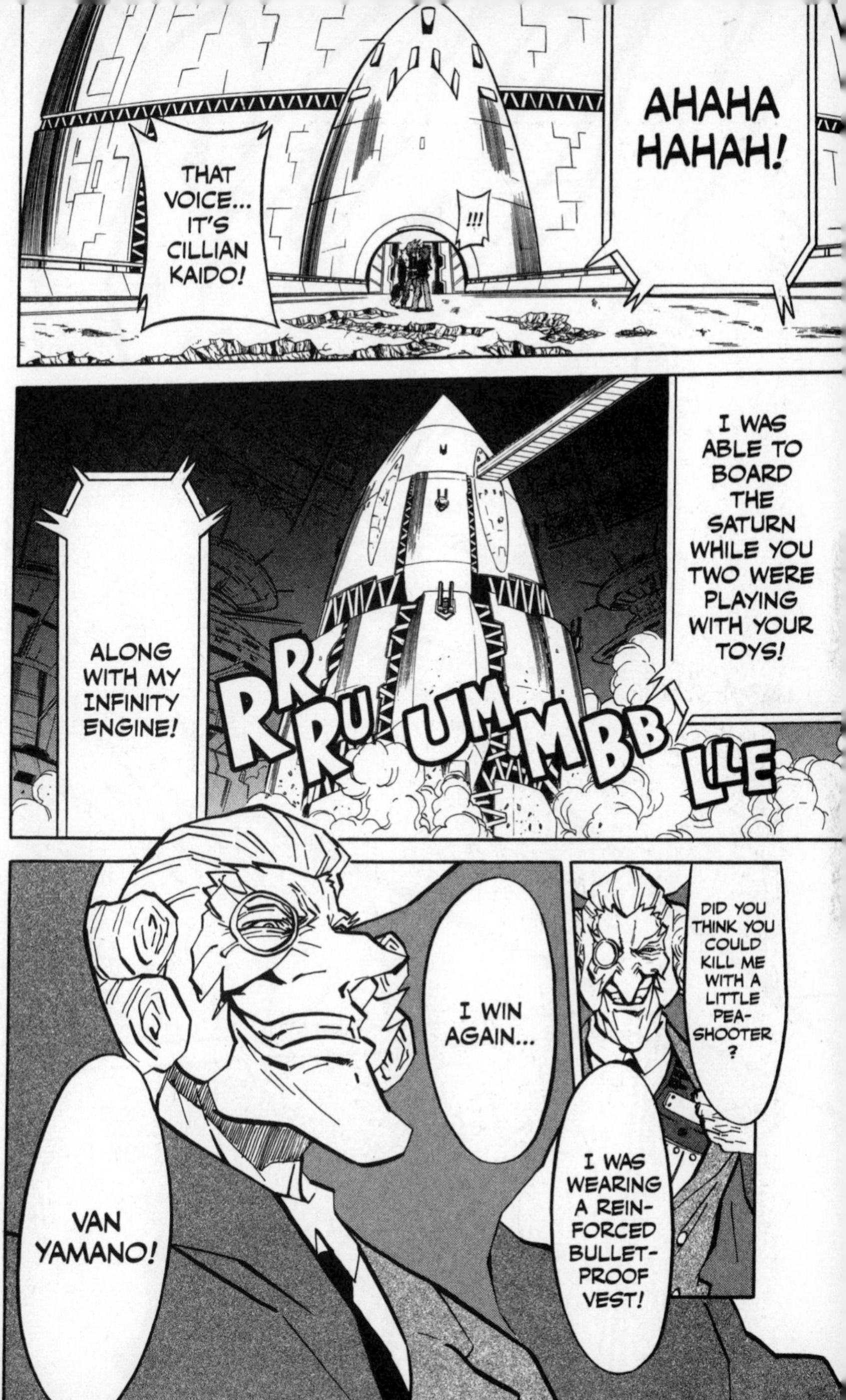
AHAHA HAHAH!
!!!
THAT VOICE... IT'S CILLIAN KAIDO!
I WAS ABLE TO BOARD THE SATURN WHILE YOU TWO WERE PLAYING WITH YOUR TOYS!
RRRUUMMBBLLE
ALONG WITH MY INFINITY ENGINE!
DID YOU THINK YOU COULD KILL ME WITH A LITTLE PEA-SHOOTER?
I WAS WEARING A REIN-FORCED BULLET-PROOF VEST!
I WIN AGAIN...
VAN YAMANO!

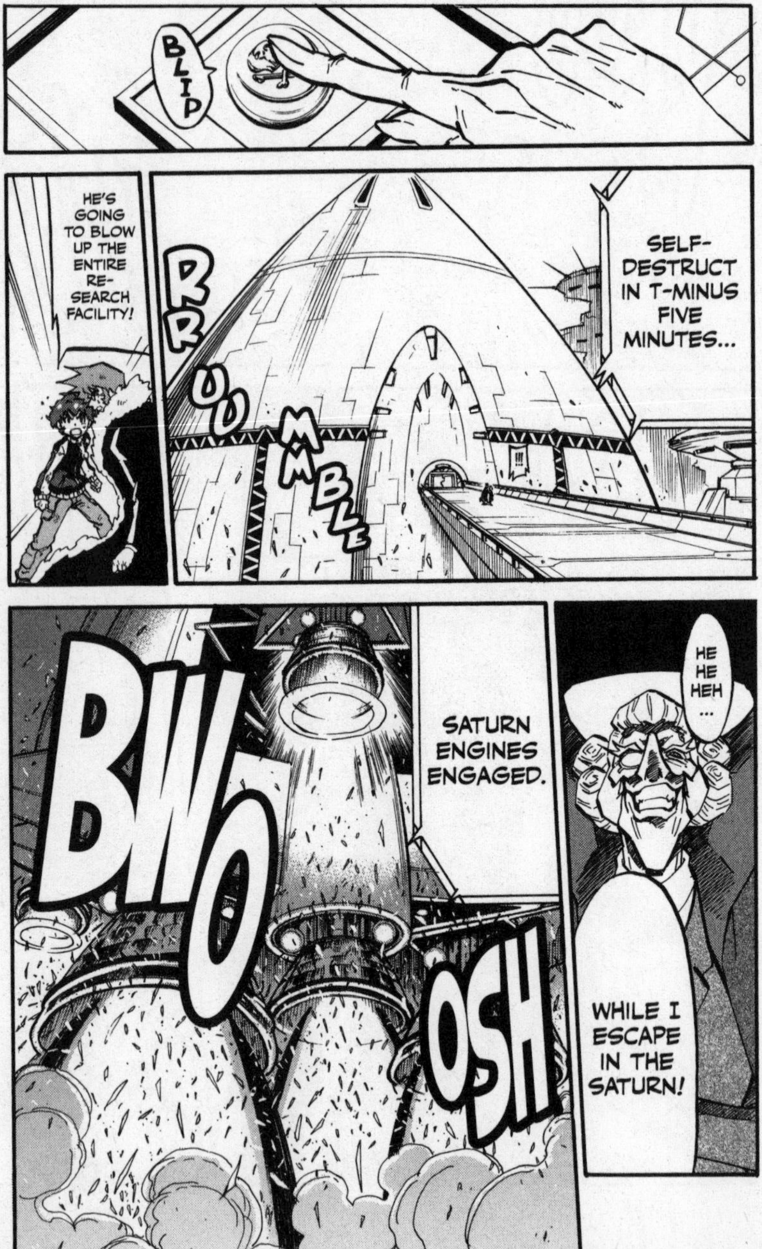
BLIP
SELF-DESTRUCT IN T-MINUS FIVE MINUTES...
RRUUMMBLE
!!!
HE'S GOING TO BLOW UP THE ENTIRE RE-SEARCH FACILITY!
HE HE HEH...
WHILE I ESCAPE IN THE SATURN!
SATURN ENGINES ENGAGED.
BWOOSH

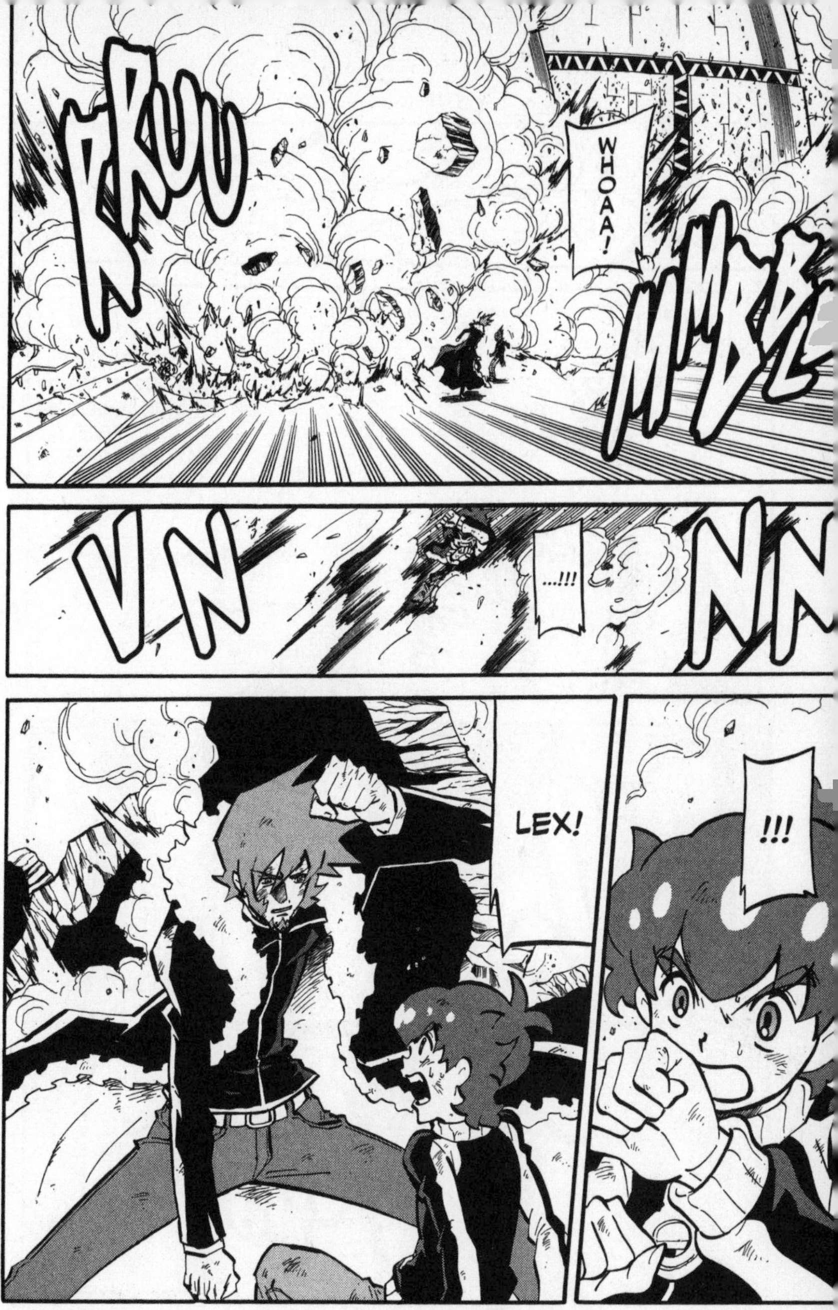
RRUU
WHOAA!
MMBL
VN
...!!!
NN
!!!
LEX!

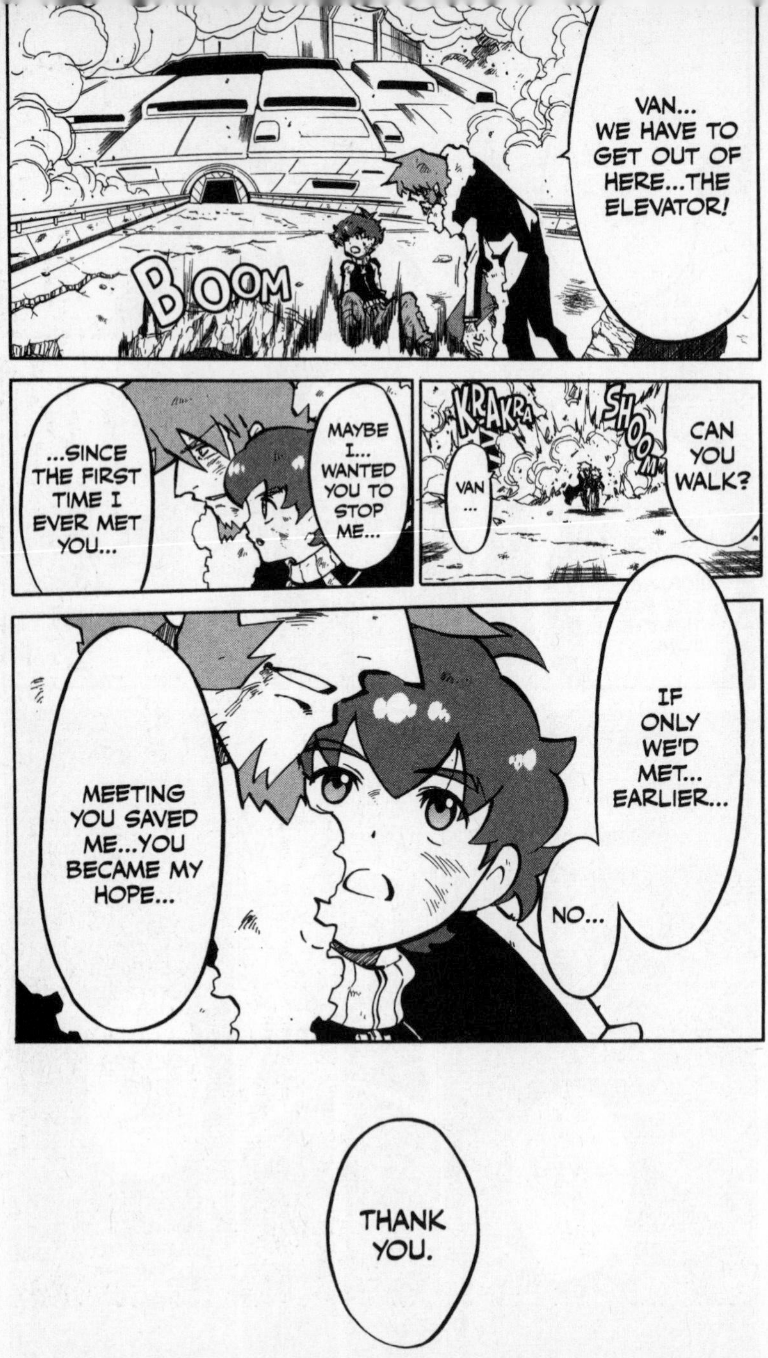
VAN... WE HAVE TO GET OUT OF HERE...THE ELEVATOR!
BOOM
SHOOM
CAN YOU WALK?
KRAKRA
VAN...
MAYBE I... WANTED YOU TO STOP ME...
...SINCE THE FIRST TIME I EVER MET YOU...
IF ONLY WE'D MET... EARLIER...
NO...
MEETING YOU SAVED ME...YOU BECAME MY HOPE...
THANK YOU.

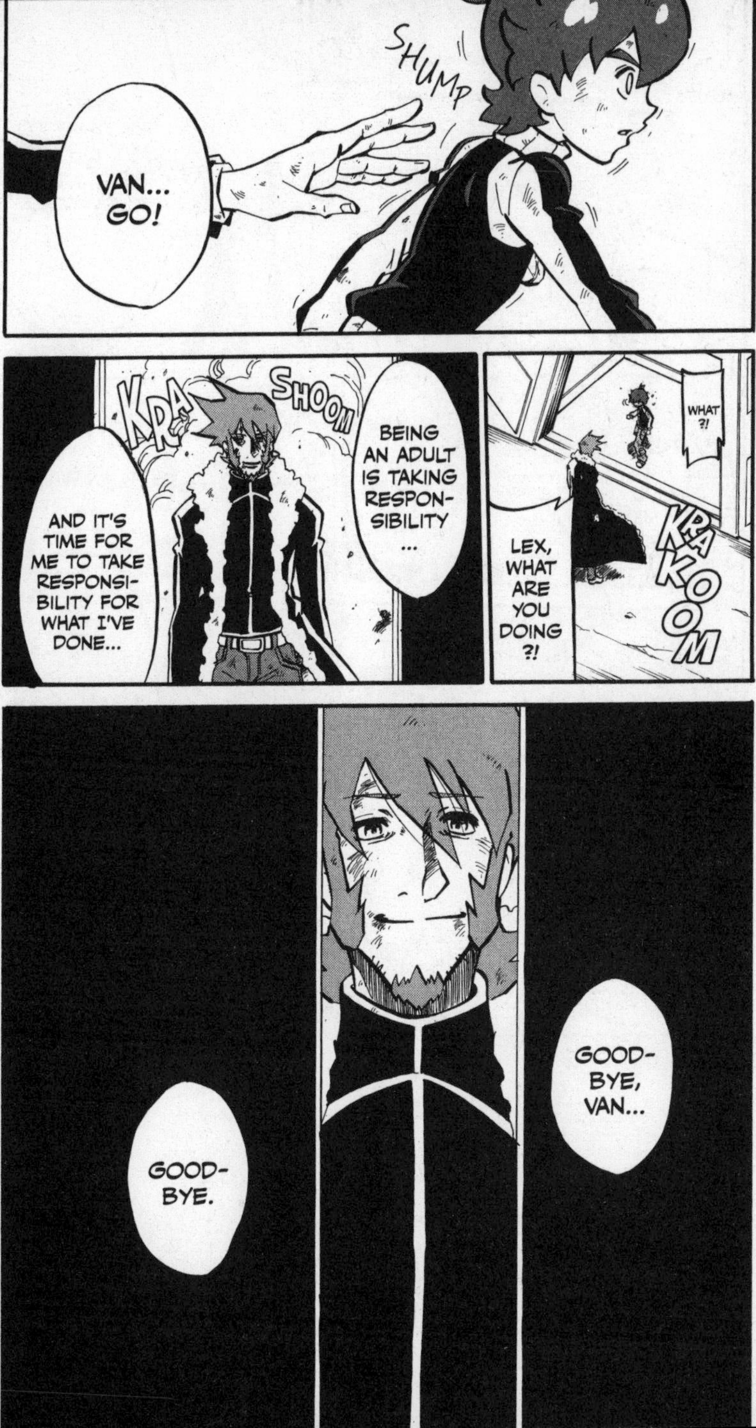
SHUMP
VAN... GO!
WHAT?!
KRAKOOM
LEX, WHAT ARE YOU DOING?!
SHOOM
BEING AN ADULT IS TAKING RESPONSIBILITY...
KRA
AND IT'S TIME FOR ME TO TAKE RESPONSIBILITY FOR WHAT I'VE DONE...
GOOD-BYE, VAN...
GOOD-BYE.

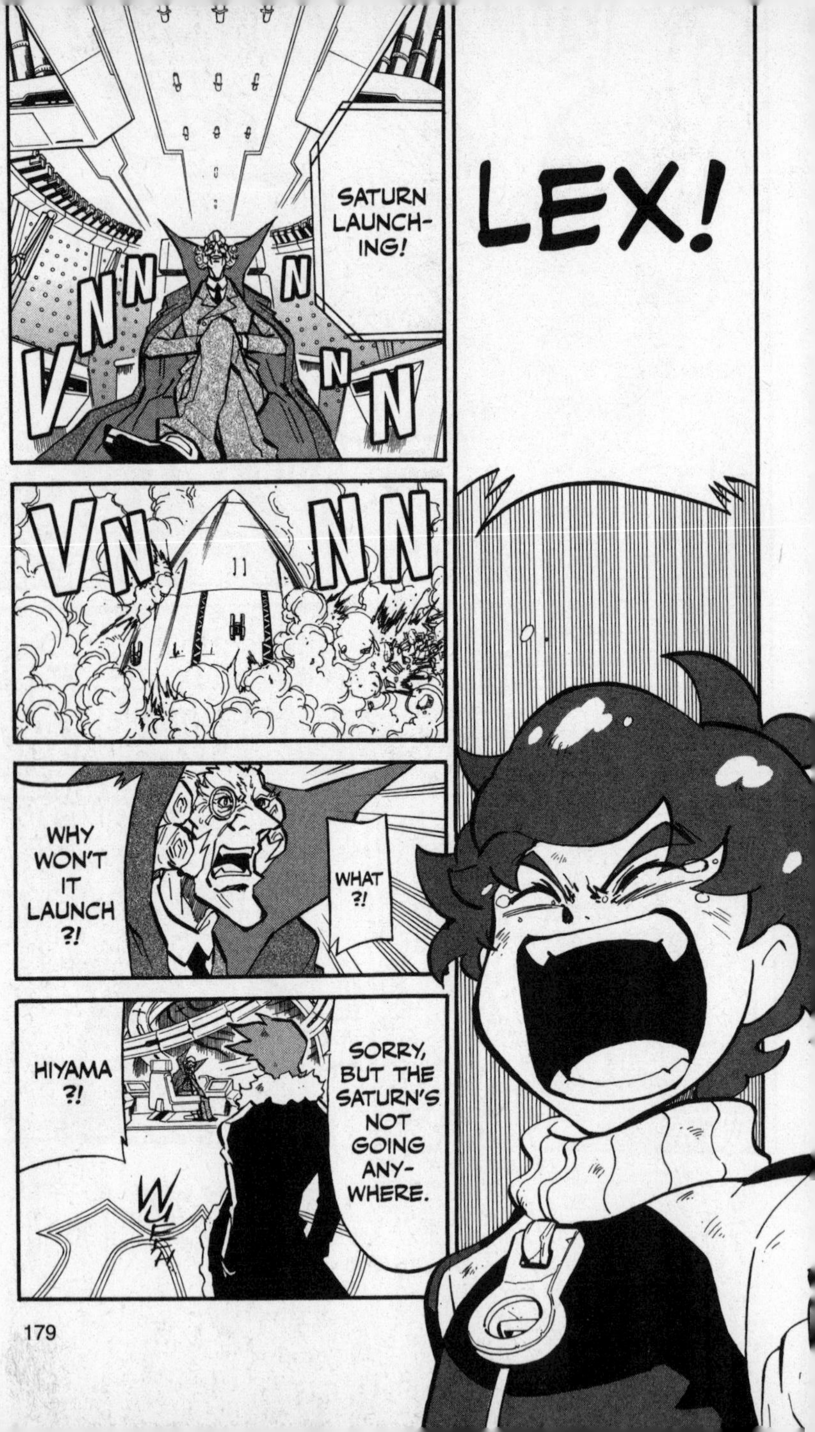
LEX!
SATURN LAUNCHING!
VNNNNN
VNNN
WHAT ?!
WHY WON'T IT LAUNCH ?!
SORRY, BUT THE SATURN'S NOT GOING ANYWHERE.
HIYAMA ?!

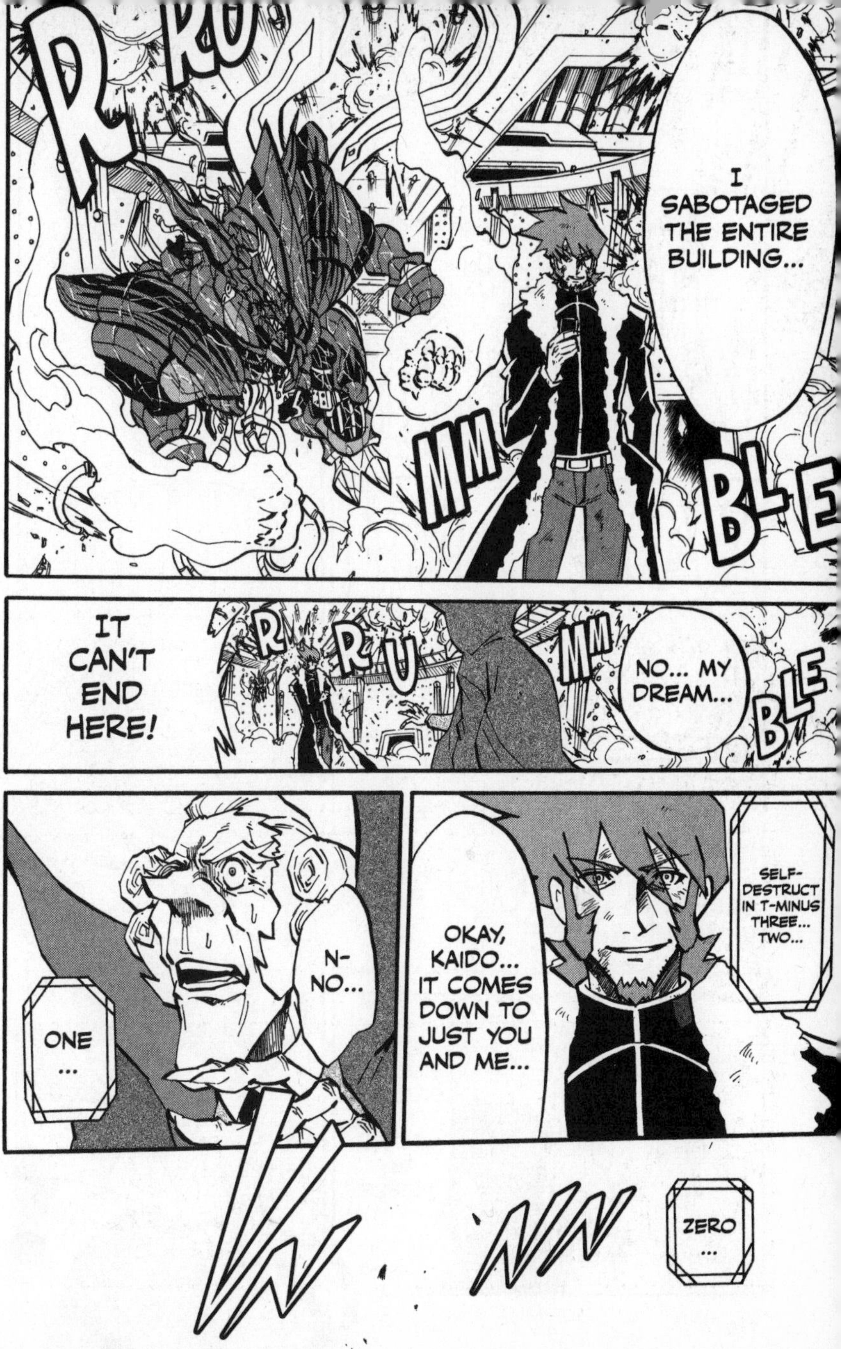
I SABOTAGED THE ENTIRE BUILDING...
R RU MM BLE
NO... MY DREAM...
R R U MM BLE
IT CAN'T END HERE!
SELF-DESTRUCT IN T-MINUS THREE... TWO...
OKAY, KAIDO... IT COMES DOWN TO JUST YOU AND ME...
N- NO...
ONE ...
ZERO ...
W NN

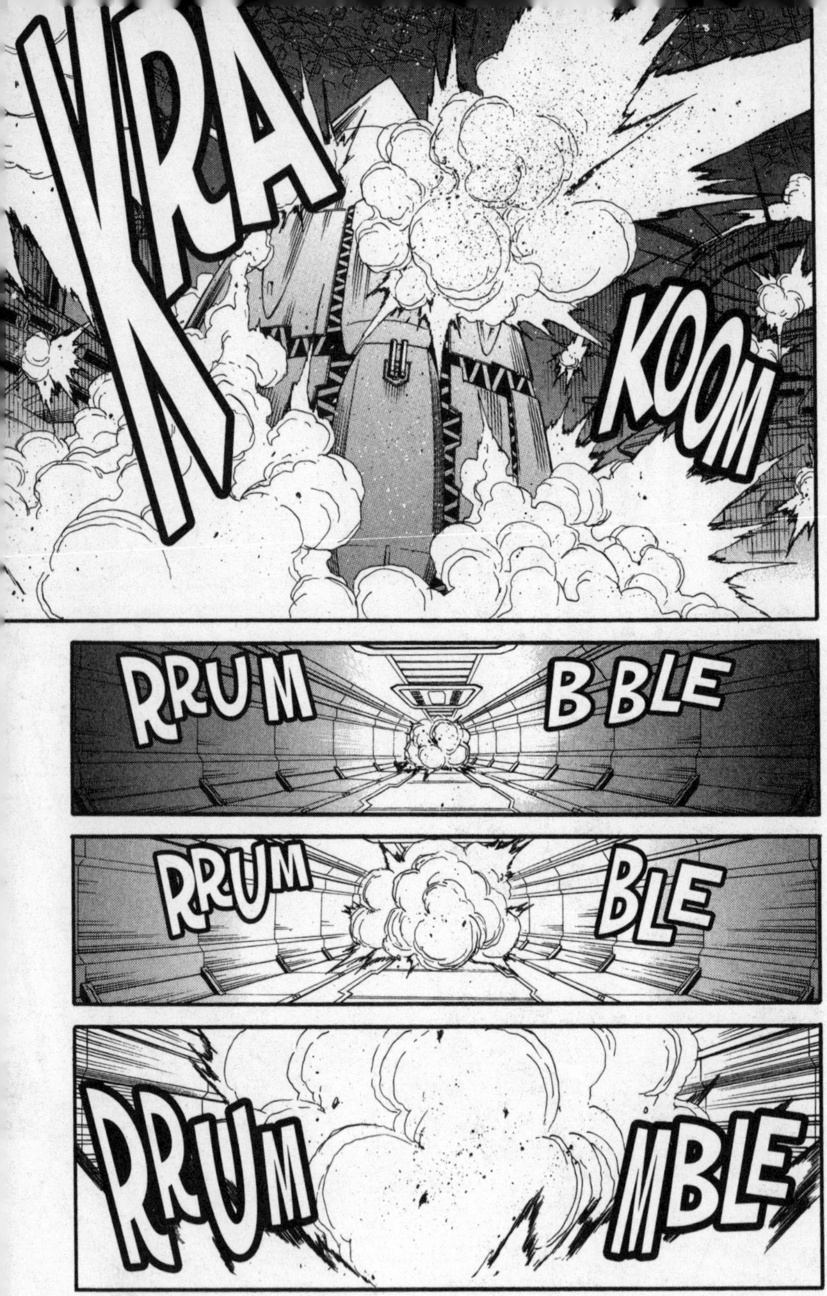
KRA
KOOM
RRUM
BBLE
RRUM
BLE
RRUM
MBLE

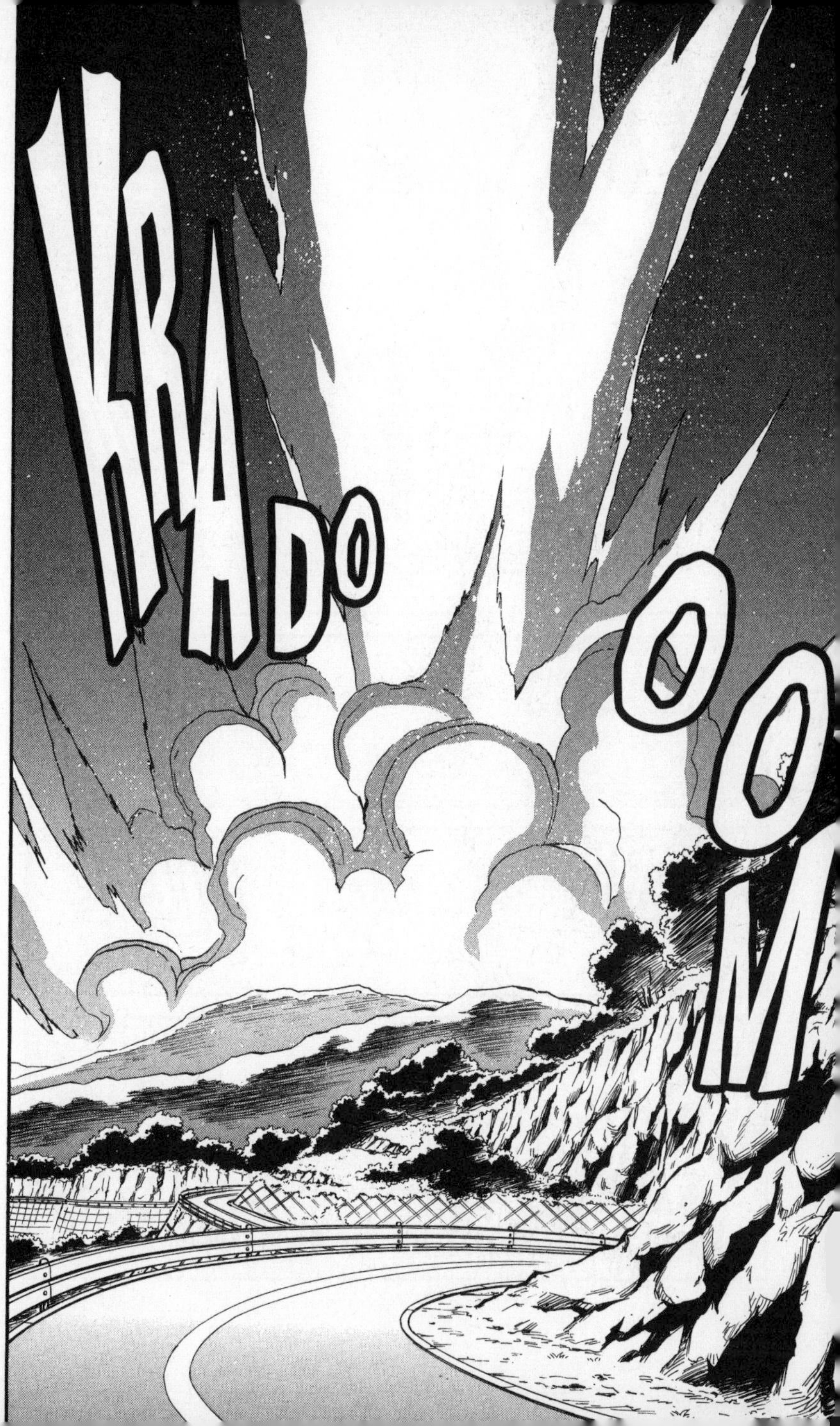
KRADOOOM

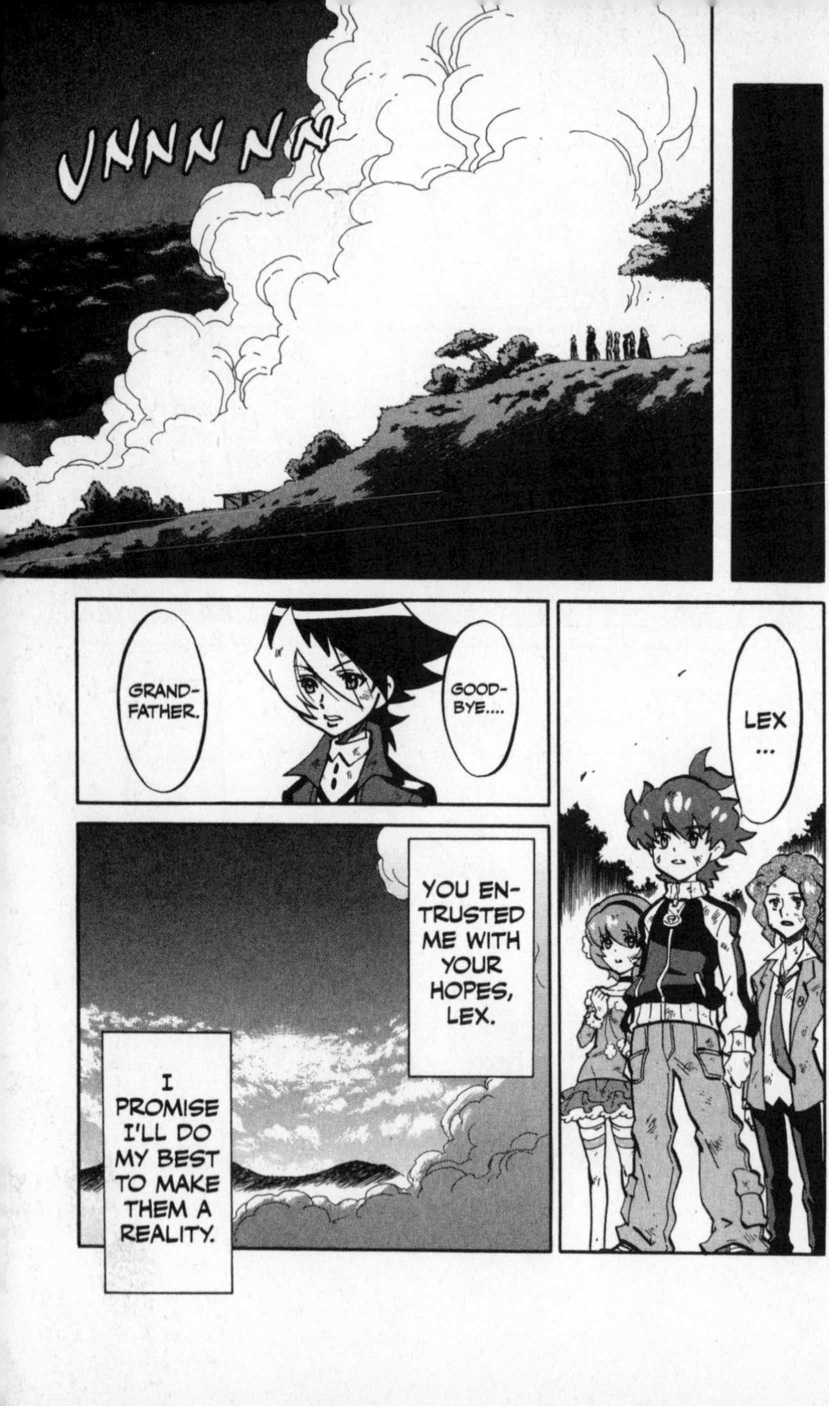
VNNNNN
LEX ...
GOOD-BYE....
GRAND-FATHER.
YOU EN-TRUSTED ME WITH YOUR HOPES, LEX.
I PROMISE I'LL DO MY BEST TO MAKE THEM A REALITY.

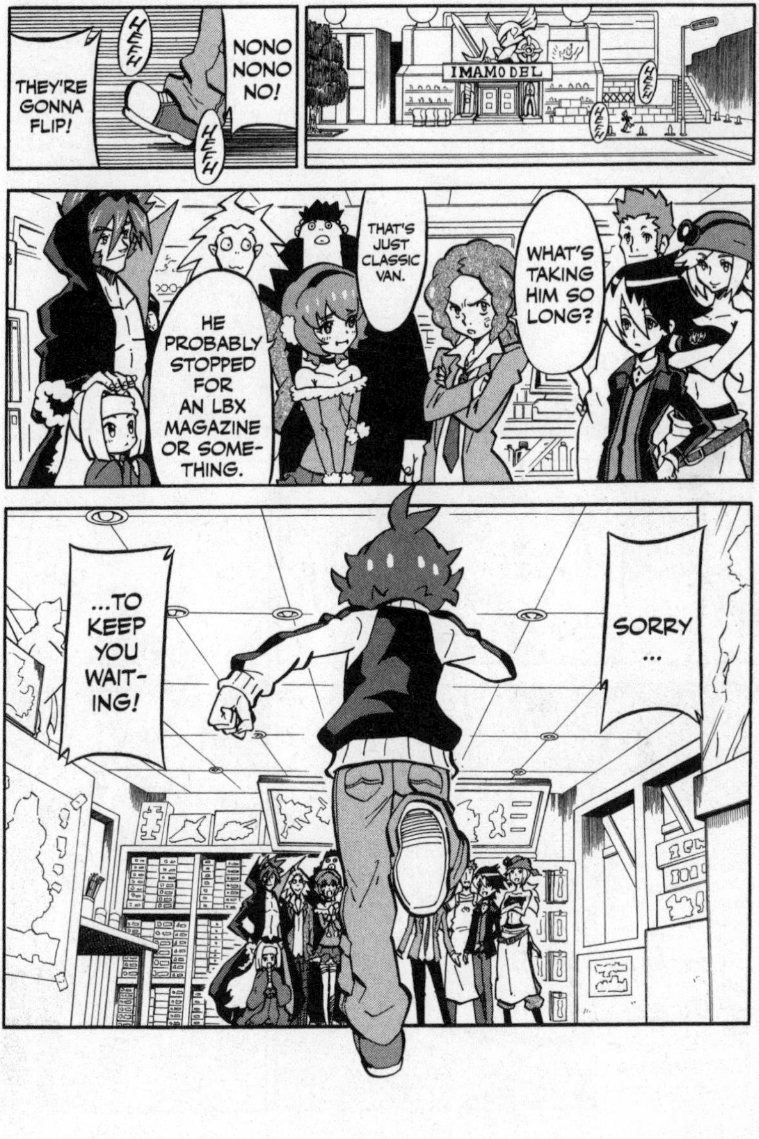
IMAMODEL
HEFH
HEFH
NONO NONO NO!
HEFH
THEY'RE GONNA FLIP!
HEFH
WHAT'S TAKING HIM SO LONG?
THAT'S JUST CLASSIC VAN.
HE PROBABLY STOPPED FOR AN LBX MAGAZINE OR SOME-THING.
SORRY ...
...TO KEEP YOU WAIT-ING!

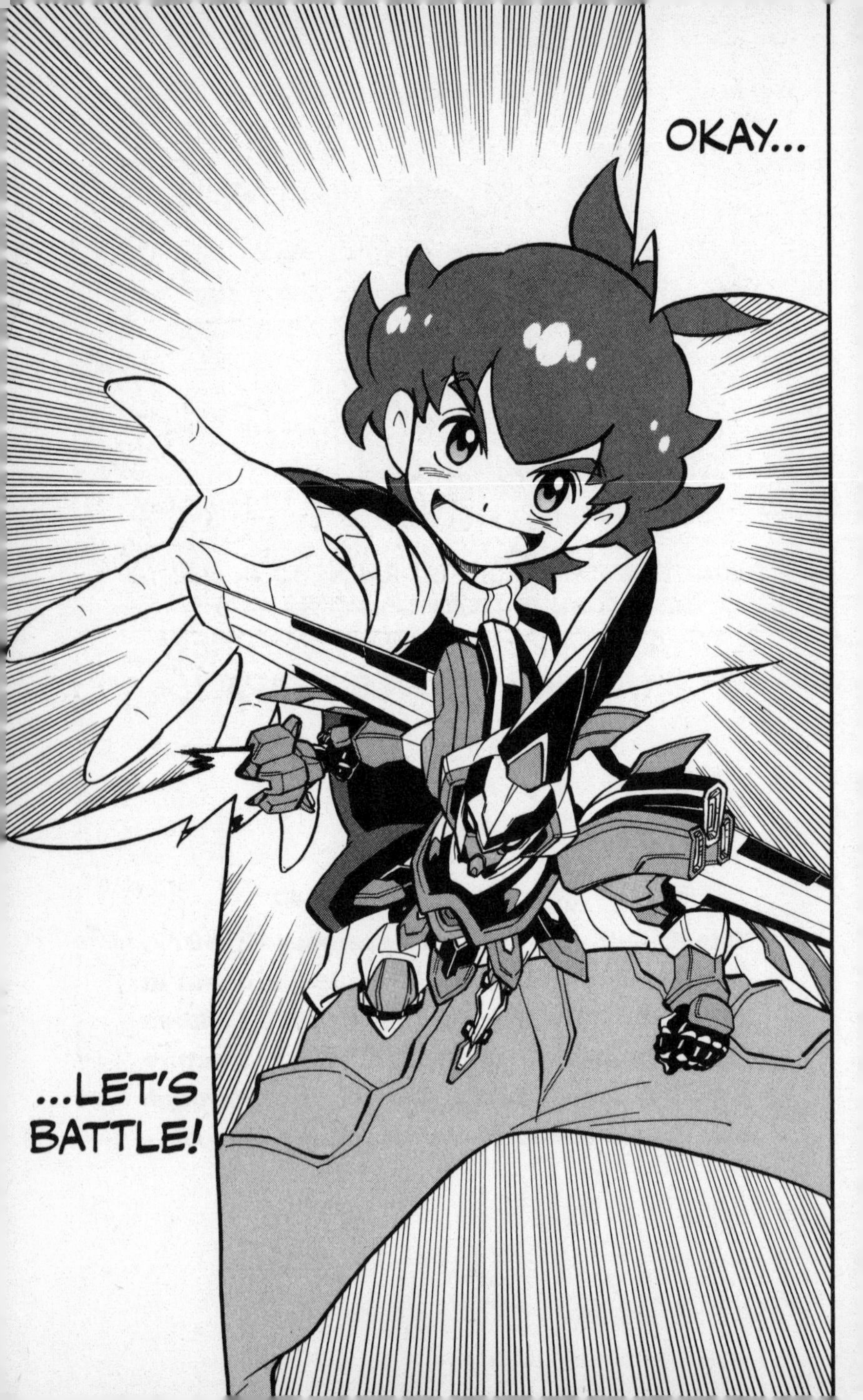
OKAY...
...LET'S BATTLE!

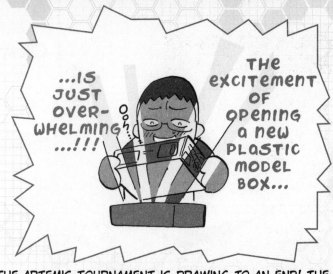

THE EXCITEMENT OF OPENING A NEW PLASTIC MODEL BOX...
...IS JUST OVER-WHELMING...!!!
Ooh...

THE ARTEMIS TOURNAMENT IS DRAWING TO AN END! THE COUNTDOWN TO DESPAIR IS TICKING AWAY!!

IT ALL DEPENDS ON VAN'S NEW LBX, ODIN... BATTLE START!!!

Hideaki Fujii

Hideaki Fujii was born on December 12, 1977, in Miyazaki Prefecture. He made his debut in 2000 with *Shin Megami Tensei: Devil Children* (*Monthly Comic BomBom*). His signature works include *Battle Spirits: Breakthrough Boy Bashin* and many others. Blood type A.

KAIDO'S TRUMP CARD

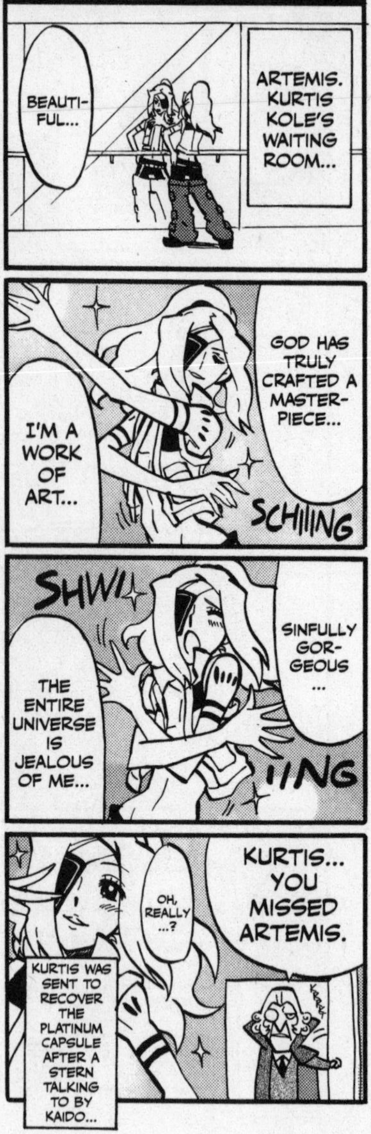
ARTEMIS. KURTIS KOLE'S WAITING ROOM...
BEAUTIFUL...
GOD HAS TRULY CRAFTED A MASTERPIECE...
I'M A WORK OF ART...
SCHIIING
SINFULLY GORGEOUS...
SHWI
THE ENTIRE UNIVERSE IS JEALOUS OF ME...
IING
KURTIS... YOU MISSED ARTEMIS.
OH, REALLY...?
KURTIS WAS SENT TO RECOVER THE PLATINUM CAPSULE AFTER A STERN TALKING TO BY KAIDO...

THE MONSTER AWAKENS

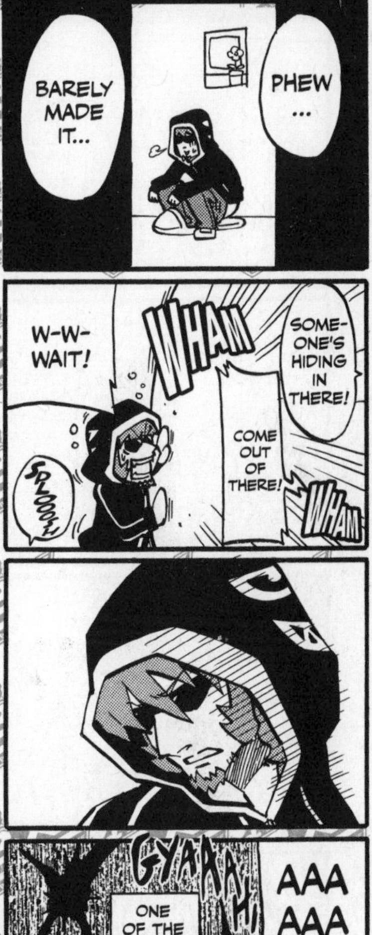
PHEW ...
BARELY MADE IT...
SOME-ONE'S HIDING IN THERE!
WHAM
COME OUT OF THERE!
WHAM
W-W-WAIT!
AAA AAA RRR GH!
GYAAAAH!
ONE OF THE GRAVE-DIGGER THUGS LATER CLAIMED ...
"IT WAS... A MON-STER!"

IT WASN'T MEANT TO BE LIKE THIS...

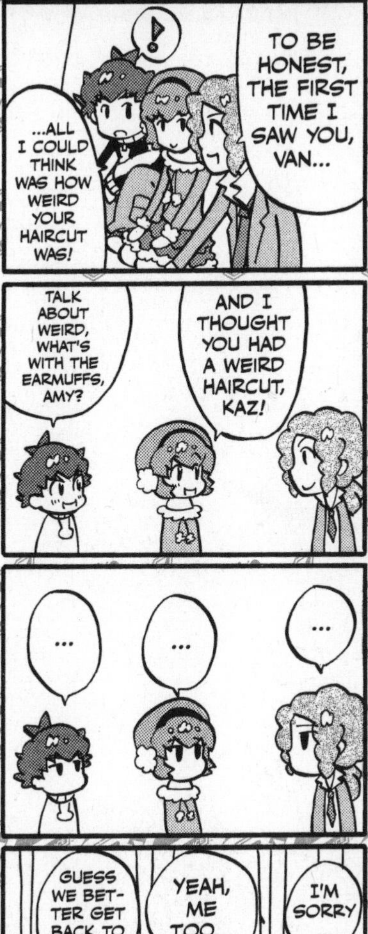
TO BE HONEST, THE FIRST TIME I SAW YOU, VAN...
!
...ALL I COULD THINK WAS HOW WEIRD YOUR HAIRCUT WAS!
AND I THOUGHT YOU HAD A WEIRD HAIRCUT, KAZ!
TALK ABOUT WEIRD, WHAT'S WITH THE EARMUFFS, AMY?
...
...
...
I'M SORRY ...
YEAH, ME TOO...
GUESS WE BET-TER GET BACK TO WORK...
Awwwwwk-waaaaaard!

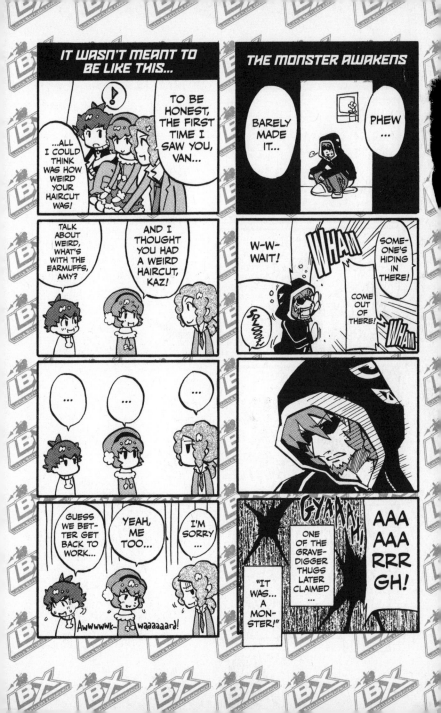

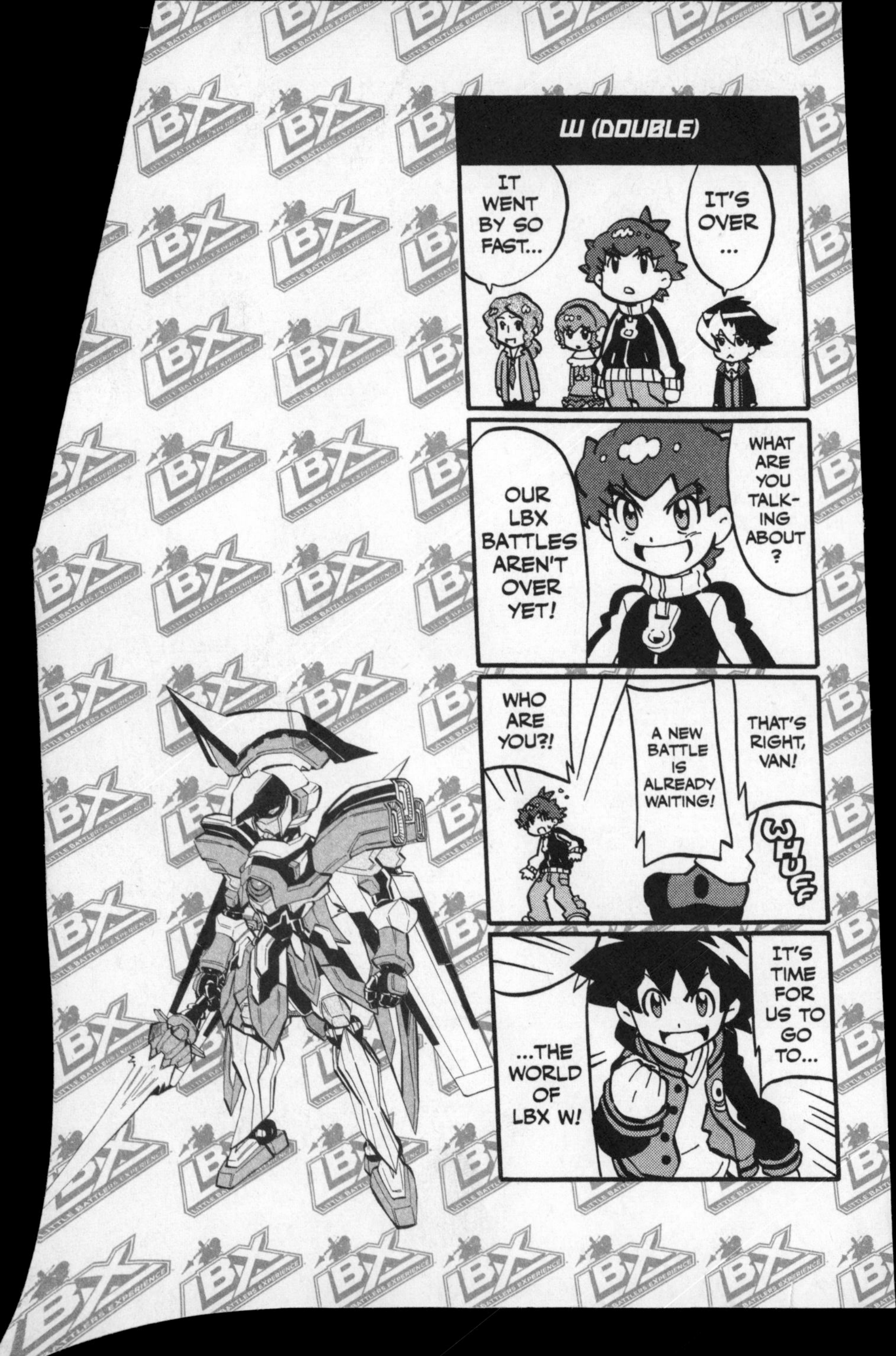
W (DOUBLE)
IT'S OVER ...
IT WENT BY SO FAST...
WHAT ARE YOU TALKING ABOUT?
OUR LBX BATTLES AREN'T OVER YET!
THAT'S RIGHT, VAN!
WHUFF
A NEW BATTLE IS ALREADY WAITING!
WHO ARE YOU?!
IT'S TIME FOR US TO GO TO...
...THE WORLD OF LBX W!

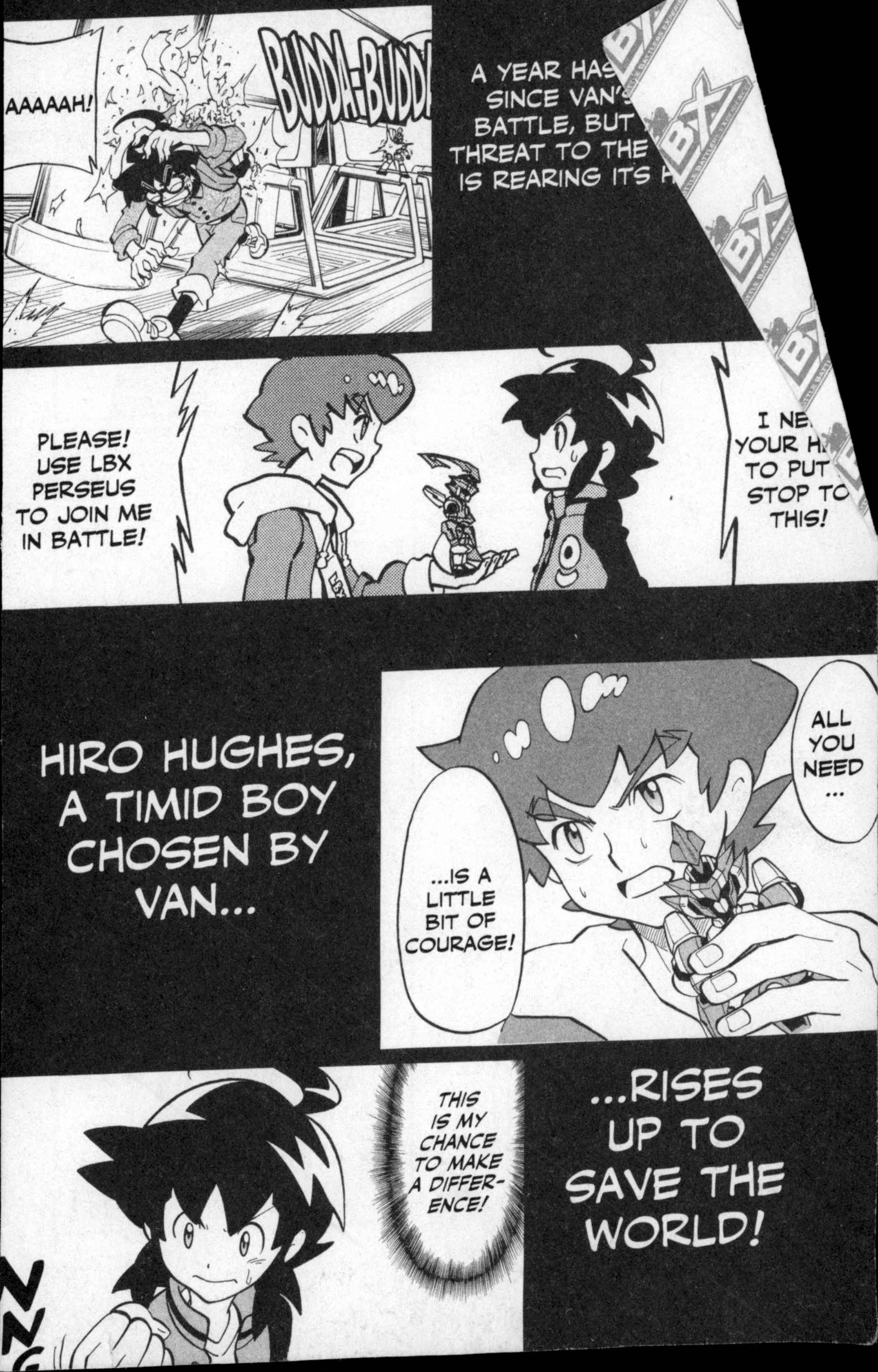
A YEAR HAS SINCE VAN'S BATTLE, BUT THREAT TO THE IS REARING ITS H
BUDDA-BUDD
AAAAAH!
I NE YOUR H TO PUT STOP TO THIS!
PLEASE! USE LBX PERSEUS TO JOIN ME IN BATTLE!
LBX
ALL YOU NEED ...
...IS A LITTLE BIT OF COURAGE!
HIRO HUGHES, A TIMID BOY CHOSEN BY VAN...
...RISES UP TO SAVE THE WORLD!
THIS IS MY CHANCE TO MAKE A DIFFERENCE!
NNG

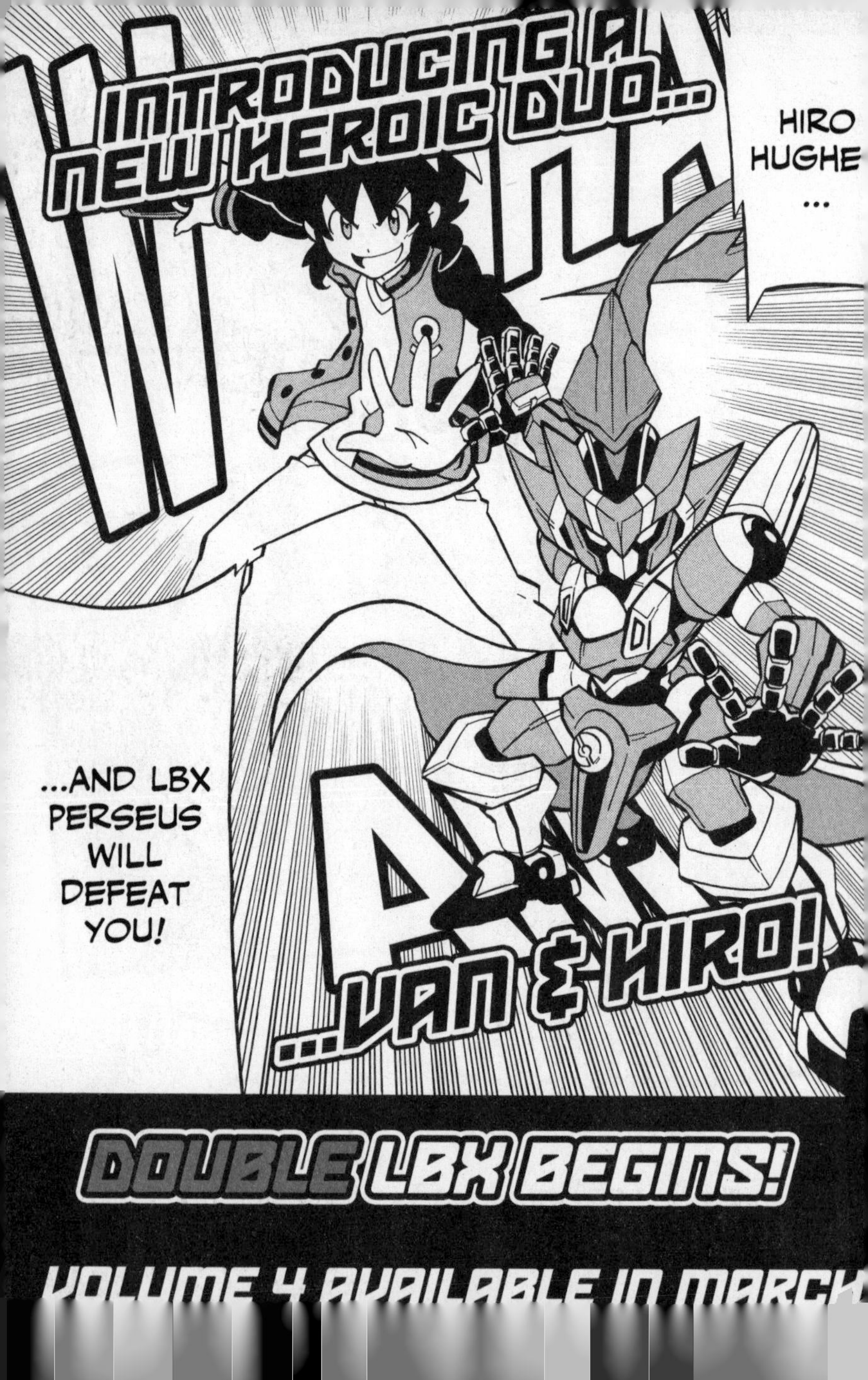

INTRODUCING A NEW HEROIC DUO...
HIRO HUGHE ...
...AND LBX PERSEUS WILL DEFEAT YOU!
...VAN & HIRO!
DOUBLE LBX BEGINS!
VOLUME 4 AVAILABLE IN MARCH

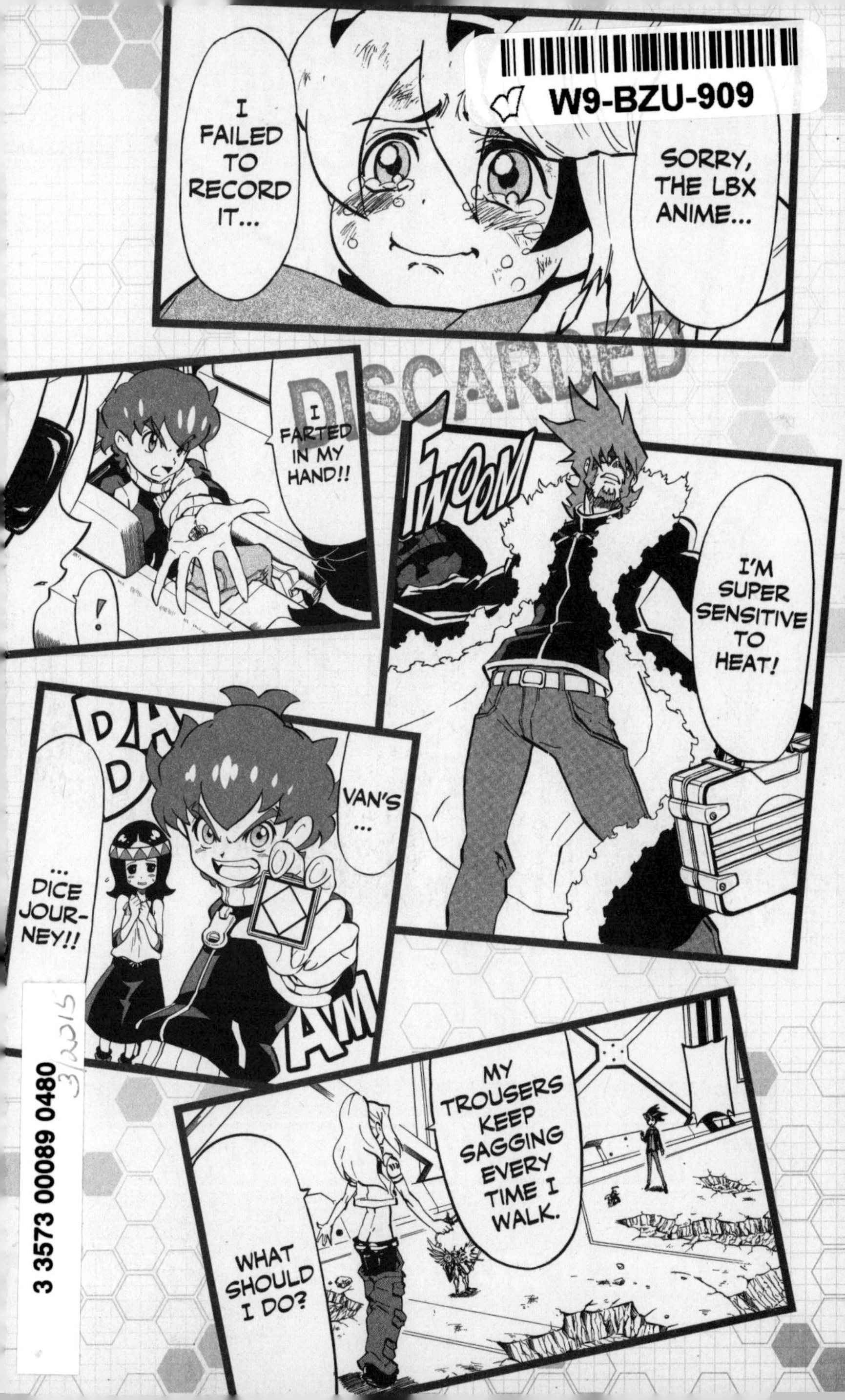
SORRY, THE LBX ANIME...
I FAILED TO RECORD IT...
TWOOM
I'M SUPER SENSITIVE TO HEAT!
I FARTED IN MY HAND!!
!
VAN'S ...
... DICE JOURNEY!!
AM
MY TROUSERS KEEP SAGGING EVERY TIME I WALK.
WHAT SHOULD I DO?